THE COMING OF THE
TERRAPHILES

'Here we have one of science fiction and fantasy's most respected and well-loved authors writing *Doctor Who*. What could possibly go wrong? The answer is absolutely nothing. This is a phenomenal book. 10/10.'
Total Sci Fi

'Exhilarating, funny and deeply peculiar… It's been years since the *Doctor Who* range put out anything as smart and engaging as this. Fingers crossed it's the first of many such volumes.'
SFX

'A bold, eccentric quasi space opera'
Doctor Who Magazine

'The great Michael Moorcock has written a *Doctor Who* book which is like Burt Bacharach knocking out an album for Lady Gaga.'
Word Magazine

DOCTOR WHO

THE COMING OF THE TERRAPHILES

Or, Pirates of the Second Aether!!

MICHAEL
MOORCOCK

BOOKS

1 3 5 7 9 10 8 6 4 2

Published in 2010 by BBC Books, an imprint of Ebury Publishing.
A Random House Group Company

This paperback edition first published in 2011

Doctor Who is a BBC Wales production for BBC One.
Executive producers: Steven Moffat, Piers Wenger and Beth Willis

The Random House Group Limited Reg. No. 954009

Addresses for companies within the Random House Group can be found
at www.randomhouse.co.uk

A CIP catalogue record for this book is available from the British Library.

ISBN 978 1 849 90140 6

Commissioning editor: Albert DePetrillo
Editor and series consultant: Justin Richards
Project editor: Steve Tribe
Editorial manager: Nicholas Payne
Cover design: Lee Binding © Woodlands Books Ltd, 2010
Production: Rebecca Jones

Printed and bound in Great Britain by CPI Cox & Wyman, Reading, RG1 8EX

To buy books by your favourite authors and register for offers,
visit www.randomhouse.co.uk

For all the Chabons

WHOEVER NAMED THE PLANET Venice named her well. Her golden surface was crossed by a million regular waterways so that from space she resembled a papal orb. Clouds followed the canals in season and emphasised rather than obscured her geometric character. Venice was a rich and lively world. More space travellers deserted to her than to any other of her nine or so rivals in the star system of Calypso V, whose ranks included Ur XVII and the extraordinarily beautiful New Venus where colonists risked every danger to enjoy her yearningly lovely landscapes.

Like all inhabited worlds, Venice was forbidden to the great rockets of the IGP and the larger interstellar mercantile vessels of the Terran service, whose routes were frequently challenged by privateers in their subtler, sometimes faster ships, some of which still used the increasingly erratic solar winds for power. The twelfth intergalactic war, which had destroyed whole star systems, left by common consent the planetary prizes unspoiled, and surface conflicts were confined to the legally conventional weapons of the region. In Venice's case, these included battle barges of enormous dimensions, their hulls driven by massive sails whose

7

canvas covered distances measured in fractions of square miles rather than cubed metres, and speedy little gondolas employing oars as regularly as they used wind. These boats darted along the wide natural waterways like bugs, their sweeps so many articulated limbs. From space, on the great V-screens, they appeared as creatures endowed with minds and purposes of their own. Cornelius the pirate had once employed those gondolas very successfully in pursuit of his trade, taking full advantage of the confusions and disguises offered by war. For the past half-century, however, he had made little use of them.

There were few land wars on Venice, few conflicts of any kind now. All traffic was conducted by water. Canals occupied four-fifths of the planet's surface. Venice was not one of the many terraformed planets created by the great commercial world-building companies. Whatever gravities had shaped her had done so naturally. People had long since discovered that symmetry was characteristic of most planets, formed in the nativity of their geology. Even the howling, fruitful terraces of Arcturus-and-Arcturus owed their existence to this familiar phenomenon and were merely exploited by the commercial terraforming families who created mainly Earth-like worlds for a planet-hungry universe.

In his long *Epiconeon*, Cornelius, nicknamed 'the Dutchman', wrote:

> *Catching the solar winds, the vessel brakes and turns*
> *Upon the brane and all the multiverse is hers.*
> *The yearning void calls out, gloriously perverse,*
> *She spurns a dozen planetary advances.*
> *This latticed orb of silver, gold and glowing pearl*
> *Sustains all reverses and her purse remains*
> *Both threatening prize and perilous temptation.*
> *Yet still my patronage and brain are hers.*

8

> *There can be no occasion, no threat or lure*
> *To drive me from my chosen station.*

His ship is called *Paine*. His hand light on his great wheel, he stands at her bridge, proud and insouciant, glorying in the beauty he commands. She is the most peerlessly perfect light-powered vessel in all space-time.

Her sails strain against the pressure of countless billion winking photons; her holds are already crowded with the invaluable and exotic booty of a hundred beautiful worlds. Within her mysterious envelope of atmosphere, created from stolen technologies, her multifarious crew, flesh, metal and petal, drawn from almost all the sentient creatures of the galaxy, crowd her decks to look down on a world they have come to consider their own.

'Ironface' is their name for the man who wears a Pierrot mask of brazen metal in the style of the ancient Italian comedy. Cornelius the pirate, ruthless poet, courteous thief, commander of a vessel feared and familiar, envied as much for her ethereal loveliness as for the accuracy of her destructive arsenal, motions with his hand, giving the order for his men's descent. Only *Remembered Lombardy* under her buccaneer captain Hong Hunter could hope to challenge *Paine* in open space. It is with relief that Venetians, training their radio-optics upon her as she appears in their upper stratosphere, understand how firmly her captain honours the conventions of his trade. She comes to take her tribute fair and square, according to the articles signed by all the brotherhood save the rogue Cervantes. Cervantes claims to own the one thing Cornelius covets, but neither pirate will describe it or admit they know what it is.

Captain Cornelius remains as mysterious a figure to his men as to his mistresses. His posted verse, studied so they might know him better, only serves to add to his mystique.

It says little of his character save that he favours beauty over sentiment. A lonely figure, he stands chewing a stick of oily black tope, offering his commands with quiet economy. He dines alone or with his bosun Peet Aviv, a woman almost as distant from the crew as himself, and as respected. None can say they like their captain or his bosun, but they obey both with a confidence they offer no other commanders and their loyalty is well rewarded. When the *Paine* completes her long tour of violent adventure every member of her crew will be worth a fortune great enough to buy presidents and kings. But Cornelius, they are sure, will not yet have found what or whom he seeks. Most say it's a woman, maybe his vanished wife. Some say it's an artefact, once the plaything of a god.

Cornelius gives the order. The ebony boats break free of their mother ship and sail down, through blazing, sun-tinged clouds, to fill Venice's morning with all their sad, commanding dignity.

The pirates, drawn from a hundred worlds and a dozen space-time continua, have come at last. Only a few, watching them from their decks and towpaths, refuse to acknowledge their power. Some even drop to their knees, bowing in respect to the inevitable, as peasants paying homage to a feudal lord.

By evening Cornelius is among them, broadcasting his formal greeting to all the rival factions on the planet, telling them, canal by canal, how much they must give and in what form, be it an ingot of newtonium, platinum bullion, provisions or crew. (Always he requests that ingot. Surely he knows there is not that much newtonium in existence?) His price is high, but the price of defiance would be higher.

When the barges are filled and brought to the great central basin called Grande Bayou, inventories are carefully made and receipts supplied. Then the recruiting begins to replace any skilled complement killed in battle or retired.

Peet Aviv, nicknamed 'the Locust', stands on her elegant prosthetics, making notes, quietly relaying orders, while Cornelius, his features engulfed within the plain, etched mask he always adopts in public, sits to one side of her desk, his glowing, melancholy eyes fixed on the distance, looking towards Saint Marx's islet where once, it is said, he courted a novice and lost her to the only enemy whose superiority he has ever acknowledged and whom he calls God.

One burgher, in a hasty attempt to demonstrate his compliance, offers to show off a marvel to the captain alone. He leaves a wealthy man, but perhaps a marked man, too. Captain Cornelius frowns and puts what could be a string of beads into his pocket, rattling them while brooding on another matter.

At last, after a week, the peaceful tension is dispelled and the pirates prepare to leave, their tolls all gathered, while Saint Marx's bells sound the end of the tax-taking. In return for this price, Venice will know protection for another decade. Captain Cornelius nods to Peet Aviv. The ledgers are signed off by pirates and canal captains in a flurry of silken pomp and brilliant armour. Then the skiffs rise skyward and are gone amongst the broad ribbons of cloud. And those whose eyes strain at their scopes see the *Paine* standing for a moment to catch the solar winds, her wide sails filling, her instruments glowing and winking in the shrouded, perpetual twilight of her decks. Then she's gone, too, a vast and fleeting glow against the black glare of space, no doubt making for her home base in the dwarf galaxy of Canis.

A memory of loss and glory. As if the multiverse had allowed Venice an audience with her own proud, cold soul.

Captain Cornelius inspects certain items of treasure, searching for that fabulously valuable ingot of newtonium, puzzles over his data and his charts, confers with Peet Aviv and begins to understand that fear he has always exploited

11

but never until now known. For there are dark tides running through the universe; currents so powerful they drag whole galaxies with them, streaming gravities so strong they swallow light and threaten Captain Cornelius's familiar existence; ultimately they threaten every form of sentient existence and if unchecked will absorb the whole of Creation. But for now the photons press against his sails as he once presumed they would do for ever, and he tacks into the solar winds, continuing his long search for the one artefact which might lead him to something and guarantee his life, his ship's life and the life of the universe he loves. He sails in from the Rim, daring the drag of the galactic Hub, still searching. Searching for the only being he acknowledges as his peer, who might join him or at least help him; who is known simply as 'the Doctor'.

Chapter 1

Green

SPRAWLING BACK IN HIS brightly coloured lawn chair and tipping his panama just a fraction lower over his eyes, Urquart Banning-Cannon decided there was nothing like the crack of oak on willow and the smell of new-mown grass to make a chap feel that all's well with the worlds and probably nothing too much wrong with the universe in general. His sigh of contentment was considerable, if a trifle cautious; he feared that Mrs Enola Banning-Cannon might lift her head 'as a questing deer' and draw the natural conclusion that he was not sufficiently busy, for it is a truism in the lives of most wives that if a man is content then he is not doing enough to take care of his spouse. A wary glimpse from under his hat's brim reassured him. Mrs B-C's substantial bosom was rising and falling at a regular rate and what could reasonably be called a soft, ladylike snore indicated that she was taking a short sojourn in the region of semi-consciousness she still liked to call 'the Land of Nod'. So far this holiday, he had to admit, was delivering its promise like a champ.

Before the happy pair a game was being played by sports people of an unusually high level of skill and watched in the main by a bunch of experts who, at irregular intervals,

13

would murmur praise or clap in polite acknowledgement of a particularly well-played moment in a match by now in its third day and coming to a stately close. This was galaxy-class sport enjoyed by super-dedicated aficionados.

The greens and whites of the men were brightened by a flock of top-class pretty girls in lavender, rose, buttercup and apricot wearing hats mostly of straw known in the millinery trade as 'cloche'. Mrs Banning-Cannon had already given this headgear an expert once-over and determined it to be beneath the interest of a true connoisseur.

Amy Pond was thoroughly enjoying what was a bit of a holiday for her, too. She liked her comfortable cloche bonnet and her silky frock, and was even learning the Charleston. She and the Doctor had spent the past week on Peers while he got some solid practice in. He was due to shoot next. She glimpsed him among the players on the veranda of the pavilion as she came to watch the game. An armoured Judoon ambled down the pavilion steps and onto the pitch swinging his whackit and acknowledging the odd bit of polite clapping from the spectators, while, heading to the other end, trotted a six-limbed dog-man from Chardoné, a bow in his forepaw, a quiver of tournament arrows on his back.

Amy had to admit she was finding it hard to get used to all the races of the galaxy taking part in this essentially British game. She was rather glad the Doctor had proven to have enough pull to bring her on tour with him. She'd fallen in love with this bizarre mish-mash of misunderstood mostly early twentieth-century English culture.

Had they only been doing this for a few days? Was it less than a week ago that she had been woken up on board the TARDIS by the sound of loud static? A crackling voice had been speaking a tongue she could not get her head around but which the Doctor, or someone sounding like the Doctor, was answering using the same language:

'Urdle durdle durdle, duroo. Comics. Snap, crackle and pop; hiss, wow and flutter; shriek, scream and twitter. Zekuneefer. Harrow after me. Sagging lorries. I am a...'

It wasn't a fun mixture of noises to unglue your eyes to.

By the time she joined the Doctor at the TARDIS console, Amy had swigged some coffee and munched some muesli and was better equipped to face the barrage of sight and sound which had his attention. He signed for her to help. He was speaking English again or at least something similar to English, playing his nouveau retro control boards and typewriters and clapometers like a Wurlitzer organ, desperately trying to keep the images and voices coming, but he was losing them rapidly. He ripped off his jacket and threw it to the floor. He rolled up his sleeves while she held the coordinates steady.

'No!' The breakup finally came with a horrible shriek which sounded to her as if it had issued from a metallic throat. 'Hey! Duroo!' cried the Doctor, both hands struggling to hold down a big plunger. 'Don't fade on me now! Dor – ic – valley – rum – ginnan Tom Mix. You're still not coming through properly. Was that something about the *colour* pools?' The chilling shriek sounded again and then slowly faded. 'No. No. No. No.' He glanced over to where she was standing. 'I'll swear they said Tom Mix. He was a silent movie film star. You know him?'

'Never heard of him.'

'We know *where* they are. Now we need to know *who*!'

Grimly he tried to re-establish contact for a while until in the end she brought him a cup of tea and some pop-tarts. Despite his protests, she made him sit down. Surely those weren't tears in his eyes?

From what she could tell he was worried about some bad guys called General Frank/Freddie Force and his Antimatter Men, who had ventured over to our side of a super-dense black hole in Sagittarius. They had been there in the far, far future for some time, apparently, and their malign influence was spreading backwards to the here-and-now.

'Up to their old-fashioned dirty work,' the Doctor said, 'those Antimatter Men. Dipping in and out of the "Second Aether". And my guess is they're probably not the only ones.' He chewed thoughtfully on his pop-tart. 'Someone's messing with the normal rules of energy flow. Time and space are all over the place. Quite literally, I mean. Growing increasingly unstable.'

The Doctor leaped to his feet before Amy could tell him he was talking what was to her nonsense.

'I suspect,' he went on, stabbing an accusing finger at her, 'that the General's old girlfriend Peggy Steel – the Invisible Lady Steel – is with them, too. A pretty unsavoury gang. And Quelchy's up to something, no doubt. You never know what side he'll take. This isn't looking good for us, no matter how you look at it.'

He went back to munching his pop-tart, worried eyes returning to the screens. 'They must know they're risking their own lives as well as everyone else's. Or do they think they've discovered a way of staying clear of cosmic destruction? You never know with that lot. Risking perpetual life at the moment of death – for what? Eternal and physical torment…' He waved his hand in the air dismissively, sending crumbs towards Amy.

He was as fired up as she had ever known him. But underneath it all, he sounded frightened too. She didn't like to hear him like that.

Of course it wasn't in his nature to stay fearful for long.

'I think I'd better get my mail,' he said a bit later, whistling *Mister Mailman* to himself and straightening his bow tie without much effect.

This was such a mundane remark that she hardly knew

how to respond. 'Your *mail*?' She was having a hard time keeping from laughing. 'I didn't know you got *mail*!'

He was embarrassed, responding by mocking her. 'Why shouldn't I get *mail*? It's information and I depend on information.' He had dragged an old laptop out of a drawer and was murmuring a password while winding it up with a little crank handle. A pixelated face appeared on the old-fashioned screen and welcomed him. 'Good morning, Doctor. You have approximately eighty-two million new mails. Shall I download?'

'Thanks, yes.' The screen was teeming with messages, a babble of different images, voices and languages. Horrible! He leaned forward, frowning as he tried to concentrate on them. Finally he said: 'Terraphiles, please.'

The screen suddenly stopped, grumbled to itself, almost sneered, Amy thought, and reluctantly brought up a flashing, busy site.

Now Amy was beginning to grin. She heard him give another password and peeked over his shoulder. 'Oho! What's this?' she teased. 'You're a member of the Desperate Dan Pie Eater's Club? They knew I'd spill your secret for enough cow pies!'

She leaned over his tweedy shoulder to peer more closely at the screen. 'Blimey! Let's see? *The All-Galaxy Legion of Terraphiles*? *Your dues should be paid in by the following date…?*'

She read on, feeling more and more cheerful as she often did when she discovered new aspects of the Doctor's complex personality.

'What *is* this? '*Greetings fellow Earth-worms! There's news of the latest and greatest intergalactic RENAISSANCE TOURNAMENTS!!!*'

(This was accompanied by a picture of a Judoon, a centaur, two women, two men and a canine, all clad in bright greens and glaring whites.)

A voice-over explained who they were but she hardly understood a word. The Doctor wasn't happy about her looking on but was too busy taking notes to remonstrate.

'*THE TERRAPHILES ARE GOING TO THE "GHOST WORLDS"!!!! Three great teams will play for the legendary Silver Arrow of Artemis, said to be of immeasurable value, in the Terraphile All-Galaxy Renaissance Re-Enactments Interworld Series Tournament, which resolves on that weird system Miggea at the centre of our galaxy. You know the one. Scene of a dozen planetary thrillers? Sexton Blake in the Ghost Worlds? "Nobody dare live there more than a year and a day…" They say it's fair to all players, a planet as close to the centre of the galaxy as you can get!!! Apparently the Arrow of Artemis is well worth winning, and the team that wins it gets all kinds of profitable endorsements for the next two-and-a-half Terra-centuries. We'll keep you posted, fellow Earth-worms, as the teams make their way to Miggea, named, we understand, for an old Earth warrior-goddess. Anyone care to send more details…? – The Head Wriggler!!!!*'

She was shaking her own head now. 'I get it. This is a site for Earth-nerds. People in the future, yeah? Who like to dress up in what they think are human clothes –' She pretended to give his own clothes the once-over, then returned her attention to the screen, which was threatening to collapse on them. 'You're a – what? – you put out fanzines called –' she read the screen – '*EarthWormer* and *Novae Terrae*?'

'It's just one organisation.' He was defensive. 'I joined while I was in the future a few years ago. I was curious, that's all.'

Very defensive. She gave him one of her looks. She couldn't resist getting another rise out of him.

'I make it my business to be informed of what's going on in the –'

She was smiling at him affectionately again. 'A Terraphile, eh? That explains a lot! You're a fan-boy, aren't you? A fan of my silly little planet. That's why you've spent so much time saving us from all those terrors and invasions. It's because we're your HOBBY! Isn't it? Own up!'

'Oh, no, not *that*, I promise you.' He was suddenly serious. 'But as for the rest,' he gave her a slightly self-mocking, hang-dog look, 'it's even worse than you think. Maybe... it's how I first became interested in Earth – the real Earth, not the one these fans believe existed. They've got Terraphilia, yes, but based on what people in 51007 thought old Terra was like. A bit similar to people's guesses in your time about what Ur might be like. Or Atlantis. Or Barsoom. Only the Terraphiles had it a bit easier because they had a few books to consult...' The screen began to fade.

'What sort of books?'

'A pretty miscellaneous bunch. The books are a sort of Rosetta Stone for academics in the fifty-first-thousandth century. The entire remaining printed texts that were found on Old Old Earth, sealed deep in a natural cave in Arctic Skipton. *The Story of Robin Hood* is one of them. *Boys' Friend. Thriller Picture Library. The Captain. The British Boys' Book of Our Empire. Captain Justice and the Submarine Gunboat. Sexton Blake and the Terror of the Tongs*. Some people think that last one is the greatest epic poem in any language,' the Doctor said, in a tone that suggested he probably agreed with them. 'Then there's a collection of cigarette cards from between about 1919 and 1940. My guess is they were unconsidered stock from some old Old Yorkshire newsagent's. If the shop was built over a cave system, as so many were, the whole thing could have been swallowed up in one of the massive earthquakes following the comet strike.' He caught her expression and added quickly: 'Yeah, well, don't worry about that. Not yet, anyway. But they've all been invaluable to the study of ancient Earth. I joined the Terraphiles ages ago, so long ago I can't remember. I still keep up my sub to the LOT.

Out of nostalgia as much as anything.'

'The lot?'

'The League of Terraphiles. They're the ones who are the keenest Re-Enactors. Most of their legendary sports are derived from those books.'

'A bit Brit-centric aren't they? Is that a word? Still, that explains it.'

'Explains what?'

'Why you show so little interest in the rest of the planet!'

'That's not true!'

'Well, you seem to like America, too. But as for China, say...'

'I'm *very* interested in China!'

'Oh, really?'

'Really. I wish I had more time to argue.'

'You're a Time Lord, you should have all the time in the universe!'

'That would be nice.' His voice became distant, distracted again as he returned his attention to his main instruments and screens. 'But 51007's the date. Now I have to refine that and pick a place. Ah! I know...'

'What?'

'They're playing a friendly match on a Planet of the Peers. There's several of them. Peers™' – he actually said the 'TM' – 'is a concession which creates a sort of never-never England. It's a laugh. You'd love it. Better than Disneyland, I promise. Well, different, anyway. We could join them there. That way Frank/Freddie and the gang wouldn't know we were taking a special interest in the Miggean "Ghost Worlds" and get the jump on us.' He clicked his tongue thoughtfully. 'I'll have to brush up on my sledgehammer skills.'

'Sledgehammer?'

'Cracking the nut. It's one of my best events. I hate the broadswording, though.'

Watching as he set new coordinates, Amy had little time to think about what he meant. Only after they reached the space-time coordinates he had plotted for them did she ask him: 'Why are you worrying about something happening so far in the future? How does it affect us?'

'Well, like everything else, the future is relative. Time moves at different "speeds" in different sections of the galaxy. What takes place at the centre of our galaxy affects the past as well as the future. Like ripples extending out from a dropped stone, you know?'

'And it's powerful enough to ripple through *all* time and space? So is it dangerous to us now?'

He was honest with her. 'I'm not exactly sure. It's something the Time Lords used to worry about. That, of course, was when there were things they could do to stop the phenomenon happening. Psychologists, mythologists, metaphysicists, historians, astrophysicists... Thousands of brilliant altruistic minds all focused on the same problem. But now it's just down to me.'

'Hey! I'm here, too.'

'And I'm sure you'll be just as brilliant.' He smiled. 'Even brillianter, probably. Now, we need to get hold of that Silver Arrow first. That seems to hold the power the guy sending that message was trying to tell us about.'

'Off we go, then?' She felt an odd flutter in her stomach.

'Yes,' he said. 'You and me and whatever rag, tag and bobtail bunch of allies we can rustle up in a hurry. Oh, we probably need an army to help us out. But we'll be in 51007 in a whisper and all the armies who might do me a favour are dead. Occupational hazard, I suppose. Unless I can contact Captain Abberley and the Bubbly Boys, of course... Oh, you'd love them. Heard of them? Some call them the Chaos Kids... Sorry. Twenty-first century. I forgot. There's three of them. And their uncle – or possibly their dad – Captain Abberley.

21

Two brothers and a cousin. They – oops…' The TARDIS gave a skittish flick to the right. 'Oof.' One back to the left.

It was going to be another smooth ride, she realised.

Amy helped the Doctor brush up on his Tournament sports for the period they were visiting. He was delighted in her. She was naturally good at almost everything – even getting proficient at many games – but Barrers and Bludgeons stumped her. She understood most of the other games which combined to produce the galaxy-wide sport favoured mostly by Terraphiles of this far future that bore such a strange out-of-synch familiarity to her own not-so-distant past. She also shared his disgust for the broadsword event.

As soon as he was ready, they took the TARDIS to a particular Peers™ planet and the Doctor, claiming to have come from another Peers™ and desperate for a game of Arrers, or indeed a game of anything, immediately tried out for the 'Gentlemen'. He proved himself a fine all-rounder with a special penchant for Hammer and Nut. As a result he was picked for the First Fifteen, which, in spite of his heavy use of nano-technical learning methods, made him a lot prouder than Amy thought was really healthy. Up to then soccer had seemed to be his game of choice. But now the important thing they had to do was (a) play for the mysterious Silver Arrow and win and (b) discover the whereabouts of Frank/Freddie Force and his/their horrible Antimatter Men to thwart whatever part of their/his scheme they could fathom. If, of course, Force and Co actually had a plan. Or even existed.

'Or else…' The Doctor spoke wearily to Amy in a tone of voice which had experienced every terror *except* this. '… it's curtains for all life in the universe. Phut! And no chance of a comeback this time.'

'Now you're being melodramatic,' she said.

'Hadn't you noticed?' His eyes twinkled for a moment.

'We're living in a *permanent* melodrama. I'm the madman with the box, remember?'

'That's all right, then.' She smiled.

Chapter 2

Blue

HARI AGINCOURT WAS BLUE. To say he felt the colour of a Mediterranean sky at noon would be somewhat to understate his mood. If he had studied English or some other ancient language a little more assiduously at school he would have been able to think of something profound by Self or Lester that described his condition. Lying not far from the whackit pitch beside the river, he was sucking his stylo and pondering an elusive rhyme for 'snake in the grass' when, with a red rose in her smart black Eton crop and clad in the flimsiest lavender frock of her chosen year's latest Loondoon collection, Jane 'Flapper' Banning-Cannon, the stunning subject of his pensée, sailed by, poling a punt and singing 'I'm A Hip Swaying Honey From Honalu-la-lu-la' in a high, clear soprano. Her companion was a rather good-looking but seemingly vacant young man wearing a bright green blazer and matching straw hat, lounging on a pile of pillows, playing an expensive ukulele and staring in a somewhat studied manner at the middle distance.

(Jane, whose romantic obsession with the Middle Edwardian Ages had caused her to adopt one of the most popular girls' names of the period, had naturally fallen in love with the handsome Hari the moment he strode onto the Archery Court. After several failures, she had hit on the plan to persuade poor Bingo to become her reluctant ukulelist in the very punt at that moment being observed by the terrifically blue Hari Agincourt, as jealous as Flapper had intended him to be, but not about, as she had hoped, to fling himself from cover and declare his undying love.)

Hari glared morbidly at the ukulelist, his fellow team member and best friend (or ex-best friend as he now preferred to think of him) Lord Robin of Sherwood, Earl of Lockesley. 'Bingo' Lockesley was the finest archer on Peers™ (XXII) and the only other local in the intergalactic team known as the Gentlemen (though the name was a bit misleading).

Apparently unnoticed on the bank, largely because of the tall reeds, Hari, it is safe to say, was now replete in his blueness. Hari existed in a universe of blue. Had he been an advanced musician of the old Berlin school, he would there and then have produced a 12-tone concerto called *Blues for my Blues* for oboe and stirrup pump and been invited to take a prestigious tour of the galaxy's major suicide salons. But, sadly, he was merely an impoverished all-round gentleman archer whom you might employ to improve your nephew's target averages and bowing stance but not pay a fortune for the privilege. After that, there were just the usual junior teaching jobs and so forth. Not enough to pay for a third-hand air-mobile and a decent room in a reasonably cheerful level of the city, let alone keep self, spouse and offspring in comfort. Which he mused sadly wasn't even Problem One.

Problem One came in three parts: (a) how to win the affections of the lady in question, (b) how to achieve a softening of attitude in his loved one's doting father, who had not unreasonably been described as a blazing boil on the face of a universe of boils and so far seemed to regard Hari, when he regarded him at all, as less than worthless and with a criminal mouth to boot; certainly not in the running as a suitable spouse for the apple of his eye, and (c) ditto re his loved one's doting mother. Even the most fearsome of tigers was not as protective of its cub as Mr U.J. Banning-Cannon IV of Great Hamptons, Long Island, USA, Earth Regenerated, the terraforming tycoon. As it happened, Mr B-C was a cooing dove compared to Mrs B-C, a stately lady with a powerful right hook, who carried with her the air of a famished giant pterodactyl upon whom one calls unexpectedly as she moodily tears apart a small tyrannosaurus to provide her chicks with an inadequate lunch.

Mrs B-C was an Orion Tarbutton, a family, it was said, of unadulterated iron dipped in arsenic, with a murky and murderous past and carrying the Curse of the Tarbuttons from one generation to the next. Said Curse could, it was true, begin as a virtue (or at least a way of making sackfuls of dosh) but end as a vice, being, of course, pursuit of gambling. Unlike Mrs B-C's Other Weakness, her gambling was, most of the time, kept firmly under control.

Unknown to her husband and daughter, Mrs Banning-Cannon had proposed this Galactic Nostalgia Tour precisely because she felt the old urge rising in her, threatening to burst the bonds she had mentally cast around it. Only moments before the decision to embark on this educational luxury cruise, while despairing over her daughter's prospects of marriage, she had caught herself watching the *First Past the Post* feature by the Major on her V. The Major recommended Warp Factor Ten in the 2.30 at Gorgon Gap Park, Heaven on Earth, Aldebaran, the acknowledged centre of koop-koop racing. Her hand had reached unconsciously for her holo-V. Her glance shot like summer lightning towards the bookmaker ikon. She was a few short seconds from placing five K each way on the filly in question when she was saved by the sound of very loud travelogue commentary in her ear.

Earlier she had forgotten to close the appropriate function.

Thank Mercury it wasn't a koop-koop race, she thought, but merely a report of the All-Galaxy Sporting Re-Enactment Society's current tour, which was reaching its close, as was traditional, on Flynn in the rather hairy system of Miggea, close to the Galactic Hub, with only three games left to play. The three teams in question were the Gentlemen, the Tourists and the Visitors. They were pretty evenly matched and no one in particular tipped to win the coveted 'Big Arrer', more formally known sometimes as the Jewelled Arrow of Artemis or simply the Silver Shaft, so rarely seen except during its presentation to the winner. Had she not been painfully bored by that particular sport – individual matches of which could be played over periods of weeks, sometimes months, and included tie-breakers involving archaic and baffling skills resurrected from the Home Planet's dim past – she might just have considered a flutter on the outcome. Large sums were said to change hands amongst enthusiasts…

No!

Had she slipped and V'd her bookie, her five full years of refusing so much as to buy a lottery ticket would have been as dishwater down the drain. Happily a re-enactment game of, say, nutcracking filled her with instant ennui and quivering disgust so, with a blink, it was easy enough to turn off her V.

She turned it on again almost at once as a solution to her problems popped into her consciousness. She checked her V-mail for a letter she half-remembered receiving. Someone from the Terraphiles whom she had planned to ignore as firmly as only the wealthy can. Ah, there it was. An oddly dressed bleating old fogey asking her to present the prize to the winner of the 15th Quarter-Millennium Terraphile Re-Enactment Tournament on Flynn. They were offering all expenses paid for two and space travel to Flynn in the

Miggea system aboard the luxury tour liner the ISS *Gargantua*, stopping at a number of picturesque planets designed to replicate the beauties and customs of Ancient Earth, courtesy Messrs TipTop Travel, Inc.

Like most rich people, Mrs Banning-Cannon loved a bargain. What could be better than a free holiday? And, including their daughter, two-thirds paid for by someone other than herself or her husband?

An ancestor might have cried 'Eureka!' As it was, she was momentarily consumed with admiration of her own astonishing intellect.

In a matter of minutes, she had replied to the Terraphiles to say that she would be delighted to accept their offer to present the Silver Arrow at the conclusion of their Great Tournament. She would make travel arrangements and send the bill to their appropriate department. Then she committed herself, her husband Urquart and her beautiful daughter Jane (aka 'Flapper') to what she was assured was Messrs TipTop Travel Inc.'s deluxe Galactic Re-Enactment Tours. Messrs TipTop assured the public that their tour was the finest and most select available, being both educational and healthy. Everything would be provided, including the latest and most sophisticated nano-tech translation pill, cultural information and style advice.

In other words, she thought, Mr Banning-Cannon and the apple of their eye could educate themselves at a substantial discount while she, Mrs B-C, took a well-earned doze in the suns of a score of sultry systems while occasionally indulging in her Other Vice, clinically known as *millinerophilia*, the ancient compulsion to shop for hats. What was more, she had a good chance of solving her remaining problem: her daughter might, with luck, find and marry a Peer. (She was, she admitted to herself, just a little hazy about what a Peer actually was, but she knew her friends would be envious.)

The advantage also being that her husband's firm owned the Peer™ concessions, thus continuing, also, to keep the money in the family.

It had been another advantage in her eyes that 'Tournaments Mediaeval (Archery Plus)' was a sport she had never wanted to bet on. Not only was it one of the few sports rarely offered in her bookmaker's menu of choices, it was also very slow and unexciting. She fancied it to be played almost entirely by titled toffs. Its teams were likely to be crammed with members of what she still called the Brutish aristocracy, thanks to a fault in her nano-translator.

Also reassuring to Mrs B-C was that many of the other planets they would visit had been created by her husband's family company TerraForma™, which made its main profits from taming various intergalactic hellspots into Earth-like speciality worlds, mostly on sporting themes. Thus the TFIII series was largely devoted to gulf, the TFVI series to chicklit, the TFVXI series to fruitball, and so on. The TFXX series, featuring Archery and Middle Ages Tournament Re-Enactments, was perhaps the least popular and therefore unlikely to be swamped with tourists. Like most tourists, Mrs Banning-Cannon loathed tourists and tried to avoid them at all costs. Therefore she was further delighted that the Terraphiles had chosen the cruise-ship *Gargantua* on which to make the Re-Enactment Tour, conveniently beginning on Cygnus 34, not far from their home in Barnard's Star, and due to end, as stated, in Miggea in Sagittarius, close to the galaxy's centre, where she would present the victorious team with the coveted Jewelled Arrow of Artemis.

As previously stated, she and her husband were currently enjoying a pleasant snooze in lawn chairs on this regenerated English village green where handsome young men in whackit pullovers and blazers and pretty young women in cloche straws and filmy silk frocks stood cheering for their team or for individual players. There were a few strict Terraphile conservatives insisting on authentic tournament formals, including 'page boy' haircuts, Wedgewood plate armour, long velvet dresses, the odd wimple, long strings of pearls, habits, top hats, bloomers and so forth taken from the earliest surviving pictures of Earth between the years 1430 and 1930, a period described by tour operators as Merrie Eusa. Behind them, on the veranda of the pavilion, from which waved various banners, chaps of many planets wearing feathered green pointed caps, crenellated capes, green baggy trousers and the loud multicoloured blazers of the Ancient and Most Honourable Order of Toxopholite Terraphiles, were relishing shants of VW Best while occasionally casting an eye on the 'Friendly', enjoying its third day played by the Gentlemen against their old rivals the Tourists.

The players consisted of more chaps in glaring Lincoln Green, their trousers, where they had any, held up by old school ties, shooting blunted wooden arrows at two other chaps, one of them a rhinocerid Judoon and the other a canine Pilparque, in heavily padded armour, helmet and gloves, situated at either end of the field and holding large whackits in their hands. These two attempted to stop the 'shooters' from hitting the 'wotsit' or board (three legs supporting a round, straw-filled object divided into many numbered sections) behind which stood 'wotsit keepers', whose job appeared to be to catch the arrows which missed and stick them in the said wotsit. Whoever scored 380 first would, Mrs Banning-Cannon understood, be declared the winner. It was a wonder, she thought wearily, that the bookies took any interest in the sport at all.

Although this Planet of the Peers™ had been chosen from the itinerary because the great matriarch assumed it to have been populated by human bluebloods, actually it was mostly colonised by archery enthusiasts wishing to honour the great

Mr Peer, founder of the original London archery ground bearing his name, but she had struck lucky in her choice even though she hadn't quite got it right. Everywhere on Peers™ chaps, mostly humanoid or at least bipedal, were shooting, whacking, fielding, wotsit-keeping or imbibing pints in one of the many pavilions in a few thousand Tournament Renaissance grounds on a franchise world which had been let for the last nine millennia to a 'regrown' family with undisputed DNA links to England in Old Old Earth. The Lockesley family's current concessionaire-in-chief in the old huntin', shootin' and fishin' tradition was Lord Robin of Sherwood, Earl of Lockesley, a keen archer on a world almost entirely given over to bowmanship and a public school education, what some called a shaftin', runnin', jumpin', crammin' and whackin' planet. Those who were not enjoying tournaments were either 'gated' for some misdemeanour at school or mooning miserably over a pretty 'stunner' with which the planet was plentifully seeded in order to keep up the supply of new chaps and stunners to attend schools and play the great and noble Tournament or the Grand Old Whack as devotees called it.

Peers™ was one of several concessions built by the Banning-Cannon family in the Moravian Cluster. All were called Peers™ and were pretty much identical, with a good supply (in appropriate species) of Decent Chaps, Silly Asses, Pretty Girls and, of course, Fearsome Magistrates, Kindly Uncles and Terrifying Aunts, Fogeys (Old) and Fogeys (Young), not to mention Policemen (Helmeted) and Policemen (Unhelmeted) as well as Marryin' Maids, Littlejohns, Scarlet Will O'Haras, Magnum Carters and all the other characters and accoutrements likely to be needed to sustain what most Decent Chaps agreed was a pretty spiffin' sort of a planet, created for the TerraForma™ company by Algernon Pine, a reconstituted writer of OE's Mediaeval English Edwardian school defrosted on Old Old Mars about ten thousand years ago.

Pine, that honest soul, had been a bit miffed to find his suggestions tweaked here and there until it was explained to him that democracy demands you give the public what it wants. Little remained of the original at such a distant date in the future of Old Old Earth's history. It should be pointed out that, allowing for public taste, the reconstructors had done their best. The concession had been pieced together by experts in what was known these days as the History Entertainment business, providing excellent templates for many nicely, and safely, made new worlds. That most of them recollected a relatively short, yet lively, period between European fifteenth and twentieth centuries was because of Original Terra's (Old Old Earth's) thoroughly frozen state. A couple of nuclear winters and a large comet had seen to that.

Having established through careful research that the game of *arrers* or *archery* was the most popular of olden times, the experts had skilfully reconstructed it as the grand finale game of the Renaissance Tournamentors, establishing The Rules of Tournament (2137) by which everyone nowadays played. TerraForma™ guaranteed their remade worlds were as much like the originals as possible.

The Society of Terraphiles held a Grand Tourney, currently the most exclusive game in the universe, every two and a half centuries, playing for the ancient Silver Arrow of Artemis (the Big Arrer), whose origins were lost in the mists of time. Some said it was of supernatural manufacture. Players often belonged to the other galaxy-wide re-enactment society, the Ancient and Most Honourable Order of Toxopholite Terraphiles, who prided themselves on following the customs, costumes and manners of the Original Olde English archers and knights. Before the main games began, several other events had to be played out, including Quartering the

33

Knave, Broadswording, Charging the Peasant, Stiffing the Publican, Dungeoning the Dragon, Swatting the Quintain and, most popular of all, Using a Sledgehammer to Crack a Nut, plus various contests involving axes, dragon-lances, swords, war-hammers and several other means of ancient human conflict.

Which was about the most Mrs Banning-Cannon understood or wished to understand of the Grand Old Whack. All this and considerably more had been explained to her by the agreeable Bingo, Lord Sherwood, Peer™ being his home world, who had the advantage in her eyes of being an acknowledged pedigree Peer of the Realm, unmarried and heir to a huge castle known as Lockesley Hall with grounds as extensive as a moderately sized country, somewhere on this side of the planet. Not only was he therefore An Eligible Bachelor, but he was also reasonably good looking, if a bit dim and over-eloquent on the subject of the Ancient Tourney of Archerie on which, it emerged, he had written several papers well reviewed in *The Whacksman's Wisdom*, the best-regarded V-journal on the subject. That he was by his own admission as poor as a church mouse and urgently in need of what he called variously 'dosh', 'tin', 'lolly' or 'argent' only enhanced his eligibility in her view because, as every plutocrat knows, the once-wealthy destitute are always more malleable than the poor who have never been anything else. And, while she wanted a blueblood for a son-in-law, she did not want a stroppy one who would talk back. It had not occurred to her that such a weak-knee would not exactly be a type her strong-willed daughter favoured for a spouse.

Her eyes half-closed against the balmy light, Mrs Banning-Cannon smiled favourably on a heavily padded and helmeted whacksman who currently defended what she understood to be the Gentleman's End against a famously keen canine player, G.H. O'Gruffy, whose tail was waving in what might

34

have been triumph and who let out loud, challenging barks as he again took aim with his bow at a wotsit defended by the rival whacker, whose protective clothing was now stuck with so many arrows he resembled a porcupine in the prime of its porcupinehood and whom Mrs Banning-Cannon fondly believed to be her anticipated son-in-law but was actually the Hon. Old Bill Told, standing in for Bingo.

The Silver Arrow of Artemis, having been stashed with other valuables in a super-secure time-locked travel-vault and sent ahead to Flynn to be opened immediately before its presentation to the winning team, Mrs Banning-Cannon was determined to enjoy the tour in the ways she loved best. The attractions of this game were becoming clearer to her, now that she realised that it was almost demanded of spectators that they sit in lawn chairs and snooze through much of every match. She had almost accidentally picked up some of the rules and objects and now even had a favourite team. The one she favoured (i.e. Lord Bingo's First Fifteen) was the Gentlemen. They were one of three which had been tipped from the start to win the All-Galaxy Tournament, though at present slightly better odds were being offered on the present Arrow holders, the Tourists. Not, she told herself firmly, that odds had anything to do with it given that this was anyway a mere *friendly*. These players, she had read, were so devoted to their sport that some members even went so far as to take nano-identity pills so that they believed they were human. Not a few were academics from all over the galaxy. These chose to immerse themselves in alien cultures and so learn through experience.

A rather disproportionate number of Tourists were Judoon, whose rhinocerid appearance made them particularly suited for the whacker's armour. Generally the Judoon had a taste for the more warlike sports of their home world, which had banned some of them for fear of exterminating their entire population and planet. Nukeball, for instance, was played only illegally and then on a few remote Rim worlds. Occasionally a distant exploding star system would indicate a somewhat Pyrrhic win.

While Mr B-C had no objection to holidaying on his own company's worlds and thus keeping the money, as he always liked to do, in the family, nor to indulging his wife's every whim in the matter of hat collections or other foibles, he was unhappy about her choice of suitors for his daughter's hand, whom his wife had insisted on parading before him. For one thing he saw most of them as employees or at least customers and as such harbouring notions of furthering their fortunes by becoming his son-in-law. He did not understand that the very thought of such a union caused most eligible candidates considerable collywobbles. For another, he had already picked out his nephew Hamlet Tarbutton as his personal choice.

Young Ham had the advantage of being as putty in his uncle's hands, not too bright and possessed of a large fortune of his own from Mr B-C's chief rival, his sister-in-law, the big boss of Earthmakers™ Inc. who specialised in remaking and restocking worlds in the image of legendary golden ages, including *The Glory That Was Rome*, *The Marvel of Mogal India*, *The Beauty of Buffalo*, *The Gods of Ancient Greece* and so on. The merging of two such mighty empires would become inevitable if Ham could be persuaded to pop the question and Jane to accept. It would also banish his monetary losses in a flash. It is fair to say that had he known Flapper had set her sights on an untitled amateur archer, whom she had met only six days earlier at a Higher Tea put on in their honour by the local Squire and who was even more impoverished than Bingo Lockesley, he would have given the nearest supernova a run for its money. Happily for the fate of this particular bit of the universe, Flapper had not yet been able to force her heart's desire to pop the question and had resorted to persuading young Agincourt's best friend to pretend to be sweet on her, thus, she perceived, stimulating the object of her affections to be spurred on by jealousy instead, it seemed, of moping about in the bulrushes like a pining frog.

Another circumstance which had caused Flapper's paterfamilias to descend into a glumness as deep as Hari Agincourt's was the new hat his wife had bought for herself on the previous day and which she had announced she intended to wear at the next day's Garden Party at Lord Sherwood's but given by the local bigwig, known as the Omar of Notts, by way of a farewell ceremony to which both Gentlemen and Tourists had all been invited. This had put Mr B-C in an even poorer mental condition than usual.

It is not unfair to say that his default state was generally that of a Spanish bull, who, already in a blood-maddened rage, has taken exception to a toreador waving a silly red silk cape under his nose. Save where the sole fruit of his loins was concerned, he was inclined to regard the galaxy's younger billions as decidedly inferior specimens. The inhabitants of this particular world he considered especially unworthy, not only lazy but vacuous, a planetful of wasters. To be asked for his daughter's hand by one of them would be harder to swallow than a whole Gouda cheese washed down with a pint of malt vinegar, and he should know because he had attempted this feat in earlier and happier days as the family's prodigal. So his wife's tendency to millinerophilia was in comparison a cooing dove and a balmy breeze to Mr B-C's soul. Except, that is, for the most recent outbreak of her maniacal ability to pick and purchase the largest, ugliest and most expensive hats in the known universe and, he suspected, beyond.

This he was still brooding upon as he lay back in his chair

and listened to the restful twang of the yew and the calming thump of the oak. Until now he had known neither rest nor calm. On the previous day, Enola Banning-Cannon had returned to their hotel apartments followed by two sturdy bots carrying between them a monstrous hatbox.

When opened, the box revealed the most stomach-turning confection of poisonous colours, ebony, feathers, gauze, ivory, bits of silver, gold and presumably platinum wire plus a whole shower of precious stones mined from the bowels of a hundred planets, four multifaceted gems resembling eyes, the whole more than adequately arching over its generous brim of about a metre and a half around his spouse's head and bearing an uncanny likeness to a *Shummyunny*, the predatory arachnid occupant of Perseus IX, which was actually the creature of nightmares. Certainly of Mr B-C's nightmares. These said creatures were inclined to fill him with a mixture of nausea, dizziness and an irresistible tendency to race into the world cawing like a rook and tearing off all his clothes until he had located a small, dark space into which he could lock himself and give vent to his inevitable diarrhoea. He had barely been able to control himself when, suspecting his dislike of a confection squatting on her head like a spider poised to leap, she had ordered it back in its box saying she was humouring him now, but –

'I shall of course be wearing it for the Earl of Lockesley's Garden Party.'

'I thought you said he was a Lord,' murmured Mr B-C before the rest of her meaning had sunk in.

'He's both. And more. The bluer the blood, I gather, the more names and titles you're allowed. Anyway, I intend to make a splash at Castle Lockesley Hall tomorrow. I've heard these titled types like to sport spectacular hats at important dates in the social calendar. This is the biggest event after the Three Legged water-ski race held in Aquarius every spring. My hat, I have every confidence, will slaughter all opposition.'

And then the shock hit the elder Banning-Cannon. And he reeled. In fact he reeled several times as he tried to find breath.

'Urk,' he said in tones of absolute panic.

She had no trouble understanding this. Nor did she have any difficulty in shaking her head and repeating her intention to sport the hideous concoction at the next day's farewell ceremony.

'It *shall* be worn,' she announced firmly. 'It is a Diana prize-winning original. It's called *Variations on a Theme by Aristophanes*. A classic title, Diana herself assured me.'

Glowing bright red before fading to a rather delicate mauve, Mr B-C had threatened and been ignored, begged and been greeted with a sniff of disdain. He had wept, only to be spurned contemptuously by this *belle dame sans merci*. He had reminded her of his phobia and been told to pull himself together. He had warned her that he would become the laughing stock of the entire galaxy, and she had retorted that it was probably no less than he deserved. He had offered bribes, only to be reminded that his recent losses on the plan to turn Sculum Crux into one vast rose garden measuring light years across had made him for the time being somewhat dependent on her fortune.

His plans for financial recovery, he had told her miserably, would probably be scotched for ever if he was to be seen mewling like a baby and tearing off his clothes while heading blindly for the Earl's nearest ornamental rain barrel. This she had pooh-poohed as nothing less than emotional blackmail. She had paid a great deal of money for her hat, an original creation, she reminded him again, of the immeasurably fashionable Diana of Loondoon, and she knew it would make her costume the talking point of the Season. Which, he knew full well, could only be good for his business.

He answered darkly that if there was to be a talking point at all it would come a poor second to the anecdotes concerning his running about naked giving impressions of rooks and badgers which would lead to his irrecoverable ruin. What was worse, assuming he would be admitted back through the doors, he would become the laughing stock of his club, the Senior Oligarch's.

Her advice to him was to take a pill. He reminded her of the dozens of doctors he had seen and how no pill had yet been made that would do the job apart from one which produced symptoms even more dramatic than the original condition. He tried pathos:

'I couldn't bear to have Jane see me like that!'

'Then make sure you control yourself!'

Stern threat:

'Enola! For the sake of both our great families and their future, you shall not wear that hat tomorrow!'

'Urquart! I shall!'

This exchange was elaborated along similar lines for some while until Urquart Banning-Cannon played his trump card (or at least the only card he had):

'In which case,' he had announced, drawing himself up to his full one and three quarter metres, 'I shall be unable to accompany you. I am already feeling queasy. By tomorrow afternoon I expect to be running a high fever and be confined to my bed.'

To which she had replied:

'Balderdash!'

And allowed a silence to follow which clearly let it be known the argument was over. Then, wordlessly, this Boadicea of the boardroom rose and walked determinedly in the direction of the refreshment pavilion.

Now, he thought dumbly, only suicide could save him. In

which case he was in a horrible double bind. Jane, under no circumstances, should carry that stigma. Daughters of self-murderers rarely married well in his social circles. He loved her above all else and all others. He must consider another strategy. And, as he sat in apparent half-slumber, a solution to his problem slowly began to germinate in his close-cropped head.

At which point a lanky, beaky, Harris tweed-jacketed individual wearing a rudely laundered grey-striped shirt and a small, not to say dowdy, maroon bow tie flung itself across his field of vision and snatched an arrow from the air just before it landed a few inches from his nose. The lanky individual then fitted the arrow into a bow he carried, drew back the string, aimed for the wotsit, hit it squarely in the centre before the bewildered gaze of the Judoon whackit keeper, and uttered a triumphant, if mysterious cry.

'Three hundred and *eighty*! Howzat?'

Chapter 3

Red

'**AND WHO MIGHT YOU** be?' Mr Banning-Cannon was unaware that this apparently young man had become pretty well used to that question and knew, if nothing else, how to answer it concisely.

'I,' said the young man, squinting down the field in a slightly self-congratulatory way to ascertain his score, 'am the Doctor...'

Mr B-C regarded the newcomer with fresh eyes, rather in the manner of a besieged commander who, having given up hope of his fort being relieved and feeling a prophetic itch in the region of his scalp, learns at last that the 7th Cavalry, and maybe the 6th and 8th, are best friends with the Indians and everything's OK.

'A doctor, did you say? Do you know much about *Perseum Arachnophobia*?' asked Urquart hopefully.

'A bit,' the Doctor replied carefully. 'Why do you ask?' He saw that his score had been accepted so, flinging down his bow, settled into the lawn chair recently vacated by Mrs B-C. 'That's it. Game over. We won. You were saying?'

'Oh.' Mr B-C coughed and shrugged his shoulders. 'There's always the chance one might run into an expert. Just making conversation…'

'I know what you mean,' agreed the Doctor. 'I'm constantly hoping for someone with a fresh subject or at least a new angle on an old one. I think it gets harder and harder to find as you get older. Seems like we have something in common.'

But Mr B-C was already returning to his more familiar mental state.

'I doubt it,' he said, now seeing little more than another skinny young wastrel, perhaps with designs on Jane like most of the inhabitants of this miserable planet. 'Unless you've done much terraforming.'

The Doctor gave this some thought. 'Not recently. I've been in a war or two. Which is apt to change a planet's appearance, of course, though not usually for the better. That's your line of work, is it? Terraforming, I mean – not war.'

'As a matter of fact we created *this* world. Moreover, my company owns the entire Peers™ concession. And quite a few others.'

The young doctor did his best to sound impressed. 'You recreated the sports and all that?'

'Well, my company did. Some of them. Broadswording, for instance. Here's my card. TerraForma™. You've probably heard of us.' Mr Banning-Cannon was glad of the distraction and even found himself warming a little towards the newcomer. He had a certain air about him, as of one not unused to authority. 'We're the second-largest firm in the business. And my wife Elona is the Tarbutton heiress. They're the largest.'

'You've got a fair bit of power and experience between you, then. You don't do those literary worlds, I suppose? The free-ranging ones, where you get to play a serious part in Balzac, or Disney, or Austin, or Meredith, or James, or Lansdale, or Mieville, or Pynchon, or Mann, or Sinclair, or Calderon, or Gygax, or Moore, or—'

There was no sign of him stopping so Urquart cut in. 'I'm not much of a literary buff,' he admitted proudly. 'We're more practical. Engineering's my game. Or was originally. There's precious little demand for highbrow stuff, these days.'

'I suppose you're right. I'm inclined to watch mostly non-fiction. And brush up on the rules, of course.'

'You're with the local team?'

'The Gentlemen. So… you suffer from phobias, do you? Frightened of spiders, is that right? Any allergies at all?'

Banning-Cannon cleared his throat. 'Oh, not really. So you've been back home with a bunch of other whackers after winning a lot of local games. Which makes you eligible for the big games being held in Miggea. You and the Tourists are travelling on the *Gargantua* same as us, I understand?'

'That's the plan. You're right about us already making the finals in Sagittarius. One more game to go, then we play either the Visitors or the Tourists. The Tourists will give us a run for our money. They almost beat us at that last friendly. We'll both be practising on the *Gargantua*. They say she has a full-size Tournament Court. We should all be in pretty good shape, everything being equal.' He waved to a passing Judoon who offered him a glance of hurt outrage as he went by, pulling arrows from his body armour.

'Important tournament, I guess.'

'Oh, yeah. The big one. And we all want to get our hands on the good old arrer. The Silver Arrow of Artemis is a legend in its own right!'

Urquart Banning-Cannon let his thoughts drift as he worked out the publicity value to all the planets involved. He would call the office as soon as possible and tell them to play up the tournaments. He brought his attention back to the Doctor. 'What? Sorry. Taking it all in. So! You're competing to win, I hear, some sort of antique artefact which my wife will present? A rod of platinum imbedded with precious stones and stuff. The mythological Staff of Law owned by the Lord of the Bee Bee Sea of old Barsoom?'

'An antique arrow, actually. Sometimes also known as the Arrow of Law, and the Silver Arrow of Artemis. Which would make it from Greece originally, I suppose. Dark Ages now, of course.' He fingered his little bow tie.

'Sounds lucky.' Urquart's attention was already wandering again. Like most tycoons of inherited wealth he had never learned to disguise his boredom.

'Hope so. Supposed to be.' The Doctor seemed a little puzzled as to what was really on Mr Banning-Cannon's mind.

'Well. Have fun. If your group and mine are all taking the ISS *Gargantua* the morning after tomorrow, I expect we'll be seeing a good deal of each other.' The tycoon made to get up. He had much else concerning him and he looked like a man with a weight on his shoulders. 'But if you should hear of any arachnophobia experts within the next few hours, point them in my direction, would you? I'm staying at the Claremont. Floor 144a.'

The Doctor shook hands. 'And you're Mr...?'

'Banning-Cannon.'

'Of course. Oh, here's my – here's Miss Pond. Amy this is—'

'Nice to meet you young lady.' Mr B-C was relieved. He shook hands with the pretty redhead in the short, pleated silk frock, noting the firmness of her grip, the glint of edged steel in her otherwise amiable gaze. He guessed that here at least this doctor fellow was a man he didn't have to worry about as a contender for Jane's hand. Then he narrowed his eyes, looking suspiciously over the Doctor's shoulder.

Another young man, clad in the glaring green blazer and multicoloured hat of a local, was ambling in his direction. Something about him caused the planet-maker to think he recognised and possibly feared him. What was he going to ask for? Mr B-C measured the distance between himself and the pavilion. In a fair race he was not going to win. Even as he considered the odds, he saw his lady wife leave the pavilion and walk off in deep conversation with Jane. Having failed to get Hari to the condition of a male peacock rattling his quills in the mating season, Jane had parted sadly from Lord Sherwood and sought her mother's company in order to discuss a costume for the next day's party.

Suddenly another notion flickered in the corners of Urquart Banning-Cannon's calculating mind. Waving a dismissive hand at the departing Doctor and his pretty friend, he waited until the next young man drew alongside. To his surprise it was Bingo Lockesley, Lord Sherwood, who opened the conversation.

'Mr Banning-Cannon?'

'Mmph?'

'My name's Lockesley.'

'Uh huh?'

'I was wondering –'

Here it came. A request for his daughter's hand. His eyes hardened. 'Mm?'

'– if you and your family would care to be my guests over at Lockesley Hall this evening? A little celebration of today's victory?'

Mr B-C was puzzled. 'I thought...'

'That I was throwing the Omar's Garden Party tomorrow? That's more a sort of municipal thing paid for by the County, you understand.'

'Aha!' Again Mr B-C knew momentary relief. 'Well, I'm not sure of my wife's plans...'

'OK, sir. The invitation's there. Nothing very fancy. The Lockesley fortunes aren't what they were but...'

Mr Banning-Cannon pricked up his ears. Now he uttered

a silent 'Aha!' Maybe the lively hand of Providence had fallen at last on his noble shoulders. His first notion was beginning to take a slightly more concrete shape. Now if this rather personable if apparently dim young fellow needed money, he might have found just the right ally. But they would have to work fast. 'If you're a drinking man, Mr Lockesley, I wonder if you'd join me somewhere quiet. I have a business matter I'd like to discuss with you.'

'Um, well, I'm not exactly—'

'Half an hour of your time and the chance to help a fellow soul out of a bit of a black hole.'

Lord Sherwood shrugged cheerfully. 'That sounds like a variant of the Lockesley motto, sir. What about the pavilion? It should be empty by now!'

'Lead on, young Lockesley!' Urquart Banning-Cannon began to see a possible light at the end of his own particular tunnel of torment. He felt as if his troubles were over already. His ship of grief had her rockets warmed and rumbling and was close to escaping for ever the gravity of his world of woe, or so he believed as he flung a benevolent arm around the peer's shoulders and, jingling his change in his trouser pocket, strolled amiably in the direction of stimulating refreshment.

Lord Lockesley's other motive in making contact had been to issue invites to the various parties involved in his best pal's own particular spot of romantic drama in order perhaps to ease love's rocky path for his friend. He also hoped to get back into Hari's good books before the two rival teams and the B-C's tour group embarked for Sagittarius aboard the same vessel come the dawn after next. A few moments later, in the deserted darkness of the pavilion bar, he listened with his mouth hanging open while this perfect stranger sketched out a plot which had its origins in the only literature the desperate patriarch had ever enjoyed, namely the adventures of Sexton Blake. Many years earlier Urquart Banning-Cannon had learned that V copies of *The Sexton Blake Library* made a sound investment. He had dallied with the idea of creating a series of Mystery Worlds based on the detective fiction of Earth's distant past only to be pipped at the post by his great rival, his brother-in-law Tarbutton, who was cleaning up with a concession of role-playing worlds based on the adventures of Sherlock Holmes, once known as 'Sexton Blake's office boy'.

Now Mr B-C dragged his chair a little nearer, looked both ways to ensure he wasn't overheard, and pressed his lips close to his listener's ear.

'How,' the worldwright began, 'would you like to own this planet?'

Inadvertently he had struck imaginative pay dirt. Lord Sherwood's ambition had always been to break free of the concession owner, restore the monarch and remould his planet into something a little less brash and dependent on tourism for its chief income.

'Go on,' he said, unable to resist such bait. 'You do mean the whole world? Lock, stock and barrel? No longer dictated to by – if you'll forgive me – a bunch of money-grubbing shareholders?'

'Renamed, remodelled, in any way you like.'

'So what's the catch? *Oh, no!*'

Lord L began to rise, certain he had spotted the viper in the haystack. 'I'm afraid I couldn't! In fact I'm pretty insulted that you should think I would!'

Urquart Banning-Cannon was not used to being refused even before he got his proposal out, except by Mrs B-C, of course.

'Couldn't what?' he gasped in surprise.

'Throw the match. Though I say it myself, I'm our best archer. We'd never win the Silver Arrow, as I'm sure you've realised, without my bowmanship. I'm not boasting, sir. Wish

I were. Just luck, you know, what? Nothing would please me more than to have that burden lifted from my shoulders. But I won't do it, Mr B-C, no matter what you offer! In fact I have to inform you that it's a pretty disgusting proposition, and if it weren't for the feelings of a brother player I would expose you immediately to the AGAC!'

Urquart had heard that these English peers were a bit barmy, the problem of inevitable inbreeding which no terraforming company had yet to crack. But this behaviour was positively certifiable. Paranoia at full blast.

'I suppose you saw her buying it in the store?' he opined.

'Store?' Bingo was getting the hint that he had grasped the wrong end of the whackit.

'The Diana of Loondoon franchise in Forest Mall?'

'Which is?'

'Damn you, Sherwood or Lockesley or Lord or whatever you call yourself! I'm talking about that infernal hat shop and you know it!'

'You're not trying to bribe me to take a fall in the big tournament?'

'Do what?'

'Throw the match.'

'Throw it where?'

'I mean…' Bingo gave up on any explanation, knowing it would sail over this amateur's head. He changed his tack. 'Well, if you don't want me to try to lose the last game in Miggea in the All-Galaxy Silver Arrow Tour, what *were* you going to suggest?'

It was Mr B-C's turn to feel his jaw muscles slacken. 'Eh? Why should I want you to do that?'

'It's well known that your lady wife has what some still call "a gambling problem". If she had put a lot of money on the other team to win, well, you can see why someone close to her would like to improve her chances.'

'My wife has kicked the gambling habit. She hasn't held so much as a tiddlywinks cup in her hand in five years. She is a strong-minded and intelligent woman. Once she has made a decision she sticks to it, as I know all too well to my cost. Anyway, if that's all it was, I shouldn't care. She could put her whole fortune on you or your rivals as far as I'm concerned and you wouldn't hear as much as an "I told you so" from me as that team inevitably lost, since she is one of the unluckiest gamblers I know.'

'Then what's so valuable to you you're willing to hand me over a fine, expensively terraformed planet which my family has been trying to buy for about seven thousand years without a hint of success?'

Mr B-C saw that the Earl of Sherwood had recovered from his fit, if fit it was. He understood the trigger had been the notion that he was asking his companion to do something completely against the Code of the Sherwoods. Upon consideration, this lifted his opinion of the young man's character. Here was a partner in crime who, once his word was given, could almost certainly be trusted. He relaxed a little and began to murmur his proposition, suggesting not only the temporary theft of The Hat but a general appearance of burglary to put his spouse off the scent.

Lord Sherwood listened in thoughtful silence. Ownership of the whole planet would allow him to offer Hari a good job, maybe a bit of land. This would enable his pal to propose to Flapper. He could also, he imagined with a deep sigh of satisfaction, restore the monarchy and put a Virgin King back on the throne. King Richard was already on a nearby planet fighting some sort of local unholy war involving balloons. He could be brought back at any moment. It would make sense, of course, to maintain a parliamentary democracy and ensure that any future selection of a sovereign would be done according to a planet-wide general election. Furthermore, he thought dreamily, there would be no loss of tourist revenues. He knew from experience that all the galaxy loved a monarch. He could easily drum up a few colourful ceremonies – the Hanging of the Guard could be one such, and there were plenty of others on his V-journal…

'So what does this hat look like? What's its size? Petite? Grandé? Anything she's worn already?'

To Lord Sherwood's increasing sympathy, Mr Banning-Cannon began to describe the horrible hat. His language boiled with passion and colour. It throbbed with authentic disgust. When the would-be thief-maker had finished, Bingo Lockesley had begun to feel that kidnapping the garish confection was no mere question of one crook doing a deal with another. It had become a question of noble necessity.

Rising at last from his chair he stuck out a steady hand. 'I'm your man, sir. Never let it be said that a Lockesley lets down a fellow creature in their hour of need! It's a deal.'

Indeed, thought Bingo seriously, even without the proffered lure, it was a chap's solemn duty to do what his new boss proposed. Urquart had revealed a side of his character that was both compassionate and sporting. Mrs B-C would only temporarily lose the company of her freshly purchased monster.

The hat would be returned to her perhaps with a witty, courteous note attached as soon as his garden party was over, and Mr B-C could rest easy, knowing that the hat could not be worn in public for some time after the *Gargantua* had reached Flynn.

As he left the pavilion, Lord Bingo relished the deep breaths of air he gulped from his surroundings, still smelling strongly of freshly cut grass, and looked up at a sky of deepening blue in which a glorious westerly sun was beginning to fall slowly towards the horizon. The plans had been discussed and finalised. The Banning-Cannons would be invited to spend their last nights on the planet at Lockesley Hall, as would the Gentlemen. The Tourists had already been invited and had refused in, Bingo thought, a slightly surly manner, but he wasn't worried about that. He was already in his imagination remodelling and renaming the old homestead. He was thinking of calling the whole world Knots, the city on Old Old Earth from which, legend said, his DNA had originally come. But the Virgin King would be the rightful ruler. Bingo had no ambitions in that direction. Every merry monarch required a serious subject. A grand title would be required, of course: Richard, King of Knots and Ruggery, had a certain ring to it. The Ancient Dynasty of Terra would begin anew. A magnificent new era would glorify the galaxy!

And all because, reflected Lord Sherwood, strolling cheerfully home through the gloom, a lady's husband had taken exception to one hat in thousands. On such slender threads, after all, did the plots of great histories hang.

Chapter 4

White

BACK AT THE SHERWOOD ranch, things were developing at a rapid pace. Mrs B-C, hearing in her mind's ear a title for her little girl (Earlette?) was ecstatic and had checked out of the Claremont and into Lockesley Hall at what some might consider unseemly speed. Finally, she congratulated herself, for it was she who had trained him, Urquart had done something right. Overseeing the arrival and distribution of her luggage, she was in several heavens at the same time. Sunset being a little extended on this planet, the sky was still a deep royal blue with a few well-formed clouds adding dramatic effect to an already splendid scene. Lockesley Hall cast an impressive shadow. Her Gothic-Baroque towers and battlements gave the nearby lake and surrounding parkland a phantasmagoric atmosphere, while the perfume of various night-scented lavenders, stocks and jasmines lulled one even further into euphoria.

V-ing ahead, Lord Sherwood had ordered a few simple dishes. His cook was told to break out the best foie gras, the finest smoked salmon and grade A caviar, also the great haunch of Boeuf de Campagne and its attendants which his grandfather had left in his will, stipulating it be cooked and eaten only when Independence seemed within reach. The Sherwoods had been royalist Virginistas for centuries. One couldn't take culinary risks when the soul of one's home planet was at stake. By a single scarcely criminal act, little more than a prank, really, he could buy that soul back and restore honour and virtue to the family name.

Admittedly, a small, still voice did from time to time whisper in his ear and warn of the potential consequences of what it insisted on calling 'the deed'.

At such moments Sherwood's outer voice answered his inner voice rather irritably, pointing out that he was not going to murder the King of Scotland or anyone else for that matter and that Banquo's ghost was unlikely to turn up as his guests tackled the meat and potatoes. As for three witches, they could only lend Olde Worlde charm to the scene and they were a very long way from Dunsinane. Besides which, this was not a melodrama. It was more of a romantic comedy, in which star-crossed lovers would be reconciled, fortunes restored, parents overjoyed and any hint of Grand Guignol wiped from the slate of events. The same small, still voice continued to insist that thievery was specifically understood to be a crime, no matter how much the poor, as it were, benefitted from the robbing of the rich. What was more, as Lord Sherwood's ancestral voices all agreed, the laws of hospitality were pretty generally defied when your host slipped into your bedroom during the hours of darkness and snaffled your favourite hat. Yet, even if he carried the crime on his conscience to his grave, Bingo Lockesley's mind was made up. Chances like this arrived once in a million years. His ancestors and his children's children would feel nothing but gratitude if they knew what he was doing for them. Should she hear his story, even Mrs Enola Banning-Cannon (née Tarbutton) would probably forgive him instantly.

*

Mr Banning-Cannon's mind, too, was made up. It had to be said that to be thwarted, as she would see it, of an earldom as well as a chance to out-hat all the other ladies at the next day's party would not fit easily into Mrs B-C's general view of what the world ought to be. Were she ever to discover that she had been duped she would be unlikely to laugh it off with a cheerful quip and a gentle, chiding tap of her fan on young Lockesley's cheek. More probably she would not rest until her Tarbutton relatives had reduced his world to ashes.

Of course, Urquart Banning-Cannon knew all this, which was why he was offering such a hefty reward for the successful accomplishment of the hat-napping. The odds favoured Lockesley considerably since he knew the house inside out. He could only hope the boy had somewhere to hide the thing once the deed was done. There would be a search. Questions would be asked. Accusations would be made. Threats would fly. Sabres would rattle.

Urquart felt a chill in his veins, a desire perhaps to rethink. Was it too late to turn back now? Usually his wife would have noticed his slightly shifty demeanour, his tendency to sweat a bit, his wet dry lips. She would have been certain something was up, but she was too distracted by imagining what she could tell her envious lady friends at home to spot the tell-tale signs.

Soon they were settled in their adjoining suites getting ready for dinner. Once or twice Mr B-C wandered into his wife's rooms and made a casual enquiry while in actuality casing the joint, getting the exact emplacement of what he came to think of as the swag.

This swag remained in a gaudy hatbox measuring more than a metre across and almost another metre deep. Not something to be easily snatched and pocketed by a professional cracksman, let alone an amateur. But Urquart had a healthy respect for Bingo's skills and knowledge of this rambling old run-down place he called home –

– while, at the same moment as Mr B-C stood before the dressing table mirror tying his ties and buttoning up his waistcoat, Bingo was wondering if he had bitten off more than he could chew.

What if he were caught? He gulped inwardly. The Lockesley name would be blackened for ever. He needed an accomplice, and accomplices were hard to come by, especially on a planet like this where pretty much everyone was a Decent Chap. He sighed. There were few candidates for the position. None could be local, of course. He had to recruit someone from the team. And his estranged pal Hari Agincourt could not be involved.

The list of candidates had narrowed down. The members of the Tournament First Fifteen consisted of seven humans, including himself, Hari and Old Bill Told, three rhinocerids (the Judoon), a canine (Uff Nuf O'Kay, their star wotsit keeper), a centaur (H'hn'ee), a bovine (N'hoo), and an avian predator or hawk-person (DikMik Aaak) who was a splendid bowman but obviously not much good at hefting one end of a heavy hatbox. There was also Masher Dubloon, the skunkoid: excellent fielder and very strong for his size. However, in spite of all attempts at de-scenting, Masher still left a distinctive smell behind him.

William 'Old Bill' Told was planning to start a skiing planet after this and could not risk blackening his name, which he had already put into the past tense. Similarly Donna Bradmann of the Second Fifteen had taken Holy Orders and planned to fill the position of Top Chider in Fingerwagger, New North Whales, after this. Dougy Fairbanks, also of the Second Fifteen, was a pretty good all-rounder on the field and specialised in lance-and-quintain, knocking up a consistently good score, but she was inclined to make even the darkest of his friends' secrets into an anecdote before remembering

she'd been sworn to total silence on ‹···›
Doctor whatsit, their newest recruit an ‹···›
rounder, as he had shown on the field t‹···›
where his loyalties lay? And, again in t‹···›
Françoise and Jessie, the James sisters, belo‹···›
of sect that forbade them from doing anythin‹···›
except eat and make love. Which left the non-hu‹···› ‹···›eral
of whom were good chaps, up for any bit of fu‹···› but each
with drawbacks.

The problem of recruiting a Judoon was weight – they
could be heard clumping along nearly half a mile away.
They took a nano-personality changer when playing, which
evened up their weight and power on the tournament field,
but here they were who they were. The bovines also carried
a characteristic smell which would give them away. So it had
to be a human. W.G. Grace had the muscles…

At that moment a discreet knock on the door interrupted
his train of thought. He crossed to answer it and stared up
into the amiable face of the team's latest recruit. 'The Doctor',
with his pretty lady friend Amy, had joined the team after
their ship had crashed here. Apparently they had been
travelling in some kind of experimental two-person craft en
route from the Greater Oort in Orion where the remains of
Original Terra could be found. He was an historian, judging
from his knowledge of O.T. and her remaining neighbours.
He had shown his ID, but for some reason Lord Sherwood
could never remember his name: probably one of those bizarre
affectations some students of the Old Worlds seemed to relish
simply because everyone else found it unpronounceable.
The Doctor was a fine all-rounder, a pleasant fellow and a
jolly lucky one, with an absolute stunner of a girlfriend. In
fact, Bingo had to admit that if Amy were not attached to the
Doctor he would even now be leaving his card on her hall
table.

he said, a little surprised. 'Ah…' Then, remembering manners, 'Do come in…'

The pair trooped through and sat a little uncomfortably on the edge of his bed. In response to Bingo's lifted eyebrow and downcast eye, Amy said:

'As you're captain of the team, we thought we ought…' She turned to the Doctor. 'Well…'

'We ought to tell you. You ought to know that we think you have some sort of – I don't know – spanner in your works – a bit of a – what's the word?'

'Spy in the ointment?' Initially tending towards roughly the colour of uncooked sausages, Bingo had, he was pretty sure, paled at this. Sure that he had somehow been overheard plotting with Mr B-C and his action interpreted as a scheme to throw the game, he now found himself in a double bind.

To dispel any rumour about traitors in the team's ranks, Bingo would have to tell the truth. Or, he thought, getting into the swing of things the way liars often do, and, enjoying a buzz from the sheer exhilaration of inventing a story, he could tell some of the truth (chatting to Urquart Banning-Cannon) and make up the rest. This seemed the preferred option. He lifted his eyes to face Amy and the Doctor and, scarcely having finished blanching, he blushed again. 'Um. Fly in the amber, eh?' he babbled inanely, blushing deeper still at his own apparently uncontrollable foolishness. 'I mean sparrow in the soup.' He looked from one baffled face to the other. 'Don't I?'

The Doctor scratched his handsome nose. 'I'm not sure,' he said. He and Amy exchanged a glance. 'See, that's the reason we're here. You might have spotted something and be able to add to what we heard… It's not very clear, really, but we think someone's trying to pinch something from you.'

'P-p-pinch?' babbled the 507th Earl of Lockesley.

'Something of yours.'

'Not – not a h-hat?' Bingo had, for the moment at least, moment, crumbled.

'A bat? I don't think so. Though it could be disguised as a bit of equipment. The trouble is, we don't know what it looks like...'

'Oh, it's pretty horrible, I promise you that.' He blanched again. 'Or so I was told. I haven't actually seen it yet myself. D-did you say *bat*?' He blushed. At this rate he could hire himself out as a space beacon. 'Bat?'

'No, *you* said bat.' Amy raised both eyebrows. 'It was a pretty good guess.'

'But the fact is we don't know,' said the Doctor. 'My friend Amy here thought it could be anything, but I'm inclined to narrow the search...'

'Um – friend did you say?' Bingo blushed again. 'Amy? Miss Pond?'

'Yes. Are you OK?'

'Oh, yes. Much better, thank you. Not your *girl*friend?' He frowned hard at the Doctor.

'Is that a problem?'

'Far from it, Doctor.' Bingo had by now pretty much given up paling and was glowing a steady red. 'Anyway, this plot?'

'We think those involved could bring about the destruction of our galaxy.' The Doctor looked towards the door as if he suspected they in turn were being overheard. 'Perhaps even the universe,' he added, apparently as a vague afterthought.

'Oh, come on now!' Bingo was about to say that even the most horrible of hats could not make the Milky Way have a style breakdown, when something stopped him. 'Oh, really? This object, you mean. This bat. Or artefact. Or whatever...'

'We thought we ought to warn you.' The Doctor rose to leave. Lord Sherwood was clearly distracted. 'It *is* only a rumour...'

'Of course. Of course. As captain and all that, I'm responsible for the actions of the whole team.'

'Quite,' said the Doctor. 'Well...' He extended his hand. 'If you hear of anything odd going on, or see anything strange...'

'Or some sixth sense is triggered,' added Amy. 'It could be anything.'

'Anything?'

'Anything general, you know. Or something singular, of course.'

'Single,' babbled Bingo. 'Quite. Absolutely. Wonderful. I'm your man. Is it hot in here?' He went to the big French doors leading to his balcony. 'Mind if I open a window? Keep my eye on the arrow, eh? Both hands on the bat. Sticky whackit, mm? Rely on me.' He began tugging at the handles. 'Good. Got it. Oh, you're leaving! Cheerio for the moment, eh? Pip pip...'

When the door closed behind them, the Doctor and Amy exchanged another glance.

'Barmy,' murmured Amy, 'if cute. Pity.'

'I think we caught him at a bad time.' The Doctor scratched his unruly head. 'Why was he going on about a bat? Maybe Frank/Freddie Force and his Antimatter Men got to Bingo ahead of us. Maybe they've nobbled him.'

'That would be a shame,' said Amy vaguely. 'OK. So who should we check out next?'

'I've told you everything that was in the message. Everything I could understand. It had to be sent by someone who knows me, and thought I'd know what they were on about. I've checked out the humanoids, and they all seem all right. Hari Agincourt is Lord Bingo's cousin and best friend. W.G. Grace is easily their finest whacker.'

Amy glanced at him. 'Hmm. And quite some beard.'

'Bit eccentric?' said the Doctor.

'And enormous,' agreed Amy.

'You'd be eccentric if you'd swallowed so many identity pills you'd been a hundred personalities in Earth's distant history in almost a decade,' he told her. 'She's by far the best historian here. And there's almost nothing she doesn't know about mythology. She's obsessed. Like those other three in the Second Team back-ups. Drake, Stanley and de Gama. Explorers? Myth figures?' He shook his head, sending his floppy hair flying. 'All completely barmy. Unless they're very clever at hiding their real personalities. But they are very, very brilliant sports people.'

'Did Lord Sherwood's manner strike you as guilty?' Amy wondered.

'At first. Maybe we'd caught him admiring his own archer's stances in his mirror? Or doing his hair? Is that natural, do you think? That shock of white blond hair?'

'There's definitely something or someone on his mind. Or, if not exactly his mind… Anyway, he's clearly sweet on someone. They've got the poor beggar poleaxed.'

'What do you mean "someone"?'

'Someone. A person. He's got a crush on somebody in the team, I'll bet you!'

'Really? Man or woman? Alien or human?' The Doctor smiled to himself. 'I'm sure we'll find out soon, if we stick around long enough.'

'You think we might be on a wild goose chase, Doctor?'

'No. The message was pretty convincing. And its location. Miggea's a significant star. It's right at the centre of the Ghost Worlds, so it's close to the apex.' He steepled his hands to show her. 'Do you see? And when a trusted informant tells you that General Frank/Freddie Force and his Antimatter Men have crossed into our space, it's important to believe them. Especially when that someone is talking from a point just barely on the right side of the Schwarzschild Radius in the Sagittarian cloud and has a familiar and particular note of fear in their voice.' He stared off thoughtfully into the distance. 'They say old Renark, Lord of the Rim, the first man to try to enter a black hole, is still in there, stuck for ever between his last moment of life and his first moment of death. And of course General Frank/Freddie and Co won't be too far from that black hole, either, for fear of being stranded. You see our problem?'

'Um. Not really.' Amy wasn't quite sure where to start, but she took a deep breath and asked: 'What's matter and antimatter? How do they work?'

'Look at this – my bow tie. The central knot's the black hole. This side of the triangular bow is matter. This other side is antimatter. They are self-perpetuating, like Law and Chaos. Same thing, see?'

Amy nodded sagely. She hoped. She certainly wished she looked sager than she felt.

Chapter 5

Black

AS SOON AS THE Doctor and his unnervingly beautiful friend had disappeared, probably to do some further sleuthing, Bingo Lockesley put his mind to the problem in hand. He was pretty sure that not only had he thrown them off the scent, but also that his scent was not in fact the one they happened to be casting around for.

Robin, Lord Sherwood, Earl of Lockesley, had struck upon an entirely new plan which would not involve him in asking for extra assistance. The rooms between his room and Mrs Banning-Cannon's suite would soon be empty, since it currently contained Mr Banning-Cannon. Bingo was certain that Mrs B-C would not be so rude as to turn up late for her first meal at Lockesley Hall. All he had to do, Bingo reasoned, was to wait until the pair leapt at the sound of the dinner gong and went haring on their way to the source of the delicious smells already wafting from below. The coast clear, he could slip through, using his master key, drag the hatbox onto the rug, drag the rug complete with hatbox through Mr Banning-Cannon's room into his own and hide it in his grandfather's old space-chest situated at the end of his bed. Or maybe on the balcony, if dry. *A piece of cake!* he thought, salivating. The smells of rich old-fashioned food permeating his family castle were distracting him.

He drew another breath. Not good enough. He went to his French windows opening onto a balcony and flung them as wide as possible. Now they too were ready for his daring theft.

A few minutes later the dinner gong boomed from below, its sonorous tones echoing through the landings and chambers of Lockesley Hall as they had boomed for decades of yore, causing an almost unseemly rattling of door handles and squeaking of hinges as the many guests, their taste buds driven to madness by those delicious traditional scents, which made them drool rather as Serbian wolves had drooled when a rare troika full of wealthy kulaks sped over the snow on silver runners, her tinkling sleigh bells reminding them what fresh horse-and-peasant tasted like.

Bending his eye to the big keyhole which gave him a sight of the outside landing, Lord Sherwood saw Mrs Banning-Cannon slow to half-speed as her spouse, splendid in traditional white-tie supper attire, emerged to offer her his arm, causing a minor jam as guests in rooms, almost all of traditional carnivore strains, fell in at their rear. The centaur, H'hn'ee, immediately behind them in splendid black and white, was forced to dig in his hoofs pretty rapidly to avoid colliding with the over-eager canine, Uff Nuf O'Kay, next to him. Together Mr and Mrs Banning-Cannon proceeded towards the banisters of the main staircase to arrive at the top and pause there in a stately manner. Her expression was that of one who had finally made it to top Indian on the totem pole, whereas her husband wore a grin set in what used to be called 'the rictus of death'. As it happened, Urquart Banning-Cannon felt in fairly excellent spirits but had never been very good at smiling. His wife had insisted on the smile.

They seemed to sail past at an incredibly slow rate of

knots. It was, Bingo could have sworn, five full minutes before they began to descend. The other guests were starting to back up. He saw Flapper arrive from her room and direct an irritable glance at Hari Agincourt, who made a strange, wriggling movement and just managed a grin, appearing if anything more terrified than Mr Banning-Cannon's. Other guests rounded the corner and slowed in some surprise to see the jam. But at least it was now moving.

'Finally!' Lord Sherwood drew on a pair of white kid gloves (because he had learned from his own perusal of those ancient 'thrillers' that this was always what Fantomas did) and inserted his master key into the door which joined his room with Mr Banning-Cannon's. The wards turned slowly but smoothly with a reassuring set of clicks and clacks. The door to Mr Banning-Cannon's room swung open.

Leaving the key in the lock, Robin of Sherwood, the pride of his people, stole silently between the rooms, the smell of Mr B-C's cologne mingling with that of the antique beef and some other, less readily identifiable salty scent, to discover to his surprise that the door into the intersecting apartments had been locked from the other side by what he considered an overly suspicious guest. This meant he was forced to return for the master key by which he let himself in through the other connecting door. Seconds later, another quick snap of his elegant wrist, and he had opened the door into Mrs B-C's bedroom, a riot of brilliant colour, flashing gemstones and silks rippling in the sweet summer breeze coming through the open window.

Averting his gentlemanly eyes from the spectacle of his guest's sturdy bloomers, he raced to the wardrobe, expecting to discover a hatbox somewhere in the vicinity. He saw nothing on top. Nothing under the four-poster. In fact, no such receptacle was to be seen anywhere. He sniffed at a funny burnt toast and flowers sort of smell, maybe a new kind of perfume? His search grew increasingly desperate. In none of the rooms, on top of no cupboard, under no bed and behind no secret panel was there a sign of anything like the hat or its box, both of which had been described to him in some detail. He sniffed again. That odd smell. What *was* it? He was about to begin again when he heard a sound in the hall outside. Someone was unlocking the door leading to the landing!

They were coming in! They would discover him.

There was nowhere to hide. He looked wildly about for cover.

Then came an outraged yell from behind him. With a terrified gulp, Robin, Earl of Lockesley set off at a rapid lick back to his quarters the way he had come, ripping off his gloves, haring through Urquart Banning-Cannon's apartments to reach his own room and slamming his door behind him while, on the other side, Mrs Banning-Cannon's screams of mingled anger and terror sounded up and down the ancient halls of Lockesley. His heart beat faster and faster. All thought was driven from his head. Made dizzy by the emotional upheavals of the past hour or so, he felt his legs wobble.

The screaming grew louder and louder. A woman's voice cried: 'Through there. I saw them! They have stolen my finest hat!'

Lord Bingo's simple but, it has to be admitted, somewhat overbred system had taken all it could. Across the galaxy, on dozens of reconstituted Earth-type planets, there were peers proud to boast of the peasant blood flowing in their veins, but the Lockesleys were not among them. Neither were they a nervous family since their blood, rather than thinning, had tended to atrophy; equally the Lockesley nerves were not so much highly tuned as petrified. That said, they had also managed to avoid all major conflicts since the time of

Vortigern when an ancestor, for a bet, had stolen a Roman's helmet and had to leg it pretty fast with the best part of a Roman legion in hot pursuit. Therefore, it was something of an aberration when Bingo, his sturdy, uncomplex brain shaken at last by an overdose of imagination and unfamiliar terrors, gave up in the face of Fate's implacable workings. The legs, which had threatened to buckle, finally did. His noble brow narrowly missing the corner of the ancestral space-chest, he fell forward, struck the old Iranian carpet and remained there.

Blackness swam up to embrace him.

He welcomed oblivion. He did not welcome coming to.

He awoke after what could only have been a minute or two to hear someone's depressing declaration:

'He's dead. As a doornail. He was killed when he startled the thief and tried to intercept him... See? Those are tiny needle marks in his neck. They must have escaped through his French windows! They're wide open.'

Lord Sherwood groaned, as much for his own benefit as anyone's. 'I say! What tiny needle marks?'

'They've gone now. Must have been a mistake of your nano-razor.'

'Merely stunned,' offered another voice. 'Let's hope he saw the intruder!'

Bingo opened his eyes. Half a dozen worried faces stared down at him. He couldn't think of anything very original to say so he said, 'Where am I?' and waited for the best.

By the cooing sound of Mrs B-C somewhere in the background he could tell she did not suspect him. And, judging by Mr B-C's grotesque wink, he was already getting credit for pinching the Great Hat of Loondoon. This bothered him a bit, since he hadn't actually pinched the tile, while the expressions on his guests' faces suggested that something substantially dastardly had been achieved.

'That's the mark of your true aristocrat,' he heard Mrs Banning-Cannon declare. 'I saw him going after them. Look, his windows are open, too. They got away through them. Without thought for his own safety he tried to tackle the thieves as they made their escape! And they struck him down!'

So the hat *had* been pinched!

'He's not hurt is he?' came Amy's worried voice from the back.

The Doctor felt behind Bingo's head. 'Doesn't seem to be. Maybe we should heave him onto the bed and check.'

'Couldn't we all do this later?' suggested Uff Nuf O'Kay. 'It would be a shame if the dinner were spoiled.'

And so a compromise was struck and Robin, Lord of Sherwood, was stretched out on his bed with a flask of brandy on his nightstand, as everyone else trooped down to enjoy the feast while the soup, fish, meats and veg remained more or less at their proper temperatures.

This was a feast Bingo didn't intend to miss. He had anticipated it since boyhood when his grandfather had taken him on his knee and told him of the family's haunch of giant bison kept at optimum freshness until such time as Sherwood might be restored and a monarch sit upon the throne. Lord Sherwood rested only for a few moments before rising, straightening his ties, running a comb through his hair, checking his neck for tiny needle marks and legging it downstairs with all the dignity a hungry man could muster. A moment or two later he made his entrance into the dining room on the excuse that no true Sherwood could desert his guests on such an important occasion.

'A genuine hero!' pronounced Mrs B-C. 'If only you had arrived in my room a moment earlier! It's a wonder they didn't have a go at the vault sent ahead today. The one with the silver arrow in it! How did the thief escape, Lord

Sherwood? Did you see? Through the window and over the balcony, I take it. You heard a noise, went to investigate and – well, we know the rest. Did you see the man?'

'Man?' Bingo Lockesley took his place at the table.

'I'm assuming it was a man who stole my hat. Or two men, maybe. Or a man and a woman. Sexton Begg and Mademoiselle Yvonne? That hat was heavy! I was going to have to wear a special anti-magnetic harness under my costume tomorrow. If I had not forgotten my reticule and returned for it, there would have been no witness to your bravery. He was leaving when I went back. I was heartened to see you chasing the intruder – or perhaps intruders! Was there more than one, Lord Robin? Did you tackle them both?'

'Um,' said Bingo. His fall to the carpet had deafened him a little.

'– and, careless of their numbers, chased them through the adjoining doors,' Enola Banning-Cannon continued, glowing with hero-worship, 'and then they gave you the slip! They must have been huge. Unless there were three or four of them. In which case you were braver than ever!' she exclaimed. 'Tell us, Lord Sherwood! Did you see four or five men? Can you give us a description?'

'I regret,' he said as he sat down at the head of the table, 'that I recognised none of them.'

'They'll have escaped by now.' Mr Banning-Cannon laid down his soup spoon. 'I'd notify the local police. But if the thieves had a vehicle waiting, they could already be off-planet...'

'Of course they only needed a moment,' his wife resumed. 'And, as you say, if they had a ship waiting, perhaps another ship in space, they could be light years away! They must have known how valuable a Diana of Loondoon creation can be. They'll try to fence it, I suppose. I'd heard there were gangs of hat-snatchers all over this part of the galaxy...'

'I warned you, my dear!' Mr Banning-Cannon finished his soup.

'You warned me of no such thing! Indeed, Urquart, if you had not been with me the entire time, I might have suspected…'

'You don't think they were after the Arrow of Artemis and took the hat by mistake?' At the other end of the table, the Doctor had lifted his head from his plate. 'You said you saw no one in the gang? Nothing for the Magistrate to go on?'

'Not a shadow,' said Bingo truthfully. 'They might almost have been invisible. D-d-id you say M-m-m…?'

'Or time-trippers.' Hari Agincourt was excited by the notion. 'I once saw a V about a gang which specialised in shunting back a few minutes before a crime was committed, pinching whatever it was they wanted, hiding the swag and then shunting forward again, leaving only the tell-tale smell of burning salt behind them. Or was it pepper? Or vodka?'

Amy sniffed.

'Yes,' said the Doctor, following her logic. 'That's all your theory lacks, Mr Agincourt.'

'See what you mean.' Hari bit his lip. 'No burning seawater, eh?'

'Well, it could have been disguised by the delicious scents of our dinner, I suppose.' Mr Banning-Cannon came to Hari's help. 'You have to admit—'

'But there *was* an odd smell. We are all impressed by the dinner,' Mrs Banning-Cannon graciously acknowledged their host, 'however I am certain that few of us here could not mistake roasting beef for burnt ozone. I'm sure it wasn't ozone. Lavender, perhaps, with a hint of *Mary's Passion*. Definitely floral. If you can't be helpful in any other way, Urquart, I suggest you try not to intervene with further theories. You have done your part. The police must have been called by now and should be here in the morning, though

THE COMING OF THE TERRAPHILES

why they don't work at night I can't think. With luck, they'll already have captured the felons by then and return my hat unharmed.'

A fresh thought suddenly occurred to Bingo: Would they? Return the hat unharmed, that was? Suppose they were animal rights activists objecting to fur and feathers who merely intended to do a little unpicking or V-painting of the hat before returning it? Or hatnappers, even! Or common opportunist crooks. What if they had really been after the Silver Arrow but couldn't crack the time-sealed vault? No. That was secure and anyway he was pretty sure it had already been shunted into the future. It was likely that once aboard the *Gargantua* Mr B-C would know immediately that Bingo had nothing to do with the heist and be thoroughly within his rights in rescinding the offered reward, maybe withdrawing Bingo's concession and kicking him, de-Earled, off the planet altogether. Now he chewed his antique beef without relish... 'Mocked are the meek when caught in untruthful celebration,' as the Book of Coleman's had it.

Lord Sherwood ignored the swift glance of enquiry Mr B-C threw in his direction. At this rate the planet-moulder would give the game away. Mr B-C did not know at that stage that the Earl of Lockesley had been unsuccessful in his heist and had, indeed, been thwarted in his ambition. The great tycoon was basking in the glow of success, believing that Bingo had managed to hide the huge hat somewhere in his room and would be able to produce it, no doubt, during the following evening when the party was over and, in the words of the recently revived song, they had burst his pretty balloon and stolen the moon away. Well they'd done that aeons ago. Anyway, it was a hat in this case, rather than a moon, which could then be 'discovered' somewhere and returned. By which time the local magistrate would be able to dismiss the whole episode as an annoying prank by some of the younger members of the Second Fifteen. Don't worry, Bingo, old lad. Things were proceeding nicely.

Mr B-C's opinion of the young man as well as the entire aristocracy had risen considerably in the past hour or two. Not only had Sherwood snaffled the hideous headgear from under the nose of his guest, he had been able to hide it before Mrs Banning-Cannon had unexpectedly returned to the room to recover her forgotten reticule. That had shown remarkable resourcefulness! The captain of industry could not have done better himself. Indeed, with rare generosity, he admitted he could not have done as well. He longed to find out how the job had been accomplished. Meanwhile he returned his attention to the meal before him which had taken on something of the character of a victory feast.

Later, enjoying a cigar and a *ballon* of cognac on the terrace, he was able to catch Bingo alone for a moment and grace him with an enormous wink. 'Good show, my boy!'

At that moment W.G. Grace, smoking a large cigar and stroking her magnificent beard, sashayed round the corner of the terrace to an exchange of 'good evenings' and so forth. A couple more such interruptions and Bingo was practically tongue-tied.

At last Bingo opened his mouth to fill his patron in on the real details of the event then realised that, not only was this the wrong moment, there might never be a right one. The hat was gone, perhaps for ever. There might never come a time when it was returned. In which case, although he could be said to have failed in his commission, Mr Banning-Cannon would never know. He would hand over the keys of the desanctioned Peers™ with gratitude and good grace, and although a small mystery would remain to puzzle him, no doubt it would be solved one day when he would be the true Lord of Sherwood rather than the mere proprietor of some woods and a big house rented at a nominal sum from TerraForma™. Why someone should want to own the hat he might never know, but only Mrs B-C would be put out and doubtless not for very long. Indeed, the first chance he got he would have her a new and equally hideous hat made and sent to her home back in Cygnus or wherever it was. Everyone would be thoroughly satisfied.

What if – and here he found himself on the verge of choking on his glass of port – what if the real thief were to ransom the hat? Even now someone could be slicing a feather or two from the stolen titfer and sending a message to Mrs Banning-Cannon's personal V indicating where to leave dosh in used oncers if the apple of her eye were to be returned without further mutilation. He gulped. And this time Mrs Banning-Cannon noticed his condition, chirruping, much to Mr B-C's astonishment, an expression of concern in the direction of her host. 'My dear Lord Sherwood! You are having, I think, a reaction to the adventures of the evening! As brave a face as you are putting on things, it is clear to some of us that you are suffering a delayed shock. In other words, your encounter with the thieves, while an act of unconscious courage, has affected your highly tuned nerves.'

It came as something of a surprise amongst those who knew him that old Bingo Lockesley had any nerves, highly tuned or otherwise. He babbled something about being perfectly all right while giving his by now celebrated performance of a space-beacon on full traffic-duty, blushing red and blanching white in a matter of seconds as his conscience swung him swiftly from a state of high anxiety to one of low terror. Then, realising that he had a perfectly legitimate excuse to offer, he mentioned that he had a long game ahead of him in the morning and maybe he'd better turn in. Happily he was saved from further torment by W.G. Grace strolling round the corner, her bow-case under her arm, shrouded in a cloud of smoke from her massive cigar and talking whackit averages to one of the centaurs. Leaving them chatting, he sloped off in the direction of his bedroom.

Chapter 6

Yellow

BINGO HAD ONLY A few minutes to climb into his pyjamas before there came a tap at his door. His first impulse was to jump under the duvet and pretend to be asleep, but then he was moved by curiosity. What if this were the real thief, for whose dirty work he was receiving shares of praise and blame, come to put the squeeze on him? What if he refused to answer?

Reluctantly, Bingo turned the handle and opened the door a crack. There stood Urquart Banning-Cannon all in white ties, still nervously puffing on his cigar and fanning himself with his toppers. Only then did Bingo wonder if Mr B-C had not insured himself against his, Bingo's, failure and possibly employed a back-up.

'Pssst,' said Mr Banning-Cannon.

'Sorry?'

'Let me in, dammit!' The tycoon hurried into the room and closed the door firmly behind him. 'Congratulations,' he pumped Bingo's still-uncertain hand. 'I can only stay a few minutes. What did you do with it?'

'With –?' For a moment Bingo was blank. 'Oh! Oh! You mean the hat?'

'Naturally the hat. What else? You're a positive Svengali, the way you made it vanish! Do I mean Svengali?'

'Maybe Mantovani?'

Urquart banged the side of his head. 'These nano-translators aren't too hot on history. Oh, I know Fellini.'

'I'm coming up with Whodunit.'

'Houdini?'

'So what about him?'

'You mentioned him.'

'Did I? OK. The hat. How did you get it out of there?'

'That's a bit of a trade secret,' said Bingo, admiring his own unexpected quickness of mind.

'You'll let me know eventually, right.'

Something like steel had suddenly entered Bingo Lockesley's soul.

'Of course, old boy. As soon as I have it all signed, sealed and delivered. The contract?'

'My word is my bond. The job's done. The planet's yours.'

'I think we need something a little more concrete.'

'Anything. Believe me. I'll write you a letter. You can trust me. I'll have the contract in your hands by tomorrow.' Urquart made to leave. 'You seem different...'

'How do you mean, different?' Bingo felt his desperation-fuelled belligerence fading rapidly. He was beginning to blush again. Then he turned pale.

'I don't know. Probably cost you a lot of adrenalin, eh? Anyway, I'll have that contract for you. But meanwhile, the planet's yours. To do whatever you like with.'

Bingo cleared his throat. Urquart opened the door to his own room. 'I'll leave this way. OK? That's funny! Do you smell something? I'd better get out of here.' And he left.

Bingo knew what he meant. It *was* an odd smell. Familiar, though. He just couldn't put his finger on it. Lavender?

He stumbled back to bed and climbed under the quilt. He was beginning to worry. He felt he had received a hint of the future and he wasn't entirely sure if it was going to be quite as good as it seemed to be on the surface.

Another knock. He was determined not to answer. He remained under the quilt, safe in the knowledge that he had locked both doors to his room.

And then someone was standing over him.

'Um, Lord Sherwood? It's the Doctor. I wondered if...'

'No,' he said, then: 'Go away. I'm sleeping. I don't need a doctor. I'm right as rain. See you for breakfast. I recommend the kedgeree.'

'The police have been called. By Mrs Banning-Cannon actually. She thought Mr Banning-Cannon didn't quite understand the urgency involved. So they're coming in the morning... I thought you—'

'P-police?' The Earl of Lockesley put his nose above the duvet. 'M-me?'

'Well, yes. Mrs Banning-Cannon thought the sooner the case, as she calls it, was put into the hands of the district magistrate, the better. Between you and me, the local constables might not be taking the theft of a hat too seriously. You can see that from her point of view... Well, meanwhile, of course, everything's being turned upside down in the hope there's been an oversight...'

Reluctantly, Bingo again bade farewell to the Land of Nod. 'I was thinking that probably it's a bit soonish to be calling in the magistrates. Constables are all that are needed in the circumstances, surely? The hat'll probably turn up in the morning. Left at the hotel or something. I mean it's only a dashed *hat*!'

'Not to Mrs B-C. Do you have any idea how much those things cost? And you know how much pull she has with the authorities. I'd guess that between them, the Tarbuttons and the Banning-Cannons practically own the local law.'

'The c-constables are c-crooked?'

'Of course not.' The Doctor paused just long enough for Bingo not to believe him, before clarifying: 'They're probably like most police forces – they know whose property they're supposed to look after first and foremost. After all, they owe their jobs to the terraforming companies. The companies are the ones who make the planets and help populate them. Generally the officers do their best to keep the peace, enforce the law – and they *are* an honest bunch, all in all, I expect – but if it's a question of my lost archery cap, worth a few buttons, and a creation of Diana of Loondoon worth hundreds of thousands of bluebacks... Well, we both know which crime they'll take most seriously.'

Bingo sat up in bed. 'I hadn't thought of that. My uncle's the local Investigating Magistrate. I'll talk to him.'

The Doctor sat down on the edge of his bed. 'I understand that Mrs B-C also made Mr B-C call him. He said he'd be round in the morning. I gather he's a stickler for the letter of the law. And of course he'll want to interview you.'

'M-me?'

'Well, yes, because you overheard the thieves and tried to catch them. Even if you didn't get a glimpse of them, the police will want to go over what you might have seen. They have trained minds, you see. They're impossible to deceive, even when we are accidentally deceiving ourselves.'

'Ah, yes. N-naturally I'll do all I can. There's just that funny seaside smell. That's all I noticed, same as you.'

'It will probably mean something to a sleuth. It might even point the finger in the direction of a felon!'

'Yes, I can see that. Who might or not be human, eh?'

'Well, of course, under normal circumstances the victim's husband would most likely be the Number One Suspect...'

'Eh?'

'Think about it. He was known to hate the hat. He is, sadly, subject to some form of arachnophobia and was overheard begging his lady wife not to wear the thing tomorrow. He already asked me what I knew on the subject of fear of spiders, and he had referred to the hat as 'that great monstrous spider squatting on top of her head' to a few of his fellow travellers. He was thought to be preparing to take to his bed tomorrow rather than confront it.'

'Really? I knew nothing of this.' (Or very little, at any rate, thought Bingo in some relief). 'Afraid of hats, was he?'

'Not all hats,' said the Doctor. 'Just a certain kind of hat. Hats resembling spiders. And anything else resembling spiders. Including spiders themselves, I expect. There's a definite spider motif,' he added in case there was any doubt.

'Well, you can see how he would take against the hat, then. Shame. For a bloke to suffer so. You'd think—'

'That he'd do something about it. He'd tried. He saw many specialists all over the galaxy. He even asked my advice.'

'Makes sense. But you couldn't help him?'

'I'm not that sort of doctor.'

'Of course that does rule him out as the thief,' Bingo pointed out.

'Why so?' asked the Doctor.

'Because he couldn't get within a mile of the thing without exploding into hives and so forth.'

'Ah, yes. So they'll doubtless want to know if he had anything to do with it.'

'How do you mean?'

'If he commissioned someone to do the deed. Conspired.'

'Ah, yes.' Bingo made an odd swallowing sound.

'But they'll probably go for a different theory.'

'Yes, let's hope so!'

'Um... Why should we hope so?'

'Oh, well. Ah. Because it would be jolly awful if one of

us were to fall under the shadow of suspicion, don't you know!'

'Yes. That's true. So you can't come up with any hint? I mean, you can't guess at who amongst your guests might have left the smell of hot seawater behind them?'

'Not unless it's – ha, ha – some sort of half-baked fish, eh?'

Bingo winced at his own appalling joke. He was beginning to feel rather glad that he had been unsuccessful in managing the great hat heist, after all. Yet what if Mr Banning-Cannon pointed the finger at him and he cracked under interrogation? As he might. Thinking that Bingo had pinched the damned hat, as Bingo had allowed him to believe.

'Well,' said the Doctor rising, 'I thought I'd pop in and talk this over with you. Just in case you knew of anything. Or if I could help, perhaps?'

'Very decent of you, Doctor. Much obliged. I'll put my mind to it.'

He murmured 'Good night' to the lanky mystery man, who left, closing the door quietly behind him.

But now, of course, Bingo was wide awake. He sat upright in bed gnawing his fingernails and trying to gather his thoughts. But, try as he might, the thoughts remained ungathered. They seemed rather determined, in fact, to remain at large. He slept fitfully that night, waking from time to time to feel what might be cold steel around his wrists. His dreams, when they came, generally involved him suffering some form of incarceration. He imagined Mrs Banning-Cannon pointing an accusatory finger in the direction of Mr B-C who, in turn, was inclined to point a similar finger at him.

He awoke early the next morning muttering to himself, his head, neck and shoulders bathed in cold, clammy sweat while from dry lips came over and over again the words: 'I'm innocent, innocent. I'm innocent I tell you. Ask him. I never did it.'

Which was perfectly true, of course, but somehow didn't convince him, let alone his imagined interviewers.

Admittedly, as a local landowner, he was not likely to be accused of the petty theft of an over-large hat, but he knew that non-local owners of many planets tended to carry rather more weight than he did. His only hope, he told himself, was that his Uncle Rupoldo came in to investigate the case. He was the appropriate local magistrate and, since the Code Napoleon tended to be the legal system preferred in this part of the universe, he stood a better chance of receiving a fair trial with his uncle on the job than if Anglo-Saxon or Barsoomian law were to be utilised. As he shaved his face that morning, staring hard into the mirror to see if he looked anything like a criminal mastermind, he mulled over the chances of Sir Rupoldo de Crespigny coming up with a not-guilty verdict or whether that old incorruptible would insist on investigating every aspect of the matter. There again, with luck, the hat would turn up, having been delivered to the wrong room on its way from the Claremont to Lockesley Hall. But that wasn't very likely.

Traipsing down to breakfast a few minutes later, feeling in better spirits after his morning ablutions, he entered the room to find all eyes turned on him.

'Hello!' he cried, rather noisily. 'What's up? Hat been found I take it!'

All eyes turned back to their previous position.

Following them he saw that they had fixed on the dark blue uniform and silver buttons of a man dressed in the rather splendid scarlet-trimmed uniform of an Inspector-Magistrate in the Sussex and Surrey Bacon Street Regulators, a branch of which kept the peace in this particular arm of the galaxy and had done for several millennia since the collapse of Law soon after the last Dark Age but one in these parts following the fifth, or possibly sixth, interplanetary war. Above this livery beamed a face of such kindliness and bucolic good will that Bingo was immediately reassured. He should have been, since it belonged to Inspector-Magistrate Sir Rupoldo de Crespigny, who had not only once dandled Bingo on his knee, but, a keen sportsman, had also taught him almost everything he knew about tournament re-enactments and their associated games. Normally, Bingo would have fallen on his uncle's kindly shoulder and greeted him with nothing but hoots of happy goodwill, but today the old chap's expression was of such considerable gravity that Bingo could tell something decidedly serious was afoot.

'Ah,' he said. 'No hat's turned up, eh? That's a shame!'

'That's exactly what it is, young Rob,' declared Sir Rupoldo. 'You're going to have to call off your game, I'm afraid. And nobody's going to be allowed to leave the castle and grounds, at least not before they can explain their actions of last night.'

'You think the hat's still on the premises, do you?' Mr Banning-Cannon said, addressing his remarks to the Inspector-Magistrate but directing a look of pleading concern at his host. 'I'd be pretty sure that the crooks would have made off with it last night, wouldn't you, Lord Sherwood?'

It became immediately clear to Bingo that he had nothing much to fear from being fingered by Mr B-C, since the terraforming tycoon had as much to lose from any revelations as he himself. His spirits lifted by about a mile on realising this.

But then the horror at what he had just been told struck him. 'Did you say the match was *cancelled*?'

'I'm afraid I did.'

'So what's happening tomorrow?'

'Tomorrow? I can't say. No doubt if the hat is discovered

or we are sure it is no longer on these premises, then everyone will be permitted to go on about their business. My guess is that the investigation will take a little longer.'

'But,' said Bingo, 'that can't be!'

'I fear it is going to have to be. It shouldn't be too much of a problem. As far as we can tell, no strange ship left here last night or this morning. The shuttle is, regrettably, cancelled, of course, but another craft should be along in a week or two and I'm reliably informed that all passengers on the *Gargantua* will be offered similar berths on the *Gigantique*, her sister ship. Terraphiles and customers on the Historical Tour will not be charged any extra, since this comes under the terms of the insurance taken out on booking the tickets. Passage will simply be transferred for everyone else. No one will be out of pocket. Luckily, there are plenty of seats available on the *Gigantique* and, since she's a sister ship of the *Gargantua*, there will be no change of amenities.'

Bingo was shaking his head. 'No, no, no, no,' he said. 'Not a chance. Don't you *understand*?'

'I understand that the Law must take her course,' declared his uncle, a little grimly.

'I think what your nephew is trying to let us know,' said the Doctor, getting up from the table and dabbing at the corners of his mouth with the ends of his napkin, 'is that the *Gargantua* is due to dock above the planet Flynn in the Miggea system on the Sagittarian Rim in time for our team to play the final games in the Great Tournament. The *Gigantique* will arrive in Miggea about three weeks too late to play the Tournament! This means little, I know, to the average traveller who might otherwise be delighted at the chance of spending another fortnight or so on this lovely and picturesque planet, but for those of us anxious to get our first crack in a quarter of a millennium at the famous and mysterious Silver Arrer, it's pretty bad news. The Tourists, who did not accept Lord

Sherwood's kind invitation to stay here, will merely have to play the Visitors. You take my meaning?'

'Hmm,' said Sir Rupoldo, upon whom the full import of the news was in fact dawning. 'I do indeed. This is pretty frightful, I have to say. I mean, we were very much expecting to win the Arrer back from the Tourists this time. Oh, I say, gosh!' He pondered this for a moment. 'Oh, this is a calamity.' He turned to a mystified Mrs Banning-Cannon. 'I don't suppose you'd be willing, dear lady, to postpone this investigation on the word of the Tournamentors that they'll return here once…' Her expression went a little further than merely answering this question for him. 'Ah, well, no, I see you're rather determined…'

He cast a pleading look around the room at the team, at anyone else who might help, at pretty much every creature, alien or human, present. 'Or that whomever pinched the darn – the valuable hat – would own up to the theft on the chance that Mrs Banning-Cannon would kindly drop charges…'

'*Certainly not!*' snarled that formidable lady. 'I did not think I would have to remind everyone that my husband's company *owns* this planet.'

At which all involved gave vent to what could only be described as a collective groan.

Chapter 7

A Close Study of Timetables

'**IN WHICH CASE, I'LL** bid you good morning!' exclaimed the officer, his kindly face full of concern. 'I have to say, young Bingo – Lord Sherwood – what a shame this is and how we are going to be unable to enjoy the final friendly game in the Gentlemen versus Tourists match, but worse than that how utterly sick-making it is that our own great team is to lose its crack at the ancient Arrer. This puts a wholly different character on the situation. One might almost think our rivals pulled this stunt merely to keep us out of the matches. This is a bad day for our tournament, gentlemen. Bad indeed.'

'Not a great one for those of us who take their millinery seriously, either,' declared Mrs B-C, attempting to get some perspective on the situation.

They all stared at her in frank astonishment. H'hn'ee, the centaur put down his bucket of cereal and tried to stop his hoof from stamping heavily on the carpet. He had worn his special indoor slippers, of course, but his hoofs still made a bit of a noise. Equally, his neighbour, a Judoon, heard himself issue a noisy snort.

'By the Medici Stars!' exclaimed Uff Nuf O'Kay, the canine

DOCTOR WHO

wotsit keeper. 'If I could get my teeth into whatever catty—'
He realised that Masher Dubloon, the skunkoid fielder, was
sitting across from him. 'I mean whatever rotter…'

Masher looked up with a quiet smile. 'Perhaps we should
all put our hands into our pockets and come up with a reward
for the hat's return?'

This was a dig at O'Kay, who was notoriously tight-fisted.
But Mrs Banning-Cannon found the idea attractive.

'I am certainly prepared to pay a ransom.'

The Magistrate-Inspector, who was leaving the dining
room, paused for a moment and then continued on, as if he
had heard nothing. While he would normally hold the law to
be above such offers, he would have allowed almost anything
that helped restore Mrs B-C's hat and allowed the Gentlemen
to continue on their way aboard the *Gargantua*.

The Doctor and Amy were peering approvingly out of
the wide windows at the castle's wonderful lawn which
fanned confidently down to pretty much the entire catalogue
of colourful and aromatic flowers, rising in serried ranks as
far as the first line of blooming cedars and giant marigold
borders near the edge of the ornamental lake. Under a warm
sun, the water glittered like polished steel.

'I'd almost imagined we'd been sabotaged,' murmured the
Doctor to his friend. 'It's crucial for us to get to Flynn and win
that Arrow or who knows what havoc Frank/Freddie Force
and his mirthless Antimatter Men will create? I wonder if the
thieves have any idea what they are doing.'

'Well, Doctor, you haven't exactly filled me in with any
further details.'

He turned away from the view. 'I don't think I can yet.
All I know is what I was told. And I'm not entirely one
hundred per cent sure of that…' Then addressing the other
breakfasters he said:

'I think paying a ransom's an excellent idea. It might have

to be a pretty big sum, though.'

'I'll put in a million,' offered Mr Banning-Cannon. He, at least, was safe in knowing what the hat was worth on the market.

There came a chorus of offers for various amounts.

'We should bear in mind,' the Doctor pointed out, 'that the culprit is almost certainly one of us and could have used some sort of timemobile to steal the hat. Or an anti-gravity device, which would be obvious from its characteristic smell.'

'Anti-gravity?' croaked Mr Banning-Cannon unable to resist darting a quick, enquiring glance at Lord Sherwood. 'And this smell? Why so?'

'It's a bit like... burnt seawater. It's characteristic of displaced tempelectrons – the smell given off by most devices employing anti-gravity.' The Doctor moved into the middle of the room. 'We know that the hat was especially heavy and could only sit easily on Mrs Banning-Cannon's head if it had the necessary anti-gravity device set in its crown. I assume the thief knew this and so sneaked into Mrs Banning-Cannon's boudoir armed with one of those hand-held things they use to stock shelves in those big DIY stores. You know – you must have seen them. No? Anyway, never mind. Then, having guided it to an open window, he could have used the "floater", as they're called in the trade, to manipulate the hat in its hatbox out of the window to a waiting accomplice. A light air-car could have been standing by to receive it, and Bob's your uncle.'

'Eh?' Bingo looked up startled. 'Uncle Bob?'

'Gosh, that's amazing!' exclaimed Hari Agincourt. 'Brilliant powers of deduction, Doctor, I have to say. But now we need to know who had the resources. Anti-grav operators aren't cheap and neither are air-cars. If it's off-planet that means someone or some company got it there, so it's unlikely to be the work of just an ordinary sort of cracksman. Yet they would not have been able to move in and out of the place without raising an alarm if they weren't known to the household, and as you know we all went through recognition checks with the android staff when we got here. Nobody missed a check, did they, Mullers?' He turned to the android butler.

'All guests were introduced to staff, sir,' the dignified and kindly android became operational only when addressed. 'And both staff and guests were all accounted for. A breakdown of that system hardly seems likely, sir.'

'Anyway,' the Doctor became animated. Amy loved it when he brought his detective skills into play. 'That's almost certainly how it was moved. But how and where is the thing hidden? Well, unfortunately that's a lot harder to work out. So we have to work out *who* to work out where. Motive? OK, the hat's valuable, but there are loads of valuable things around here to steal. So why pinch it? It's not the most portable object, is it? So, let's assume there's no specific financial motive – in which case we're back at the fundamental question.'

'Which is?' Mr B-C prompted.

'Why would someone pinch a hat?'

'It's an original!' declared Mrs B-C. 'A Diana of Loondoon original! No two are alike. I can think of several collectors who would give a fortune to own one they don't have. They're like antique paintings. In fact, Diana included an entire original Rembrandt print in one of her latest models. She's an artist. The Rembrandts became her trademark for a while. At other times she used Picasso, Emin, Coca Colon – all now in museums. She takes whatever materials inspire her, although I believe the "Phobos" life-size hat she made for Lady Mars was commissioned. Many considered that ultra-vulgar. I don't know. Perhaps it is, a little. It could only be worn with the help of six anti-gravs, not one. Happily this wasn't the real Phobos, which long ago crashed to the surface of Old Barsoom.' She almost smote her forehead as inspiration dawned on her like sunrise over the Pink Alps of Caladon.

'Lady M is *so* competitive – of course!' Mrs Banning-Cannon sat up suddenly, knocking over a glass of Vortex Water. 'She could have stolen it. She's rich enough. She owns Intergalactic Air. We can't move to make an Earth-like planet without their atmosphere plants.'

'Did she want that hat?' asked the Doctor, sounding slightly surprised.

'Oh, you know, we're great rivals.' Her mascaraed eyes became two small black slugs as Mrs Banning-Cannon eased her features into the semblance of a smile. Her lip gloss gleamed like fresh blood. 'But she would have to wear it, wouldn't she? I mean, that's what hats are all about, becoming a talking point. So all she could do is spend her money on another Diana creation. That's how I'd challenge her and I'm certain that it's how she'd challenge me. Perhaps it was stolen for the precious stones and metals…'

'Except,' said the Doctor, 'a job of this kind just wouldn't be profitable to an ordinary thief. Even if the equipment were hired, you'd only just about break even. And if the anti-grav stuff and shuttles were factored in, it would still be running at a loss. No, I think there's something else going on here.'

'Doctor, if we can't get the hat back in less than twenty-four hours, we're done for.' Hari Agincourt was striding up and down beside the long breakfast sideboard. Clearly he was highly agitated about the chance of never playing the match. 'You saw them, Bingo. Any ideas?'

'Um,' said Bingo. 'Wish I could say I had actually seen 'em. But little more than a glance…'

'I was out of the room for less than five minutes, Lord Sherwood.' Mrs Banning-Cannon could not find it in herself to speak harshly to the young man she had selected for her future son-in-law. 'You heard something, surely?'

'Um. Yes. I heard a sort of hissing noise. Like a cobra, you know, or one of the larger vipers and I-I...'

'Presumably you made a dash through the connecting rooms and were just in time to – to...' the Doctor coaxed.

'To look for them. They must have been hiding. But when I turned round they...'

'They were heading back towards your rooms? So you gave chase and they escaped through your window,' Flapper Banning-Cannon kindly reminded him. Her own private theory was that poor Bingo had over-exerted himself on her behalf and was now having to deal with his friend Hari's hurt dislike because Hari had refused to understand that Bingo had simply been recruited by Flapper as a kind of stalking horse – or did she mean sacrificial goat – or, no, it was some other sort of goat – a sheep, maybe? A Judas lamb? Was that it? Ah, well. It would either come to her or it wouldn't. She uttered the jaunty sigh of a girl who viewed her educational opportunities as having had to be endured as politely as possible; now they were behind her, she felt that they could call quits and go their separate ways.

'Absolutely right,' said Bingo gratefully. 'Pretty much exactly how it went.' He darted Flapper a look which to her said 'Thanks for being a pal', but which to Hari said 'You do this because we're in love'.

'The hat and its box were still there?' asked the Doctor.

'No. That's the funny thing,' said Bingo, conscious of the close attention he was receiving from both Banning-Cannons and the Doctor and glad to be able to tell the truth. 'I didn't see it anywhere!'

'So while you checked the other rooms of Mrs Banning-Cannon's suite, they made their escape with the hat?' suggested Flapper.

At this, Hari turned his back to them and stared ferociously out of the window at a lawn and a lake which must have been wondering what they had done to inspire such ire.

'Pretty much about it, Doctor, yes.' Inwardly Bingo was writhing, aware that because of his own selfishness in taking Mr Banning-Cannon up on his offer, he had let down his own side with a vengeance. Also, he had let down Hari. And Flapper. Given different circumstances he might have begun keening wildly but he was of old English stock. He contented himself by keening silently within.

If only he had thought of the consequences for a moment! He wanted so badly to tell the truth. He had scarcely told a lie since he was 7, when he had pinched a jar of strawberry jam from the kitchen cupboard then tried to blame Cook and a housemaid for the crime, forgetting that, since both were androids, they had no taste for human food at all. He shut his mouth tightly when he remembered that moment. He ought to have realised then that he didn't have the brains or personality to be a master crook. And now his story was thinner than a Copernican gas cloud. If it weren't for Mr Banning-Cannon backing him up and the Doctor also apparently trying to help him out, he would have been up the creek and crying for a paddle. As it was, he could see himself making all sorts of slips when actually talking to the peelers. He shuddered. Not only would he lose Lockesley Hall, he would spend years on a prison planet pumping water for the tankers of Aqua Supplies to sell for vast profits to the mining worlds and the desert planets which were not worth terraforming.

In a different set of circumstances, his best friend Hari would have sensed his anxiety by now and come to stand beside him, but Hari was standing meaningfully elsewhere. At the far end of the room.

Bingo would have confessed everything if it would have done any good. The fact was there was little to confess. He hadn't stolen the bally hat. All he was guilty of was *planning* to steal the hat. If other thieves hadn't actually pipped him, he would, of course, have something to tell all those people who now stood facing him and whose lives he hadn't actually ruined. Some other rotter had done that. He wished he *could* have caught them!

He was going to get his planet and do what he liked with it in spite of not having stolen the hat. The only things he had on his conscience were that (a) he had agreed to pinch a hat but hadn't, and (b) he was going to get his lifetime's dream without having done anything dodgy to gain it. He looked around the room despondently and caught what he thought was the knowing eye of the Doctor. Who would have no chance to show off his tremendous skills as he might have done had they made planet-fall on Flynn and not been doomed never to reach Miggea and the play-offs.

So as time sauntered on and Uncle Rupoldo and his men marched behind, all the more motivated to solve the crime now that their team was in danger of never so much as getting a sniff at the Arrer, Bingo manfully played host to the Tournamentors, the Re-Enactors and the holidaymakers while checking his watch about once every minute in the hope that some news would come through concerning the whereabouts of the stolen hat. He tried to talk to Hari, but Hari was moping and would have nothing to do with him. And when the beautiful Flapper tried to talk about Hari to Bingo or to Hari about Bingo, both men, for the wrong reasons, refused to speak. It looked pretty definite that, by the time night fell, neither true love nor true sport were ever going to run smooth again.

Bingo went to bed praying that the hat would be discovered and the passengers of the *Gargantua* be allowed to leave. Gloomily he anticipated another unsleeping night.

The Doctor went to bed wondering who on earth was telling the truth and who was lying when clearly nobody he had spoken to had any reason to pinch Mrs Banning-

Cannon's horrible hat. He brooded on the possibility that this was to do with the tournament and that the Judoon, who comprised the majority of the Tourists, might have planned the whole thing in order to stop them catching the ship and so arriving in Miggea too late to play. But such tactics, he had to admit, weren't characteristic of the Judoon, who tended to have fixed, literal attitudes where the law was concerned. He racked his brain for further possibilities and spent a fretful night in the process, there being rather more rack than brain involved.

Everyone was up at dawn, which was no inconvenience to the android staff. A gloomy and generally pretty weary team met in the breakfast room. All of them had popped dust from their eyes, staring at the chronos reading off the minutes before it would be too late to solve the crime and get aboard the *Gargantua* in time. Another gorgeous sun rose over the brilliant flowers, the picturesque trees, the green lawn and the glittering blue of the Lockesley Hall ornamental lake, but it beat down not on a bunch of cheery faces remarking on the splendour of the weather and its perfection for a tournament match but on a crowd of miserable features staring into the sky watching the tenders take up their more fortunate fellows to board the *Gargantua*.

Only Mr Banning-Cannon was not grieving. If asked he would have told you that he was as cheerful as the robin which, in the words of the popular ditty, sings in the tree. Sadly, however, he could not afford to show his pleasure but must appear as grimly inflexible on most topics, especially the heisting of expensive hats, as his lady wife.

Around lunchtime, Sir Rupoldo de Crespigny dropped out of the sky, followed by a squadron of his men, to issue the happy news that Mrs Banning-Cannon's hat had been found, abandoned, though still in its hatbox, in the bushes on the far side of the lake.

'It appears,' announced Rupoldo, who felt that Mrs B-C should have been more flexible in the matter of pursuing charges and thus let the local heroes get a chance, at least, of playing for the coveted Arrer, 'that the hat in question has been found. I would be obliged, therefore, madam, if you would accompany myself and my officers to identify it.'

The hatbox was opened, the hat identified. Something, said Mrs Banning-Cannon, *could* be missing from the hat. She didn't think so. It looked bedraggled, as if part of the internal structure had been displaced. As if it had been sat on... (It still resembled a squatting spider.) Eventually she was forced to admit that the hat, though a bit battered, was hers and that charges should not be pressed in the matter of its theft. Everyone was relieved until they remembered that the intergalactic liner had already departed and with it their chances of playing an historic game –

– until the Doctor strolled onto the well-kept lawn thumbing through a copy of *Colvin's ABC, the Intergalactic Spaceship Guide for the year of 51007* and whistling happily to himself.

'What's made you Mr Happy-Face all of a sudden?' asked Amy, who was taking the situation almost as badly as everyone else, if not more so, since she had some hint of the larger stakes involved.

The Doctor looked up with a smile which he shared generously with his surroundings and the population of Lockesley Hall's beautifully manicured lawn.

'Oh, I just thought you'd like to know,' he said, continuing to beam, 'that if we catch the local between Peers™ and Poppy 100, which leaves the local spaceport at 23.33 this evening, and on Poppy pick up the 7.20 water-barge bound for Desirée in the Outer Lavum Hestes and head for Dafryd, the mining world, getting the 11.28 to Placamine then jump from Placamine in Poseidon, arriving seven days later on

Seaworld™ 5000, we should be able to get to Kali 7 20.40 by the following evening, to reach Ganesh the following night and, with a spot of luck, get there about six-and-a-half hours before the *Gargantua* is due to leave on her final leg into Sagittarius, bound to go into orbit some days later above Murphy in the Miggea system before she turns round, after being restocked and getting her spaceworthiness certificate redone, and begins her journey home.' He beamed with self-congratulation, before adding: 'Of course, it won't be very comfortable and some of those connections are a bit tight, but we should be able to get to Flynn the morning after we check in at Murphy.'

The Doctor would remark to Amy later that he had been cheered before, had been cheered quite a lot of times actually, but never quite as joyously as when he had told his team that they would, after all, have a crack at the Big Tournament.

Chapter 8

Abroad in the Aether at Last

AMY HAD RATHER ENJOYED her stay on Peers™. It wasn't every day you had a chance to see what a mish-mash people were going to make of your own history and how pointless it was to worry about literary immortality. These Re-Enactors and sports people made you realise how distorted your own ideas of the past could be. She supposed there was a slight difference here since pretty much the whole of her own era could be compressed to a slender sliver given how much time had passed between the world she had been born into and this period, some fifty thousand years into the future. And when you thought of it like that you were impressed by how long the human race had managed to endure in spite of all the wars and foolish political ideas it had seen come and go.

'I think I understand why you like us as much as you do,' she told the Doctor. 'I guess I'd take a liking to anyone who was able to survive that long.'

'Oh, you're definitely worth fighting for,' he said, fiddling with something under the main encephalog-accumulators. A hologram of a 'bucky ball' about the size of a large water-melon appeared before him.

'And that's what you've done – fought for us, I mean. Over

hundreds of thousands of years. Can I help? What's that?'

'What?' He looked up at her in some surprise. 'Oh, you mean this! I'm hiding the TARDIS.'

'Who from?'

'Oh… nasty people, nice people, me, you. I'll send it somewhere logical, in case we need it in a hurry. Just remember these words: *Mood Indigo*. That'll be our clue, OK? If Frank/Freddie Force and his Antimatter Men are knocking about I need to be super-cautious. Can't have them getting their grubby little anti-hands on the TARDIS. Here – hold this…'

She looked at the large piece of cable he had put into her hand. 'Just hold it?'

'For the moment, yes.'

'Maybe we wouldn't be so admirable if we hadn't had your help, Doctor. Ever thought of that?'

'I don't need to.' He started changing the settings on his sonic screwdriver. 'I mean, I've seen the future, pretty much the whole of the future, and I've seen the alternatives. I see thousands of alternatives. Millions. Billions. That's my talent.' He sniffed modestly. 'One of my talents. One of my many talents.'

'Is that why you seem so relaxed sometimes? Because you can see the whole universe and know what the odds are on a favourable outcome?'

'Yes. Well. More or less. Sort of… Not really,' he decided. 'More complicated than that. More sort of hit and miss. You humans can generally get yourselves out of your own messes. Sometimes you just need a bit of help. And you did – do – will do pretty well at pulling yourselves back from the brink before you disappear into nothingness. You wouldn't expect me to bet on a loser, would you?' He grinned. 'At your best you're not only smart, you're kind. And unlike most of the intelligent species I've come across, you have *imagination*.

That's probably the defining characteristic of the human race. Even the Time Lords didn't have as much imagination as you lot. That's maybe what we value most in ourselves and others. At its finest it enables you to understand how someone else feels.'

He shrugged, before ploughing on: 'Now the Daleks and all that lot – incapable of imagining a decent meal, never mind a different point of view or another species' right to exist. Imagination gives you conscience. I could go on. Or I could complain about what terrible sloths you are, taking for ever to learn the most obvious ideas. Always thinking you know what's best for people.' The Doctor turned the hologram this way and that, frowning.

'Didn't you ever think you knew that?' She offered him the cable. He rubbed his chin as he stared at it.

'Oh, in my younger days, maybe. When I was a much older man. I've made a lot of mistakes. A lot. Hiding the TARDIS from everyone might be one of them. But I'm going to do it anyway!' He grabbed the cable from her and disappeared under the desk again. 'Just remember–' he whistled a few bars of a tune '– *Mood Indigo*.'

The Doctor clapped his hands. The hologram blopped and was gone.

'So, who do *you* think pinched that hat?' He turned to her suddenly.

'And then just dumped it? I don't know. A thief with a conscience?' She laughed.

His chuckle came back up at him from the twitching darkness only he sensed at that moment. 'That rules out the Judoon, then!'

'Seriously, do you know who did it?'

'I know who *was* going to do it.'

'Really!' She was intrigued. 'Are you going to tell me?'

His smiling face disappeared and emerged slightly out of

focus in a spot behind her.

'You know I hate that,' she pretended to slap at him over her shoulder.

'I know who had a motive. Mr Banning-Cannon.'

'Sure, but you were down there with me when she went back to find her reticule thing. He was with her.'

'True. But he could have got someone else to pinch it for him. So who was the last person to come down to dinner?' Another of those sudden searching looks.

'I can't remember. His lordship? Bingo Sherwood, maybe?'

'Got it in one, Pond.' He straightened his back and stood up.

'But they'd have found it in his room,' she argued. 'The police made a thorough search.' She retaliated with one of her sideways looks. 'Are you teasing me, Doctor?'

'I didn't say Bingo did it, and I didn't say he had a motive, but he *was* the last person to come down for dinner. Perhaps the last person in Mrs B-C's room. We both thought he was behaving a bit suspiciously.'

'I said goofy.'

'And I said flaky. These chaps aren't exactly bred for their brains. Would *you* send him off to steal an expensive hat?'

'He's very cute, but I wouldn't trust him to pinch a penny bun from the baker's shop.'

'So we'll rule him out…'

'… in spite of him having the opportunity?' Amy was sceptical. 'Come on, Doctor, you're not telling me everything you know!'

'Really, Amy, I am. I'm asking you questions in the hope you'll come up with an idea I've missed. We're pretty sure a hand-held anti-grav hoist was used, judging by the smell of bouncing tempelectrons. And whoever did steal it was able to dismantle it at their leisure.'

'I get you. They weren't trying to pinch the hat itself, they were looking for something in or on the hat!'

'That would be my guess. The people with the obvious motives wouldn't have had the time to do that.'

'The whole castle was on the lookout for the hat,' Amy pointed out.

'Exactly. So the thief or thieves were able, with the help of an anti-grav gun, to spirit the hat out of Lockesley Hall, get to a safe place, find what they wanted and then abandon the rest after putting it roughly back together.'

'Then why was his lordship acting so guilty?'

'I think because he was planning to pinch the hat but when he got there it had already gone.'

'But it was *huge*. I saw it when they brought it in.'

'That's pretty much what I've been worrying about, too.'

'So? What's the answer?'

'I don't know. It's been puzzling me.' The Doctor disappeared back under the console. 'The Arrow's safe in the time vault which will be sent to an unknown time in the future. Once the winners are declared...'

'What are you doing *now*?'

'I told you. I'm taking precautions. I'm hiding the TARDIS. I was tempted to try to bring everyone to Miggea with us, which would have been very stupid. There are too many unknown factors in all this. I think we're in serious danger. And if I knew what it was, I'd feel a lot better about using the TARDIS. Given the risks, it makes sense to keep it in reserve.'

Amy nodded. Sagely, she hoped.

First Intermission

HIS SHIP IS CALLED the *Paine*, named for a hero of ancient times who suffered the fate of most heroes, dying poor and alone with half the people he'd saved hating him. She has turned away from the light of her home, the dwarf galaxy Canis, and, never travelling at less than whatever in that region is the speed of light, she gathers momentum and sets her sails for the main spiral of stars we call the Milky Way.

Her captain, the Dutchman Cornelius, takes a deep breath of her rose-scented atmosphere, itself stolen from a long-dead galaxy, which encloses her in an envelope giving life to all on board and all that sustains life on board. Ultimately he is bound for Sagittarius, near the centre of those two hundred billion stars he knows as home. He understands, perhaps more than anyone, that something terrible is happening within the Schwarzschild radius. And what is that unseen, unimaginable power which remorselessly drags this galaxy and thousands of other galaxies towards what must be the centre of the multiverse. Dark tides ripping and running through the whole of perceived reality.

Scientists in his home galaxy first noticed it. That each galaxy had a black hole into which matter was pulled had been understood for centuries. People had also known that their galaxy was in turn being drawn towards an even stronger source of gravity. Only a few, like Captain Cornelius, guessed why. Like all rational beings, he accepted that gradual cycle of regeneration, of universal life and death, as inevitable – this knowledge has existed for millennia – but of late some other less benign force was at work. The old protections of checks and balances had gone wrong. Those who dwelt around the Galactic Rim became aware of this danger first. Pirate though he was, he did all he could to warn those who would listen: the fundamental cycle of birth, death and rebirth was being threatened by this implosion's increasing rapidity. Everything was happening far too quickly. According to those few wise creatures who could sense the greater multiverse beyond our galaxy, beyond our universe, we were facing nothing less than the corruption and utter destruction of *everything*.

Cornelius knows that whatever it is which lies at the centre of the universe, what we call a super-black hole, something unimaginably dense and tinier than an atom, has become erratic: the very thing which provided balance to the universe was now unbalancing it. Captain Cornelius sought the advice of every intellectual he encountered on his voyages, frequently making piratical raids on alien fleets crossing our Milky Way, not because he was greedy for wealth but because he was desperate for information. Few were able to offer him a sufficiently satisfactory explanation, even when they themselves observed the phenomenon.

All Captain Cornelius knows concerns a legend – little more than a rumour – about a stolen artefact taken from what some identify as the Realm of Law. They insist it be returned to the heart of the multiverse. If that is not done then all living matter, all living things, the very stuff of life, will be destroyed as punishment for that theft. There will be no regeneration. There will be no multiverse.

The artefact takes many forms in our side of the universe, identified as the Realm of Chaos. Some call it simply the Regulator or, colloquially, the Roogalator. Others of a more romantic disposition call it the Newtonium Staff or the Cosmic Balance; the Balance said to sustain the equilibrium of the universe.

Cornelius has heard that when the universe we know vanishes at last it will be into Limbo, where it will *not* regenerate. There will only be death, and those of us who remain conscious will remain conscious at that frozen moment of death, knowing our fate but never able to change it. Time, of which space is a relative dimension, disintegrates and intelligent order is lost.

Captain Cornelius stands on his bridge, his home galaxy behind him, its light filling his sails with the solar wind, and he stares into the deep, deep darkness ahead of him: the silent and near-infinite reaches of intergalactic space, which reflect the Dutchman's own desolate, inconsolable heart.

Other legends say that it is Cornelius himself who stole the artefact and is doomed to know the consequences of his action but never correct it. He knows guilt without end, torment for ever.

A touch of the wheel, an order to his sailors, and the *Paine* banks slightly against the infinite silence, driven by light, into that barely endurable darkness. The heavy tides are running. Time and space become erratic, insane. Dark tides running, destroying everything we ever valued. A flume of thousands of slain suns washes around his hull. Black suns collapse and vanish. He must not risk his ship. He must find some other way of reaching the centre. Dark tides are eating the multiverse.

In spite of all threats and dangers, Ironface the Dutchman is heading for the Hub.

Chapter 9

Dancing with the Galaxies

THERE IS LITTLE MORE alarming, on an ordinary day-to-day level, than living and working aboard an old nuke-burning, cadmium-dampened space-bucket in which our kind first sought to conquer the stars. They make noises whose source is untraceable. You see odd things. They seem to have a will, even an imagination, of their own. Known as nukers, the tramps are largely non-existent these days, but there was a time when the galaxy was full of them, pounding and battering new routes between the suns and mapping not only the systems they found but describing previously inconceivable horrors. On board as well as outside…

Amy had experienced only the sophisticated technologies which allowed the TARDIS to manipulate her way through time and her many dimensions which is somewhat naively called 'space'. She had known not only wonder but also a certain security being, as she was, the guest of a Time Lord. Now, as she lay in a narrow bunk, having awakened in something resembling a glass coffin, she wondered if she shouldn't regret her decision to accompany the Doctor on this adventure.

The ship they had picked up from Peers™ was a C-class nuker, crewed by as slovenly a bunch of spacerats as ever sailed between the stars, travelling from the water world of Palahendra to Desirée, the 'rendezvous' world, where merchants came to trade and have their ships repaired. The cargo would probably be sold to representatives from the mining planets of Outer Lavum Hestes where water was quite literally worth its weight in platinum. In spite of this, most captains would not waste their fuel or their time on the water-trade, chiefly because such ships were always in danger of attack by pirates who merely wished to restock their own supplies and who could not care less whether the old crates made it back to a safe berth. Many of the crew quite happily moved between work on water-barges and pirate ships, since pay and conditions were about the same.

But this consideration had not been regarded as a drawback to the Gentlemen. Their match in Miggea was more important than life itself, and Mr and Mrs Banning-Cannon, whose considerable luggage was stowed wherever it was relatively safe against mould, rust, buckling plates and popping rivets, had known nothing about the existence of such ships, until the moment they stepped aboard and asked where their suite might be. The laughter greeting this request was tribute to the many times the story would be told over and over again in the disgusting dives and low 'pessy' joints scattered across those parts of the galaxy still permitting the passage of such vessels as the K1-32. The best this ship could offer by way of luxuries were a working fire extinguisher and a couple of toilets which did not threaten to suck you out into space whenever you pressed the Flush button.

Mrs B-C's first action had been to threaten the captain and then, when this did not work, to complain to the Doctor, accusing him of being in league with the 'scum' to fleece them of their hard-won billions. The Doctor had gravely promised to register their complaint as soon as they reached 'civilisation'. Then he had suggested they freeze themselves for the duration, which they had declined to do because they feared they would be robbed in their sleep.

Their daughter Jane had been perfectly sanguine about this method of travel and had used the confined quarters to get to know Hari better. Hari had warmed a little but still believed that she was playing fast and loose with his and Bingo's emotions, though he no longer saw Lord Sherwood as his enemy, merely as a fellow dupe of a heartless siren of the spaceways.

With his friend bonding thus, Bingo at least attempted to set matters straight but was feeling so guilty about his part in making them lose their flight on the *Gargantua* that it seemed obvious to Hari that he was lying, though perhaps for noble reasons.

'Look here, old bean, I never intended to flirt with Flapper,' Bingo had begun after their fourth day on board, 'she merely suggested that I give her a ride on one of our punts. Her object, if you must know—'

His boyhood chum had responded frostily. 'Oh, I'm well aware of her object, old man. I assure you I have no intention of stepping between you. Let nobody, I hope, call me a duck in the mango. Or do I mean "mangey"?'

'Hari! You must believe there is nothing between myself and Miss Banning-Cannon. My heart, I assure you, belongs to quite another person, quite as beautiful – in fact even more beautiful – um, no, that sounds wrong – but anyway, another equally stunning girl...'

At which Hari had raised a sad, silencing hand. He suggested they drop the subject, go into the larboard companionway and try those new shots he had been talking about long before the Banning-Cannon party had turned up on their home planet.

In the moaning semi-darkness of the companionway, the two friends shot and caught 'safety arrows' almost automatically, neither able to continue the kind of casual conversation which was normal to them in these circumstances. Crew members would pause and watch them for a moment or two, sometimes commenting on their game before continuing about their duties. The steady 'twang' and slap of an arrow shot and an arrow whacked was soothing as the horrible old tub ploughed through the void at speeds once considered impossible, catching the currents of time itself and using them as all such ships did, to cross the great distances from one star system to another.

Wandering past the patched conduits and re-riveted plates of the bulky tanker, Amy found it hard to get used to the idea that this ship operated on technology that had once been innovative and magical but was now as outmoded as the first aeroplanes seemed to her. She wondered what a person from her own time would have thought of the machinery. Perhaps they would have dismissed it as magic, some kind of jiggery-pokery, an illusion. In spite of her own direct experience, in spite of having already seen many strange and wonderful things, she still had the occasional feeling of being in some sort of Alice in Wonderland dream. She smiled to herself. If there was a Queen of Hearts on board then she could be heard at this moment up in the control room.

'I demand to see the captain! Don't be insolent to me, young man. I could have you and your entire operation crushed into nothing!' Mrs Banning-Cannon had not stopped complaining since they had seen the ship drifting in shallow space and waiting for their tug. The captain, a ruggedly handsome young centaur called N'hn, at least sixteen hands high at his withers, had greeted them with a yellow bag of sweets in his big hand, his safety harness slung casually around his waist and his working overalls undone to the chest. He had been amused to see the passengers trooping aboard his ship and made a mock bow to Mrs B-C, offering one of his corn sweets. 'Weren't we at school together?'

Since then Amy had watched the centaur enjoying himself at Mrs Banning-Cannon's expense. What Amy realised and Mrs B-C did not was that Captain N'hn had nothing to lose. The centaur knew how to make his ship work and how to find a crew for her. He had fought off many pirate attacks. Most importantly, nobody else wanted his job. He drew some satisfaction from that. It gave him a power the terraform heiress could neither imagine nor ever desire.

Amy sneaked past them and carried on to one of the ship's observation ports. Space was dark and silent; the nearest spread of stars was a blur of silver in the faraway arm of a galactic spiral. She had no idea where they were and didn't much care. Some of the other passengers were nervous. One or two were positively frightened, but Amy, who in the TARDIS had never been able to look through an observation port of this kind and see the reality of size and distance, was far too fascinated to know even a shred of fear. After all, she knew what it was to hang in space with only the Doctor's hand keeping her from drifting off into the intergalactic void.

But now, watching, she observed something she had never expected to see. A swirl of darkness, like a smoke cloud millions of miles across, was obscuring her view of those distant suns, as if a great seven-fingered hand had reached up, then turned and dissolved into streamers of thick, dark gas. Those faraway stars which lay within the mass's coiling compass were behaving like nothing she had ever seen. Flickering, revolving, merging, separating, they performed what looked to her like a kind of vast cosmic dance. The dark streamers flowed amongst them, bringing them together, drawing them apart, a magnificent formal parade of countless suns moving to some unheard melody. Was this a common phenomenon, something nobody had bothered to tell her about because they were all so familiar with it?

Amy craned to see more. She had been told to look out for the so-called Great Refiguration or the Conjunction of the Million Spheres, when far more than that number of stars and their satellite planets joined to perform a stately, galaxy-wide pavane, behaving like sentient beings as they moved in a series of complex diagrams heralding, it was said, the rebirth of a universe. Everything in existence vectored to that moment when the composition of Creation changed, so some mysterious alien had once told her. She had no idea what he meant. She enjoyed her own thrilling discovery of new colours, the extraordinary distances covered by patterns made by the sinuous black smoke.

She felt the tanker quiver and become still, quiver again, grow still again. Was it, too, yearning to join the mighty formation as it changed then changed once more as if shaken in some titanic kaleidoscope?

Surely she was not the only witness? She turned and ran back down a narrow corridor festooned with pipes and wires which had come loose from their moorings. The ship continued its subtle, almost sensual shuddering, and if any of the regular crew were aware of it they gave no sign. Not until the corridor opened up into a wider gangway did she know that she was not the only observer. The captain, N'hn, his huge, healthy equine body as full of delicate tensions as his ship, stood beside the Doctor, staring through a long slot, watching the streaming galactic smoke and the shimmering, pirouetting stars.

'What is it?' she asked. 'Is it normal?'

'It depends what you mean by normal,' murmured the big centaur.

The Doctor was rubbing his face, his brows drawn in an attempt to remember something. 'I've never seen it this close inside the Rim. Why would it be speeding up now? This isn't the moment. It's not time to change.'

How old he looks now, Amy thought, and felt guilty.

'We've become used to it,' the Doctor went on. 'The phenomenon which was most people's only proof of the existence of a multiverse? Dark force! The dark tides! They told of worlds beyond the arras of "space". That's what we're seeing, much closer inside the Rim than anyone's ever reported. Usually you need an OPR telescope to watch this.'

'Doctor! What is it?'

He turned at the sound of her voice. He still looked vague, thoughtful. 'Oh, hello, Amy. Yes. You're watching what's sometimes called the Dance of the Planets, but this is a Dark Forces manifestation.'

'Dark *Forces*? You're not talking about Lucifer and the armies of Hell are you?'

He laughed. 'I hope not. This is something that was discovered in your own time – roughly – and was used to prove the existence of a largely invisible multiverse. They called those streamers "dark flow". Now they're known as dark tides. They're moved by gravity, like ocean tides. They seemed to come from nowhere and move at millions of miles an hour, dragging whole galaxies with them. We are all so delicately, so vulnerably *connected*.' He shivered. A momentary chill.

Amy shook her head. 'I've no idea what you're on about. As usual.'

The Doctor pulled a face. But it sagged into a lazy smile. 'Never mind. Think of it as a gravitational pull, only from outside your galaxy. So strong that it's tugging galaxies away while our black holes pull in the other direction. People started to call them "the black winds", which is a bit poetic but you get the idea.'

Captain N'hn continued to watch the spectacle. 'These aren't the big wind. These are like breezes compared to a hurricane. A little jig rather than the full ballet. But they're still spectacular. They represent the forces pushing us while black holes are the forces pulling us within our own galaxy.'

'And this is important, why exactly?'

The Doctor ran his fingers through his hair as he considered this. 'There are people who can use that energy to travel at millions of miles an hour in vessels which can dodge in and out of the different planes, moving between the near-infinite worlds of the multiverse and somehow navigating in order to take a kind of shortcut. Really it's mostly an astonishing skill at negotiating the gravitational pull from universes or galaxies within those universes that aren't visible to us. They've been moving away from the centre of our galaxies for at least two and a half billion light years.'

'More than I can take in,' said Amy. 'Why are they dancing like that?'

'That's just what it looks like to us. Some sort of reconfiguration where most of the essential elements can't be seen. We'd need special instruments to detect all the different gravities in play. Beautiful, isn't it?'

'And dangerous,' murmured the ship's captain. 'Something's fouling it up, setting things off too soon. It's powerful. That's just a squall. But enough to tear us apart if—'

He cursed as the ship suddenly shifted and spun, her gravity simulators working overtime, whining and throbbing as they attempted to keep her steady. Elsewhere the crew were yelling, busy with the jobs they had been trained for.

'— if they get a good grip on us.' He headed off towards his control room, galloping as fast as he dared, the sound of his hoofs growing fainter until he disappeared.

'There's a dark wind blowing through all the multiverse we know and our destinies are determined by its contrary flow. Joli grand, joli chant, joli trista, funning you, allez vous, etherista...'

The Doctor had dropped his voice again and seemed to be quoting someone. His tapping feet sounded like the distant, complex drumming of the Arcturan Cyclops as they galloped and trotted and cavorted in all their half-human glory, celebrating the great gathering which came every ten years. He continued to mumble, almost as if the words were an equation he had memorised. He looked up suddenly.

A moment later they were floating in free fall and could hear the captain yelling orders to his men. Struggling to keep their balance, they were dragged this way and that. Then the ship's gravity was restored. But Amy already had some new bruises, and she guessed she wasn't the only one.

Behind her now the Doctor was ruefully rubbing his shin. 'Hadn't expected that. Sorry.'

'Wasn't your fault,' she said. 'Or was it?'

He laughed at this.

'Wasn't your fault. Or was it?'

Why was she repeating herself?

She was back with the Doctor and Captain N'hn, looking out of the observation port. She opened her mouth to speak. Then, once more, she was floating in free fall. She was on her own, watching the star clusters begin their dance again / rubbing her bruised leg / talking to the Doctor / boarding the ship / flirting with Bingo / watching an arrow impale itself in the backside of a gaudily dressed little man she'd never seen before / leaving the TARDIS on Peers™ / practising in the grounds of the big country house...

It was too much to take in. She passed out. Red and white candy stripes twirled away in a familiar pythonoid pattern.

And her body was moving slowly in an arc which mirrored the greater arc of the ship.

She felt horribly sick
she was about to throw up...
something flung her against
yielding metal and she bounced
there over and over again
she fell down a long arc of
fierce rainbow colours
advanced towards spiralling
galaxies...

Until she was following the Doctor along a rocking gangway where strange muted golds and fiery greens attacked her, stinging her wherever they struck.

She realised she was experiencing her first real space-time storm. The ship had been caught by precisely those forces she had witnessed outside. They were pushing instead of pulling. Anti-gravity? Anti-something... She had thought that by now they would be using the pull of the black hole to rendezvous with their destination. Instead, something else was pushing them backwards, and she was again trying to visualise a cosmology so complex, so vast that their entire galaxy might be the merest speck, as invisible to others as a microbe was to her. There was no guessing the dimensions of the multiverse and no point in trying because size had no meaning to her. She wondered if it had any meaning to anyone. Everything was relative, after all. She found this enormously funny but hated the sound of her own laughter. She wanted to go home. How she longed, longed to be home where some things were more important than others. Where...

There were tears on her face and she had her head against the Doctor's shoulder, but she couldn't remember her own name as she watched scarlet words in an unknown language rush from her head and mingle with her long red-gold hair then disappear into a black funnel. 'Doctor?'

'It's all right.' His voice was warm. 'Just a minor storm.

Those awful time winds...'

'Time winds? Time tornadoes, it feels like.'

'That's closer to the truth than you know, Dorothy.' He drew a long, deep breath. 'Or, at least, I think it is.'

'I'm really trying very hard not to kill anyone,' she heard herself saying.

'Of course you are,' he said comfortingly.

From somewhere came the sound of singing. She thought at first she could hear some of the crew but then she realised the voices were too light. Too light? What was going on in her head?

'Hello, boys.' That was the Doctor. He was setting her gently into her bunk, looking at a beautiful pale blue globe containing three handsome young men whose eyes smiled into hers as they rested, apparently on currents of thin air.

'We'll spin yer there, capano, never fear, for we're the mighty Bubbly Boys, no system can confine us. Or even wine and dine us. So ask us what and ask us why, don't ask us who in case we die. Toot too a roo. How's the future looking to you, cousin? Don't worry, we'll be there to lend a hand when the time comes:

> *We're Bubbly Boys from Ketchup Cove*
> *Bright blue we are and purple too and brave*
> *enough to face the kids from Kettle Cave.*
> *Yaki do, yaki doan, yaki dye-o*
> *Yaki fight, yaki tight, yaki spy-o*
> *Song like that sing for cinco de mayo...*
> *Hoo la la, magic jar wonder why-o...*

She became horribly self-conscious. Her stomach churned and she heard herself, a little Scottish girl who had never lost her accent, asking awkwardly, 'Who did you say you were? I don't think we've been formally introduced. Or informally either, for that matter.'

She heard the Doctor's voice. 'Don't worry. They're on our side. Probably. Blood's thicker than any wild tide. Al, Tom and Bob Bubbly. Captain Abberley's crew. Three of the Famous Chaos Engineers. They know the Second Aether better than anyone.'

She turned her head. They had all gone. The ship's movement seemed slow and she was certainly steady. The storm was over. Amy got out of her bunk.

She found the Doctor in the dormitory he was sharing with another twenty or thirty men. He was leafing through star charts, making notes on a V-pad, and looked up when she came in. 'You OK now? I'd have warned you if I'd had any sense that was going to catch us. Those winds shouldn't have occurred anywhere near here. It's just plain *wrong*. Did you meet the Bubbly Boys? I asked them to keep an eye on you.'

She nodded.

'What are you doing, Doctor? Puzzles?'

'I wish. I'm too easily bored. Why is it, Amy Pond, that we're travelling at twice the speed of Earthlight and I feel like we're limping along at a snail's pace? Was that Mrs B-C out there? Before the storm caught us?'

'Yes. I think I was wrong about that theory of mine. She'd never deliberately have brought this on herself. What do you think?' It didn't seem strange to be talking normally again. Somehow the storm had refreshed her, like a long sleep.

'I'm sticking to my theory – that we're looking in the wrong places for the thief.'

He glanced up to watch cobalt blue bands of light winding themselves around knots of copper pipe. A little spillage from the nuclearoid engines which he had assured her wasn't dangerous.

'I suppose you never came across that book by Barry Pain?' he asked. '*The One Before*? I was enjoying it. Funny how nobody ever reinvented that kind of fiction. I knew most of those guys who came out in the 1890s – the New Journalism some of them called it. More than one bunch under the same tag. Like the 1960s. Nothing was around in your day that they hadn't thought of. I'd like to take you back there some time. Pett Ridge. Arthur Machen. J.M. Barrie. H.G. Wells. Jerome K. Jerome. P.G. Wodehouse. Lots of 'em, when they were all writing for the *Pall Mall* and *The Fortnightly*. Very funny, too, Pain. A lot of them…' He spoke absently, like someone trying to remember happier days.

Amy had the feeling he was reluctant to say what was really on his mind. But she knew he wouldn't tell her any more than he wanted to, unless –

'Are you trying to protect me from something?' she asked.

He looked at her with a bit of the old twinkle in his eyes. 'If I am, I haven't been very successful. I think I've told you everything I can be sure of.'

'What? Enough to alarm me?'

He smiled. 'Everything alarming you is what's alarming me. And I don't really know much more. I can't address any of the big questions, not without help from the TARDIS, and I'm still too scared to try bringing her in. I think there are powerful people looking for her. I can't afford not to keep her hidden. And the dark tides might rip the TARDIS apart. Or she could slip into another universe and we'd never see her again. The TARDIS is safest hidden from me as well as from anyone chasing us. So let's concentrate on the questions we *can* answer! Why is that hat still bothering me? It seems trivial but it's important to what we're here for, I know it is. We've worked out who planned to steal it, who was going to steal it and why. We aren't any further forward working out who *actually* stole it or why…' He was tired, leaning back on his bunk with his hands behind his head. 'I think if we had just a couple of answers we'd know better what to do. So we keep on hopping from one grubby old spaceport to another and hoping we'll find out before we get to Miggea. Do you know who the planet's named after?'

'Who?'

'A legendary Queen of Seirot. In the great fight between the forces of Law and Chaos, she stood for Law. There was a war between the Archangels of Law and the Archangels of Chaos. A bit Miltonian, but there you go. Only without all that religion, thankfully. Anyway, where was I? Oh yes, this queen led her forces into what was called the Battle for the Balance. So that was more like Ragnarok, I suppose – the end of everything. But the old chronicles rarely describe her as a force for good. Though she fought for Law, which is *supposed* to be good, right, she was seen as one who would rather kill for a principle than let an enemy live for a chance to make things better. That's Law gone sour. Function forgotten. And E.J. Milton wrote a whole epic poem about it. Her own troops stopped trusting her in the end. She spread so much carnage, they were sickened by the amount of blood she spilled for what she considered an ideal. You've heard people say: "That was positively Miggean?" Oh, you haven't. *Really*? Well, you know what I mean. Makes you think. That's why sports are so important. Well, I've just decided sports are so important. People rarely play sports for a principle, do they?'

'It depends,' she said, glad finally to get a word in and determined to make use of it, 'whether you're a Rangers or a Celtic supporter.'

She was glad when he laughed spontaneously. She realised it had been far too long since she had seen him do that.

Chapter 10

A Time to the Dance of Music

THEY WERE A GOOD few parsecs from the source of the storm when the pirates were spotted, spiralling out of a globular cluster locally known as Grone and very quickly moving in parallel to their ship.

The Doctor had been playing six-dimensional chess with the captain when the screens began to burp and sigh with warning signals.

'They're after our water, almost certainly.' N'hn brought up the visuals, a thin spread of stars, and locked them into focus. 'They have instruments that can sniff it across the whole damned Milky Way. But they have no way of sniffing the Chronii.'

'I didn't know you were carrying any.' The Doctor put his head to one side. 'I was a bit surprised when I saw your only big armament was an old-fashioned Kruppmeyer shunt-action Ganymede gun.'

'That's more for reaction than it is for defence. The quickest way of getting out of a low-grav situation I know.' The centaur had become friendly with the Doctor, recognising his know-how and grateful to find a 6D player among his passengers. 'You can play with it, if you like. It might reassure the passengers and draw their attention away from our real defences which—'

'Not really my sort of thing,' the Doctor cut in. 'Aren't exactly legal, are they? Chronii, I mean.'

'Don't ask me why we're criminals if we fly with the best protection anyone ever came up with. Mutuality. A perfect union of species.' The captain was keyboarding as he spoke. Now he started to flick unfashionable Horspool toggles and pass his free hand over his screens in configurations which once would have been thought magical.

The Doctor was more interested in staring at the screens, trying to make out the nature of their likely attackers. Crenellated jade-like figuring along the hulls of the seven ships closing in on them was a sign that they had belonged to the old Manakai invaders from the Arkwright Cluster, but that lot had been wiped out ages ago. The ships were probably owned now by renegade members of the Dructionjen clans, exiled many generations earlier for Dalek-worship, a quasi-religious cult which believed the Doctor's old enemies would one day return to take over the galaxy. The Doctor had no time for the renegades or their beliefs but he knew their potential for destruction and took them seriously.

N'hn was issuing orders in his full-throated accents, his hoofs drumming rapidly on the old insulating tiles, threatening to shake them loose again. The Dructionjen were moving into battle formation, clearly seeing the tanker as an easy mark.

The Doctor slipped out of the control cabin to check on the passengers. Pale yellow light blazed up and down her jade crenellations. They had settled down after the storm. Many were still playing various games and remained blithely unconscious of the further approaching danger. A few had been alerted by the crew's changed behaviour. As the Doctor passed by, Hari Agincourt called out to him. 'Anything up, old boy? Something we can do? I was told we weren't seriously damaged by the storm.'

'Nothing to do yet.' The Doctor slowed for a moment and lowered his voice. 'Don't say anything now, but we're about to be attacked by pirates. If we're boarded, which is unlikely, it might be a good thing to be ready to defend yourselves.'

Hari's whispered response was typical. 'Oh, gosh! That's a spiffin' bit of luck. We're going to see some action, eh? What can I do?'

'Just get some of the team together so they're ready for any emergency we have to face, OK? Have you seen Amy?'

'Down that way and to the left when I last saw her.'

'Ah, yes. That would be right.' The Doctor disappeared in search of Amy.

Although Hari had no clear idea what the pirates were like or how they could be fought, he was typically game for anything, while being perfectly aware of what the consequences could be. He had watched the optional infoscreens when he had first come aboard. They were graphic, put together at a time when the prevailing idea was that passengers had to be encouraged to fight off any attack by raiders. Nowadays the company let people watch who wanted to. Hari didn't like the look of the slimy beggars represented on the screen. He almost hoped they would be boarded so he could get a whack at them.

A few moments later, Bingo rounded the corner at a rate of knots, his eyes bright with what his ancestors might have called battle lust. 'Seen my bow-case, old boy?'

'I think you left it in that bit of the inspection gangway, old man.'

'Thanks, old boy.'

'Don't mention it, old man.'

It was impossible not to bond under these circumstances.

*

The Doctor had found Amy and they were on their way back to the bridge when they passed Hari and Bingo again.

Bingo's heart did some Olympic-standard aerobatics in his chest. He was determined to defend Amy, come what may. The fact that she was probably better equipped to defend Bingo never once occurred to him.

When they reached the bridge, Amy helped the Doctor close the door behind them. The big centaur was sitting in his long bucket-seat, humming a tune to himself and stroking his holographs gently, carefully. As the pirates outside formed a cage around his ship, his instruments and screens gathered to their captain like obedient pets.

He seemed unconcerned by the pirates' tactics. But Amy felt a new kind of tension in him in spite of his apparently relaxed attitude. He began to murmur rapidly into his main board, leaning forward, his tail perked high. 'OK.'

The attacking ships were glittering with zigzagging bolts of pure gold and green energy. In another instant they would start firing, set at a factor designed to kill or stun passengers but leave the ship and cargo intact.

The captain was snorting and tossing his long locks back from his eyes. Then he spoke in his own language, a series of high-pitched ululations, long snorts and grunts, rising to a loud and rather raucous whinny which had a note of challenge in it.

At the same moment, the skipping lines of light along the hulls of the pirate vessels began to straighten and become still.

Amy felt the Doctor tense. She guessed he knew what was coming.

'Chronii!' he murmured to himself. 'I thought...'

All at once the pirate ships swung in closer. Rapidly the energy along their hulls rearranged itself, uniting into one large beam which moved gradually away from each ship like a kind of searchlight until all were pointed in at the water tanker, threatening her and broadcasting a flashing blue and dark yellow signal to heave to, over and over: *Heave to, Heave to.*

The centaur's hands began to drum out a series of rapid beats, those movements bringing him views of his own ship's exterior which had become spotted with coppery splotches, like a form of rust. But the rust, or whatever it was, had started to move, each patch crawling independently, seemingly of its own volition, slowly turning into bright, roughly spheroid, red and white shapes.

Suddenly the rays moved out from the pirate ships, pencilling tighter, brilliant against the flat blackness of the universe until they all threatened the tanker.

No message had come from the pirate fleet because none was needed. Everyone involved was aware of what passed between the predator and its prey. The thieves were giving the ship a chance to let them come aboard and pump out their water. But clearly Captain N'hn was not prepared to let them do this and was revealing whatever protection he possessed. That they were unimpressed was obvious, too. They hadn't recognised the odd, globular energy creatures carried by the tanker which the Doctor had earlier identified as Chronii.

'Why's water so valuable to them?' Amy asked, finding the tension hard to bear. 'You'd hardly think it was worth fighting for. All they need is a decent recycling system.'

'Modern ships have near-perfect recycling systems.' The Doctor spoke distantly, his eyes intent on the screens. 'But even they need to top up. These old ships use almost as much water as people do where you come from. Their recycling units are shot. So whenever a pirate gets a water alert, this is what happens. They must have some pretty sophisticated detection gear. But there's something else going on here…'

'Yeah. They're going to kill us.'

DOCTOR WHO

'They don't care. They think their force beams will stun us long enough for them to come aboard, pinch the water and leave. Usually they're not bothered whether the occupants live or die. Generally, they die.'

'What can we do?'

'Not a thing. Watch for an opportunity. But there's nothing we can do right now.'

Amy opened her mouth to ask another question and then closed it. The rays were darting across the darkness as the clusters of light on the tanker's hull broke clear, apparently deliberately moving towards the rays, forming a kind of link-mail armour around the ship. The rays met the clusters, spread and then somehow seemed to writhe and bend, unable to pass the balls of light. The captain was yelling now, what appeared to be challenges in his own resonant language. The rays suddenly began to turn outwards, away from the tanker. Very quickly they were cut off on the ships. The pirate vessels began to fan out urgently, as if they had only now realised what was happening.

But the tanker's weird globes had swiftly turned the same colour as the rays. The globes actually raced upwards, like bowling pins up an alley, using the attackers' own force beams to *climb* towards the ships!

'What are they, Doctor?' She was fascinated, still not sure how safe they were from the pirates.

The attacking ships were now taking evasive action. They twirled and bucked through space at a rate which threatened to break them apart. They tried to angle themselves so that they would be virtually invisible but still they could not escape the strangely bending verdigris and mustard rays which their own beams had become. Nor could they get away from the globes which used the beams as roads, rolling up them, blending their own colours with those of the attackers.

The Doctor bent forward, his eyes on the main screen,

leaning over the captain's shoulder as the handsome centaur chuckled and neighed and continued to caress his keys.

'So you really *do* carry Chronii,' said the Doctor.

The captain shrugged.

'Why are they illegal, Doctor?' Amy wanted to know.

'I think the authorities are scared of a public outcry. They're hard to understand, the Chronii.'

'Are they – what? – sentient? Can they think?' she asked

'Oh, yes. They're sentient all right. Pretty intelligent. Their own planet's out near the Rosette Nebula. It's off-limits to any member of the Galactic Union, which is almost every inhabited world in this era. They turn a blind eye to what they call Crucial Services using them. Not many do, because you have to make deals with the Chronii. They don't work for nothing and they're all volunteers.'

'Why would they volunteer?'

'There's a trade-off. I suppose you could call them gourmets.'

Now the rays were arcing around so that they were spearing straight towards the pirates who were putting their craft through all kinds of complicated manoeuvres in an effort to get out of their way.

The globes began to drift back towards their own ship. They no longer twinkled with verdigris and mustard but had a greyish tinge.

'They're exhausted,' said the Doctor. 'They've done their best. Now we have to wait and see if that best was good enough.'

Even as he spoke the nearest pirate ship was struck by its own armaments, bent back on themselves. The ship flickered with scarlet and emerald flames and then began to drift away, clearly out of control.

'What's happened to it, Doctor? Have the Chronii killed them?'

'Probably not. What's happened to them is what they expected to happen to us. At least until they spotted the Chronii. Then it was too late for them to get away.'

'I *still* don't understand.'

'Well, they have, so to speak, been hoist by their own petards.'

'What's a petard?'

'Look it up on the internet when you get the chance.'

'You don't know, do you?'

'I used to know. I've forgotten. Some sort of bomb or booby trap, I think. Anyway, it means that what the pirates planned for us is now happening to them instead, because the Chronii, who are wonderful little beings, can turn almost any form of aggression away from themselves and direct it back at the aggressor, usually in a more powerful form.'

The pirates were now all spinning helplessly out of control, their formation completely broken. The only reason they remained nearby was because the tanker's gravity held them.

From somewhere in the distant bowels of the K1-32 came the sound of wild, raucous cheering.

Captain N'hn turned, grinning at Amy. 'There you are, girlie. That's what a ship without guns can do. If she has friends. And the Chronii are the best friends any spacer could come by, eh, Doctor?'

'While you're alive. Where did you find them?' The Doctor continued to keep his eye on the helpless pirates. 'Not the Rosette.'

'Right. They found us. They wanted a trade and I was willing to give them one. They save our lives and they get whatever spoils there are. Look, they're heading out for that ship.' It was true. The globes of silver and copper had regained a little of their lustre and were disappearing through the hull of the nearest predator.

Amy was still puzzled. 'I don't get it. What do they want? How are they paid?'

'They eat our waste,' murmured the Doctor, a little disgustedly.

Captain N'hn began to laugh at what he obviously regarded as the Doctor's delicacy of expression.

'They love the taste of humans,' said the captain. 'They get to eat the fresh corpses of the dead – either side – after a battle. That's where they're going now.'

'But what if they're not dead?' Amy wanted to know.

'Oh, they will be soon enough,' the captain reassured her. He laughed loudly again when he saw her horrified expression.

'Hang on,' said the Doctor staring hard at a screen. 'What's happening there?'

Chapter 11

Antimatters

THE SCREEN SHOWED A length of the tanker's hull and, some distance away, the leading pirate ship. From out of that ship another beam connected with the shadowy rays left behind by the Chronii. This brightened suddenly into white and red rays, intertwined. The beam had reached the K1-32 and spread around one of the rear airlocks.

The captain cursed and looked about under his desk, grabbing a big old-fashioned NE-gun from the floor and running out of the control cabin hastily followed by the Doctor.

'What is it?' Amy wanted to know, following as fast as she could. 'Captain? Doctor? What's going on?'

The captain was too distracted to answer, talking into a microphone, issuing rapid orders to his crew. The Doctor did his best to respond while looking wildly around him for anything that might help. Seeing a discarded bow and a quiver of arrows, he snatched it up.

'Defend yourself!' he told Amy. 'Any way you can.'

'And why? What should I be worrying about?' she wanted to know.

'Boarders!' Was all he had time to tell her.

'We've been *boarded*? Who by? I thought the Chronii had dealt with them.'

'They dealt with the pirates. What none of us knew was that the pirates were carrying passengers.'

'You know who they are?'

'That candy-striped ray could only come from one source. I'm hoping I'm wrong…'

'And here we are, Doctor dear.' A strange, growling voice, full of mockery, with a slight, metallic lisp. 'Here we are again, darling. Ready to straighten you all out.'

The voice came from around the corner of a corridor. Captain N'hn, who had been galloping ahead of them, his big rifle ready, came to a sudden swerving halt, throwing up his hand to stop them following. He shouted to a group of his men who had appeared ahead of them. 'Stop. It's too late. They're in.' Lowering the gun he turned to glance at the Doctor, shrugging. He carried an air of hopelessness completely at odds with his earlier manner. He drew a great breath and let it out slowly. 'They're in.'

The Doctor shrugged. 'We did our best. We didn't know.' He raised his voice: 'Good afternoon, General Force. How's life on the other side?'

'Safe, warm and beautifully predictable, thanks for asking, Doctor. No need for me to enquire how life is for you. Chaotic as usual, I'm sure. Well, we're here to help.' He seemed to speak with two synchronised voices.

They reached a part of the ship used as a kind of makeshift gym. Several crew members and a few of the Tournament team looked helplessly on at the weird group who stood there. They were uniformed and carried wide-nozzled weapons a bit like old blunderbusses, and they seemed unnaturally pale; even the men with darker skins had an oddly grey appearance. At first glance they resembled a theatrical troupe. Their uniforms were garish reds, golds, blues and green. They wore peaked high-crowned dark blue military caps with sweeping plumes. The gold braid on their sleeves, jacket fronts, collars and shoulders was almost blinding. Yet the men were each surrounded by a strange, pinkish aura, covering them from head to foot.

Amy looked at the Doctor. 'How did they escape the Chronii?'

'The Chronii didn't recognise them. Without those skinsuits they're wearing – not the comic opera uniforms but the pink aura – they would disintegrate. They'd implode and take us with them. Sometimes two or more have to share the same body but they must be related. Something to do with their DNA. Or is that anti-DNA? That's why Frank/Freddie sound as if they are talking in an echo chamber. They are literally brothers under the skin. They carry a subcutaneous energy pack to create that aura, which in turn gives them the means, quite literally, of hanging together. It's a pseudo-skin. Switches on and off. It allows them to enter our space. If we managed to break down an aura with some sort of energy weapon or even the sonic screwdriver we'd destroy them very quickly, but we'd also destroy ourselves. There's only one safe way…'

One of the men spoke. 'Succinctly put, Doctor.' Amy guessed he was the leader, because his voice had that same echo and he wore a vast amount of gold frogging across his chest and a multitude of twirls on his mustachios. He put a short-fingered hand to his soup-strainer and laughed into Amy's face. 'Who's your new gal?'

The Doctor ignored this but inserted himself between Amy and the newcomer. 'None of that, General Force. What do you want here?'

So this was the infamous Frank/Freddie Force, thought Amy, and those comic opera soldiers behind him had to be his Antimatter Men.

'Those suits are their defence *and* a potential suicide weapon,' the Doctor continued, his eyes cold as he glared at General Force. 'It's like a personal protective field. The Chronii didn't realise Force and his boys were aboard. They couldn't have done much against them if they *had* known. Unless you know where the umbilical's hidden, breaking down that skin even slightly would cause a massive implosion drawing everything into itself and turning it into one vile mess of formless flesh. Inside out.'

'Exactly so, Doctor. In other words, my dear, destroy us and you destroy yourselves. Here –' He/they held up his/their hand so that his/their sleeves fell back, revealing his/their skin with its strange pewter-coloured radiance. 'That's what antimatter looks like when it's controlled by the power of Law.'

'Law?' Amy was outraged. 'Law? You think putting on a circus ringmaster's uniform and invading a peaceful ship in deep space is *legal*?'

'I'm referring, Missy, to a higher form of Law. To the highest form of Law which counters the kind of Chaos your master so enjoys spreading through the cosmos.'

Amy's red hair might have been on fire as she stepped forward. 'What did you call me? What did you call him? You little creep! I'm going to rip that silly hat off your head and —'

'Hat?' said Frank/Freddie Force, glancing around.

'No!' This time it was the captain who put his huge body between them. 'Miss Amy. It's not – not —' He seemed lost for words.

'Safe?' Frank/Freddie Force chuckled. 'Not at all safe for any of us. We're taking considerable risks, you know. We've never sailed this near to the Rim.'

'Why *are* you so far from home, Frank/Freddie?' the Doctor wanted to know. 'Keeping company with the worst

136

pirates. Risking our lives and yours. I suppose you had no choice. There isn't a ship from your own hemisphere could get you here. I didn't expect you ever to want to fly so close to the edge of this galaxy.'

'I enjoy a surprise, don't you? It should be obvious. We knew you'd start falling back in around this time. So we came as far as sanity allowed us and waited for you. Duty, Doctor dear, makes us take unusual risks, *n'est-ce pas*?'

The Doctor glared. 'Spare us your hypocrisy, Frank/ Freddie. What are you hoping to steal from this ship?'

'Steal? Come along, Doctor. Let's not get on high horses here. We'd be wise to keep our tempers, too. This is what you could call a tense, even implosive, situation, tee hee. If either of us gets too touchy we'll all be in the treacle, eh?' His men exchanged insane grins, enjoying their leader's humour. 'Golly,' they said. 'Oh Golly! Ha ha ha!'

Amy thought the scene disturbing in a number of ways, not least the conscious theatricality assumed by Force and Co. That was more than a bit creepy. Yet it was hard for her to see as a serious threat this sinister little man, with his curling mustachios and his ringmaster's coat, his bright crimson trousers with the sharp blue stripe tucked into gleaming black boots with huge spurs jingling on them; but she could tell from the Doctor's body language that this was about as serious as it got. He had already hinted as much, hoping that he would never have to do more than hint. But now they faced each other in a stalemate.

Amy had picked up a little about the antimatter universe from the Doctor, and they'd met an old philosophical jummybug on Latest Io who had explained to her about Law and Chaos; how the universe maintained stability and creativity, balancing between Law on the one hand and Chaos on the other. But they were not the same thing. Professor Ormic, the learned jummybug, had given the impression that philosophically he saw their universe not in terms of good and evil, but in terms of the fundamentals of the multiverse. Law and Chaos – order and creativity – matter and antimatter were qualities which became good or evil depending on their context.

In balance, Professor Ormic had told her, these qualities kept the multiverse from becoming too rigidly organised or too disorganised. Constant regeneration. There had always been people of quite disparate origins who dedicated their lives to maintaining the status quo, explained the professor. In the history of the cosmos the balance tilted sometimes one way, sometimes another. The Time Lords had once helped to maintain that balance. The professor pointed out that what he called the Cosmic Balance was a symbolic construct for something enormously complex. He could have told her more, but the maths would have been overwhelming. The Balance was the way in which the multiverse maintained its equilibrium so that neither side tilted too far in one direction or another, since these were the two more or less equal forces which kept the multiverse from collapsing into nothingness. Matter and antimatter were not the same as Law and Chaos, of course. Law and Chaos existed in both spheres.

Amy had become used to some strange experiences in the Doctor's company and this was one of the strangest: to be standing listening to these two humanoids, one of them representing Law, the other Chaos, discussing the weirdest philosophical and metaphysical ideas as if they were tangible realities.

There was something hallucinatory about this moment. Minutes earlier Amy had watched coloured rods of light climb along a ray of energy and enter their ship. Now a villain – actually two villains – Frank/Freddie Force, had materialised before her eyes. She had faced far worse monsters, without a doubt, but for some reason she was as scared of this bizarrely uniformed little man (or strictly two little *men* in one body) and his gang as she had ever been of anything. Everything about Frank/Freddie was *wrong*: the pink and pewter glaze of his skin, constantly squirming and wriggling as it quite literally kept the brothers together; the oddly coloured face that might have been painted on using clown make-up; the bright pantomime tints of that uniform, all clashing in subtle ways she could not quite describe; and the way the Antimatter Men imitated General Force, even echoing his gestures from time to time. Amy felt physically sick when she looked at them. She glanced at Captain N'hn and the Doctor to see if they too were experiencing the same sensations.

Certainly there was an expression of intense loathing on the centaur's face. Of course he might have looked the same at any invader who'd tried to take over his tanker. The Doctor's face was an angry mask.

'What possesses you to continue these assaults on us?' He gestured with the bow and arrows still clutched in his right hand. 'Why can't you stay in your own sphere of the multiverse?' He glared at General Force. 'We have never once attempted to invade you or change you, yet you're obsessed with invading us. *Why*?'

'It is in the nature of Law, Doctor.' Frank/Freddie Force's over-bright features split in a grin of challenging mockery. 'We are concerned with what you might do some day. What you *might* do. We cannot help ourselves. It is a constant irritant – an itch which demands to be scratched. Be Prepared. We are driven to make neat as strongly as you, Doctor, are driven to put cats among pigeons, throw spanners in works!'

'Except that I'm *not* driven to create strife where there is peace. I don't feel an irresistible urge to spill the milk or stir a pot or whatever else you imply I love to do. I don't travel about the universe constantly seeking the moribund and trying to quicken pulses. Yet you are apparently maddened by the unpredictable, disturbed by everything which isn't thoroughly straightened and mapped and catalogued and – what?'

'Controlled is the word you're looking for, Doctor. Without the proper controls we can't see ahead – we can't make accurate predictions. The Future goes dreadfully, terribly, miserably wonky! Can't you see that? You and your "empathy"? Can't you sense how horrible that makes us feel? How can I make you understand the uncertainties of an intelligent antimatter being? Fish gotta swim and birds gotta fly, Doctor. I gotta do one thing till I die. I can't help myself. It's in my anti-DNA. I am who I am. I'm General Force for Law. We are the Forces for Law. We work in the name of the Law and in the name of the Law I demand that you give me—'

'You'll not take our cargo,' swore Captain N'hn. 'I'll blow us all up before I let you.'

'Absolutely! Don't let the beggars threaten you, captain!' Bingo Lockesley spoke from behind Amy. The other Gentlemen had turned up and were crowding around the door. 'I heard all that rot. We don't like your kind of cop. Every system needs its elements of irregularity in order to flourish. That's natural.'

'Who are these comic opera bounders?' demanded Hari Agincourt. 'Surely you're not going to take them seriously, captain?'

'Oh, I'm taking them *seriously*,' said the captain grimly.

'So am I,' agreed the Doctor. 'So am I.'

'All we want from this ship, Doctor, is what our instruments detected.' Freddie gestured with his ringmaster's whip. 'East is West and West is East and the right way we have chosen. What we came here to find. Once we have it, we'll leave you in peace, I promise. It's nothing. A trifle. Less than a trifle. A mere confection made from silks and satins, buttons and bows, rings and things, felt and strings and bits of wire. Not worth the life of one of the least of your people. Indeed—'

'What is it?' The Doctor's voice held a grim, threatening note now. 'You are a cynic and a sadist, General Force, for all your claims. What is it you want from us?'

'An item of clothing, that's all. Something one of your passengers brought aboard. We've crossed half a universe to find it. A lady's hat, no more. The kind of decoration I love to affect, as you know.' He doffed his own shako, its plume nodding and bobbing. The shivering energy skin, which held him together, formed a kind of peak at the top of his head before flattening off and squirming just above the surface of his well-creamed hair. 'A hat. A milliner's confection.'

'Gosh!' Bingo, still in the doorway, was momentarily taken aback. 'I say!' But, as various sets of eyes focused on him, the presence of mind which made him a great Tournament Captain came to his aid quickly, and he added. 'Is that why you've gone to so much trouble? I have to say it seems a bit unlikely, what?' He looked about him a little uncertainly, as if half-expecting Mrs Banning-Cannon to emerge from the crowd. 'A lady's hat, did you say?'

'Were you on Peers™ a few days ago?' asked Flapper Banning-Cannon from behind Hari. 'Pinching people's titfers and chapeaux all over the bally place? If so, I think my mother would like a word with you. Stay right there, please. I'll fetch her!'

General Force appeared to grow a little warm. 'Don't you play games with me, Missy. I haven't time for games. If you know where the hat is, I would advise you to come clean at once!'

'It's not your bally hat!' cried Hari protectively. 'And if you continue offering these young ladies threats, I'll have to ask you to place the matter with me! We don't take kindly to hat thieves in these parts.'

He stood with his hands on his hips ready to face the

Hounds of Hell, the Armies of the Night, the Gadarene Swine and any other bunch of barmy bozos who thought they could threaten the love of his life. 'You're a bounder, that's what you are!'

'A dashed bounder,' echoed his friend. (There is no tighter bond than that of the recently rebonded.)

'All for one and one for all,' said Flapper firmly. 'I'm so glad you two are chums again.' She turned to face the minuscule general. 'So was it you?'

'Was it me what?'

'Was it you who pinched my poor, distraught mother's favourite headgear?'

Frank/Freddie Force scowled.

'Well? Was it?' Flapper demanded

'I don't know what you're talking about. What I'm asking is, you must admit, not exactly stripping this ship to the bone. I'm asking you to deliver to myself and my men, so that we can all continue about our business, one hat, label of Diana of Loondoon. It's easily recognised. Pink ribbons. A large bow. About fifty feathers. Clouds of yellowish lace...' He waved a gauntleted hand. 'You know the sort of thing.'

'Not so fast, young buffoon, whoever you are!' came the booming tones of Flapper's formidable dam. 'If indeed it *was* you who had the nerve, the temerity to steal my hat when we were staying at Lockesley Hall, I shall ensure that you are charged with the crime and punished to the fullest extent of the Law!'

'Oh, this is nonsense!' swore General Force. 'I represent Law, madam and that hat is – is...'

'What? Evidence in a case? That's absolutely correct, my good lunatic. A case of theft, not to mention damage to a work of art, gross negligence in the question of leaving the said work of art to be left out in all weathers, which led to further damage and—'

'Madam! Be silent!' Frank/Freddie Force squeaked. 'If you possess the hat I demand that you—'

'*Demand*, is it? Be *silent* is it?' By the sheer power of her personality Enola Banning-Cannon forced herself to the front rank where she stood glaring over the military man, made utterly fearless by her firm knowledge of her own righteousness. 'You sneak into a respectable woman's private apartments, rummage through her wardrobe, purloin an expensive item of clothing, are unable to escape with your spoils, abandon them to the elements and then chase off into space, sneaking around until you find a second opportunity and then descend to make threats – coarse threats – to her friends and loved ones in an attempt to lay hands on her hat for the second time in a fortnight – whereupon you—'

'Madam!' Beneath the wriggling protective armour, Frank/Freddie Force's skin glowed an unprepossessing peach, clashing with his coat and causing his companions to stare at him in alarm. 'I DID NOT STEAL YOUR HAT!!!'

'Raise your voice to me now, would you, you nasty little upstart?' trumpeted the mighty matriarch. 'And what's more you utter the grossest of lies. I am stunned into silence at such disgusting, ungentlemanly behaviour. When I left home to begin this tour, I never anticipated for a moment that I would encounter someone who rushes around the universe stealing the personal clothing of poor, fragile females who rely only on male chivalry for protection!'

The Doctor seemed rather shamefacedly to withdraw from this exchange, thoughtfully fingering his bow tie with one hand and his borrowed bow and arrows with the other.

'Where is the hat? If you would save yourselves and your ship, you will give me that hat.' Frank/Freddie Force took a step towards Mrs Banning-Cannon but was intercepted by Hari Agincourt.

'You jolly well shan't have anything on this ship if you

continue to make such threats,' said Hari firmly. 'You're clearly no gentleman.'

This piqued the general. For any biologist wondering if it was possible to flush over a blush, Frank/Freddie Force demonstrated indisputably that it could be done. And he growled a response.

'Clearly,' agreed Amy, her eyes widening as General Force rounded on her.

Which brought Bingo Lockesley to the fore. 'Don't you dare threaten this – this – angel!'

Force began to unbutton the holster on his belt.

'Careful now!' The centaur saw Force's intention. 'He'll – qah!' He stepped aside, tail swirling, his face suffused with horror as the Doctor coolly fitted a practice arrow to his bow and, drawing back the string, let fly at a particular point on Frank/Freddie Force's left buttock.

The arrow reached its target and stuck there, quivering. The 'skin' had not been pierced, but the blunt arrow had found the subcutaneous so-called umbilical. A sudden silence fell. The Antimatter Men stared at their wounded leader who very carefully turned, disbelievingly, one hand around the shaft of the arrow.

Nothing happened.

Frank/Freddie Force drew a tight, shaky breath and looked behind him. 'Golly! Oh, golly! Oh, golly, golly, golly!'

He gulped.

Then he began very slowly to walk towards the nearest outer bulkhead. 'Very well, Doctor. Very well.' His tone was suddenly measured, cautious. 'You have found my Achilles heel, as it were. Clever. You know far too much about us. *Far too much.*'

Silence continued to shoulder in on the scene. Everyone held their breath.

Still keeping the long arrow in place, Frank/Freddie

Force continued to make his way crabwise to the bulkhead, his astonished men, unsure of what was happening, but understanding that they were all in serious danger, formed a semicircle around him. He reached the ship's inner hull and spread himself against it. His men followed his example. Then, to Amy's utter surprise, the Antimatter Men and their leader slowly turned into hazy outlines of pink and white and faded from sight into the bulkhead until they vanished.

The arrow shot at Frank/Freddie by the Doctor clattered to the metal floor. Captain N'hn ran back towards his bridge, yelling orders to his crew with the Doctor and Amy following rapidly in his wake.

The centaur flung himself into his big bucket seat and threw every lever and switch, turned every dial on his boards, until a high, musical whine filled the ship. She bucked forward under more pressures than she had ever been designed to stand, putting a great many parsecs between herself and the pirates, while General Frank/Freddie Force and his men turned once more into candy-striped ribbons of energy and fled through the void in an effort to get to safety before the emergency batteries in their pseudo-skins' power packs gave out. The captain whinnied with amusement, though he kept his eyes on the screens and continued to check the distance between his tanker and the disabled pirate craft.

'Well done, Doctor,' Amy cried. 'How did you know he was bluffing?'

Captain N'hn shook his head. 'He wasn't bluffing! He wasn't bluffing! What I want to know is how you knew where the power for his faux derm was coming from, Doctor.'

'It had to be an implant point and it had to be protected as much as possible by fat. Logic! And eyes. I used my eyes. The rest was hoping I could aim decently while he was distracted.'

'Will he try again?' Amy wanted to know.

'I'm certain he will. Probably not immediately. He's taking quite serious risks already. And we're letting ourselves gain momentum as the black hole draws us in.'

'What on earth could he want with that awful hat? And why pinch it twice?' Amy peered at the screens. General Frank/Freddie Force and his followers were well behind them at last. All she could see were the faint and distant stars.

'I don't think he did pinch it first. He wouldn't need *two* goes at it once he had it in his hands. So someone else must have made the first attempt. They might have been working for Force and Co. It's hard to say. If Lady Peggy Steel, the Invisible Thief, was with him... As far as I know, this is the first time he's risked coming so far away from that black hole. That hole is the core of our universe, as an even denser one exists for the whole multiverse. Both lie at the centre of our universe *and* Frank/Freddie Force's antimatter universe. Don't worry about it. OK? He's taking extraordinary risks – chancing suicide with every move he makes out here. Even to go a little way into such a completely alien environment takes either a lot of courage... Or considerable desperation...' The Doctor shook his head. 'What does that hat represent?'

The door opened and Mrs Banning-Cannon stood there. 'About two million bluebacks,' she said. 'Some believe no one's ever paid so much for one of Diana's hats. She refused to sell it. I told her how I wanted it for the prizegiving in Miggea, and she relented. But that silly little man surely wouldn't have gone to such lengths just to steal a hat for ransom or to give it to a lady friend. The materials are worth a great deal, of course. It contains living organisms. Could the hat contain a rarer precious stone or metal than even Diana knew about when she sold it to me? I inspected it thoroughly, of course, the moment it was in my hands again. It did, I will admit, look a bit like a dead spider. But I found nothing. I was indeed a little disappointed when I examined the materials. In artificial light it appears rather tawdry. Mere platinum and a few rare stones. Oh, all the usual junk. I suppose her artistry lies in what she does with them. All ruined now of course. Once a hat has shown its furniture I fear it has become unwearable. Still, the principle remains.'

Mrs Banning-Cannon sighed deeply. 'I came to thank you, Doctor. There are few men who would so readily take such risks as you did to defend a lady's honour. Ah, if there were only a planet where men and women of courage could retire... some Old Barsoom brought back to life.'

The Doctor cleared his throat. 'Well, er, I – that is, I'm sure...'

Amy gave Mrs B-C her best and most winning smile. 'He's like that,' she said. 'Chivalrous. Impulsive. A bit of a Don Quixote. That's why I'm just happy sometimes to be his little Sancho Panza.'

'Is that a sort of secretary or PA?' asked Captain N'hn, who took little interest in ancient texts.

'Something like that,' agreed Amy showing her teeth.

Chapter 12

That Old Spaceship Shuffle

'I SAY, DOCTOR, THAT was a smashin' bit of shootin',' said W.G. Grace, the Bearded Lady and the best whacker on the team, resting her arm over her beloved antique bow-case and letting her spare hand lift a cup of Assam to her hirsute lips.

'At this rate you'll become a pretty useful second-best bowman, eh?' Bingo winked at his new friend.

'Don't overdo it, chaps,' added Hari, 'or his head will swell until we're able to use it for a target.'

By now the boys of the First Fifteen were bonding like billy-o, all differences forgotten over a pint or two of tea and a fruit bun at the temporary mess reserved precisely for this function. Within hours they had joined in the old debate concerning broadswords. Bingo thought they should remain at a metre wide and about a third of a metre long. Hari felt they should be shorter. The broadswording event required extraordinary skill but was not a sport popular with spectators. There was talk of dropping it from the programmes in future. Others wanted to change it. Donna Bradmann fried sausages over a single-burner portable heat canister. The Doctor rather enjoyed the sensation of retreat into an Edwardian school story. He was getting the kind of rest he needed, but soon he would have to sleep and think.

Meanwhile, Amy was enjoying the non-players' company, with not quite as much tea being consumed and a little more Vortex Water, as issues of the day were discussed, such as whether Allardyce had any chance against Preston in next year's intergalactic home game. Flapper wondered what the General Ejection in Nova Roma would mean for the galactic council. Seventy-eight members were up for ejection in the coming year. Amy was fascinated. She had not realised that the galaxy was actually democratic.

'If you can *call* it democratic,' said Flapper bitterly and launched into a long and somewhat parochial attack on a great many people with unpronounceable names whom she assumed Amy knew.

'... and Mummy's paying far too much for the old ones,' she complained.

'The old ones?'

'Yes, the ones being ejected. That's how you pay for the new ones' campaigns. By selling off the previous incumbents who then have to work for a person rather than the people. They're called lobbyists.'

'I'm only buying fifty this time,' declared Mrs Banning-Cannon. 'The last lot were a complete waste of money.' She frowned. She was still trying to work out what Frank/Freddie Force had wanted with her hat. But she was full of praise for the Doctor, whom she declared to be a knight in a shining armoire. Which, for Amy, brought up the image of the Doctor attired in a natty French wardrobe.

She smiled. 'Did you actually buy that hat on Peers™, Mrs Banning-Cannon?'

'I ordered it when we stopped on Loondoon for the Heart of the Blitz re-enactments. Diana herself was there – a woman of extraordinary beauty – and promised to send the hat by Gbot to Peers™, where I could pick it up at her branch in the

Forest Mall. Which, of course, I did, planning to wear it for the Highest Tea ceremony.'

'Gbot?'

'You know, one of those warpers that make holes in space. The kind of holes which form vortices and kill human messengers.'

Amy deduced she was talking about a robot courier. 'And it was never out of your possession until it was stolen?'

'Exactly.'

'But it was made in Loondoon?'

'So I understood. You don't suppose Diana or one of her staff used my hat to get through customs on Peers™, do you?'

'That's a thought,' said Amy. 'Suppose something was smuggled in the lining – something that Frank/Freddie Force and the rest wanted badly, but which someone else stole. That would mean your hat no longer carries the contraband but that the thief now has it. And the thief's on this ship.'

'Why do you assume that?'

'Because Frank/Freddie Force detected what he was after and assumed that the hat still had its secret intact.'

'Ah, of course. Well, I have to admit that the hat was returned to me in poor condition. The great central arc sagged a little. And the decorations were all over the place.'

'Could it be possible that part of your hat has come adrift?' Amy was still a little vague about her theory. She wished she were bouncing ideas off the Doctor.

But the Doctor was still bonding, swapping tall stories with his new buddies, and scoffing crumpets and teacakes. That is to say, *their* tales were tall and *his* happened to be true but sounded tall. Everybody knew about the legendary Daleks who had once sought to invade and inhabit the galaxy. But few had heard the stories he had to tell. Not that anyone believed him, which was why they admired him.

'You ought to be writing for the Vs, Doctor,' roared W.G. Grace, slapping her not inconsiderable thigh.

'Rather!' declared Donna, detaching another crumpet from her toasting fork and handing it to W.G., who delicately wiped crumbs from her magnificent face foliage.

'You can tell 'em all right, Doctor,' declared Denise Compton, the Second Fifteen's second-best whackswoman. 'You've done some space travelling in your time, I'd guess.'

'I like to travel,' the Doctor admitted. 'I have what you might call an enquiring nature.' As if to demonstrate, he became suddenly thoughtful. 'I was trying to work out how they could disseminate long enough to cross space on a photon beam. They expected to leave that way, though with the hat, having taken horrible risks to acquire it. They had less than a twenty-five per cent chance of survival, same as they gave us. So what makes it so *valuable*?'

The company had become infected by his mood. 'By George, that was the spookiest bally thing I ever saw in my life and all of them dressed up like organ grinders' monkeys!' declared Denise. She was still a little shaky from the encounter. 'Was it an illusion, Doctor? I mean, if we looked around, would we discover it was a bunch of your old mates putting on a show to liven up this boring voyage?'

The Doctor allowed himself a smirk. 'I wish I had that level of creativity.'

Somehow the subject got changed to archery techniques in enclosed spaces and how you could rig up a perfectly good quintain if you didn't mind using the casing of the ship's nuker. A chap someone knew knew of a chap who had used the cadmium rods at full draw to give him eighteen hits or rolls. Sadly they'd blown up passing Kali 4.

At length, feigning tiredness, the hero of the hour made an excuse and left musing for bed. Stooping uncomfortably, he was met in the gangway by a slightly flushed and cheerful Amy, whose unruly red hair stood on end as she realised that they had both been wondering the same thing: what could be worth risking the death of the universe for? Because Frank/Freddie Force, the Antimatter Men and Lady Peggy Steel, the Invisible Crackswoman, reportedly often in his company, all wanted what was hidden aboard this ship.

'They gambled their own lives on it being here. And ours,' said Amy. 'And if you hadn't happened to be carrying a bow and arrows and acted with unusual presence of mind –' her grin widened – 'who knows what would have happened?'

By now they were sitting in the makeshift gaming room where a few other parties were playing virtual machines. Some machines were so threadbare they were barely visible to anyone but the users. The pair sat in the darkness, well to the back, and talked quietly.

'It would have produced a totally chaotic effect swiftly followed by a collapse into permanent stasis. Caused by an in-turned war of the very forces evolved to maintain the great multiverse in perpetuity,' the Doctor murmured. 'We're going to need assistance from the Second Aether. Those brawly boys are mad as moonbeams and as hard to catch long enough to question and see if they'll help us.'

He'd already told her that only in those spaces lying between the twin planes of matter and antimatter, Law and Chaos, was this war understood and exploited in full. The Second Aether was the realm *between* space and time where the Famous Chaos Engineers performed their morphing miracles. They called themselves names like *The Secondaries* or *The Preprincipleasures* and lived in a dimension not even Morphail's wizard scientists could explain. This environment was thought to be the legendary spaces of the *inbetween*, which could be traversed by winding roads of energy and where peoples of every species, race and creed walked between the worlds. To some they were known simply as the Spaces, but to the more romantically inclined, the Second Aether.

Home to the totally opposed immeasurable entities generally known as the Spammer Gain and the Original Insect, the Second Aether sheltered many a corsair tribe but in the main the inhabitants left the real fighting, the blood feuding and the empire building to their associates. They took sides fighting for those they called the Principles.

The Doctor sighed and grimaced, his eyes opening wide as another thought struck him. 'We know they don't side with Law or Chaos, Matter or Antimatter, Reason or Romance. But most of them *will* rally to a call. They need Law as life needs death and as waking needs sleeping. I'll see what I can do. It's risky, but it's worth a try. Meanwhile we're somehow hosting a mystery beacon radiating to every millinery freak for umpteen billion parsecs and we don't know where to look for it. Desperate measures, Amy. What do you call those odds?'

'Oh, be generous,' she said, her spirits rising. 'Fifty-fifty?'

'Let's make it more interesting,' he said, running through his pockets until he found a live card, flashing and gaudy in the light. 'Neither side will be happy with a tie in these circumstances. Let's say fifty-one to forty nine, eh?'

'Don't tell me.' She was sardonic. 'You're the fifty-one per cent?'

'Let's find out.' He leaned forward, smiling like a Fool, and winked.

She took his proffered arm and quietly stood up. They had barely reached their own section when the darkness was split by bolts of the richest indigo, by zigzags of scarlet and oscillating, impossible greens.

'At last!' The Doctor lifted his head like a predator detecting a change in the wind, the sound of distant thunder. Amy half-expected him to lift up one arm, the way a dog or cat might lift a forepaw and sniff at the territory ahead. He helped her brace against the gangway plates as they turned slowly so she immediately recovered her balance.

'What is it, Doctor?'

He cocked his head a little to one side and grinned at her.

'The *Fall!*'

Chapter 13

Bingo's Bit of a Bloomer

SEEING SHE WAS STILL mystified, the Doctor looked at her in delight. 'We've started the Fall,' he said again. '*The Fall!*'

And then she remembered being warned about what was happening.

The nukes now damped off, they quickly achieved 'deep fall'. That meant they had positioned themselves above a so-called gravity well, a dangerous manoeuvre but commonly made by commercial ships. It would allow them to gather momentum from what these spacers called Little Rock, the local black hole, so small it was invisible to the naked eye, yet so dense as to be the gravitational core of the galaxy.

Gravity remained the most mysterious power in the multiverse but they used it as casually as their ancestors had used electricity. Now Little Rock drew them *downdowndowndowndowndowndown drew them down, drew them down* towards its almost inconceivable mass. 'A glitch...' *he felt pinned.* 'Can you feel it? Is it?' *He felt sick. What was that? A glitch. Scritch the glitch? His memory was wrong His senses... Had he fallen asleep Why was he getting so much wrong?*

The Doctor's head cleared. What had happened in those few seconds?

The red-brown and yellowish tanker had not been built to run on *colour*, that mysterious energy leaking through from the Second Aether. But she would repower long before she came anywhere near the Schwarzschild Radius. Meanwhile she used the latent and most mysterious energy in this universe to drag them 'down' to their next port, turning slowly, end over end to preserve her interior stability and keep her auxiliaries powered.

Now their only vision of the great vastness of interstellar space came to them framed by their Vs. Hard experience had told them what happened if you did not lock down the portholes on an old ship (new ships lacked observation domes altogether). Most sentient creatures who tried to use an open observation dome, housing the majority of the ship's 'eyes', their viewing and registering instruments, found themselves staring into the near-infinite and going irredeemably mad.

The Doctor yawned. The chances of being attacked in the space lanes were gone for the time being and everybody could relax. *Or almost everybody.*

For a while he wrote calculations in tiny print in a little black notebook, his face twisting with the exertions of his massive brain. Drawing on life experiences denied most sentient creatures, he concentrated on the many complicated layers of existence, intratemporally occupying the same space, nesting one within the other, each generally invisible to the other.

Only a few were blessed or damned with the Doctor's power to see the multiverse in all its vast, beautiful, bountiful, exotically coloured aspects, its glamouring glory. Those few knew how many truths could exist at once: the countless alternatives, the infinity of paradoxes, the billion twists of fate. That power only came with an understanding of how space could be a dimension of time, still hard for the average head to handle.

That was why the Doctor could be so apparently nonchalant on occasions, frustratingly enjoying his insouciance, when other people were going mad with terror. The ancestors of the first interstellar human voyagers had been called Guide Sensors. They'd had the same talent as the Doctor. Sensors could plot courses through the cosmos others could not even detect. These were the people who had once mapped the multiverse and discovered another kind of space altogether.

This 'other' space was known as the Second Aether. There were stories that the Doctor had actually named the region, but he always denied it.

Of those who travelled on that tiny splinter of red and yellow turning gently end over end through space, only the Doctor could sense all the alternatives, weigh all the odds and therefore make decisions impossible for anyone else. But he, better than anyone, knew that he was not infallible. The risks were horrible.

He slipped his notebook back into his pocket and seemed to be sleeping with a look of astonishing serenity on his face.

Watching him, Amy found herself imagining him as a speck of glowing indigo, locked in a single stitch at the centre of a swirling, glittering, multicoloured tapestry representing all possible versions of all possible events, the alternate planes of the multiverse, beginning and ending in dimensions too vast or too tiny for the human senses to comprehend. How was it, wondered Amy, that ordinary creatures like herself could be aware of such vastness, almost beyond comprehension, and still remain sane, still be concerned about their fate?

How could you take yourself and your own desires and ambitions seriously? Amy wanted to know. *How could you expect to have any effect at all on major events?* Then she shrugged as she had often shrugged before. The answer was, of course, very simple: in spite of your being so apparently insignificant, every action you or any other being took in the multiverse had meaning and effect, and was echoed in every other version of reality. Everyone was their own multiverse, just as the peak of Everest contained fragments that were models of the whole.

A spec of indigo. A distant horn.

In that wash of brilliantly coloured near-infinite geometry, reflecting on all the dangers which might threaten humanity, whose actions were mirrored and echoed almost to infinity, the Doctor, that twin-hearted, generous alien, had entered a world of near-infinite possibility. Amy did her best to imagine what he saw and all the possibilities of which he was aware. The Doctor was even now trying to work out the specifics of the threat against all the millions of worlds inhabited by intelligent species. He was doing what no computer could do. Not for the first time her heart went out to him, the last of his kind. He no longer had a single equal he could talk to.

Yet she was pretty sure he relished his life more than he mourned it. If only she could follow him into those rich and solitary places. She could probably help him to help himself. But she knew much of her motive was to do with how she envied him and almost resented the fact that he would never be able to share his vision of the multiverse. Suddenly she felt shut out and alone. Would she ever see her old, ordinary, normal, shabby home world again?

At that point she saw the captain galloping past, his hoofs muffled in huge, soft slippers. 'Anything wrong, captain?'

He glanced back at her, his voice quiet and controlled. 'Oh, we're falling faster than normal. Can't work it out. We need to slow her down a touch, that's all. No danger, Miss. Nothing for you to worry about.'

She was about to sneak off to her hammock in her own quarters when she bumped into Bingo Lockesley whose effect on her self-esteem had, she was forced to tell herself, been putting her ego into double digits of late. Just the sight of him cheered her up.

He had come in quietly. 'Is the Doctor snoozing?' he whispered.

'Resting the mighty brain,' she told him.

'Apparently that fireworks display wasn't anything to worry about,' Bingo informed her reassuringly. 'The ship has switched into what the captain calls "Fall mode". I keep thinking he's talking about girls' frocks. You know – "Spring fashions"?' He was clearly cheered by her response. 'It was almost like dreaming while awake. Felt like that to me, anyway! Nice to see you smiling again, what? Mind if I join you for a few minutes?'

'Not at all.' She had to stop herself flirting with him to take their minds off all that had happened to them since they had boarded the water tanker. 'Have you had your tea?'

His happy, innocent face cheered her up. 'Rather!' he declared.

'Ah. I haven't.'

'Oh, gosh. Neither have I. Or rather I mean. Tea! Sounds gripping.' He paused. 'Um, shouldn't we – I mean – you know, pop the Doctor into his hammock?'

'He's hard to lift up,' she said. 'He tends to bend in the middle.'

'Right-o. Leave him, then, shall we?'

'Probably best,' she said. Amy suspected the Doctor had not picked that odd posture at random.

They were halfway up the corridor when she found herself saying: 'So what do you think was in that hat?' And cursed herself for an idiot. She had planned to stay away from any serious conversation for a bit.

'Contraband?'

'Sure, that'll be it,' she said.

'It would have to have been something very valuable,

don't you think, eh? I mean, I can't see that General Force and his gang taking all those risks just for a bit of canny-canny or Jhivan honey.'

'Oh, yes,' she said, reaching the battered TeezUp and selecting an Assam no milk/no sugar. She loved these retro-nouveaux gadgets. They had the strangest appeal. She held the big china cup in both hands and sipped while Bingo went off to look for tokens so that he could buy her a bun.

She was wondering if the Doctor knew more than he was telling. There were still a few mysteries to be solved.

Bingo returned in triumph, buns in hand. And before he could sit down she had a question for him.

'Flapper's ma still has her hat with her, doesn't she?'

'Oh, of course, of course. Got it from Uncle – from the IM – almost as soon as it was found.'

'Nothing was missing?'

'Mrs Banning-Cannon checked all that out and was satisfied. It was messed up, that's all. I know. And Mr Banning-Cannon said it was just as hideous and stomach churning as it had always been.'

'He hated it that much?'

'Absolutely. Loathed it. Gave him the willies.'

'Something about it?'

'Said it reminded him of spiders.'

'But there weren't any spiders on it, surely? I mean, did Diana of Loondoon have a Hat of the Arachne line?' *Why, why, why didn't she have the common sense to stop asking questions?*

Bingo found this amusing. He laughed a little too long and hard for his own ears and began to wonder if he was in danger of giving himself away. He was relieved when Mr Banning-Cannon turned up.

'Ah, there you are, sir!' Bingo cried. 'Everything tickety-boo?'

'Eh? Oh, certainly. Never been ticketier or more boo.' The

great patriarch was in high spirits. The return of his wife's hat and the fact that all suspicion was now focused on Frank/ Freddie Force had relieved him of most of his worries. He was humming to himself, pottering about in a bit of a reverie. His wife was no longer, as he put it, 'on his case' and his daughter was in love with his wife's choice – hang on!

'Hang on,' he said. 'Aren't you the young chap our Flapper's got her eye on?'

'Oh, gosh, no, sir. You must be thinking of Hari Agincourt. He's the bloke sweet on Flapper. I'm – I mean – she's – that is – Oh, cripes!' And Bingo again gave his celebrated impression of a stop light. He had forgotten that Hari had specifically asked him to say nothing until he had his promised job back on Knots née Peer™.

Mr Banning-Cannon couldn't face another drama.

'This chap any sort of Lord or such, like yourself?'

'You mean a member of the Peer Age, sir?'

'If that's what you are?'

'No, sir.'

'No? Oh, Lor'.' Mr Banning-Cannon's eyes took on their old hunted look. 'Not an aristo?'

'He will be, sir. Now the planet's mine, I intend to make a few changes, and one of the first is to restore the monarchy and the peerage. I could do it now, I suppose, but it would be nicer to have a ceremony of some sort. Hari, for services to his planet, will definitely be knighted, sir, but my guess is he'll receive an earldom before Yule.'

'Is that what you've got?'

'An earldom? Yes, sir.'

'And what's this "Yule"?'

'Yule's a kind of log, sir.'

'Really? Then everything will be fine. Bit o' money goes with that, eh?'

'Fishing rights, touring rights, renaissance and re-enactment rights. All of that, sir.'

'Splendid. So all's well that ends well, it looks like, right?'

'Spot on, sir.' Beaming, Bingo let his hand be shaken chirpily by Mr Banning-Cannon.

He turned to share his pleasure with Amy.

But she had gone, hotfooting it back to her quarters.

Bingo frowned. 'Must have been something I said,' he opined. And returned, a little fuddled, to the cabin he shared with Hari and Co.

Chapter 14

All Changed

THE SPACEPORT ON DESIRÉE was so vast it occupied half the land surface of the planet. Coming to rest on the very edge of Left Field, as it was called, the passengers eagerly unstrapped themselves from their harnesses and, while they waited for Customs and Immigration, crowded up to the observation dome, no longer out of bounds.

The Doctor hadn't been to Desirée for many years and he remained deeply impressed. The spaceport offered an endless landscape of ships. Ships stood beside fuelling and repair derricks, their prows pointing proudly into the loud and glaring sky. Ships lay at anchor above and below the clouds, or within the clouds, their hulls sparkling with unnameable radiations, or pouring blue, purple and green smoke into the disturbed atmosphere, coiling to mix with the subtler shades of lavender, dove grey, pale green and liquid blue torn by constant lightning storms in its upper reaches.

The huge yellow moon with its silvery red rings was clearly visible on the horizon, silhouetting the slender golden snub-nosed Graham-White superfast interceptor rockets of the IPC, sporting beautifully tapered stabilising wings and festooned with bulbous gun turrets. These were dwarfed by tall, asymmetrical djonkers ships, flown by bots and crewed by Ramimeds, capable of surviving without air for hours at a time and needing little sleep. The long-run spacers could cross from one galaxy to another but were unable to carry living creatures other than Ramimeds, whose home planet spun about a sunless region of the galaxy and was essentially a giant comet. Between these flew buzzing tenders, loading and unloading, bringing passengers off or putting them on. Hari Agincourt, with Flapper beside him, pointed excitedly at ships he recognised.

'Look, Flapper, that's a giant De Havilland! And there's a Dumont F-22! That's a modified Farnsworth Wright and Wright. Gosh, that's a Judoon interceptor. A double-hulled Ban'sh star cruiser. An old Comer ring-rider. An M-type Galinax. A Vickers 12-30M. This is amazing. I never thought I'd see any of these in real life. I have the *I-Spy* Vs, of course. Oh, wow!'

Flapper did her best to seem interested but she was beginning to long for a few hours' solitude and a nice bit of good escapist V-fiction. Love covered many a well-earned yawn.

She had to admit the sight was stunning, though. There were squat ships and circular ships, brightly coloured ships and severe black, white and grey ships, ships made to resemble birds or giant fish; there were ships which seemed spun from spiders' webs and hung with silvery droplets of dew, ships so massive they looked as if they would sink into the super-reinforced concrete of their pads. A million shades of metal flashed and clashed in the crowded port. Peoples of every race and manufacture walked between the gantries or sailed above them in open air-cars leaking *colour*. And when the atmosphere testers came on, the new arrivals were hit by a sea of scents out of which it was possible to detect burning metal, fuels of every kind, plants, bodies, cooking food, the life-gasses of a thousand worlds.

'Atrocious!' Flapper's mother put a handkerchief to her mouth and nose. 'Why do the authorities permit this stink?'

'Believe it or not,' Captain N'hn stopped at the open door, swinging a bag over his shoulder, 'it used to be worse. They have planetary deodorisers on full blast and air conditioning at every major subfield. See those funnels of smoke at intervals across the field? This is what space would smell like, lady, if it wasn't almost wholly airless!'

Captain N'hn was in great spirits, having repelled pirates and completed a successful run. He was already in the process of selling his cargo to a broker and would soon transfer it. He had a sweet little filly, an administrator in the NNE sector, whom he had V'd earlier, and she was more than glad to help him enjoy the fleshpots of Desirée as soon as possible. But there was one thing he had to do first. He delayed long enough to squeeze through the crowd, shake the Doctor's hand enthusiastically and thank him again. 'If you shoot that well in the last games, Doctor, you're bound to win the Arrow. The first thing I'm going to do when I leave is get to Ferdii's and put a hefty bet on your team before I blow the rest of my tin!'

'We'll try not to let you down.' The Doctor laughed with the big centaur. 'And good luck on your next trip, captain. I'm sure we'll do our best to live up to your faith in us.'

The captain pushed his way back to the gangplank where an anti-gee raft floated in readiness and, with a typical bit of centaur bravado, threw his knapsack on ahead of him then jumped the gap, mane and tail flying.

Between the parked spaceships were busy V-boards advertising all the pleasures the planet had to offer. The crew were already watching them, murmuring notes into their implanted Vs, reading off numbers and street names as they waited impatiently for the cages to be run up beside their hull. 'The warm weather's coming,' muttered one, as he squeezed past the Doctor and Amy, 'and the buds are on the vine!' He uttered a strange, panting noise and gave Mrs Banning-Cannon a leer as he went by. 'Night, Missus. Aye aye.' A parting wink.

'Oh, my goodness!' Mrs B-C recoiled in disgust. 'I hope I never have to travel with that bunch of ruffians again. Promise me, Doctor, that you haven't booked us on another ship like this one. Look!' She peered down hopefully. 'Those must be the porters I asked for.'

Disembarking from an open airbus advertising the Djinn Inn, and crossing over to the nearest of the tanker's causeways, came a group of uniformed giants with numbers stamped on their chests, their backs advertising 'the best hotel on Desirée'. They were massive. Their heads were shaven of all hair and they had distinctly simian faces. Mrs Banning-Cannon waved and pointed. 'Here! Here!' she cried until they looked up and raised their thumbs to her. The leader spoke to the others and their huge mouths split in laughter.

Suddenly a big, blue, blocky air-car dropped down to hover on a level with the observation dome and in a moment the Customs and Immigration boys came aboard, asking questions, scanning bodies, demanding dockets, feeling alien, unfamiliar flesh. The Customs men were mostly halbots, half-robots of flesh and steel, their eyes modified to make them more efficient, sending information back to the central ordinats. When they got to the Doctor and Amy, the immigration people were confused.

'There are some odd discrepancies,' one murmured. 'Your passport documentation won't register.' He blinked hard, trying to re-scan the psychic paper the Doctor had handed him.

'They're the new kind,' explained Amy. 'Issued through OE.'

'Olde Englande?'

'Of course not,' snapped the Doctor in apparent ill-temper. 'Original Earth.'

'I didn't know it had been finished.'

'Just,' said Amy.

'You must have had the codes through by now.' The Doctor pretended to be increasingly impatient.

The official was baffled. Over his shoulder, Mrs Banning-Cannon looked at the Doctor's papers. 'Why, what's the trouble?' She was at her haughtiest. '*This* man is a well-known doctor, and *I* am Mrs Banning-Cannon.'

The immigration official recognised her name. For all he knew her family already owned Desirée. TerraForma™ was probably the parent company. 'Doctor, sir? Of course, sir.' He scratched the back of his head, looking at Amy. 'And you're his nurse, are you? Ah, yes.' His face cleared as he was at last able to read the passport properly. He put his palm against the documents. 'That should do it.'

'Thank you.' The Doctor turned to the matriarch. 'You saved us some embarrassment.'

'As you saved me, Doctor.' Her smile was almost charming. This holiday seemed to be doing her good.

The transporter arrived to take them to the West Field on the other side of the planet.

Amy was still finding it difficult to get over the size of these vast terminals. She had seen big cities on big planets but nothing like this devoted entirely to the shipping of the interstellar spaceways.

The Doctor enjoyed her astonishment. 'And these are often only the tenders of the large ships like the *Gargantua*. All the really gigantic ones are out there in space. To say nothing of the large patrol ships of the IGP. There are all kinds of refuelling stations, including a massive *colour* pool further in towards the sun. I believe that this was the biggest spaceport in the entire sector.'

'What if someone decided to take a shot at it? Sabotage?'

'If someone thought it worth blowing up Desirée, they'd either destroy half the galaxy or wake up the day before in a police cell. Desirée's on a time fault, and they've managed to harness some of its power. They've invented all sorts of temporal alarm systems. They can actually go back and deal with a problem before it happens, and they've got a constant forward time-loop working for them. No way that I know of fooling those. To my knowledge, there have been fifty-two thwarted attempts since the port was founded.'

'You've been here before?'

'As a youngster, yes. In my gap century. I had a job once as a courier, taking bills of lading out to the ships. I got lost too many times. Ships were delayed. They fired me.'

Amy laughed at this, not believing a word of it. 'You're having me on again, aren't you?' She shook an admonishing finger.

She was relieved when a special car came for the Banning-Cannons and took them away to their hotel. She would be glad of the relative peace. Since the Doctor had saved them from Frank/Freddie Force, Mrs Banning-Cannon had cultivated his and Amy's company.

Most of the other passengers had not bothered to book accommodation, since the hotels were extraordinarily expensive. They were heading straight for their connection, to board early and be ready for take-off in about twelve hours.

'I hope nobody tries to steal that again.' The Doctor nodded towards the huge hatbox being carried aboard the hotel's tender. 'I wish we could get her to give the thing up and leave it here. I'm sure Mr Banning-Cannon would love to see the back of it.'

'So are we sure he paid young Bingo to pinch it?'

THE COMING OF THE TERRAPHILES

'Oh, I think so. Paid him in planets! Well, in *a* planet.

'Yeah, Bingo's already decided to give Hari a knighthood, quickly followed by an earldom, so that Hari will be able to reassure Mrs B-C that he's the stuff that sons-in-law are made of…'

'And meanwhile Bingo's trying to land you and take you up the aisle, Amy Pond.' The Doctor grinned.

Amy kept a straight face. 'Well, I am rather fond of him, Doctor. Don't you like the sound of Amelia, Countess of Sherwood. Or is it Earl-ess? Can you have an Earl-ess? Anyway, he's sweet. And very enthusiastic.'

'Oh, yes. I saw he was enthusiastic. Here's our taxi.'

A battered air-car drew up at the gangplank and the Doctor helped Amy into it. She tried to avoid sitting on the split maroon fake zylorian myatt covering of the bench seat. The driver was a huge Unshim-Anlinite sucking a three-foot long chirpy. Apart from her face, which looked more like a human skull, she had most of the features of an earthly praying mantis, which told them she was from one of the colonised planets of Anlin. An albino with several sets of ruby-red eyes, she greeted them cheerfully, commenting on the improvement they had seen in the weather. 'Had a hot oil storm a week ago. The stuff was everywhere. It would have been funny if there hadn't been so many accidents. Big Brunk went over a walkway. Fell almost a mile. Wasn't much to clean up after that.'

The air-car started up with a lurch, throwing them forward. The Anlinite used one of her sets of arms to stop Amy falling while the Doctor helped her get settled in her seat. 'Wow!' she exclaimed. 'It's enormous!'

The mantis made hissing and clacking sounds which were probably laughter. 'You should have been here last month. We had almost double this volume. Time storms! Unusual number of crashes, apparently. People having hallucinations and so on. Piggo went totally crazy and pinched an ippy cruiser. You know what the cops have become. Everyone jittery. Something to do with the dark tide's sudden speed. Pulling them in. Gravity increase? I doubt it's as big a deal as they're making it out to be. Fuel crisis? There's more *colour* pools, not fewer! I don't really understand these things. I mean, what's gravity? Does anyone *know*? Causing some serious turbulence, though, they say.'

'We noticed a bit of that,' said the Doctor. 'We arrived ahead of schedule. Had to settle back and use our thrusters.'

The car made its way through mile after mile of battered, oil-streaked commercial ships, many of them undergoing minor repairs, others being refinished or refitted, with the sky belching and cackling and sending streaks of lightning in all directions, while the combined stinks of thousands upon thousands of ships from any number of distant worlds formed a heavy blanket below, hiding the hulls from view. Every so often a blob of rainbow-streaked *colour* wallowed by, floating like a giant, irregularly shaped, grimy, soap bubble. Dangerous. The stuff was the best fuel ever discovered but to drop into it meant you passed through into dimensions not always compatible with any known life.

The smog eventually grew so thick that the Doctor pulled over the car's canopy to protect them from a sudden isolated shower of what was only partly water. The smells seemed to get stronger the further they went. He wrinkled his nose. 'Maybe we should have taken the Gentlemen's bus,' he said. 'I just wasn't sure if we'd get any time alone on the Dafryd boat.'

'Will it be as cramped as the tanker?'

'Well, she's designed for passengers, but she's not a luxury liner. A bit basic. I'm afraid Mrs B-C will be upset with me all over again when she sees the vessel.'

'Oh, God, I can't imagine!' Amy began to laugh.

'Get some sleep,' said the Doctor. 'It's at least a couple of hours until we pick up the 11-28 to Placamine.'

Resigned, she settled back in her cushions while the Doctor continued to look around him at the great port, identifying ships which had been built sometimes two or three hundred years before.

The Doctor sighed, suddenly remembering a day, so long ago, when everything in time and space had been new to him. He'd been so excited then, and the universe was so mysterious. There had been so much for him to explore, and he'd had a long, long lifetime ahead to enjoy it all in. Now, he thought with some sadness, he had seen far too much of it to retain the same early sense of wonder. But then – how different had he really been in those early days of wonder? He might never know. There were not many people left to ask.

He looked out at all the odd designs of ships and thought about the thousands of cultures they represented. Rank upon rank, mile upon mile the car flew on, past an enormous liner, its dull metal giving it an oddly organic sense of sickness, dwarfing the very planet itself, as it came down for serious repairs which couldn't be made in free space. When the Doctor asked the driver why the ship was in dry dock, the praying mantis answered that she understood it had been attacked by something down near the Inner Suns.

'Know what it was?' the Doctor asked casually.

'I heard they hit a *colour* pool,' said the driver. 'Though with all her sophisticated instruments, I'm surprised they didn't spot it.'

Colour lakes were found everywhere throughout the galaxy. They were patches of pure energy which could be parsecs across or, if found on a planet, only a few feet wide and a few inches deep. They supplied almost all the post-nukers, since the famous inventor O'Bean the Younger had developed engines capable of using the raw stuff. It was extremely difficult to refine. Almost singlehandedly O'Bean had drawn the human race from its last long Dark Age.

Their driver drove her car between two identical ships, whose noses disappeared in a blood-red cloud of roiling gas. 'The captain had to do some snappy steering to get her out of the pool,' she told them.

The Doctor craned his long neck to look back at the big ship. 'What was her name?'

'I forget, cit. One of that class of supers. Super-luxury. Super-speed. All of that. I saw a V about her. Didn't you? I know they made a lot of fuss. She was a C-class. Belonged to the Aristophanes family, I know. I bet she was insured for a bundle!'

'I bet,' agreed the Doctor. 'But I'm surprised her captain let her get into a *colour* pool and so close to the Inner Suns.'

'You must have heard, cit. There's a lot of stuff going on down there. Funny stuff you never hear about on the V. Just rumours. But they add up. Sightings of ghost-planets, weird distortions in the charts, whole planets changing position or else vanishing altogether. Conflicting currents bad enough to pull an ordinary ship apart. Dark flow forming pictures as if it was intelligent, trying to communicate. I'm surprised you don't know about any of that stuff. Where have you been?'

'You saw the old tanker you picked us up from. We started speeding up for a while, too. Something sent her communications all over the place. Time winds blowing every which way. She had no high-speed, no real contact with anyone or anything. How long have you been hearing stories like that out here?'

'Quite a while. But that's real time. Our time. Months ago for you.'

'It's all relative.' With a sigh, the Doctor sat back and closed his eyes.

'Don't talk to me about relatives,' said the driver feelingly. 'Did I tell you about my husbands? Ex-husbands, I should say.' She leaned forward to tap a control irritably. And began to wheeze, then to cough. There is no stranger sight than a mantis cabbie in full exoskeleton shake. But she kept steering steady, to Amy's amazement.

That was all the Doctor needed to help him keep his eyes closed and get the forty winks he had been promising himself for ages. What was going wrong with the *colour* pools? If they disappeared or became contaminated it could mean vast changes in the economics of the entire galaxy.

He was awakened by the driver yelling: 'Here we are, cit! Forty-seven red ones, if you please, thank you!'

Leaning forward the Doctor handed her a yellow. 'Keep the change,' he said, as the driver started to punch the numbers into her wrist bank.

He looked with some relief at the relatively modern spacebus which was going to take them to Placamine in Poseidon.

They were not the first passengers. The Doctor cocked his head when he heard something half-familiar.

'What was that?' he asked the neatly uniformed steward who checked their tickets and directed them to their cabins. 'Voices?'

'Oh, just the miners singing, cit. The Desirée All Male National Eisteddfod Deputation. They're lovely to listen to, aren't they? Representing Desirée in the Interstellar Eisteddfod. Great lads, sir. There's a strong chance they'll bring back the *ab Ithil cardigan* if not the Yellow Leek itself. You're very lucky they had some spare seats from what I heard, cit. Those lads will be singing, singing all the way.'

'All the way?'

'If I know them,' said the steward fondly, opening the cowl. 'You won't be able to stop them.'

'I thought I heard a choir of angels in the distance,' said Amy. She looked around the boarding lobby. 'Oh, this is much better. Clean and tidy, at least.'

'I think you'll find us very comfortable, ma'am,' said the steward. 'You'll be with us for the next seven days, won't you?' Getting off on Glub Glub, I understand.' He grinned. 'Sorry, ma'am, just my joke. Seaworld, I mean. A pity you can't go all the way with us to New Llareggub. You must get someone to introduce you to old Taffy Sinclair. He's a doctor, too. And a plotsman. But he's also the choirmaster.'

'Oh, I'm not that kind of doctor,' the Doctor said hastily.

'Neither would he be, sir. You're with the Gentlemen, I understand. You going to the black hole, are you? These lads know all about black holes, sir. We follow all the big Renaissance Re-Enactments we do, the lads on board. We're all big Terraphiles here, sir. We have a lot of very good amateur players. Any tips for a cit who might be thinking of placing a small wager?'

'Oh, you'd be wise to bet on us.' The Doctor looked up through the agitated, multicoloured sky as if he could see their destination from here. 'The way everything's going, it's more important than ever that we win that Arrow.'

Amy glanced at him, suddenly alert.

Chapter 15

Luxury Class

APART FROM MRS BANNING-CANNON'S occasional complaint about the choir practising in the common rooms of the spacebus and a bit of an argy-bargy between W.G. Grace and her chums, who had accused one of the other players – Pavli-Pavli – of licking their arrow flights during a friendly on the faded artificial green provided by the bus, the journey was largely without incident. Poseidon had experienced an horrendous space tornado and was out of bounds to civilians.

Amy was sure Frank/Freddie Force and Co had been given the slip, but the Doctor wasn't quite so optimistic. 'Once he's after you, that one, he becomes a bloodhound. If I didn't know better, I'd say he had somehow attached himself to our hull and Lady Peggy had made them all invisible.'

'You're not serious?' Sitting next to him, Amy stirred her kashions. She would have been glad to have a bit more variety in her diet, wholesome as the food was.

They were feathering down against the huge, glowing world of Pangloss. They would not actually land but had arranged to meet the *Gargantua* here. As they swung round into Pangloss's night side they spotted the mighty liner lying along the line of the planet's twin rings, hardly visible at first until their own reflected light suddenly struck her and made her blaze like a star, all silver and rubies in the depths of night.

'Wow,' said Amy. 'Whenever I start to get blasé, something like that happens. Is she the *Gargantua*? Gosh, she's the size of Earth!'

The Doctor smiled. 'Aren't you glad you didn't miss the chance to go aboard her? Even if it's only for a few days. I'm surprised she's here ahead of us. She wasn't supposed to arrive until tomorrow, I thought. I must have got the schedules wrong.'

'It'll be good to take a shower,' Amy said, 'without worrying about seventy miners queuing to use it after you. Did you say they have showers en suite?'

'I think the A-class cabins have two,' he told her. 'But that's only for the family apartments. Mr and Mrs Banning-Cannon and their daughter are in one of those.'

'On a different deck to ours I hope.' She smiled.

'At least one removed. Probably twenty or so. I think it says somewhere on our tickets.' He consulted his pocket-V, then put it away, grinning. 'They're on Deck Four and we're on Deck Hundred and Two!'

'Result!'

'Yes, that's six decks away from the B-Cs.'

'Six?' She shook her head. 'You're a whizz at maths, Doctor, but even I know that four from a hundred and two makes a ninety-eight!'

'Think about it,' he said. 'The ship's a huge tube. She has a hundred and ten decks.'

'Oh!' she felt like an idiot. 'So the poshest deck is next to the lowest economy?'

'Not exactly.' He seemed puzzled. Something about the massive planet had intrigued him. Then he turned his attention back, watching as their tender swept gracefully around the golden ship while she drifted into dock.

Her wonderful nouveau baroque stylings made Amy gasp in delight.

'They're the G-class. The most up-to-date ships in the galaxy. Safe, luxurious even on the cheapest decks. Nothing spared. Planets bought and sold to pay for them,' the Doctor told her. 'There are five of them in all. Commissioned by Meng and Ecker. Built by Mhuta and Shang. Fitted by Jon-Jon Coolart & Co. And we get to travel free.'

'Free? How come?'

'M&S – Mhuta and Shang – are one of our sponsors. There's a full-size Tournament court on board. You name it. Nutcracking. Arrers. Jesting.'

'Jesting? What? Joke-telling competitions?'

'Um. Maybe I mean Jousting? Quintain, where you have to charge at a straw man with your lance and try to make sure he doesn't swing round with that long arm of his and knock you off your saddle. That's harder than it looks. Everyone's a bit rusty at the mounted events because there was no chance to practise until now.'

'They have horses here?'

'Of course not! We use centaurs.'

'I can see why Mrs Banning-Cannon was fed up, if this is what she's used to.' Amy gazed wide-eyed at the *Gargantua*. 'She's as big as – I don't know – the Moon?'

'Roughly the size of four moons. In volume. She'll last for ever.' He shared Amy's pleasure in the glowing golds of the *Gargantua*'s exoskeleton, the brass and platinum pipes curving and curling to form a tight bailiwick between hulls and the infinite galaxy-splashed blackness of eternity. Nothing in the known universe could kill her. 'Even if she's badly mauled by something or drawn into a star, she'll live. She's been through five suns and still come out in one piece with all functions unharmed. Five suns, two of them ten sols strong! She can survive anything!'

'And black holes?' asked Amy. 'What about those?'

The Doctor made a face. 'Maybe even one black hole. But I think it would be risky to bet on two.' He was peering past the ship at the planet hanging in space behind it. A huge, dark disc. And he frowned. 'That's funny. If I didn't know better I'd say that Pangloss was deserted.'

'How can you tell?'

'Light. No reflected light, even.'

'And that means...?'

'Could be anything. Maybe nothing. I'll check the gazetteer on my V. Hmm. Nothing. Tourist world specialising in architecture from the Third Islamic Empire. Soft stone sculptures. Nothing much a gang of asset-strippers would need.' He tapped his head. 'Very strange.'

He pointed as a tender emerged from the gates, tiny beside the massive ship. 'Here comes the Transfer Officer. We'll ask him.'

As the TO came aboard the Doctor introduced himself, wanting to know what had happened.

'Difficult to say, Doctor. We arrived on schedule to find the entire planet deserted. Actually a desert! Nothing growing. No sign of a battle of any kind. No messages we could capture. We had agents down there. Vantul, Malli, Poshnam. All good friends. Gone. Together with the rest of the population. Dust. That's all that's down there now.'

'Really? Nothing living?'

'It's as if she's been sucked dry of every bit of energy. I called it all in, of course. We haven't been here more than half a day. There should be a path but we haven't traced it through if there is one. I wouldn't be surprised if something or someone has made a corridor for itself, eating up planets as it goes. Maybe dark flow grazing? But I've never heard of anything like it this close to the galactic Hub. We only had a handful of passengers due to be getting off here. They're in very poor shape, I fear. In shock. A lot of questions we can't answer. We have plenty of empty berths, of course, because there were over a hundred bookings to the Tournament in Miggea, and your berths haven't been resold. We can only hope whatever it was isn't going anywhere else on our course.'

Gravely the Doctor took all this in. He was very thoughtful when he talked to some of the other passengers. The *Gargantua* was continuing on course, making her way to Miggea. She would then take on new passengers and return, keeping the same course which had brought her here, though she would bypass Pangloss. The IPC was sending a team to investigate. With luck, they would discover what had happened. It usually turned out to be a disease or a big comet, a natural phenomenon. Sometimes, however, they had no way of finding out the cause of something like this. Space was full of these mysteries. Many would probably remain unsolved.

Amy voiced what he was probably thinking. 'Anything to do with Frank/Freddie Force and Co?'

'Could be. But did he come out this way? I don't know. But this looks like one of his attacks. The whole thing stinks of a matter clash.'

'Well, he was going in the opposite direction to us, wasn't he? That means he's probably already failed to find the hat – or whatever was hidden in the hat. He'll have given up, surely?'

'That makes sense,' said the Doctor.

But his frown did not lift. He remained in this mood for some time. Only when they were enjoying a tasty dinner in the elegant restaurant with its murals depicting all the peoples of the galaxy did he manage to cheer up. The few former inhabitants of Pangloss were keeping to themselves and had no wish to discuss what had happened. Some of them had elected to wait in a capsule until the IPC arrived.

By the time the *Gargantua* was on her way to Miggea, all talk was of the Tournaments and how the teams would do.

Amy certainly hoped that what had happened to Pangloss was a fluke. She wasn't sure she could take another pirate attack. She supposed the decision of the *Gargantua*'s officers to make light of what had happened was the right one. No point, as they used to say, alarming the shadies and frightening the phonies.

Chapter 16

Dark Tidings: The Tsunami of Time

THE WHOOPS OF JOY with which the Gentlemen greeted their first sight of the Tournament Court reflected the general mood of everyone who had suffered the more spartan amenities of the various ships used to get them back on course.

The court was the latest in artificial environments, with grass indistinguishable from the best natural turf, a beautiful quintain run which could easily be turned into a jousting alley, a full-length arrers pitch, broadswording mats, quarterstaff grounds, nutcracker enclosures and all the other facilities required to put on an entire set of practice rallies, with the Tourists there to play against while each team got the other's measure. Wearing practice 'pads', a full suit of which could be slipped over one's ordinary clothes, they could play all day.

The Doctor was a bit of a dark horse and was being kept back as much as possible so that rival players would not be able to judge all his skills. He spent more time on the nutcracker enclosure than anywhere else. He knew he might be weak in that area. Almost as soon as they had boarded, he was down in the 'pegs', carefully swinging his sledgehammer to hit practice nuts designed to register the most feather-light strikes. Although the Arrer – the beautiful silver Arrow of

Artemis – was awarded principally for the final whackit match, all scores in the games played were taken into consideration and there were too few really good nutcracker players for any team to ignore this aspect of the 'Renaissance Rally', as the V-commentators liked to call it. In another part of the court, Judoon quarterstaff aces were having at it with loud snorts of triumph or grunts of effort, while centaurs galloped up and down the quintain course, narrowly missed by the swinging arms of the target or 'man'.

Amy watched from the bleachers with an especially critical eye for the archers. She had tried a bit of archery as well as hockey at school and felt that the Gentlemen, though strong on bats, were still a little short of really good bows. Bingo, of course, was an astonishing shot, but after that the Doctor and Hari ran him only a fairly close second. She had known nothing of the games involved in a Renaissance Rally before the Doctor began his crash course, but now she had all the expertise of a valuable punter, a punter, in fact, of the best kind, who believed in their own ability to outplay every professional and make far better decisions than the interstellar referees brought in to judge the matches.

She was filled with the excitement building now all over the ship. While audiences were discouraged from attending the early practice games, they were banned altogether from the later ones for fear they might gain advantages for use when wagering. Amy, however, was understood to be the Doctor's nutcracker trainer and had been issued with an official Terraphile Re-Enactment Society pass to all practice events. It was clear to her that the teams were well-matched and that there was little between them. It was going to be tough to win that all-important Silver Arrow. Why was it so all-important? The Doctor himself still did not seem to know why he needed it.

Meanwhile, during their time off, Hari Agincourt,

reassured by Bingo that their home planet was in the bag and an earldom on the horizon, continued to woo Flapper Banning-Cannon, who was relieved that at last there were no more spaceships for him to admire and identify. She was glad, of course, that he had hobbies. A man with hobbies could be trusted and you always had an idea what to buy him for his birthday or a Mass-X holiday. While she thought she could never get thoroughly involved in ship-spotting, she felt that life on Notts (or whatever Bingo chose to call it) would probably keep him busy enough, and she rather liked the idea of learning some of those games. She was not a great lover of cities. Hari shared her taste for the rural life, so that wasn't a problem. Now all she had to do was get him to pop the question and hope that Pop continued to smile as benignly on their potential union as he seemed to be doing at present.

To his relief, Bingo Lockesley was beginning to find Amy's company relaxing. Not that she wasn't already the easiest girl in the world to get on with. The tension had all been his. He hadn't known how she felt about him. At least he could now breathe without his chest constricting. He no longer felt his body tie itself into small, tight knots of the kind that would baffle the most dedicated boy scout, whenever Amy hove into view. Like Hari, he looked on the prospect of the future with this angel and it was good. Jolly good, in fact. Of course, he hadn't asked her and she hadn't shown a great deal of interest in settling down to a long and restful life at Lockesley Hall, but he thought there was a more than fifty-fifty chance of her helping him pick suitable dates and banging the posts, as the quaint old expression had it when it came to traditional marriages, preparations for.

Life had become pretty idyllic now they were settled aboard the mighty *Gargantua*, a ship designed to instil feelings of tranquillity and wellbeing in its pampered passengers and almost guaranteed to turn the least likely of shipboard romances into something permanent and beautiful (or so it said in the brochure). Hari told Bingo that one of the regular travellers on the monster ship had told him that there was some sort of relaxing scent the owners put through the air supply. Certainly, he was pretty sure he had been smelling wonderful roses since he had come aboard. The awful fate of Pangloss was no longer the main topic of conversation.

Bingo and Hari were not the only bachelors looking forward to the joys of matrimony. Even W.G. Grace had trimmed her magnificent chin topiary and was eyeing a tall and handsome running fielder, David Saint Roberts, who had paid her the compliment of saying she was probably the greatest all-rounder since Myfanwy Bannarji, the legendary Whistling Whacker of Haverford West, an obscure planet in the Murgatroyd system, since carried off by a powerful pumper and sold for scrap.

Elsewhere the lads of both teams were all taking advantage of *Gargantua*'s many entertainments and were getting along famously. The rival teams were on excellent terms and the many other passengers, most of whom were travelling to attend the Terraphile Renaissance Re-Enactments, were in various states of happy anticipation. Only one Panglossian remained awake after a week in space. The others had elected for a light cryosleep. The *Gargantua* was a happy ship again. If space liners could smile, whistle and snap cheerful fingers then there was no doubt that the massive ship would soon be doing the hoochie coochie as she slipped magnificently through the star lanes.

The Doctor, although frequently turning his thoughts to the various mysteries engaging him, was determined to enjoy himself while he could. He discovered that he had an aptitude for nutcracking that would almost certainly advance his team's chances in the coming games. His archery skills had been honed and he was presently concentrating on the subtleties of jousting. The joust was perhaps the hardest aspect of Tournamenting because it involved the 'iron mule', an extremely hard seat and a two-stroke 'Wasp' engine which was inclined to spray hot oil whenever it got overexcited. He made the most of all these pastimes in the sure knowledge that, the nearer they came to Miggea, the tougher things were going to get.

Even Mr and Mrs Banning-Cannon were enjoying the trip. The tycoon had found a bar where he could hobnob with fellow captains of industry, and Mrs B-C had found the ship's milliner, whom she considered something more than a mere Diana-in-waiting. She felt a little as Prince Lobkowicz must have felt when he realised he had become Beethoven's patron. She was undoubtedly a patron to Genius. Mr Toni Woni had a splendid way with hats. He was a natural. Not only had he completely recreated and indeed improved her stolen and recovered chapeau, he had made her several new hats which, he was forced to admit to himself, were his finest creations.

This was not surprising. Just as Leonardo needed his Medicis and Borgias, so had Toni been awaiting his own particular muse and patron. Together they talked brims, crowns, veils, buttons, bows and bands and every evening Toni retired to his studio to work. Never thoroughly appreciated until now, he flourished. Where he had been admired, now he was worshipped. And so he bloomed. Felt, lace and feathers came to fresh life at his touch. The spirit of his household goddess, Donna Coco Colombino, imbued him with fresh inspiration every morning as he woke to accept his breakfast tray. Mrs Banning-Cannon was inexhaustible on the subject of *boaters*, *fedoras*, *pork pies* and *bowlers*. Toni had but to name an obscure hatter of history to find she knew all about them, including Dr Lock St James, inventor of the

Piccadilly *topée* and Fly-in-Squatt, the infamous Mad Hatter of Fleet Street who had designed the gruesome *de-cap-i-tator*.

The great matriarch felt she had at last discovered a true fellow spirit. And, what was more, she was a very generous fellow spirit, her coffers apparently unlimited, her mighty head always ready to accept fresh décor. If she were not a natural, capable of carrying the most elaborate summer *gainsborough* to the simplest formal *pillbox*, she would have been in danger of becoming something of a butt of the other women's disdain; but there was no getting away from it, she was a woman who could wear a hat in a world where that art had come dangerously close to being forgotten. When she appeared at a *friendly* between the Gentlemen and the Tourists, her inventive *Colonel Jack tricorne* became the centre of attention, at least until the match started, and there was scarcely a dowager or a debutante who did not yearn to learn the great lady's way with a *mop* or a *tiara*.

Well aware of this, Enola Banning-Cannon was content. All previous upsets and disappointments were forgotten. She was setting the tone. She was leading the pack. She was establishing her milliner not merely as Diana's equal but as her superior. There was scarcely a woman aboard who was not a trendsetter in her own circle and acknowledged Mrs B-C as mistress of mistresses. Mr Toni Woni had it, as his chief trimmer reminded him almost daily, well and truly made.

If a ship could radiate peace, love and happiness, then the *Gargantua* was pumping the stuff out into the near-vacuum and covering every passing planet with joy, leaving the suns and the moons singing 'I'm aitch ay pee pee wy' at full volume. So immensely H-A-P-P-Y was that enormous liner that she might have had the whole galaxy yodelling and tap-dancing by the termination of her cruise, had she been permitted by Fate. But Fate, who never misses the chance to slip a bluebottle into the Vaseline, had other plans.

Out near the Sagittarius Schwarzschild Radius, a storm was brewing, created by forces which had always been there but were now growing increasingly less stable as they shifted in and out of their own space-time continua, making a very dangerous place in which to know perfect bliss. Even the captain, a Polynuraied and therefore naturally given to anticipating the darkest and most unlikely dangers, was whistling as he checked his autopilots and supervised his incredibly intelligent and well-programmed bots. He repeated jokes told him at his table the previous evening (they were rather lost on the bots) and made remarks such as 'It's going to be a very pretty evening' when his second officer, Mr Tr'r'r'r an insectoid Bruzh of an equally gloomy disposition, sat down with him to enjoy their afternoon tea. Designed, as her architect had put it, to 'calm and relax the customer at every turn', the *Gargantua* was pulling out all the stops as far as helping her passengers forget the shadows lying in her wake.

It would be an exaggeration to describe that gorgeous liner as 'doomed' but it is fair to say that, within the next few thousand parsecs, she was going to find herself in some pretty thick and steaming soup.

It began to dawn on the Doctor that he was under the influence of the *Gargantua*'s reassuring spell when, settling back into the comfort of his specially programmed armchair and sipping a cooling drink, he sighed contentedly and said: 'Well, I have to say it looks as if the worst could be behind us.'

Hearing himself speak, he knew he should have at the very least crossed his fingers.

Awakened by the alarms from the control room, Captain Snarri bundled out of bed, hastily climbed into his uniform and hurried at once to where the bots were processing the information.

Mr Tr'r'r'r was already there, spraying his facetted eyes with pep fizz.

'Show the captain what's up, lads.'

The bots indicated the screens they had materialised for him. 'Storms ahead, sir. Moving into all quadrants.'

Captain Snarri coughed and accepted the Vortex Water his steward, the twin-headed Lio Jir Kahpeth, offered him. He and Mr Tr'r'r'r were both used to storms and invariably found the means of taking the ship around them. The first rule on a G-class M&S was never to disturb the passengers.

Captain Snarri noted some peculiar fluctuations in his bank of barometers, designed to register the slightest changes in the weather and anticipate their likely effect on the areas of space through which they intended to pass. This was unusual. They were surrounded by the storm. There was no avenue open to them. They were going to have to go through.

With a deep sigh he had the bots plot the best course.

Except there was no best course. The storm was fierce and implacable, streaming from the direction they planned to take. The spattering of galaxies was obscured by what might have been heaving waves of black smoke. That smoke was already coiling around the forward hull, clinging to the complicated filigree, spreading across the observation ports.

In a moment the Doctor arrived, pulling on his jacket. 'Oops,' he said, craning forward. 'I *think* I've seen this before.' He drew closer. 'In fact, I *know* I've seen it before.'

This was the same phenomenon he had spotted from the bridge of the water tanker when they were much closer to the Rim than they were now. He had an unhappy feeling that things were getting worse.

'So what do we do, Doctor?' The captain was used to moving through some of the worst fluctuations the void could offer. He took another pull on his Vortex Water. Although he commanded a luxury liner, he had a great deal of experience and knew how to remain cool through any circumstances in which he found himself. The rest of his staff were arriving now. He indicated the information which was now coming in rapidly. 'Any point in warning the passengers?'

'I think there is.' The Doctor fingered his chin. 'They need to know. It could get a bit rough.'

The ship was falling into a well of darkness, flying entirely by her instruments. All that could be seen of the outside was the occasional flash of light as the blackness sagged open to reveal clusters of stars, miniature galaxies pouring ahead of them so that the Doctor realised for the first time that they were not being drawn into the gravitational systems but were being forced through them. Something was pushing them back away from their destination. Not pulling them down towards the black hole at the centre of their galaxy, as he had thought, but drawing them out to the Rim, to the unknown regions of intergalactic space. How could that be?

Pulling on her big red sweater, Amy entered the now dark control room. 'I thought everything was all right?'

There came a shuddering blow to the hull. Another.

And another.

It felt as if a giant dampened hammer were repeatedly striking the ship. The captain cleared his throat and spoke calmly to the passengers via the internal V.

'Sorry you're being disturbed, folks. Just a spot of turbulence. We expect to be through it very soon now.'

The ship's alarm systems began to scream as the *Gargantua* was tossed up and down, turning from side to side. Amy grasped the Doctor as the nearest thing she could cling to. 'This is like the last time. Only worse. I thought you said this ship was unsinkable – or whatever a spaceship is. Not like the *Titanic*, I hope. Oh God – what is that stink?'

The smell of candyfloss, cloyingly sweet and chemically flavoured, came and went and now something pale blue fading to a paler green was filling up the control room like foam. Surprisingly she could still breathe, but she could no longer see the Doctor.

She was in her police uniform, running for the TARDIS. She was in the high-street beauty parlour wondering how to tell them she didn't like their cut. She was in the TARDIS, reading an Agatha Christie. She was getting ready to go to sleep. She was running across a limestone pavement in the Yorkshire Dales and there was a pack of woad-painted Iceni coming after her. When had this happened? She couldn't remember. Now she was sitting at a desk, writing. Now she was outside the spaceship, this spaceship, the *Gargantua*.

The plumber was lecturing her on the proper maintenance of her hot-water heater and she was a creature of air and darkness slipping somehow through a gap in the hull which only she could see or use. She was big. An undine as big as the universe and able to see galaxy after galaxy after galaxy all streaming towards an invisible source of gravity. A supermassive, infinitely tiny presence, smaller and heavier than any black hole at the centre of any single galaxy. She realised this presence was the nucleus and everything else was moving according to its extraordinary density, its immeasurable gravity. And suddenly she was heavy, too, watching as she spun clusters of galaxies in her gigantic hands, blew out the flames and the heat of suns, made chains of white dwarf stars and played bowls with quasars until she sat under a tree in a park, perhaps in Africa, as lazy lions licked their chops and moved their heads to show they were ignoring her.

She was a soldier in Afghanistan, desperately trying to reach cover as she crawled from her wrecked tank. She was a little girl, an old lady and suddenly, after millennia, herself, her own age, and still the huge ship bucked and rocked and spun like a stick being thrown from hand to hand. And she realised that 'size' was an illusion, that it did not matter how big or heavy or fast anything was, it was all relative, for the multiverse around her only got smaller and smaller in some directions, bigger and bigger in others and that she had just as much effect on this quasi-infinite environment as a sentient being a fraction of her size or someone living in a universe vastly bigger than this one.

She understood that it had something to do with self-similarity. Her actions affected every aspect of the multiverse, were echoed on every plane, every alternative. Whatever danger threatened them now would threaten them everywhere. These other universes were no more independent of the presence to which they were drawn than her Earth was independent of the sun. It had nothing to do with size. If she pushed, the whole multiverse responded. If she slept in this aspect of herself then she probably slept in all other aspects. And how many were there? Millions? Billions? Probably. But was this also true of the Doctor who she could see now doing something with his sonic screwdriver?

The ship divided and became many ships, each one a fraction bigger than the next. Each one containing an Amy, but not a Doctor. Where was he? Was he independent of the multiverse? The only one of his kind?

This made sudden sense.

Something began to come clear in her head as the ship's captain took hold of her arm.

'Are you all right, Miss?'

He had interrupted her at the very point of understanding. She rounded on him angrily.

But he had become the tall French guy she met on holiday and it was impossible for her to tell him off. 'I was trying to do a sum…'

A sickening groan erupted from the middle of the ship and

it began to bend. Everywhere people were screaming. The screams became a bleating alarm and suddenly the control room was full of passengers struggling into the emergency suits they found in their cabins.

Again the captain was shouting at her. Telling her to go back to her room. Go back and put on her suit, prepare to get in the lifeboats, but before she could do that the hull straightened out, though they were still bound by the black ropes and rearing waves of the intergalactic tsunami.

The Doctor was also not wearing a suit. Grabbing her arm he supported her on his shoulder and helped her back to their cabins. The ship was roaring, squealing, scraping at the fabric of the cosmos. Every so often the black clouds parted to reveal streaming galaxies, their light leaving strange trails, almost like handwriting, across the captive stars, able to behave only as the tsunami demanded.

'Are we breaking up, Doctor?'

'We're very strong. Should be able to withstand a time storm.'

'Is that what we're in?'

'Something worse. I'm not sure. But when the time currents combine like this, everything is confused. Space is affected by time. It's a dimension of time and it also has its own dimensions. It has to obey whatever rules apply. In Chaos, these storms are usually benign. In Law they aren't. Far from it. So if this quadrant is controlled by Frank/Freddie Force and his Antimatter Men, we're probably in serious trouble.'

'Is there anyone out there who can save us?'

'Probably.' He was helping her into her suit. 'Like I said, it depends who's in control. I've already sent out a wide-band SOS. We'll have to wait and see who picks it up. If it's Frank/Freddie or Lady Peggy the Invisible, don't hold your breath. I'm trying to get us into the Second Aether. If that works, at least we'll be in territory occupied by both Law and

Chaos, Matter and Antimatter. You'd better hope Captain Abberley and the Bubbly Boys hear my SOS first. The sonic screwdriver's been set to that signal for ten minutes.'

The ship stopped bucking. Outside, the strands of the black tide had vanished. They were drifting against a field of intense scarlet. *Cosmic no man's land*, thought Amy.

The Doctor was gleeful. 'I did it! Didn't think I could. Are you amazed?'

'But where are we, Doctor? Have you any idea?'

'I certainly have, Amy. See over there?' The blurred outline of what looked like a seagoing yacht, somehow behind one layer of scarlet with many more layers on the other side of it. 'That's old Quelch's ship, as I live and breathe.'

'Who's *Quelch*?'

'Captain Quelch? Chaos Engineer. A possible enemy if there's something in it for him. But then he'd do pretty much anything if there was something in it for him. Good rule of thumb – don't trust him. Don't believe a word he says. He's as likely to be in league with Frank/ Freddie Force as not.'

'And where *are* we?'

'Oh, sorry. I got us into the Second Aether. It's how we escaped from the storm. It was so violent it might even have destroyed us. I've never known a time storm like it. Not in this region, anyway. That ship was built to survive the hearts of stars and she's about to be smashed to bits! I don't know if I can get us out.' He peered through the observation V. 'Ouch! It hurts your eyes, doesn't it?' He turned, frowning, pursing his lips, thinking hard. 'We're in a rendezvous point. You have to have them in this kind of environment.'

'Which is?'

'Didn't I tell you? Should be obvious.' He allowed himself a hint of self-congratulation for getting them there. 'That, Amy, is Ketchup Cove!'

Chapter 17

The Red and the Black

KETCHUP COVE GLITTERED WITH a thousand shades of scarlet, twisting and rolling. Amy made out tiny specks drifting in it, specks which converged and came closer. Soon she realised that each one was a vessel of some kind. Yet not one of the ships resembled anything she had ever seen in space before. These were old-fashioned schooners and steam tugs and slender yachts. They moved up and down slowly as if riding at anchor upon some gentle sea. Other ships fashioned of ebony and ivory, onyx and coral were not so familiar but were as bizarre and beautiful as anything she had ever seen in all her travels with the Doctor. She realised she was outside the *Gargantua* standing on her endless hull.

'We can't be in the Second Aether long,' the Doctor was saying. 'Not now. We might be able to get back here. In fact we *have* to get back here at some stage. But those plates have popped and others could still go. They need time to make repairs.'

'Why, Doctor, why?' / 'Why, Doctor, wh-?'/ 'Wh-?' She shook her head, trying to clear it of the echoes filling it.

A small skiff skipped past, skimming the scarlet and pink waters of a bloody lake. A great roaring of surf filled her ears,

197

growing louder and louder, yet still her own voice continued to echo as she watched his lips moving, forming words she could not hear. It was her own voice roaring.

'Nowhere else is as safe,' he said, very clearly and calmly. 'And even here we are going to find as many enemies as friends.'

'What is, what is, what is, what is…' She drew a deep breath and forced herself to stop.

'The Second Aether? It's the space between. It's where I think we'll find the Roogalater. The Regulator. In that space.'

'Between what?'

'Between everything. Between the First Aether and the Third. Between Law and Chaos. Between Life and Death. Between Matter and Antimatter. Between Dreams and Waking. You name it, Amy…'

'Me name it? I can't name anything. I don't even know where we are.'

'I told you.'

'The centre? The centre of the multiverse? The centre of reality? The centre of nowhere? How did we get here?'

He brandished his sonic screwdriver and winked. Reflected light gave his face a bloody appearance. Then he vanished.

Suddenly she was terrified. She had no resources left, no courage, no intelligence, no physical energy. Nothing.

She felt that she was buoyed up on water. She was swimming. Doing her best to stay afloat. A mist was rising and there was something coming up under her feet. A ship? No. It was a man. A man she had never seen before. He had a sallow hatchet face with cold, mocking eyes. He wore a crumpled linen suit, a white cotton shirt, a dark blue bow tie and on his head was a white naval cap. At first he seemed to be standing on a small wooden platform but, as he rose up towards her through clouds tinged with pink, she saw that he was standing on the deck of a small seagoing launch.

He raised his hat and held out his hand to help her aboard. 'Good day to you, Missy.' His voice was oddly cultivated, sarcastic. 'Welcome aboard my little ship. Captain Horatio Quelch at your service. What brings you to our part of Creation?'

Amy felt frightened. Where was the Doctor? Had something happened to him? She hardly knew how to respond. 'We were in a storm. I'm looking for my friend,' she said. She desperately wanted the Doctor to find her. She had no idea what to do here. 'I'm looking for the Doctor. Do you know him?'

'Know him? Why, of course. He's an old pard. Is he here?'

'He's somewhere around.'

Suddenly she heard the distant sound of an engine. She tried to see through the mist.

'Well,' said Horatio Quelch. 'Let's get you to a place of safety.' Raising his cap again, he opened the wheelhouse door for her but she held back, calling towards the sound of the engine.

'Doctor! Doctor! I'm here.'

Lifting and falling on invisible waves, a small paddle-wheeler, like the old Thames pleasure boats, came chugging towards her, its engines clanking, its funnel pouring grey steam against the scarlet. She could make out a big, hearty, bearded man wearing an old naval cap on the back of his curly hair, standing in the wheelhouse, his meaty hands steering the boat towards her.

And, gathered on the foredeck, waving their hats, were the three boys she had seen before. What had the Doctor called them? No. They had named themselves. The Bubbly Boys? A crazy little rhyme they'd sung which she couldn't remember.

'Bah! Oh, blooming bah!' With a pettish spin of his wheel, Quelch and his boat vanished, leaving her sinking into scarlet goo.

Then her feet were on deck again.

Not Quelch's deck, however. The Bubbly Boys stuck their faces around a funnel. They were still singing. She could hear them now:

We're the Bubbly Boys from Relish Ridge
That's Old Grandpa Quelchy on yonder bridge
Hot as an oven, cold as a fridge.

The voice that boomed out of the wheelhouse was not one of theirs. It was a big, rich Yorkshire voice. 'Make way there. Look lively, yon lads. How do, Doctor. Dost tha know me? It's Cap'n Brian Abberley. Abberley, come to visit. And here's me boys. Tha knows t' Chaos Kids, 'appen.'

The Doctor was beside her on the deck of the *Now the Clouds Have Meaning*, laughing. 'What's all this about, Captain Abberley? Have you come to do us a good turn?'

'Wish I could, Doctor. Anything to disoblige the Original Insect. Anything to help an old pal. And I'd be helping the Spammer Gain herself, what's more. But we're only just in alignment here. We need to be in deeper space than this. Old Quelchy's got your Roogalator. That's my guess. Got it off his lady friend, Peg the Unseeable. I'll look out for that, never fear. Meantime tha ship's about to give at t'seams. Big 'un, too, she looks from here. Oops. Sorry. Dialect. Just trying to fit in, lad.'

'We can't drop any deeper, captain. Not with the storm so bad. Have you any idea where you're heading?'

'Back to the centre. Too fast. Too soon. Why?'

'You know why. I think Quelchy's pinched the Roogalator, but he can't want to destroy everything including himself,

200

can he? So who would?'

Abberley drew his great grey brows together, took off his cap, yawned. 'Only the Force.'

The Doctor took her hand. 'Come on, Amy.'

They were back on the hull of the *Gargantua*. The little paddle-wheeler chugged alongside.

'Madness.' Amy held on to the Doctor as he inched his way up the slick coppery hull of the *Gargantua*.

'Do you still have the beads they gave you?' he asked.

'Not yet,' she said.

'Here,' said Captain Abberley. 'I'll take those for you.'

'Take *what*?'

'Doesn't she know yet?' The captain stepped outside his wheelhouse.

'How can she?' said the Doctor. 'I don't. Time's all over the shop and so are we! Without the Regulator in place it's only going to get worse! Trust is all we have now, Cap'n Abberley.'

The big Yorkshireman stuck his cap on the back of his head while the three Chaos Kids, grinning, grouped themselves on the deck.

We are the merry Chaos Kids
Our friends are all around us.
The very merry Chaos Kids
Old Quelchy's out to hound us.

'Where are we, captain?' Amy asked. 'Can't you help us?'

'Just told yer, Miss!' he shouted over the swelling sound of the Bubbly Boys:

We'll spinyer there capan, never fear
For we're the mighty Bubbly Boys,
No system can confine us

201

Or even wine and dine us
So ask us what and ask us why
Don't ask us Who in case we cry
Toot oo ta toot
How's the future looking down there, cousin?

They held up cages containing four lizards wearing smart little spacesuits. One of them squeaked at Amy. 'If you can understand me, you must help. We're well educated, ma'am, and captives of barbarian lunatics, as you can tell. We had never heard of a Roogalator until recently. We have no business in the Second Aether. We lived peaceful lives until—'

'Until t'little buggers blew themselves up trying to destroy a rival asteroid,' chortled Captain Abberley affectionately, steering in alongside. 'We'll drop 'em somewhere safe. Beg pardon, Miss.'

'We really do need help,' said Amy. 'The outside air's getting thinner.'

'In the soup, are we, Missy?' Captain Abberley scratched his chin. 'We can't help you out. But we *can* help you in.'

He felt around in his pockets, found what he wanted, and threw them to her.

She caught them one by one. Five – or was it six – beautiful glass marbles.

'Old Q's lost his marbles again. Try those! Sort of ball bearings.'

She lifted them close to her face. They began to spin in the air, four around the fifth, and maybe cycling around a sixth, she couldn't be quite sure. She saw that they were a necklace strung on a strand of pure silvery energy and she put it on.

A brilliant mustard yellow spread across the scarlet. 'If old Quelchy's gone off with it, we'll find him. He doesn't know we pinched his maps. He probably pinched them from someone else. You'll have it in time for the Big Match. Ho yus! Don't worry. He'll lead us to Force.' And the paddle-wheeler turned, sending up a swirl of scarlet spray, and pounded off.

'That's the Second Aether for you,' said the Doctor.

Wearing her suit, Amy waited in the big control cabin watching the beads flickering and turning and then snatched them off and put them in her pocket. Captain Snarri stood in the centre issuing orders to his bots and crew.

'Please make sure all surviving passengers gather at the central core. In the gymnasium. It's the safest place in the ship.'

She still felt a little sick but she knew somehow that the worst was over. Captain Abberley and the Bubbly Boys had got her back to the *Gargantua*.

How can these weird people manipulate matter like that? she wondered. But for some reason she was now even more frightened than before. *What's happened to the Doctor?*

The Doctor hung somewhere outside space and time, drifting, drifting...

He had fallen asleep. He hung above time, above space, and he looked down towards the scarlet expanse that wound into the quaking greenness of Emerald Edge. Here was now and no longer. Here, only the scarlet expanse of Ketchup Cove was stable, the old rendezvous point of the Chaos Engineers. Here were four quasi-planets circling a heavy sun. A star circling a black spot. One place. One time. Into which everything used him as the node. The focus of all the worlds of the multiverse. Stretches of yellow-silver spread everywhere. The so-called moonbeam roads. Summer, Autumn. Everything else was lighter or darker. Sooner or later. Bigger or smaller. This was where it focused and from where it all radiated. And he thought his thoughts, reviewing a million or more options. The Roogalator. The Silver Arrow. Four planets circling a single star. Miggea, Circling a tiny black sun. The time vault. A bucky ball, stronger than any known metal. The – He considered his action. Acted. It would kill him one day. Again.

Amy was gone. Captain Abberley and the Chaos Kids were gone. Quelch had gone. Where was the Roogalator? It could only be here, surely? He could smell it. But the ship itself was gone. Somewhere unseen overhead came a grating squeal. The Doctor awoke; looked up. He saw nothing there but a slurry of grey-white. A conjunction of galaxies and a fine rain falling. He wiped his eyes clear of the water and clambered along the slippery outside of the space liner, a tiny figure like a flea on a cat. Was Amy all right? He scratched the back of his hand.

He was still in his spacesuit. He recognised a time-twister when he was caught in one. Well, what had got him into this would very likely get him out. He reached into his pouch for his sonic screwdriver. So far it had served him well.

He had no idea how he had found himself outside the ship, but the screwdriver should get him in. Amy was the one to worry about. The *Gargantua* was safe for the moment, drifting in the Second Aether, where neither rule nor misrule applied. Captain Abberley and the Chaos Kids had guided them out of immediate danger. Now the entire ship drifted against the glaring scarlets and crimsons of Ketchup Cove, the safest rendezvous for everyone who cruised the Second Aether.

Barley sugar melted out of his mouth and coiled into space.

But how were they going to get back? Was the big ship still spaceworthy? She looked pretty battered. That was the worst storm he had ever lived through. Assuming he *was* alive.

He found a little one-man airlock in the big ship's hull and set to work with his screwdriver. A series of lights flashed as it undid the locks from inside. A pressure from his gloved hand and the circular hatch opened away from him. He slipped in, closing the hatch behind him, rebolting it manually. He slipped back down the hull's companionways and found a lock into the main ship. The spacesuit and helmet were slowing him down a little, but he decided to err on the side of caution for now. He headed for the gymnasium as quickly as he could. As he'd suspected, all the passengers and several of the crew were assembled there.

He removed his helmet and found Amy. She was still in her spacesuit. She was baffled.

'They can't see us. What's happening, Doctor? Where are we? Who was that?'

'You've met the Boys before. The Chaos Kids and Captain Abberley pulled us out of trouble. We're still in the Second Aether, running parallel to the ship's regular course but a scale or two over. We can't stay here much longer. Quelch knows about the Regulator, I'm sure. He might even have it. Or maybe he knows where it is and he's just biding his time. But we can't follow him – we'll have to leave it to the Bubbly Boys. They're after Force too. Those ships of theirs can morph and warp in this stuff, but we need to be back in the First Aether. I think we've just about survived the storm. Good. The kids are all right. We're there.'

He signed to her to come with him as he made his way to where the captain and his officers were conferring. He told them quickly what had happened. 'I got us through the storm. We can go into Fall as soon as we're out of here. Is that OK with you?'

'Fall? Are you sure we have enough thrust to pull us free once we're there?' The captain was studying hastily thrown up power screens.

'I'm fairly sure.' The Doctor lost his balance for a moment and steadied himself.

'We've leaked a lot of power, Doctor. There's *colour* dripping from half the tanks. Our protective shields are buzzing, which means they're working at half-power or less. How do I know there isn't a fleet of enemy ships back there just waiting to attack?'

'Because there isn't. I have one friendly ship keeping an eye on us and there are some others that might not be particularly friendly but will probably support us because they don't like Frank/Freddie Force.'

'Is that who attacked us?'

'No. We were trapped in a space-time super storm, that's all. It shouldn't have caught us because it shouldn't have been in this region, but it did and that's all there is to it. Dark tides running. I told you. No other regular ship could possibly have survived. But this one lived up to her reputation.'

'Can we still make it to Miggea?'

'I hope so. Get the screens in place so we can see what's going on outside. As many as possible. The storm has to have passed us or we quite simply wouldn't be here any more.'

'We're safe then?'

'At least until another storm comes. We'll have to run ahead of that one if it finds us.'

Amy said: 'If we're safe in the Second Aether, why can't we stay here?'

'Because we're almost out of the Second Aether and we're not designed for it, Amy. Those Second Aether ships survive by constantly changing shape. Adaptation's the name of their game. That's the way they move. Not because they have enemies to deceive but because the rules of time and space are different here. Everything flows, remakes itself, alters its constituents. If, like us, it kept the same appearance the space would essentially harden around it, crushing it. Can't you hear that creaking now? They go with the flow. And look at those prediction charts! We're going to break apart if we stay in this area of space. In our own space-time we can probably limp on to Miggea, or another system if we have to, and get help there. It might be possible to put all the passengers off and then make a dash back to Desirée, where we could be decently patched up. As it is, we just about have enough food, fuel and equipment to make it to our destination.'

Although the captain commanded a luxury liner now, there had been a time when he had been in charge of warships. He knew the Doctor was telling the truth.

'So how do I do it? How do I get us out of one space-time continuum and into another?'

'If you'll let me take over your controls, captain, I think I can do it for you.'

'Be my guest, Doctor.'

Either the captain trusted the Doctor implicitly or he had no options left. He stood back as the Doctor and his friend got into the high-speed elevator which would take them rapidly to the control deck.

Almost everything the captain had believed was now in question. His first duty remained to his passengers and his ship. This strange man and woman in their retro costumes were now the only hope he had.

Chapter 18

Captain Cornelius, the Pirate

'THAT'S IT, I THINK.' The Doctor leaned forward in his seat, slipping the sonic screwdriver back into his pocket and staring hopefully up at the screen. They had emerged in an area of space which was crowded with stars, rich with flickering golds and silvers, with quivering rubies and emeralds, with every kind of planet and satellite.

'Looks beautiful, doesn't it? And now we've got to find our original sector. The storm will have passed by now. I love this part of space, don't you? We've shifted a fair bit from our original position, but at least we're almost out of the Second Aether.'

'So what's happening, Doctor?' Amy was determined to get some answers. 'It's serious, isn't it?'

'Oh, yes.'

She waited, but he didn't elaborate.

'So why is it serious, Doctor?'

Like her, he had still not taken off his spacesuit, though neither now wore a helmet. He sighed, staring at the V on which pictures of outer space flicked and refocused.

'You know how we – my people, that is – can – could – live a very long time, don't you?'

'You sort of explained it, but I didn't really understand. Kind of like some reptiles or insects...?'

In spite of the seriousness of the situation, he grinned. 'You make parthenogenesis sound so attractive.' He touched a screen to bring up another sector. 'Well, that form of regeneration is also what the universe does. In fact it's not just the universe but all scales of the multiverse. Some cultures have observed this without fully understanding it. They call it the Great ReCreation, the Conjunction of the Million Spheres – all sorts of fanciful names. At a natural point in her cycle, the multiverse begins a process of recreation to make herself afresh. There is an exchange, of sorts. Some matter becomes antimatter; Law becomes Chaos – everything – well almost everything – is "reversed". This happens so slowly most sentient creatures hardly notice it. Evolution. Some intelligences will often work out what's happening. It's not a secret. It's a constant, ongoing process and it guarantees our existence – multiversal immortality, if you like.'

'So, it's not exactly immortality. Not the kind where we remember all that we've learned or all that's happened...'

'Right. Not that kind. Even Time Lords couldn't recall everything from a former existence. I certainly can't. Anyway, that's the fundamentals of life and regeneration in the multiverse. It's a fine equilibrium, regulated by what some people call the Balance, a semi-abstract visualisation which can be said to act like the beam, fulcrum and pans on an ordinary pair of old-fashioned scales to maintain everything in equilibrium.'

'I'm still having a hard time getting my head around it.'

'Well, to put it as simply as I can, somehow, through interference by something or somebody, the process of regeneration has been speeded up. Speeded up so much that parts of the process have not had a chance to develop and degenerate and therefore *re*generate naturally. It feels as if the Balance has been pulled apart. Instead of expanding and contracting, as it should, the multiverse has gone out of kilter. These storms are partly the result of antimatter "infecting" matter. Matter is corrupting antimatter. Law is infecting Chaos, and Chaos is infecting Law. We need to find out why. And we *have* to restore the Balance, otherwise the entire cosmos will become infected until it rapidly degenerates and collapses into inchoate matter – *nothingness*. The conquest of Death over Life. Anything remaining sensate long enough to witness this process *would live that moment of dying for ever!*'

She shuddered. 'And what would have happened to the rest of us before it came to that?'

'Hard to say... With the destruction of time comes the collapse of space.' He was still checking the screens as he spoke. 'Nothing pleasant. A few hundred years at most in which the multiverse will witness some really horrible permutations!' He looked up at the screens again. 'I mean *really* horrible stuff. Mutations that would make us mad just by glancing at them. Chaos and Law in their extremes.' He checked off figures on another screen. 'I can't help thinking Frank/Freddie Force has something to do this. Those Law-birds always believe they know better than the rest of us. It's in their nature to *impose*. Chaos prefers to go with the flow, like Captain Abberley and the Bubbly Boys. That's how they travel. Frank/Freddie and his lot don't mind about the damage they cause in the fabric of time and space. Like driving a straight, flat highway through forests and hills and towns, careless of whatever destruction is created. They make holes in the multiverse. Their ships shred it. Turn it into scrap.'

'So why do you think Miggea's the key?'

'Because Miggea is the only "rogue system" that still exists in the multiverse. Miggea is able to move in an eccentric orbit which passes through all aspects of reality somehow without being destroyed. If, while we're in that system, we can – I don't know – re-adjust the cosmos, restore the Balance, then we stand a chance of surviving. Of everything surviving. That system's as far as you get until you come directly under the influence of the black hole.'

'So that's why we're heading for Miggea. Using the Re-Enactors as a disguise!'

'Sort of. Yes.'

'And you sent the TARDIS off on a false trail because you're afraid that whatever is trying to destroy the multiverse thinks you can stop them.'

'I thought it was Frank/Freddie Force, but now I'm not sure. He's after the same thing as I am. Or seems to be. I suspect others are after it, too. See, this has been going on for a long time. Since your time, in fact. When you and I first got the message. Oops! Look out!'

The huge ship was suddenly spinning while also turning over end on end. From somewhere came the voice of the captain issuing rapid instructions. Alarms began to sound. A fierce cacophony.

And then it stopped.

They were drifting in space in what was surely the same area they had left when the time storm struck. Except that there were now no streamers of dark matter threatening to wrap themselves around the *Gargantua*. They were moving along peacefully while the distant suns glimmered far away.

Captain Snarri joined them. 'I'm not sure where you qualified, Doctor, but that's the finest bit of navigation I've ever witnessed. And with no further damage to the ship.'

'Thanks, captain. I suppose you noticed that only a few of your hull plates look strong enough to sustain a long trip. One section has sprung completely. You'll need to get some repair bots outside as well as in.'

'I'm already on it. I'm surprised there weren't more casualties. Our hospital was twisted, lost some plates, but we've done our best to patch her up.'

Somewhere out in the shadows a darker shape moved gracefully, turning slowly, as if against a wind, and Amy had a sinking feeling deep in the pit of her stomach that she had seen that shape before, either in the distant past or in her dreams, she could not be sure which. Why she was alarmed she couldn't tell. But when she looked away for a moment and looked back the shadow was gone.

The Doctor was busy with some calculations. More screens picked up interior scenes on board. The passengers were unwinding, obviously relieved and only just realising they had survived. Bots bustled everywhere on the huge liner, repairing what they could. Mostly they concentrated on the triple hull, their r-guns pulling plates together, resealing any cracks, aligning Vs both outside and inside, straightening tubes, tightening nuts.

In a moment, carrying their suits and helmets, Mr Tr'r'r'r and some of his officers joined the Doctor and Amy. They stowed their protective clothing and crowded around the Doctor asking for advice. Only then did Amy mention what she had seen on the screen. She pointed, but whatever was there had not returned. Maybe she had imagined it. After all that business with the Chaos Kids, she would not be surprised. She felt stupid when she pointed and there was nothing there.

'Oh, I'm sorry,' she said. 'I must be hallucinating. I wonder if that's not what I'm doing all the time these days.'

But the Doctor had learned to trust her senses, even if she didn't. 'What did it look like?'

'Shadows,' she said. 'Just a lot of shadows. Probably nothing, just marks on the screen. Sorry.'

'Well, let us know if you see it again,' he said. He turned

back to the second officer. 'Where did you say that pinhole was?'

Amy concentrated on the screen where she had seen the shadows. A glint of silver, nothing else.

She heard the Doctor ask the captain a question and the captain answer: 'Never had any use for them. We had strong defensive screens, of course, but those generators were all damaged. We were sure we'd need nothing else. We're too big and we never carry any cargo of much value. So why do you ask, Doctor?'

The Doctor scratched his unruly head. 'Because we're looking vulnerable. We sustained a lot of damage in that storm. How many were injured? Was anyone killed?'

One of the ship's doctors had blood on his white uniform coat. He was unhappy. 'I've been trying to find out. Several of our elderly passengers had serious heart episodes when we weren't there to treat them. We never expected to lose patients in this day and age. Quite a few resurrection caskets are out of commission. Most of our instruments rely on the power supply. When that went out, we were pretty helpless. I feel like a fraud, calling myself a doctor.'

'I know what you mean.' The Doctor looked away. 'Have you managed a count yet?'

'I think it's at least forty people. We've frozen them now, but probably too late for a few of them. The 200-year-olds are all right. We had some youngsters with bad injuries. No chance of helping them until we get back to civilisation. Which isn't likely to be Miggea. Ships usually wait for us or some other big liner to turn up and take their troubles to us. We're well ahead of them, certainly in technology. They're pretty primitive. My sister did a year there for her interstellar service job. She said it was like going back in time.'

W.G. Grace came in carrying her treasured bow-case under her arm as if ready for a fight. The other players had laughed at her because throughout the entire storm she had never let go of it. She had speedskin over a big gash in her arm but she reassured everyone that no muscles needed replacing. 'Back in time?' She laughed heartily, her big beard wagging. 'That's no problem for the Terraphiles.'

She did not know until they told her that they had lost the whole of the Second Fifteen, sucked out of the ship when two triple-fitted plates in their quarters blew. The heroes who had tried to go back in to that section and save them had been outstanding players – Donna Bradmann, one of their best fielders, and Shanasakar Greeb, the Second's skunkoid archer. The other casualty, a Judoon, had not died like the rest of the players but had been found in another section and was caught in some sort of hallucination, drinking *colour* from the leaking fuel tanks, thinking it was Vortex Water. Unrefined *colour* wouldn't kill you if only a little was ingested. But this was powerful extra-refined super and had to be contained in special vats. Mr Tr'r'r'r came up to inform them that no other player had been especially badly hurt.

When Amy heard all this she was horrified. All those poor players killed! They had come all this way, across vast swathes of space just to die in this horrible accident.

'It must jeopardize your chances of playing the Tournament,' Tr'r'r'r was saying, but she hardly heard him. Some of those who had died had almost been her friends.

Then she wondered how much of her experience out there in the Second Aether had been hallucinatory? She made her way through to the Doctor and asked him the first chance she got. He too was mourning the dead, but he reassured her.

'Don't worry,' he said, 'I've known Captain Abberley and the Bubbly Boys for a very long time. That's the advantage of travelling via Miggea. They're really all right. Sad as I am, Mr Tr'r'r'r is correct: it could have been an attempt to sabotage the team.'

Amy was almost crying, angry. 'Someone would kill all those people just because of this Tournament?'

'I don't know, Amy.' The Doctor sighed heavily. 'We could be disqualified if we don't turn up with a full team. And we have to win that arrer. That's still the most important thing.'

Amy felt obliged to step up. 'I'll help out if you need me. I was a pretty good fielder during the rehearsals, wasn't I?' Then she became embarrassed. How could she possibly be any better than the tried and true players of the Second Fifteen, let alone the surviving First Fifteen?

He understood and patted her on the shoulder. 'Thanks, Amy. I'll remember that.'

She felt like biting her tongue.

As she looked up at the dark screen again she could have sworn that she saw another shadow fall across it. The outline was familiar. Were they still in the Second Aether? Had she just spotted a Chaos ship?

And there it was, suddenly clear, filling the screen, turning gracefully against a star cluster. Seemingly only a few parsecs away.

'*Look!*'

They turned, surprised by her emphasis.

'A ship,' she shouted, then dropped her tone. 'Isn't it? I mean, do they have ships like that in space? It's like an old galleon! With huge sails and stuff?'

'Oh, dear me,' said the Doctor. 'You're right about it being a ship, Amy. And I know her master. He's a very old acquaintance of mine. I was rather hoping he wouldn't find us. Not in our weakened condition. He's a long way from his usual hunting grounds. He used to cruise the Rim worlds at this time of year. Collecting his rents. Looking for prey. They're closer to home for him. He's fast and he's very, very dangerous. The IPC have sent whole fleets after him, but he has his ship and his little galaxy well defended!'

'Little galaxy?' She was bewildered by this. 'Can you have a *little* galaxy?'

'Dwarf galaxies. Groups of star systems caught in our galaxy's gravity. Sort of islands off the coast of the Milky Way. Remember?'

She was sure he hadn't told her about them, but that was typical. She suspected him of mixing her up with some other girl he'd known. At first she had resented his confusion. Now she understood it better and was more forgiving. She no longer bothered to correct him.

The others were joining them to stare at the screen. 'What is it?' W.G. Grace wanted to know. 'It's huge, isn't it. Looks like an old-time clipper ship, though considerably bigger. Hard to tell, of course.'

'Oh, she's big.' The Doctor took a deep breath. 'Yeah. And fast, too. A beauty, isn't she? I remember a time when—' He caught himself. 'There was an era long ago, when space was full of them. They called them "starjammers".'

'Can she help us, Doctor?' asked Amy.

'I'm not sure she intends to offer help exactly,' he answered. 'She's the *Paine* out of the dwarf galaxy Canis. Commanded by Captain Cornelius. That's what he calls himself. An old acquaintance of mine. A sort of enemy, you could say. Or a rival. Depending on the circumstances. He doesn't do a lot of universe saving, Amy, that's for sure. He must have been following behind the storm. Waiting. Keeping out of the way. A dark wind is the last thing he needs. Light's totally important to him. Still, I doubt he has any plans to attack us. I bet he wasn't expecting to find the biggest liner in the galaxy helpless as a newborn baby, just waiting for him to take her.'

'A prize?' W.G. Grace leaned her bow-case carefully against a console. 'You make her sound like a pirate, Doctor.'

'That's because she *is* a pirate. The most infamous and

217

feared pirate in the galaxy.' The Doctor was grim. 'I've come up against her in the past. There's only one other ship like her in the entire pirate brotherhood. *Remembered Lombardy*. And I suppose we should be grateful it's not her. Colonel Gaspard Reynauld would be shooting at us by now.'

He sharpened the picture.

'She's an old Rim clipper. I doubt if there's another living person in conventional space-time who has seen a ship like that in the ordinary way of things. Powered by photons. By the power of suns. By light itself! Built before the *colour-engine* was invented and made her obsolete, at least as far as the major shipbuilders were concerned. Imagine a whole fleet of them! They were formidable. Oh, yes! I've tangled with Captain Cornelius more than once. He's known as Ironface, because of the metal mask he used to wear in battle. A sort of phantom of the space opera.' He winced at his own joke. 'But I've never had so much to lose before. Or so many other lives in immediate danger to think about.'

W.G. clasped her fancy bow-case to her. 'But by definition she can't travel faster than light. We can. Or could. We can get away, can't we?'

'You didn't study relative relativity at school, did you W.G.?' The Doctor was rubbing his face, as if to get circulation back into it. 'Light travels at many different speeds, depending on context. We just use the old Einsteinian speed to make certain calculations, the way we use Earth kilometres or litres or parsecs. Or Anglo-Saxons used their feet. Same as time. You know that time moves at different speeds, don't you? If it didn't, there wouldn't be any space as such. No *matter*, as we understand it. Does your enthusiasm for the past, W.G., mean that you only went to schools which taught Dark Age science?'

Grace turned a substantial shade of puce and would not reply.

The *Paine* banked again, sweetly, elegantly. These jammers were the first ships Earth had used for deep-space exploration. Those great fleets moved before winds of light radiating from the stars, the way old-time galleons used the wind. At some point, decades or centuries earlier, the *Paine* had been built in space and then towed or boosted up to speed until she could sail under the power of light alone. She never stopped moving, circling planets while her tenders went back and forth, using the power of galaxies to travel.

Amy wondered if the *Paine* was really their enemy. After all, if dark matter spread to dominate the universe, the *Paine* would become incapable of movement and drift for ever in the doldrums of space. But maybe Captain Cornelius did not care what happened in the future. What if he lived merely to enjoy the moment and refused to worry about any consequences? Already Amy was becoming intrigued by a man she had never seen...

'Oh, thank goodness! You're safe. I looked for you everywhere and was beginning to think – oh – you know...' Bingo Lockesley was trembling. He seemed on the verge of tears. He still wore his emergency suit, splashed with blood. He was horribly pale.

'Are you all right, Bingo?' Not wanting to hurt him if he was wounded, she hesitated before hugging him.

He looked down at the blood. 'Gosh, no! Ha, ha. That's not me. Poor old gent broke his arm, got some cuts from a ripped inner plate. Medics fixed him up pretty much on the spot. I've just come from the hospital section. All I got was a bump on the head. Knocked me out for a few minutes, that's all. It's the others need our help. A nightmare, what?'

'Old Bingo's been a brick!' Hari joined them, wiping his hands on a rag.

Flapper was with him. She wore nurse's overalls and her hair was hidden under a blue hat. 'Glad you're safe,' she said. 'Some people were actually sucked out through the hull and into space. Others were seriously injured. They had to go into the cryogenic bay. We did everything we could do until the medics had things under control. We heard some of our own people were killed. We thought we'd better come up here and look for you and met old Bingo on the way. Thank goodness you're safe. Ah, there's the Doctor. How is he?'

'A bit tired.' Amy was delighted to see them. She was reminded of the first and second world wars, when the unlikeliest people suddenly became heroes. 'His steering saved our lives. He got us out of the storm.' She knew she would never be able to explain the Second Aether.

'I hear Greeb and Donna bought it, what?' Hari Agincourt was embarrassed at his show of emotion. 'Jolly bad break. Somebody said that the whole Second Fifteen were lost. Is that true?'

'Yes, poor devils.' Bingo kicked at the floor.

'Those two were both ace players, weren't they?' asked Flapper. 'I mean they're a serious loss. I know it's not good form to talk about the team's chances at a time like this, but isn't this going to make it difficult for the Gentlemen?'

'It will a bit. I think the casualties – those who weren't sucked into space – will be all right, of course, when we get back to a civilised world. But meanwhile things are a looking a bit sticky, yes. Miggea's not exactly advanced as far as medicine's involved. For the sake of Donny and Masher we can't risk resurrecting them there, can we?'

The Doctor nodded vaguely, studying the banking space-clipper.

Amy realised that the mood in the control room had changed. There was a sudden silence. Everyone was now looking at the screen on which she had seen the sailing ship.

'Big, isn't she?' said Bingo quietly, rubbing his head. He looked about him for a seat

'Rather!' agreed Hari. He glanced at Flapper. 'You all right, old thing?'

'She might be here to help.' Flapper shivered and drew closer to a manly Hari. 'I mean, it's possible, isn't it?'

'I don't think so.' Amy clutched at the 'celestial' necklace in her pocket, suddenly wishing she too had a manly arm to gather her in. For reasons obscure to her, she took out the necklace and put it on. 'That's the *Paine*. She's a pirate ship, captained by a villain they call Ironface. Because of his mask.'

'Oh, Lord!' exclaimed Bingo. 'I've heard of him. I say, Hari, I think we'd better get our bows and a couple of quivers of arrows. Stand by to repel boarders and all that.'

The Doctor heard him. 'Not much chance we can chase off Ironface the way we did General Force. His grapple beams could crush us like a tin can. And we're already pretty much in the position of a can someone's trodden on. Half the force screens are down. Our hull plates were seriously damaged in the storm. We're a sitting duck for any predator. We can only hope he doesn't *think* of us as prey.'

The ship's monstrous black sails bulged as she came about. Her masts were hundreds of metres high, her sails miles across. Yet, because the *Gargantua* was herself such a gigantic ship, the *Paine* seemed relatively small in comparison. Apart from dark brass furnishings, she was all black. Any light not directly used to sail her was saved in energy converters deep in her slender hull. She had two *colour* engines as auxiliaries. Her gun ports gleamed, showing just a hint of her banned Mann and Robersons. The energy cannons inflicted worse than death on any living thing they as much as brushed with their radiation. They were considered the best armament in the universe, hugely effective, but nobody had used them in centuries because of the terrible torture they inflicted. Nobody died quickly from a Mann and Roberson shot, but they did, inevitably, die. It was unwise to engage the *Paine* in battle. She never lost. And fluttering unostentatiously from her foretop was a black flag on which a skull and bones had been embroidered in pure white thread.

The *Paine* kept close to the *Gargantua*. She sailed beside the liner but made no threats, took no action, simply continued to shadow her. Only the *Gargantua*'s own flickering lights and the glimmering of faraway stars made the pirate visible. Passengers and crew crowded to look at her, craning their necks to follow the masts and get some measure of the size of her sails.

All was silence.

Finally Captain Snarri wiped his huge mouth and said wearily, 'Normally we could probably outrun her, but she can see we've been hurt. I can't engage her because we're a civilian ship and my first duty is to the passengers. So. I can't run. I can't fight. I suppose I'm going to have to barter. Pirates have kidnapped rich passengers in the past and held them to ransom. We'll probably be made to surrender volunteers. Generally most of them have been returned in one piece. Ironface might be satisfied with any treasure the passengers have.' Snarri took a deep breath. His sigh was long and bitter. 'I've had no training for this situation. I am responsible. Yet I have no idea, Doctor, what to do.'

'Perhaps I can negotiate a way out.' The Doctor put a comforting hand on Snarri's shoulder. 'Cornelius and I have crossed swords before. Quite literally on one occasion. In a coalmine. Near Newcastle. About 1918. Leopard Men.'

'I can't think of an alternative.' The captain appeared to sag. He sat down in a chair just as a resonant, ironic voice came in over their communicators:

'Captain Cornelius of the privateer *Paine* wishing to establish contact. Do I have *Gargantua*'s permission?' At least he was following the polite protocol of the space lanes.

Captain Snarri pulled himself together, licked dry lips and said softly: 'Permission granted, captain.'

He signalled to the bots and the busy little machines tuned the *Paine* in and trained their V on Captain Snarri. 'Good evening to you, Captain Cornelius. I am Captain Snarri, commander of this ship.'

'And to you, Captain Snarri.' Unexpectedly a head, covered by a tight leather helmet and a simple, white papier maché Arlecchino mask from the Italian Commedia dell'arte, filled the screen, as if he had deliberately chosen a less menacing persona. He wore an undecorated dark blue naval jacket buttoned to the chin. 'I apologise for the rather melodramatic hiding of my face. I like to travel and that would be impossible if anyone recognised me. Might I express my regret at your misfortune?'

'Let's not resort to hypocrisy, Captain Cornelius. I know you for a pirate and you know my ship as one of the greatest passenger liners in the galaxy, protected by intergalactic law. Which I invoke. Your ship has a duty to rescue mine.' Snarri could not easily hide his anxiety for his ship and passengers and was doing the only thing he knew to try to protect them.

'Put me on now,' murmured the Doctor. At a sign from the captain the V now showed both men and Amy on the pirate's screen. 'Good evening, Captain Ironface. We've been thrashed, I'm afraid. Black storm. We're pretty much out of commission. I suppose there's no chance of your giving us a hand?'

For a moment the pirate captain's gaze moved from Snarri, to the Doctor and lingered a moment on Amy, making her shiver. Then, letting his attention return to the Doctor, he let a shadow of a smile cross his face.

'Why, Doctor! What a compliment. But you forget my calling, surely? I'm a star thief. We wish to board. If you refuse – well, I'm sure I don't need to make the conventional threats. We've both seen Mann and Robersons at work. There's not a survivor of the Rim Wars who hasn't. However, if your captain will give us his word, I'll leave my men on my ship and merely bring my bosun. What do you say? I've no intention of doing you further violence. But I think you'll admit we have the advantage.'

Captain Snarri made a noise in his throat. He glared at the screen, then at the Doctor. His shrug was angry.

Second Intermission

OUT OF THE DARKNESS and silence of the intergalactic void, breaking through the thin membrane between one universe and the next, the oddly shaped ship pauses, its engines cackling faintly like distant geese, wisps of dark energy moving around it like tentacles feeling its odd angles and appendages. Within, faces sad, speculative, smiling, silently contemplate the cosmos. Then comes the noise of raised voices, arguing their position until a decision is reached and the ship warps again, fading into the perpetual night. It makes a sound like an angry donkey, suggesting to anyone looking out at it that it is at least part organic, which in a sense it is.

Millions of light years away, more than one set of instruments detect the ship and speculative minds debate its origins, sending probes to examine it but in truth they are relieved to remain in ignorance, at least for the moment.

The ship spins and vanishes again, registering on only the most sophisticated detectors.

Bosun Peet Aviv of the star-clipper *Paine* relays the news to her captain, murmuring of the Second Aether and those who hunt between the worlds and in turn are hunted. They speak of Lady Peg the Invisible, of Frank/Freddie Force and the others who move between the worlds using atmospheres which, passing from one gateway to another, make corridors, whole universes, of breathable gasses. Their instruments again pick up the ship, but its occupants are gone. Where? What have they chosen to do? Are they already walking between the worlds, leaving that strangely shaped vessel adrift or anchored in some clever configuration which, like a supernatural incantation, they can turn into speech and thus return? Magic or science, it's all the same to the passengers of that ship or her watchers, for this is the far future where a spell can be a mathematical formula and a song can work a miracle.

Peet Aviv relays her sightings to her master, reluctantly admitting her mystification. But the pirate captain has other business on his mind and pays poor attention to the matter. He commands Peet Aviv to wear her red and blue formal uniform and to be vigilant. They could be trapped still, and their ship consigned to some other universe, a speck of heavy dust travelling through the shadows of worlds too large for their eyes or their instruments to measure.

Or are there plans to lure them down into the region of the black hole where they will sail for ever in the same terrible moment?

More than once the great starjammer has sensed a trap and barely escaped it.

Captain Cornelius knows he is taking a great risk in leaving his ship, but he would not do so unless the stakes were the highest he had ever known.

Chapter 19

Conversation in the Captain's Cabin

WITH JUST A SUGGESTION of *noblesse oblige*, Ironface the pirate ducked his helmeted head beneath the lip of the airlock and raised his hand in an old-fashioned peace gesture. 'I am grateful for your hospitality. May I introduce my bosun in all my adventures? Mademoiselle Peet Aviv, Captain Snarri, the Doctor and...?'

'Mademoiselle Amelia Pond,' said Amy firmly. '*Enchantée, monsieur.*' She was delighted to see a glint of humour in the Doctor's eye.

'If we're parlaying, we'll go this way into my state room,' Captain Snarri said, with a sharp whisk of his tail.

Captain Cornelius and Peet Aviv fell in behind the *Gargantua*'s commander, the Doctor and Amy bringing up the rear. Amy was fascinated by the bosun of the *Paine*. Peet Aviv was one of the strangest and most beautiful creatures Amy had ever seen. She wore a copper and platinum exoskeleton over most of her upper body. The exoskeleton resembled the carapace of a gigantic locust but her elongated head had been modelled on Modigliani's *Woman with a Fan*. Peet Aviv's legs were elegantly curved steel springs so she moved in long, bouncing, graceful strides. Her voice was sweetly musical.

Had she not worn a banned neutron pistol at her side, she would not have been recognised as a pirate.

The captain's state room was luxurious but had the air of being rarely used. A bot brought a fire to life in the elaborate Style Liberty grate, and all five sat down in deep armchairs with broad arms of oak and dark burgundy plush. The fire threw warm shadows into the room, and Captain Snarri raised and lowered his hands bringing the lamps to soft light. His long legs carried him gracefully to the cabinet where he poured their requested drinks and brought them personally to his guests.

In his usual realistic, unemotional tone he opened the conversation. 'We've survived the worst space-time storm I've ever experienced. No doubt you've been listening on your eavesbots, Captain Cornelius, so you know our situation. We can't fight you. We can't outrun you. I've been broadcasting signals, but the storm obviously wiped out potential assistance from nearby. Any police help is days or more away. So we're at your mercy, sir.'

'My word's given, sir.' Cornelius sipped his Vortex Water. 'I'll demand a small enough price. Matter of professional honour.' Again a shadow smile. 'But that wasn't my reason for requesting your permission to board.' He gestured to Peet Aviv who apologetically unbuttoned her neutron gun's holster and rose to put it on the mantle beside the Scottish clock. As she sat down again she raised her VW in a genial, unsmiling toast.

Amy found her mind growing more alert but was not really sure why. The rest of her was very much relaxed, enjoying and admiring the room. The big cabin was beautifully furnished with large, comfortable chairs, mostly in the style, or so the Doctor whispered when she mentioned it, of Morris and Stickley, the old Arts and Crafts designers. All dark oak and glinting copper, the furniture reflected the light from the fire basket in the grate. Amy was grateful for the luxury. This was the first time since the storm she had been able to sit down and, as far as it was possible in the circumstances, unwind. The huge bowl of old-fashioned pink and white roses on the centre table looked real and their scent was gorgeous, adding further to her sense of wellbeing.

'You won't hear the faintest buzz from our Mann and Robersons, captain, no matter what ensues today. I'm unarmed. You'll hear no intended threats from us, and I apologise for and withdraw any unintended threats. Save in one small matter, which I'll announce in due course.

'I'm glad to see you, Doctor. You knew I'd recognise you, I suspect.' He chuckled. 'Do you find it as hard as I do to discover suitable intellectual company, these days? I remember our last meeting with pleasure, for you, too, are a sensitive like me. I hope you have a little time to spare me.'

'I'll happily spare as much as necessary, if you'll help our ship, Captain Cornelius.'

'Then let us discuss just that. Will anyone mind if I smoke? I have a splendid Meng and Ecker's heavy tobacco.' Having received their permission, he stuffed his long-stemmed meerschaum. 'It's obvious you've seen a storm or two by the look of your ship. I never thought one of these G-class monsters could be caught by man or force of nature. They said she could go into a black hole and come out unscathed. Yet here she is.' Captain Cornelius placed his pipe in a pewter ashtray. 'It seemed to me that you were off course when we sighted you.'

The Doctor crossed his gangling legs, his long fingers pushing back a flop of hair from his face. 'Exactly right, captain. Did you also encounter a storm? You're some distance from your preferred routes.'

'Indeed we are, sir. The dark currents swept in and caught us just after we'd left our home port in Canis. We'd only seen the currents from a safe distance. As you may know, there have been many more such storms beyond the Rim than near the Hub. Even so, they appeared to be threatening deeper space only and, until recently, we had little to fear. We have been extremely lucky up to now. You can imagine what those currents mean to us. We depend on light. Light is even more important to us than it is to *colour*-fuelled vessels. Without it, we could not move at all. We could, I suppose, convert solely to *colour*. But the prospect of the galaxy going dark is one guaranteed to alarm any intelligent creature.'

The Doctor smiled. 'Dark means cold. Cold means death.' He leaned back in his chair admiring the paintings on the walls. He was doing his best to show no emotion. 'What was your course, may I ask, when you saw the tide?'

'I was heading for Miggea, at the Hub. She orbits the Schwarzschild Radius, as you know. The Ghost Worlds? I'm a keen Tournament watcher, and I gathered the three finalists were going to be playing on Flynn this year. I had hoped to be there.' His smile was self-mocking. 'Not as myself, of course. I used to have a certain amount of skill with the bow. I had no plans to take part in the Tournament proper, but there are archery contests arranged around the perimeter. I'd imagined perhaps I could try my luck at one or two of those.'

'That would have been dangerous,' the Doctor observed with an answering smile, 'given that there's a high price on your head. You must know that.'

'I'm rather flattered, in fact. But I'm an incorrigible romantic and have to admit I relished the risk.'

'Like Robin Hood,' said Amy suddenly.

They both turned to her enquiringly.

'Robin Hood, the outlaw archer. The Sheriff of Nottingham put on an archery match and Robin Hood went there in disguise to see if he could win. They show it all the time –

well, they used to. Flynn! That's it! I knew that was ringing a bell. Errol Flynn. Basil Rathbone. Olivia de Havilland? Galloping through the Green Wood? Trigger?'

'Trigger?' exclaimed the Doctor. 'Really? The horse? Roy Rogers?'

'I recognised him,' she said. 'I was rather proud of myself. It was Aunt Sharon's favourite film.'

'Film?' murmured Cornelius enquiringly.

'Twentieth-century Earth art form,' the Doctor told him. 'An early type of V drama.'

'So...' The Dutchman showed a deeper interest in Amy. 'You're a time traveller, then? Like the Doctor?'

'Errol Flynn and that,' said Amy, feeling awkward. 'I'm from...'

'Old Old Earth,' put in the Doctor hastily, turning back. 'Her subject at university. Dark Age studies. You know what we Terraphiles are like with our love of minutiae.'

'I, too, must study this Robin Woods. Prowling through the jungle, eh? He sounds like something of a tiger. Forgive me for my rudeness, Captain Snarri. I only want a small price for helping you reach your next destination. Part of that is one thing you're carrying which I learned about from a mutual acquaintance. General Force. Frank/Freddie Force came to me a while ago and suggested he and I combine our energies to take it. I have to admit, I was tempted. Then I decided that would be unsporting, since I had already decided to claim it for myself. Also, to be perfectly honest with you, I don't like the fellow. I don't think I'd want to do business with him. He was looking, as you surely have guessed, for the legendary Arrow of Law. The Silver Arrow for which your teams are competing.'

The Doctor carefully set his glass of Vortex Water down on the wide arm of his Stickley chair. 'The Arrow? You think we have it on board the *Gargantua*?'

Captain Cornelius looked surprised by the Doctor's reaction. 'You don't know you're carrying it with you?'

'I'm not sure what game Frank/Freddie Force is playing with us both,' replied the Doctor, 'but we are not carrying the so-called Arrow of Law. It's in a travelling time vault which will only arrive when the last game's played on Flynn. We can't get it until then. That's precisely to stop it being stolen or the presenter being tempted to nick it themselves. I saw it placed in the vault. Many of us did.'

'Surely you know what that arrow is? Or what it represents, Doctor?'

Amy wondered if the Doctor intended to tell Captain Cornelius about the message he had received from the Hub of the galaxy, or whether he intended to play what few cards he held close to his chest.

The Doctor's face was expressionless when he replied. 'Of course I do.'

Captain Cornelius broke into a spontaneous laugh. 'Of course you do! Then perhaps you can tell me where it comes from and who now possesses it?'

'It's the prize for which teams of Terraphiles play a series of archaic games. The games are played once every quarter-millennium. The team which wins those games receives the Silver Arrow of Artemis from the previous winners. Until the last game, it remains kept out of time and space. The team who last won it are known as the Visitors and are probably already on Flynn. Surely you know all this?'

The captain ignored the question. 'Your reason for joining the team?'

'To have a bit of fun, you know. Get some exercise. I can always do with that.'

'So you crossed time and space in your TARDIS, risked your life more than once, just for a bit of fun? To get some exercise?'

'You know that one, surely? A person gets bored...'

'That's your entire reason? I doubt you're being entirely frank with me, Doctor. My instruments detected no sign of your TARDIS. As for the Arrow...'

In the ensuing silence Amy looked from one man to the other, wondering who would speak first.

Eventually the Doctor said: 'This is all I know. I got a long-distance message from someone who understood how to contact me. The message was broken. Partly common galactic from this period. I half-recognised the voice, but I can't say for certain who it was. I didn't recognise all the language. Their signal came from Miggea's Schwarzschild Radius. They mentioned Tom Mix, an ancient actor, Flynn in Miggea and the Cosmic Roogalator or Regulator. Then they mentioned Frank/Freddie Force's name. That worried me, because Force is crazy enough to bring about the death of the multiverse – all time and space, matter and antimatter. The death of everything. That would suit his ego. He's one of the few creatures I can believe mad enough to destroy us all.

'I also knew from my own observations that the dark tides are running – running through time and space – which suggested something had gone wrong, since they were *already* moving at unprecedented speeds. The message came from the centre, so I decided to go there and see if I could find out what was causing all this. And I wanted to fix that irregularity, if I could. From what signals I could decipher, that Silver Arrow is somehow linked to the dark currents. I thought if we won it I could examine it and see exactly what it was...'

Captain Cornelius broke into easy laughter. 'That's "all", is it, my dear Doctor? You speak of a horrifying ego! Yet you crossed vast distances of space and time on the off-chance of being able to fix something at the centre of the multiverse without knowing exactly what you were going to remedy?'

'Well, yes.' Awkwardly, the Doctor straightened in his chair. 'Not for the first time. That's what I do. Does it amuse you to patronise me?'

'Forgive me, but it does sound unlikely. If you detected irregularities why didn't you try to adjust them there and then?'

'I followed the signal. It led me into that sector. I think you know me as well as I know you, captain.'

'Indeed. Don Quixote. Righter of wrongs. Rescuer of those in distress. A man driven by infinite curiosity.' He raised his hand. 'No, no, I'm not mocking you, Doctor. We are natural brothers. I am confrontational, as you know, by nature. You are not a man who turns away from conflict. So you followed the message. What else did it tell you?'

'As I said, I couldn't see who was sending it. The Terraphile Re-Enactors were mentioned, Tom Mix, Dissolution... A few names. So the only thing to do was to go there and find out.'

'And what have you found out so far?'

'That the dark tides are certainly running. Leaking into our hemisphere. Wide and deep. A million currents all at different speeds. Different times. Faster than I realised. Dangerously fast. Way beyond any previously noted speeds. Which essentially means everything will vanish from the universe, maybe even the multiverse, long before their natural, expected time. A thousand years or less instead of billions...'

'And you know what the dark tides are?'

'As much as anyone. They give out no light though they absorb light. They attract, much as gravity attracts. A dark current creates storms in space when it meets with the elements defining the environment we both inhabit. With anything defying gravity. Beyond our sphere it pulls whole galaxies with it, presumably into the powerful black hole none of us has ever seen. Around that all matter revolves.

In our own galaxy our black hole is the best-known gateway into the antimatter multiverse, which exists in opposition to our own. It is, I believe, one of a series orbiting that larger phenomenon. Opposition is what guarantees the survival of everything in Creation. Without it the multiverse would collapse into inchoate primal matter and antimatter which in turn would dissipate into nothingness – a multiverse without shape or meaning – or intelligence.'

'Intelligence, Doctor. There's the key, eh? It would cease to be. Whatever you call that fundamental power of reason and creation is what allows the multiverse to exist. Without it we are condemned, essentially, to non-existence. Whatever our motives or ambitions, they are meaningless without an ordered multiverse where Law balances Chaos, matter balances antimatter, Life balances Death. One cannot exist without the other. And somehow, as you've observed, antimatter is infecting matter, Law and Chaos are confused and soon – what?'

'Life and death will become indistinguishable. Matter and antimatter, law and chaos, good and evil, become indistinguishable. All the opposing qualities which at present are in balance, which give meaning to existence, will disappear.'

'And this process is rapidly increasing, eh? Do you know why that is, Doctor?'

'I'm here to find out.'

'That's the spirit, Doctor.' His voice was grim now without a hint of sarcasm. 'So have you discovered why, in your efforts to return the cycle to its natural speed, Miggea is important?'

'Because she is the nearest star system to the Hub. Because she has unusual properties.'

'True. But that's all you know?'

'She has an eccentric orbit and her orbit takes her closer

to the multiversal Hub than any other body.' The Doctor studied the masked man's eyes.

'Why are you playing these contests in Miggea?'

'Why? That's obvious, captain. To win the Silver Arrow.' The Doctor was frowning, curious. He shifted in his chair. 'I suppose.'

'To win an arrow which has been the prize in an archery tournament held every two hundred and fifty years for the last few thousand or so. Not legendary for that reason, surely? The arrow has qualities. Associations. And could be what – a million years old? Fifty thousand at least. That's how long scientists have noted the dark currents dragging our universe in.' Captain Cornelius shrugged to himself, reaching over to the table for the flask of Vortex Water. He offered to refresh their glasses but they refused. 'So – the dark tide has been running for at least fifty thousand years! Admittedly running faster and more ferociously than when we of this galaxy first noticed what was happening. From Earth in the post-enlightenment period, mm?'

'That's right. On Earth they only had the means of identifying it by the year 2010. I've been trying to understand it ever since. Do you know why this is happening, captain? Is that why you're here?'

'This is my native space-time sector. My scientists have had a chance to study the dark tides at some proximity. As the scientific community has observed, there is no doubt that the tide or tides have enormous powers of gravity. The dark tides could be a quality of gravity. Gravity is a quality of matter. Matter is a quality of time. Gravity makes the universe go round. Without it, everything would collapse, as you've said. Anti-gravity cannot, of course, exist without gravity. Everything is comprised of opposites. Destroy that opposition and you destroy – well, as you said, Doctor – everything, as we've discussed.' He reached for his pipe, changed his mind.

'Now, what if the balance, on which we depend, were maintained by something more than a metaphysical idea but by a *physical* element? Let's call that element a "regulator" – the same sort of thing they put on primitive beam engines to make them work at a desired speed and so on. Clocks, too. This regulator maintains the multiverse theoretically through eternity. The universe of matter slowly becomes antimatter and the universe of antimatter turns into matter? Out of death comes life and out of life comes death. Opposites sustain existence.'

'That's not a profound notion, captain. We're agreed on that. You asked what if this "regulator" were something physical?'

'Or something, at any rate, which could assume physical shape.'

'Fine, yes, all right. But does it change itself? Or is its shape determined by the will of a sentient creature, or a number of sentient creatures? Do you have a theory about what that shape could be?'

'I think you know what I think. The story I like best is that to protect itself your so called Roogalator can shift shape, the way a cuttlefish, for instance, can disguise itself in both colour and shape when it recognises potential danger.' The captain leaned forward. 'But perhaps it takes time to change. We know that some of us can come and go across the worlds of matter and antimatter. What if one such person found that regulator and, not really knowing its function, stole it? What would happen then?'

'I don't know...' mused the Doctor. 'I'd guess it would return automatically to its place at the centre of existence.'

'Perhaps. But it might need a similar means of returning. A carrier to take its physical manifestation back to its natural environment. An intelligent agent – something or someone who could replace it and put the multiverse back on course again?'

The Doctor's face showed that he understood, though Amy was struggling to keep up.

'You're no doubt suggesting this prize arrow you're seeking is also the missing regulator?' The Doctor fingered his chin. 'But that doesn't make sense. They've only been running these matches for a few thousand years or so, and the irregularities were first observed in the twenty-first century. Even if you understand that time flows at different speeds and space has moments of intense malleability, it still doesn't explain what's going on. Oh!' He brightened. 'Unless there are two arrows, or one—'

'— has assumed the identity of the other,' Cornelius finished. 'Perhaps to disguise itself from the original thief, who is looking for it still.' He leaned his strange, masked head on his hand.

'Frank/Freddie Force again!' exclaimed the Doctor.

The captain nodded. 'Apparently it has changed hands several times. It wound up in the shop of an antiquities dealer on Venice and then seems to have disappeared. We were on Venice not so long ago. I hoped to find it. Well, Force and his men followed us into deep space and requested a conference. I saw nothing to lose. He told me what he sought and I was curious, though I didn't have it. And wouldn't have traded it to him if I had. He's one of the few beings we know with the arrogance to think he can return order to the cosmos. That's my theory.'

'He's been looking for it effectively for ever – dodging in and out of Chaos space and antimatter space, searching for that regulator.' The Doctor was enjoying this exchange. 'He's discovered a little information here, a little there, every time he makes a foray into our universe. Maybe he was the original thief? Unlike most of us, he can travel between the hemispheres of matter and antimatter and remain alive. The Arrow, if that's what it is, has the power to change its shape if it is threatened. We know that much, at least, from legend. Not *exactly* a thinking object but capable of hiding itself from those who would use it for their own ends? Cup, sword, animal, even human form when useful. Does it think as we think? I don't know.'

'What if Force was the one who stole it?' suggested Cornelius. 'And then he lost it and has been hunting for it across time and space, making expeditions into our hemisphere whenever he dares or has a clue. If so, then he still believes possession of it will allow him the power to control it.'

'That's impossible. Insane!' The Doctor's face cleared. 'Ah! Frank/Freddie's never been sane. And the very act of stealing the regulator would have increased his delusion. But why would he believe we carried it with us?'

'He told me he'd smelled it. Not literally, I'm sure. But through some sixth sense – an affinity he achieved through the very act of trying to make it his own. He sensed it was with you. I don't know, because he is moving in and out of time and is most likely the unwitting cause of some of these storms? The regulator—let's say it is that – has changed shape more than once in its efforts to elude him...'

'So there could be two arrows?' The Doctor nodded slowly. 'One is this mysterious shape-changing regulator and the other is the one we're playing for? Or—' The Doctor was becoming excited. He broke into a delighted laugh. 'Or the regulator somehow was passed over to Mrs Banning-Cannon. We all saw it go in the vault.' The Doctor shook his head. 'He must have looked for it there first. But the vault is outside time and space. That could mean the arrow in the vault that I'm going to play for isn't the one he's after. It's no more than what we always thought it was. In which case none of us has the faintest idea where the Roogalator is. It's not an arrow. It could have taken any form. A nano-dot or a planet.'

Captain Cornelius smiled. 'Oh, we really should see more of one another, Doctor! There are few with our knowledge of the multiverse's quirks!' He got to his feet and, watched vigilantly by Captain Snarri, began to pace the cabin, the flickering firelight creating expressive reflections and shadows on his mask. 'Well, well. So General Force is playing a deeper game than we know, eh? Or he *thinks* he's playing a deeper game. Hmmm.' A small, slightly sinister laugh. 'He plays a subtle game, at the very least. But why should he take such a risk to board your ship if the arrow wasn't on it?'

'I'm not sure he *is* that subtle. Perhaps he honestly believed we were carrying the arrow.' The Doctor hesitated. 'He attacked our ship clearly believing that what he sought was hidden in the hat one of our passengers had had stolen but which was recovered before we left Peer™.'

'A *hat*? He was after a *hat*?'

'Exactly,' said the Doctor. 'And who knows how long he has been pursuing the hat or whatever part of the hat had the arrow in it?'

'The arrow was a decoration, perhaps?'

'But if so it must have been well hidden in the rest of the decoration because no one remarked on its being missing. In fact Mrs B-C, the owner of the hat, was clear that, as far as she could tell, *nothing* was missing. There was evidence that someone looked for an object hidden in the hat and didn't find it. It wasn't there or she would have said something.'

'She's not a lady to keep any disappointment to herself,' added Amy, fingering her necklace.

'And why would the prize for the contest we'll be playing when we reach Miggea be hidden amongst us?' asked the Doctor. 'It doesn't make any kind of sense.'

The captain nodded slowly. 'So we have a mystery. How, I wonder, are we going to solve it?'

Amy felt suddenly tired. She wanted to curl up in the big Stickley chair and drift off to sleep. She was finding it hard to be terrified by the most feared pirate in the galaxy. She was growing used to this, though; if she had learned one thing in her relatively short career it was to do with powerful men. Their actions might be dreadful, both ruthless and cruel, but they were sometimes surprisingly charming in person. And Captain Cornelius, there was no doubt, was very charming indeed.

Captain Snarri stood up to replenish their drinks. It was evident he was unhappy about the trend of the conversation.

'You're certain that Arrow isn't aboard your ship, Doctor?' Captain Cornelius accepted the VW.

'As certain as I can be, captain.' The Doctor took a sip of Vortex Water. 'As certain as I am that your old-fashioned sense of chivalry ensures us our freedom. We have nothing you want.'

Captain Cornelius sat down again, crossed his legs and stared thoughtfully into his fire. 'You're wrong there, Doctor.'

'Do you know where Frank/Freddie Force and their men are now?' asked the Doctor.

'We tracked them as far as Cygnus and then lost them. We thought they might be going home.'

'No clear idea of the system he was headed for?'

'I'm afraid not.' The captain reached to knock out his long-stemmed pipe in the grate. 'He was showing – you know – matter-chill they call it. Why he was so far out I didn't ask. I assumed his mission was of some importance. Maybe he'd brought his ship in via Cygnus. They can do that, I'm told. He had tracked us out from Venice. He followed the usual etiquette so we allowed him to board, though some of my men were against it. They had a notion the skins of Force's men would burst and send us all to our reward. Which, as you can imagine, is not likely to be a comfortable one for us. Are you a praying man, Doctor? You, captain? you Mlle Pond? Are any of you in the habit of ascribing a maker to all that?' And he waved his pipe to indicate eternity.

The Doctor did not answer. 'Did he come because you had something he wanted?' he asked instead.

'He offered me a huge reward if I could help him find it. I fear I sent him on his way. But I don't deny I was intrigued. If he has a method of sensing the thing he seeks, he must have known I did not have it.'

'He returned towards the Hub, you say.'

'Yes. I assume so. Our instruments lost him.'

The Doctor took another sip of Vortex Water.

'We are all seeking the same thing, yet not one of us has a clear idea what it is. Or, indeed, who has it. I only know we have a chance of winning it, fair and square, if we can get good enough replacements for those we lost in the storm.'

Captain Cornelius laughed spontaneously. 'You plan to win it?'

'Fair and square. How else can we get hold of it?'

'And if another team wins?'

'We explain that we need it?'

'For what?'

'If it is the stolen regulator or contains the elements of whatever mysterious stuff constitutes the regulator, we need to get it into the heart of the black hole where its components will presumably do their job and restore a proper sequence to the multiverse.'

'You think they'll agree?'

'I can only hope we will be able to demonstrate our need.' The Doctor sat back in his chair. He grinned. He shrugged.

'Hope for the best.'

Captain Cornelius drew on his pipe. It was impossible to judge his expression behind the mask.

'We'll get it,' Amy said. 'I know we will. Most followers of tournaments like this say we're the favourites.' She grinned. 'And I have a good-luck charm from the Bubbly Boys!' She tapped her necklace making the spheres rotate. She was showing off, she knew, and silently admonished herself. She was 21 and still behaving like a kid.

Captain Cornelius returned her smile. 'But you're two key players short. Your entire Second Fifteen is gone. Yes. I eavesdropped. If you'll forgive my presumption, you sound a little desperate, Mlle Pond. Even with a good-luck charm from Abberley and Co. What is it, by the way?'

Automatically she covered it with her spread hand. 'A very strange bit of jewellery,' she said, glaring at him. 'Some beads, which they pinched, as far as I could tell, from that horrible Captain Quelch. And gave to me. We have plan B.' She added, changing the subject so violently it left skid marks in the air.

Captain Cornelius's attitude had changed subtly. He seemed at once more alert and more relaxed.

'And if we fail,' put in the Doctor, 'what will happen to you in particular, captain, when dark tides run across the entire galaxy sucking out the light?'

'I rarely leave my ship, even when we reach our island port in the Dwarf.' The pirate shrugged. 'Without light we are nothing. We long ago let our auxiliaries run almost to empty. All that *colour* was dangerous on a ship of our kind. No doubt we'll freeze and die. The heat death of a star clipper, eh?' And he laughed. 'But the multiverse will die soon after, and I would hate to witness that. Only General Force is mad enough to crave that experience. I think we do have interests in common.'

'So you're proposing a compact of some kind?' The Doctor stood up and warmed his back against the fire before stepping politely aside.

'You seem to understand me pretty well, Doctor. I suppose you should. What do you say, Mlle Pond? Should we all join forces? It would be the end of me if the light went out. The end of us all, I'd guess. And what if we survived the end of the universe – the destruction of the multiverse, even – would we not be even more bored than we are now?'

'Perhaps.' The Doctor was thoughtful. 'I'm surprised that you, of all people, are seriously proposing we form an alliance.'

'It might be the only solution to any future difficulties. That arrow could be the oldest artefact in existence. Or it was stolen from our future and the ripples come all the way back to our here and now, mm?'

The Doctor lifted a sceptical eyebrow. 'Now we're getting into the realms of the supernatural, captain.'

'My scientists suggest the *materials* which constitute it are the key to understanding it, not the *form itself...*'

Impatiently, Captain Snarri stood up. 'If I could have your word that this is not a diversion to hold our attention while your pirates board our ship...'

'Certainly, captain.' The tall man put a forefinger under his Arlecchino mask and scratched his nose. He took a pull on his pipe. 'At some point, long ago, your Roogalator was removed from the very Hub of our cosmos and carried off. The thief who took it was an adventurer with no special motive except curiosity, the ability to negotiate an environment which would destroy the likes of us, and a greed for the power his curiosity brought him. He had discovered a kind of map which in turn led him to the regulator. He knew he had something crucial to the fundamental mechanics of the multiverse. So he tried to exert his own will upon it. By doing that he caused it to evade him by, of course, *changing its shape*.

'Because it was never replaced, the multiverse became less and less stable. Either Frank/Freddie Force is the original thief or he learned about the object *from* the original thief. Either way, he still believes he can use it to gain total power over Creation. And that, I fear, is the sum of what I know or have guessed.'

The Doctor rubbed his jaw. 'I can see how it is in our mutual interest. What do you say, Captain Snarri?'

'I say we've little choice and if the pirate wants neither blood, souls nor treasure, I'll cooperate to do what's in the best interests of my passengers.'

'Perhaps,' said Cornelius, 'we should settle details when we discover the Regulator and work out how to re-establish it at the centre of the multiverse? Assuming that's still possible. So let's agree to travel on together, at least for the time being. I have a small but up-to-date hospital aboard my ship. We can treat your injured. Save a few lives, with luck. And we have bots who could help you make some running repairs. If anything, the *Paine* is even better equipped than the *Gargantua*.'

'So. Let's talk practicalities. What's your price, Captain Cornelius?' Snarri was anxious to get the pirate off his ship.

'One thing now.' The masked man looked towards Amy. Again she felt that unfamiliar frisson. 'That's what I want for my assistance.' He pointed directly at Amy.

'*What?!*'

Unconsciously the Doctor took a step back, as if from a ticking bomb. 'You can't—'

'That necklace. My price.'

Captain Snarri burst out: 'This won't do. She's just an individual. She can't... she shouldn't—'

'Don't worry.' Grimly Amy removed her 'celestial necklace' and placed it into the captain's outstretched hand.

'There. Now you'll keep your word.'

He bowed.

Amy continued sharply. 'And there's a small price for giving you that. A personal price, you could call it.'

He waited.

'Captain Cornelius, would you let me see your ship? Not her secrets or anything. Just the ship. She's so beautiful!'

The captain's laughter was spontaneous. 'Why, of course, my dear. I was forgetting my manners. And you, Doctor – you will visit us, too, I hope?'

The Doctor sighed, smiled, and gave in to temptation. He told himself it was to keep a watchful eye on Amy.

Chapter 20

Happy Ships

WHILE HIS NANO-BOTS REPAIRED the big liner's wireless links and his engineering-bots crawled all over the battered brass and silver hull, taking charge of the major damage to the ship's superstructure and plates, Captain Cornelius followed at a distance, ready to help if the *Gargantua* got into any further difficulties. Amy, meanwhile, had been taken by the noncommittal Peet Aviv on a tour of the black clipper, marvelling at the system of pulleys and counterweights used to manipulate the sails, at her lockers full of exotic treasure, her galleys and pantries, her instruments designed to work entirely on reception of certain vocal codes, her guns, her crew made up of every form of intelligent life, half-flesh, all-flesh or metallic.

The *Paine* was familiar, in that she resembled an old-time clipper, and unfamiliar in that the far-future technologies were almost impossible to understand, but Amy remained fascinated with the life forms: long-necked ostriches with simian heads, large saurians, the strange, alien beauty of snake-faced women. She saw little that seemed significant to their particular interest but she couldn't help noticing the restless atmosphere aboard. The crew seemed generally terrified. These weren't the people she had expected to find, full of mocking confidence, anticipating the great wealth every creature of flesh or metal would take home with them. She almost felt sorry for them, especially when she realised they feared the dark tide with a superstitious credulity Amy found unpleasantly infectious.

She was led past buzzing gun bubbles full of blinding multicoloured energy, workshops, repair rooms and every kind of laboratory, where blinking lights and eerily coloured liquids mingled. But the atmosphere was horribly oppressive. Eventually she felt she could take no more and was glad when Peet Aviv escorted her back to Captain Cornelius's quarters where the Doctor was ready to return with her to their own ship.

Captain Snarri still didn't trust Cornelius. The Doctor convinced him that, whatever his many crimes, Cornelius followed his own strict code and was always as good as his word. Cornelius knew what had happened on Pangloss. 'Force, in short. Either deliberately or by mistake, the Antimatter Men attracted a dark tide. The storm destroyed everything except the core of the planet itself. They're lucky the star didn't go, too. That's Frank/Freddie for you when they lose their temper.' There was a chance, thought Cornelius, that some had survived below the planet's surface, but it was unlikely.

Amy returned with the Doctor to the *Gargantua* full of the wonders she had witnessed on her tour of the great starjammer. She kept quiet about her feelings concerning the atmosphere on board the *Paine*.

'It seems almost as big as the TARDIS inside,' she told Bingo, who had been waiting nervously for her to return. 'But then you don't know what the TARDIS is, do you?'

'The *Paine* is a big ship, then?'

'Not as big as this one, but still pretty big. Sails that are miles across. Well, you've seen them. They just don't look as big as they do when you're standing right underneath them, looking up. Captain Cornelius is…' She was going to say 'dishy' but she guessed this might confuse Bingo and hurt his feelings, so she said: 'Very tall. Mysterious. Probably pretty ruthless.'

'That's what I heard, too. Bit of a swordsman, I gather.' Bingo was an expert fencer.

'I'm sure he is.'

'But why did he let you two look around his ship just like that and come back here without giving us terms or anything? I mean, he's a bally pirate, isn't he? I thought you were mad to go in there with the Doctor. I was afraid I'd never see you again!'

'He's as worried about the dark tide as we are. He wanted to join forces. He's hoping that if we stick together we'll have a better chance of surviving. Apparently those tides are even worse out near the Rim.'

'I'd guess so. What with one black hole pulling our star systems one way and being pulled by an even more powerful one the other and this bally dark tide stuff all over the place, I'm getting a bit baffled, actually.' Bingo didn't think this was that much of an admission. He'd been rather baffled most of his life. 'I say, Amy, I was awfully worried about you while you were hobnobbing with that pirate johnny. Next time you take it into your head to do something like that, you'd better take me with you, you know.'

Suppressing a smile, Amy promised to let Bingo know next time she decided to take off after a pirate. She felt rather pleased by his solicitousness. It was an odd feeling. She wasn't altogether used to it.

'Well, young lady, did you pick up any clues?' The tone took her between the shoulder blades. She stiffened. She had almost forgotten that sound.

'Hello, Mrs Banning-Cannon.' Amy turned. 'Clues?'

'About my hat,' she announced with what might almost have been pride. 'It has been stolen *again*! From my cabin!'

'Oh, really? Must have happened during the storm, yes?' Bingo was doing his best to sound concerned. Only a few weeks ago he had been watching a V, where it turned out the crook committed the crime unknowingly having been struck on the head and hypnotised by the person who didn't want to be caught. Bingo wondered if the knock he had received on the head during the storm had stunned him in the same way. He was beginning to suspect himself of the robbery.

But if so, puzzled the hapless earl, what had he done with the swag?

The Doctor was giving him suspicious looks. Or so it seemed to poor Bingo who, with a strangled word of goodwill to the baffled Love of his Life, did his best to disappear while Mrs B-C continued with her tale of the Second Theft of a hat which, even she had to admit, was no longer worthy of the name. There was, after all, a new and better hatter supplying her with exotic headgear.

Why, the Doctor wondered, was anyone still concerned about that hat? 'Is there any chance,' he suggested hopefully, 'that the hat could have been sucked out into space and is even now circling our hull?'

'Not according to the crew.'

The Doctor ran his hand through his already well-tousled hair. 'Nobody spotted a pirate lurking about, I suppose?'

'It's possible one came aboard in disguise, but unlikely,' murmured Bingo.

'Besides which, Captain Cornelius gave his word he wouldn't let his men bother us,' Amy reminded them. 'I think it's a matter of pride with him. Crooks have principles like that. It probably makes them feel virtuous.'

'So we'll have to search the ship, I suppose.' Mrs B-C

looked as if she was about to roll up her sleeves there and then.

'There are rather more important issues, mother,' suggested Flapper, who had turned up in time to hear most of the exchange, 'than hunting for hats. We are being shadowed by the most notorious and feared pirate in the known universe and our ship is in serious danger of popping half her plates and plunging us all into the depths of space!'

'Jane!' declared her mother. 'I never thought to hear such disloyal words from you, of all people.'

'I'm being practical, mother.'

With anyone else Mrs Banning-Cannon might have escalated such an exchange to Code Red, but hearing these words from the apple of her maternal eye stopped her pretty suddenly in her tracks. Her jaw dropped. Her eyes widened. Her nose froze in mid-flare. A strangled sound came out of her throat. She said something like: 'Roospikentamee?' which others would later try to interpret, the general consensus being that what she thought she had said was 'Are you speaking to me?'

'Oh, really, mother!' her daughter answered and, turning on a heel which seemed specifically designed for such a manoeuvre, she exited the hall with an almost professional sweep of her skirt, closely followed by Mrs Banning-Cannon, who was followed at what he considered a slightly safer distance by Hari Agincourt.

The silence they left behind them was filled with a collective sigh from the Doctor, Amy Pond and Bingo, Earl of Sherwood.

The hat was, as far as any reasonable search could determine, well and truly gone. Every one of the *Gargantua*'s vast decks had been searched as thoroughly as possible by passengers and specially adapted crew bots. It was even established that the hat had not been hidden on the outside of the ship's hull. Mrs Banning-Cannon had talked Urquart Banning-Cannon into offering an extraordinarily large reward for its return. In Captain Snarri's firmly held opinion the hat was even now drifting in space some light years behind them. He had even sent a skiff back to check for any remains, but they had found only a few smears of organic body parts. And now, as they approached the Ghost Worlds, the search had been abandoned. The massive gravitational pull of the black hole required considerable energy from the *Gargantua* simply to stay on course. For the *Paine* it was all but impossible to resist the power of the so-called Little Rock.

Miggea's strange qualities, which permitted her to circle the Shwarzschild Radius without being drawn in and allowed her four planets Earth-like gravity could only be counteracted by the extraordinary engines of the *Gargantua*. The 'Shifter' system, the Ghost Worlds, should not logically have existed at all – and wouldn't have, if it hadn't been for their peculiar independence.

Amy did her best to recall what the Doctor had explained to her about their nature, though she knew as well as he did that even if he had written it all out as an equation, as he had tried to do once when discussing variable time speeds, it would have made her head ache. There came a point in descriptions of certain multiversal phenomena when not even an inhabitant of Algo could have plucked a tune from the maths. Amy had always admired brainy people who could calculate but, in spite of her natural intelligence, which made her guesses frequently pretty accurate to the Doctor's great delight, formal maths made her head hurt.

Miggea's astonishing gravitation, which kept her stable under conditions which would have long since destroyed any other star system, permitted her satellites to orbit in a complicated pattern around her, although at a considerable distance from their parent star. By similar flukes of mass and evolution, she made her eccentric progress through the countless variations of the multiverse. How this had come to be was equally mysterious. Her inexplicable adaptive qualities had hardly been guessed before her settlers, of which there were relatively few, discovered to their horror that she began quite literally to fade gradually from our universe, only to reappear in another universe, then another ad infinitum. Those still living in the system were adapted descendants of the original descendants. Only a handful of newcomers had settled there in recent centuries. That her planets had kept their orbit as faithfully as she kept hers was another of her qualities still mostly unexplained.

The Doctor told Amy that the Miggea system had a way of orbiting the multiverse and surviving. The only human being to come close to formulating a satisfactory theory had been an early Guide Sensor, the semi-legendary Lord Renark of the Rim, who had led, it was said, a huge percentage of the entire human race out of its original universe and into another which had then been thought to represent the multiverse. Renark had disappeared, as had his expedition. Some believed he was still in the black hole, others that the entire expedition had been recreated as a computer program using an earlier form of nano-technology whose secret had also been lost.

Every few years some optimistic soul would seek to recreate Renark's experiment and disappear in turn. If there was a way through to what some still called 'Renark's multiverse', there was certainly no way back, leading to what certain theoretical astrophysicists still referred to as Renark's Dilemma. Many a gig of text had been written in the attempt to solve that particular puzzle. Some argued that Renark had reproduced himself, deliberately or accidentally, on every multiversal plane. Others believed he had gone beyond the Radius into the black hole itself where he now hung for eternity, neither dead nor alive.

The Ghost Worlds, as the Miggea system had been called since the discovery of those singular properties, retained their secrets, but there was no doubt at all that they existed against most of the present laws of physics. Had they come into being in this universe or another? Did they really belong to the Second Aether?

Miggea was on the screens now, magnified so that it filled the ship's huge main V, installed for the benefit of passengers. Amy bit into an apple which had been freshly grown in the *Gargantua*'s repaired hydroponics, her eyes big with astonishment. She had not expected Miggea to be such a bright, lustrous blue. The sun was dancing with fiery gasses. She could easily believe, from what little she'd seen of it, that the Ghost Worlds had been born in the so-called Second Aether, in the spaces between each plane of the multiverse. It sounded crazy until you saw it. Maybe Captain Abberley and his Bubbly Boys came from here? She sighed. Now she was getting too fanciful. She was overtired.

As the *Gargantua* began to manoeuvre into her own orbit around Miggea, and the *Paine* tacked carefully into a wider, safer orbit, they heard Captain Snarri's voice as he contacted Travel Control on Murphy, giving their call signal and destination. At the top right-hand corner of the big screen they saw a puzzled pachydermid in a loud red and yellow check sweater pop something in his mouth and speak in a typical nasal accent. 'Murphy-Ganesh calling. We have you registering as an Axil fighter, *Gargantua*. Can you confirm your visual recognition as a G-class tour-liner? Our instruments are a bit confused.'

A line of code began to chatter at the bottom of the screen. 'Thank you, *Gargantua*. The last attempt to storm Murphy was unfortunately by a whole fleet disguised as a G-class.

Not a bad try except for the polka-dots. Welcome! Are you visiting any particular planet in our system?'

'Here for the games on Flynn,' the captain replied. 'And we've been in a pretty bad storm. Need to make some repairs and transfer some of our wounded, if possible. How are you off for hospital places? We have three vacuum-burn patients and a group of otherwise pretty badly broken-up interior injuries. The *Paine* came to our assistance and helped us with some of our injured. We lost a doctor and two radiographers in the storm.'

'We run a rather primitive section down here. Nearest sophisticated medical facility is at Cocokojoj in PrimZ, if you're able to get that far.'

'No problem, Murphy. We can put the passengers who came for the sports off on Flynn, get over to Coco and be back in time to meet you on a rerun. Any idea when you start shifting?'

'Shouldn't be long now, *Gargantua*. When we come back in is a bit harder to predict as you're probably aware. Are you sending down tenders?'

'Two to Murphy. There's another due on Cohan and the majority are for Flynn. Can you take yours now?'

'Give us a couple of hours to prepare, *Gargantua*. There's always the chance that we'll start shifting before we know it, and we need to build a few emergency procedures into our receptors. OK?'

'Go ahead, Murphy. We'll wait.'

Hearing a sound behind her, Amy turned to see that Captain Cornelius had joined them on the V. He had discarded his papier maché Arlecchino and was wearing the simple metal mask which had given him his nickname 'Ironface'. Strangely it humanised him more. Amy could see why some of the Vs about him called him handsome. He was taller than anyone on the ship and exuded the air of self-containment she had first noticed about him. He wore the same dark blue uniform he had worn when they had first met.

'Hello, Captain Cornelius. What can we do for you?' The Doctor was concentrating on the other screens.

'Forgive me for interrupting, Doctor.' Cornelius spoke softly. 'I'm curious to see Miggea. I've heard so much about her over the years but of course it has never been possible for my ship to come in so close. She's an impressive star. Shall you be going down to Murphy?'

'We'll wait until we get to Flynn before making any kind of landfall. Even then the ship's too big to bring down.' The Doctor smiled. 'Chances are we'd blow Flynn out of the sky if we tried. The *Gargantua* was built in the K.H. Brunner off-world yards and like most big ships has never flown through an atmosphere. We'll be using tenders to get all the passengers down. Has the *Paine* ever made planet-fall?'

Cornelius smiled slowly. 'Only in Never-Never Land, Doctor.'

Amy was surprised by this reference. 'I didn't know you were a fan of Peter Pan, captain!'

'I wouldn't say I was a fan exactly. But we took a ship many years ago which was carrying a couple of time capsules a collector had found on one of Old Earth's neighbours. Not only the discs they used but a small player, also. I transferred them to my V-files. Part of my personal collection at home.'

'So "home" isn't your ship?'

'Let's say the *Paine's* one of my homes.' He smiled. 'I doubt if Captain Hook himself was anxious to publicise everywhere he lived.'

Amy realised she was dropping her guard. She had to be careful. Even on the V-screen Captain Cornelius was proving too charming to be trusted.

After Murphy had taken their remaining wounded, the ship began to warm up and turn for the next part of their journey to Cohan, where they stopped very briefly before continuing on to Flynn. A matter of hours. And there she was!

She did look very Earth-like. Soon they would be standing on her surface. Amy began to feel very excited. Flynn had been their destination for such a long while and there had been so many setbacks along the way, that she had begun to feel she would never see the world where the Re-Enactment Games were traditionally played. The Terraphiles themselves, of course, did not know the world except from what they had seen on the V. Where Murphy, O'Brian and Cohan had all been terraformed on Eirish themes, Flynn had been terraformed to model the English Cotswolds and the hobbitoid Shire, with rolling, grassy drumlins, woods, lakes and rivers, thatched cottages of butter-coloured stone, villages and greens, crooked chimneys blowing friendly smoke, all of it resembling a fantasy landscape even more comfortably nostalgic than the Peer™ planets.

Now they neared Flynn, she could see that parts of the planet were thickly forested and full of the kind of wildlife which had once occupied the countryside where she had spent most of her life. Unexpectedly she felt a pang of homesickness for the world she had left behind. Why on earth should she feel so sad? It wasn't as if she would never see her village again.

Or was it? Bucolic as she looked, Flynn was part of the Shifter System – the Ghost Worlds—and the Ghost Worlds could be very dangerous indeed. She, the Doctor and the Terraphiles would not be the first to ride the Miggea worlds on their 'sideways' orbit through the multiverse and never return. She had to remind herself that the TARDIS had been programmed to rendezvous on Flynn. But what had happened to those missing people she had no idea, though it was thought they had disembarked on one of billions of possible 'planes' and either settled there or perhaps even been killed. Amy experienced a rare moment of self-pity. She was far too young to die. There was so much more for her to see before she returned to the old familiar places! *If* she ever returned. Hadn't the Doctor told her that the dark tide could start spreading out – backwards and forwards? Engulfing everything that had ever existed or would ever exist in that strange, destructive gravity?

'Pull yourself together, Amy Pond!' she told herself not for the first time since she had met the Doctor in her back garden some fifty thousand years in the past. And she felt the familiar pang, that she might never be able to tell anyone about her adventures and all the things she had seen. Maybe it was for the best. What did it mean if every single world of the multiverse were to die? Never to have been? Never *to* be? That was, after all, logical. She imagined the dark tide as a kind of overflowing lake of *nothingness* which engulfed existence and then somehow engulfed itself...

She became aware of Captain Cornelius still on the V. His smile was melancholy, filled with a peculiar longing.

'Are you looking forward to putting your feet on a real planet, captain?' she asked.

He shook his head regretfully.

'You're keeping my celestial necklace, I suppose?' She still hoped he had only borrowed it.

He shook his head briefly his eyes still melancholy, sardonic, bowed and said: 'I hope to return it next time we meet in person. Assuming all our coordinates—' The signal faded. He disappeared, replaced by an image of his ship.

An hour later the PA sounded, warning them to be ready for planet-fall. A tremor ran through the *Gargantua* as the monstrous vessel was prepared again for a disembarkation. Amy had her bag packed, like the rest, and had suited up for safety during their descent. She and the Doctor joined the queue for the second tender, which would take the teams down to Flynn. The Banning-Cannons were taking the third tender. Mrs Banning-Cannon continued to complain about her stolen hat but, since she was already wearing one of Mr Toni Woni's latest exclusive creations, her protests rang a bit hollow. She saw Hari Agincourt throw one final look of anguished parting at Flapper and then they were aboard Tender 12 and the big airlocks swung shut.

As they belted themselves into their comfortable seats, Amy was sure that she caught a whiff of the sea. She was reminded of taking the hovercraft to France. She sniffed again. She had not been mistaken. Who was it the Doctor had told her about? The aliens who smelled so strongly of the sea when they were nervous? She was glad when the Doctor sat down beside her. He could be oddly comforting at times like this. His eyes twinkled and he was as excited as a schoolboy taking his first trip in an aeroplane. He winked at her as he buckled up. It seemed years since they had boarded the *Gargantua* and Amy would be glad to set foot on natural ground again. Particularly such picturesque ground. She wondered what Flynn had originally looked like before the terraformers had changed her. Perhaps she had been landscaped by the Banning-Cannons or their ancestors?

Behind her, Bingo Lockesley slid into his seat. 'Jolly exciting, what?' He frowned over his buckles and straps and eventually got the hang of them. 'We're going to have to play awfully well.' He turned to Pom'ik'ik, one of the Tourists' best fielders, whose normally yellow scales had turned a faint greenish-blue, showing that he was nervous. 'You worrying about the games, old boy, or just the trip down?'

'Actually,' said the Aldebaran, 'I was hoping Miggea wouldn't start shifting while we were in transit. Does anyone know what happens at a time like that?'

'I'm not sure anyone's survived to tell us, old man!' And

Bingo let out a loud laugh indicating something of his own nervousness. Then, remembering Amy, he leaned forward and patted her shoulder. 'Don't worry, old thing, there are plenty of warnings before she starts to move. I've read up on the whole process. The tender will be waiting. The reason she's still here is because she's somehow protected in her orbit through the multiverse. As I understand it, it's to do with the equilibrium of her various gravitational fields. I mean, she'd look like a wreck if there was any danger, wouldn't she?'

'All passengers please lock safety harness,' came a robot voice over the intercom. Amy settled deeper into her seat, thinking again how much like one of those huge new international airbuses the ferry was with her two decks. The main difference was that there were no windows. The view of the outside was shown on a large screen on the seatbacks in front of each passenger. There came a sudden throbbing sound and an electric tingling sensation. Bot attendants began to move up and down the aisles. They seemed to be checking on something. Again the robot voice sounded. 'This is our second and final message. Will passengers please lock safety harness. All passengers not already situated are kindly requested to take their places.'

The pilot's voice came over the intercom. 'Very sorry, everyone. We seem to be registering an extra passenger. Nothing to worry about. Just a glitch caused by the recent storm. We'll do a manual count and then we'll be off.'

Amy heard a buzz of enquiring voices as the bots rolled up and down the aisles checking the numbers until at last the pilot's voice came through again. 'No problem. All's well. Please prepare for take-off.'

Seconds later, the ferry to Flynn was casting off smoothly from the big passenger ship and turning sluggishly in space.

Amy watched in fascination as the ship fell through blue-white clouds into a sky as clear as a lake, then levelled off and slowly crossed a range of the same pale green hills she had seen on the V-screens. Although much of its colouring was artificial, the planet was if anything more beautiful than its pictures. Herds of deer looked up as the ship passed and flights of exotic birds floated towards them before turning away, heading for the horizon. The great sapphire-jade sun sank into the ocean and then rose again behind them as they spiraled down towards a stretch of grey-black concrete where small freighters and passenger boats stood on their launch pads.

Aboard the ferry the excited terraphiles crowded around their screens, pointing out the beauties of the planet. Amy and the Doctor speculated on the population of Flynn which could not be very considerable. The paucity of ships indicated this.

'From what I've learned,' the Doctor told her, 'there are only a few thousand inhabitants of the entire system. There were, of course, many more when the planets were first terraformed, but that was before people discovered Miggea's strange qualities. Sometimes it seems the system returns only minutes after she left but the inhabitants have gone through several generations. Even without her peculiar orbit, Miggea would still be subject to the black hole's influence on her planets. The terraformers were able to fix Flynn's appearance, but beneath those rolling hills, woods and lakes all kinds of changes are taking places. The landscapes as a result become horribly treacherous and give shelter to a whole variety of bizarre creatures. Outside the settlements you must be wary at all times. I've seen people go mad, their flesh melting and transforming before their eyes as planets like these collapse and reform in a matter of hours. What you see one moment has a very different aspect the next. Believe me, Amy, trust little – especially your senses.'

'Warning to all passengers. In five minutes we shall be coming in to land. Please prepare.'

Amy had heard little of the engines in space but now they roared and shook as the ship fired her retro-rockets, positioning herself for a landing. Then came a stomach-churning sensation of falling, a further massive blast and the ship shook as she began to descend. The shaking became a trembling, like a horse ridden too hard and then was quiet.

'Flynn,' said the Doctor a little unnecessarily.

Amy raised a sarcastic eyebrow.

She had to admit that it was good to breathe fresh, natural atmosphere after such a long time in an artificial environment. They were taken by air-buses to the special accommodation prepared for them, arranged as a series of thatched cottages. They each held up to eight people and were built around a green large enough to accommodate a ground where the players could practise all the games they would have to play in the coming Tournament.

The games were worrying Bingo Lockesley. They were still two players short and were due to begin their first serious match in two days' time. Bingo was wondering where he was going to find a good fielder and an archer before then. He was hoping that Flynn, since it was after all the major venue for the games, might have a few decent amateur players. As soon as he had put his bag in his room he left for the local hostelry, the Blue Barsoomian, to have a drink and ask a few questions.

The regulars at the tavern were delighted to be enjoying a shant with one of the stars of the following week's Tournament and, when Bingo asked, they were only too pleased to recommend their best players: 'Mad' Mac McLachan and Old Fred Townsend. A polite enquiry gave Bingo the information that Mr McLachan was their top archer and that he would be out of the lock-up in three and a half weeks, having been found guilty at the local assizes for clocking the landlord of the Three Earthlings with a two-pint shant of Peregrine's Best. But Old Fred Townsend was free and they were sure he would be honoured to substitute for the Gentlemen's missing fielder. He would be in later, if Bingo would care to wait, which he did.

When Old Fred arrived, his step was a little unsteady, partly because of his evident pleasure in the local beverages but mostly because his left eye was being regrown at the eye clinic on Murphy. Bingo wished him well and asked who he thought their second-best fielder might be.

The Doctor and Amy found Bingo later in the snug of the Blue Barsoomian. He had partaken a little too enthusiastically of Peregrine's Best and felt, as he put it, about as miserable as a three-legged cat at a greyhound race.

Bingo would later wonder if the Peregrine's plus his high regard for the young woman, rather than his good sense, played too great a part in his decision to take Amy up on her earlier offer to field for them. And, since it had seemed churlish to ask one of the women and not the other, had it been the wisest choice he could have made? Had he been nuts to suggest to Flapper that she might like to try out her archery skills at the targets the following morning?

Chapter 21

The Tournament of Terraphiles

THE COINS BEING TOSSED and the order of team play determined, all the Terraphiles, the Gentlemen, the Visitors and the Tourists, retired to Flynn's lavishly appointed pavilion to enjoy a few friendly pints of Vortex Water before beginning the serious business of broadswording, jousting, quintaining, nutcracking and, ultimately, whacking. Amy and Flapper, having done pretty well that morning, were now officially members of the First Fifteen, allowing the Gentlemen to qualify, and had confided, one to the other, that they weren't at all sure about their own sanity, having volunteered to play in matches which, the Doctor had told them, might well determine the fate of the multiverse.

At this stage the various species tended to group together. The seven humans of the Gentlemen consisted rather contradictorily of W.G. Grace, Flapper Banning-Cannon, Amelia Pond, Old Bill Told, Hari Agincourt, Bingo Lockesley and the Doctor. By far the largest non-human group were Judoon who were inclined to link arms and sing, very loudly, songs which, happily, only Judoon knew to be utterly filthy. The Gents' complement of rhinocerids were three superb and highly aggressive all-rounders. Their only canine team mate, an Arfid from Sirius, tended to prefer the company of humans. Uff Nuf O'Kay was an outstanding wotsit keeper, able to catch arrers in all four hands, his mouth and his prehensile tail. His best friend was the handsome centaur H'hn'ee. The bovine whackswoman N'hoo was inclined to hang out with the younger Judoon who were all secretly in love with her. The two avians were Aaak, the massive hawkperson, and S'ee'ee, the equally large sparrowman whose skills at archery were the subject of many songs on his own planet where at least eighty statues had been erected for him. That said, S'ee'ee was considered boastful and, while he had been cleared by a court of his peers several years earlier, was thought somewhat cold blooded and insufficiently remorseful of an accidental death during a friendly with another avian team on his home planet. He and Aaak were not close, and S'ee'ee was at the far end of the bar chatting up an attractively crested Twitterian, one of the Tourists' best whackers.

The energies of most of the humans in their team were spent telling Amy and Flapper that they were rather good and nobody could have known from their playing at the practice nets the previous couple of days that they weren't seasoned professionals. Hari and Bingo, in particular, devoted most of their waking time to getting the pair's game up to scratch. They had, in truth, become pretty passable players.

Everyone was speculating on the next morning's weather. Flynn had in fact been picked in part on account of its variable weather which was thought to be caused by Miggea's relationship to the multiverse.

The evening ended early with much shaking of hands and slapping of backs and assurances of good luck, best teams winning and so forth. Everyone went to their beds early. Only the Doctor stayed up later than the others, his eccentric and complex brain rattling away like a downhill express.

He had a feeling that this tournament was going to be the most important in the history of existence. Unless he put the pieces of the puzzle he had been working on since he and Amy first heard that oddly familiar voice from the area of the Sagittarian Schwarzschild Radius, only nothingness would extinguish their past, present and future leaving a true cold silent void.

What part did Captain Cornelius play in all this? And, most important of all, what caused the running of the dark tides through the universe, perhaps the multiverse, creating horrendously destructive storms, stealing the very light from all the worlds? How, if at all, were these events connected? Wasn't it stupid of him to play these apparently frivolous tournaments and place so much importance on winning the so-called Arrow of Artemis? Surely it couldn't be the mysterious Roogalator? The experience of almost a thousand years told him that the danger was real, yet nothing in that experience had ever brought him the problems he was now grappling with. This was nothing less than a crime against Creation. Surely even Frank/Freddie Force, insane as they were, were not capable of such an act?

Some of the puzzle's parts were beginning to come together, but he knew in his bones there was little time left to find the others. Time, in fact, was quite literally running out.

Eventually his thoughts drifted slowly into dreaming. Since the dreams were no better or worse than the realities he decided he might as well go to bed.

In the Doctor's dreams, various Greek gods and goddesses took part in the Olympic Games. The prize was Life itself. He was the only member in his team. They called him Mercury, Harlequin. Black tides curled around his feet. He walked as if in thick mud, hardly able to draw one leg after the other.

Amy was not exactly enjoying a restful sleep, either. Her dreams, however, were more immediate and to do with her failing to whack back arrow after arrow until suddenly Frank/Freddie turned up and caught the last one. Waving it, they put out Miggea's indigo sun. Then they put out Earth's. Then they put out every star in the universe and she could hear them chuckling with all the self-loathing and malice in Creation ready to suffer for eternity as long as every sentient thing suffered with them. She woke up, her hands clutching for the Arrow of Artemis.

And in his own, rather narrow bed, Robin 'Bingo' Lockesley dreamed that he had won the final game of the Tournament and Amy Pond had agreed to be his bride. But why was she wearing a black dress?

Bingo awoke next morning with mixed feelings. At his best he knew he could probably beat the finest archers in the galaxy, including W.G. Grace, but he had been known to have some very bad days. He had a horrible notion that this was going to be one of them.

Amy, on the other hand, showered with a song in her heart and another on her lips. Why she felt so cheerfully confident when she had spent such a terrible night, she had no idea. She tossed the shampoo into the air and caught it. She even tossed the slippery soap and caught that. If only she could do the same with arrows, things were going to go pretty well, she thought.

The Doctor sat on the edge of his bed trying to read back his notes. He had a nagging feeling there was something missing from them. Someone who was playing a crucial part in the whole scenario. The Force Brothers and the Antimatter Men? Peggy Steele, the Invisible Crackswoman? Brian Abberley and the Bubbly Boys? Captain Quelch, whom he was sure he'd seen lurking in Ketchup Cove? Who else? He was seriously wishing he had not hidden the TARDIS so thoroughly. He was sure it was around here somewhere. Had they stipulated an ETA? No, it was probably connected to an event. He should have thought this through, he knew, before he hid it. He had a decided feeling that this wasn't the first time he'd sort of mislaid the TARDIS.

He stumbled into the shower. He had sent his clothes for cleaning just before he had gone to bed and they were hanging outside his door, ready to wear. As he got dressed, the birds started to sing. He pressed the button to open his blinds and there was that deep blue sun rising over the dark, burnt orange and strawberry-coloured hills. He flexed his fingers.

Today was the day he swung his sledgehammer. And every nut he cracked had to be a winner. He was going up against two of the best in the game, both of them Judoon – one from the Visitors and one from their great rivals, the Tourists. They had been competing for years and had incredible muscle control, swinging huge, beautifully balanced hammers. The Doctor's hammer, of course, would not be nearly as heavy. The sport took bodyweight and species into consideration, among other things. This morning would determine which hammerer would play the other. He felt more confident than he had done the day before, even though, when he checked his V, the bookies were favouring both Judoon over him. More ominously, the bookies were giving both rival teams better odds than they were giving the Gentlemen.

He met Amy outside on her way to breakfast. She had also seen the odds, and yet she too was smiling.

'Are you reconciled to losing?' he asked.

'No way!' She laughed in his face. 'Now we know the odds we have a better idea what we're playing against. What we need to do. Is that nuts, Doctor?'

'There's no better way of taking your opponent's measure,' he said. 'That's what I used to be told at the Academy. An overconfident opponent is a beatable opponent. Of course, those professors weren't always proven right...' The Doctor shook his head as if to get rid of unwanted thoughts. He hummed to himself, avoiding Amy's eye.

She knew only a little bit about his past on Gallifrey, and she also knew there were some subjects she should not bring up.

'Let's go and get some breakfast,' she said.

Chapter 22

Tournament Time

HEFTING HIS HUGE HAMMER, the Doctor judged the nut seated at the regulation angle to the nutting pad. He had to make every crack count. The hammer had to be brought down at a particular spot and a properly judged speed or the nut as well as the shell itself would be crushed. The object was to crack the shell and leave the nut itself whole and unharmed. Few people could achieve this with ordinary nutcrackers or a fairly light coal hammer. Only thoroughly trained nutsmen (or 'crackers') could achieve what the Doctor would have to do over and over again until all ten nuts of the first round had been cracked. He was relieved when a Judoon from the Tourists won the first toss, even though he could choose the type of nut he would crack.

Watched by a keen audience of 'shell-faces', as fans of the sport were called, the huge Judoon fixed his visor in place, flexed his powerful muscles, spat on his hands and picked up his mighty hammer. The white-gloved Gondarlian nutter (who was also the umpire) stepped forward to place the regulation Brazil – a hard nut to crack at the best of times – in position and then step back. The representative of the Visitors checked the positioning of the nut to his own satisfaction and gave the thumbs-up. Taking long, deep breaths, the Judoon lifted his sledgehammer above his head. It shone like silver as he shifted his feet in the sand, wriggled his legs and arms a little and then, with a loud Judoon war-snort, brought the hammer down. The tough shell appeared to be untouched by the hammer as he stepped back. Then it fell into two neat halves, revealing a pristine nut, ready to eat. The crowd applauded loudly and enthusiastically with cries of 'Well cracked, sir!' and 'Nutted!'

A popular player with the crowd, the Judoon acknowledged its applause with a modest (for a Judoon) bow and stepped back courteously as the second coin was tossed and called. Once more the Doctor lost the toss and watched keenly while a second Judoon lumbered up to the nutting pad, cheered by a large number of the audience. He lifted his hammer in acknowledgement. He was very definitely the favourite.

Again the Brazil was placed and a white-gloved representative of the Visitors checked it. Again the huge Judoon judged it with the naked eye, hefted his sledgehammer and swung suddenly, expertly, and the nut fell into two perfect halves.

Wild cheers again for the favourite.

When his turn came, the Doctor felt like a midget up against giants. His only applause came from his team's immediate supporters. His hammer felt like lead. For a moment he hesitated, then adjusted his hands on the shaft while the white-gloved nutter stepped forward. The Brazil was placed and Bingo, representing the Gents, came to observe and then accept the positioning. Now the Doctor stepped up, lifted his hammer high over his head, shifted his feet a little in the sand, and struck. There came a gasp from the audience and for a moment he felt he had checked the blow too soon. Then, in relief, he saw the two sides fall and heard his supporters cheer. The first round was a draw.

Place. Swing. Crack. Place. Swing. Crack.

The Doctor's turn came round again. So far the cracksmen were level. All were aiming for a clean round. The Doctor was beginning to gain confidence but he knew he had to be careful and marshal all the skill he had. The game had already begun to slow. Characteristically, Judoon were naturally competitive but tended to lose self-control if put in a weak position. The Doctor knew that his best chance was to draw ahead by even the smallest margin and use the Judoon's natural impatience against them. So far he knew he had been lucky. That luck would not hold much longer, especially at Change of Nut, when the next of the four kinds of competition nuts was brought into play.

Sadly, on his fourth swing, he proved this spectacularly. The hammer came down on his first walnut. Somehow he misjudged. The muscles of his upper left arm twitched uncontrollably and the hammer descended with huge force on the nut, smashing it to pieces and sending fragments showering all over the place.

One of his opponents said something so rude in Judoon that he spluttered and almost choked on his own grunting laughter. This set the other Judoon guffawing, too, so that the pair could hardly hang on to their hammers when, to their astonishment, the Doctor said, in perfect Southern Judoon:

'Now, now, gentlemen, you would not wish such language to be heard by your mothers, I hope! Assuming you know who they are.'

Whereupon the first Judoon asserted that he would be happy to use the Doctor's head for his next turn with the hammer if that would make him feel any better, and the second added that if his rival Judoon cared to knock it off he would gladly give that head to the village children to use for their next polo match.

And so on.

273

Until the Doctor asked him if his horn had come loose and been lost amongst bits of shell because it had been so small it was impossible to tell. This made the Judoon turn bright brown. If there is one thing guaranteed to upset a member of his great race it is a disparaging remark about his horn. He offered that he would be more than willing to give the Doctor an idea about the size of his horn by, in his own coarse phrase, sticking it where the sun didn't shine. He followed this remark with a noise vaguely reminiscent of a speedboat running aground on mud, which the Doctor recognised immediately as the Judoon version of what the English once called a raspberry, the Americans knew as a Bronx cheer and the mole people of Juno Major knew as a reverse-frrrrrmp.

Eventually, the umpire stepped in and insisted all three contestants shake hands like gentlemen and apologise, which was done, not without a moment's hesitation on the part of the two Judoon.

Both Judoon then embarrassed themselves considerably by smashing their own nuts rather noisily and drawing some loud laughter not only from the Doctor's supporters but from their own. The Doctor saw that he now had the advantage. Worse than being booed for making a fault, the Judoon feared becoming the subject of amusement.

The next three games were won by the Doctor and then each of the two Judoon, so that the Gentlemen were still one game behind.

The final Change of Nut was to a pecan, the hardest regulation nut to crack with a sledgehammer owing to the relative softness of its shell. This would be the deciding Change unless they came to a draw between two of the players in which case a tie-breaker would be brought out, the most difficult of all – a chestnut. By some miracle, as the Doctor saw it, the Visitors' Judoon was eliminated. The final was now between him and the Judoon from the Tourists.

The chestnut was brought out.

Place. Swing. Crack. Place. Swing. Crack.

Another chestnut.

Place. Swing. Crack. Place. Swing. Crack.

The Doctor was sweating visibly and both competitors were flagging. Yet still no clear winner had been decided.

Place. Swing. Crack.

The Judoon was puffing and panting, frustrated that he could not easily beat the Doctor. Muttering and fuming, smelling noticeably of sweat salt, the Judoon took careful aim, swung his hammer and – smashed the chestnut to pulp.

The play had taken all afternoon. To his own utter amazement, the Doctor had squeaked into first place. The next day would be the first of the equine events played by all teams, involving the quintain, while the final event would be the jousting. This would be followed by the broadswording event. Only on the fourth day would the serious team game begin and the first of several whackit matches be played, each lasting at least three days. The Doctor was glad that there was no other part of the tournament likely to rest entirely on his shoulders, though, with untried substitutes, the Gentlemen were bound to have a very hard time of it indeed.

That evening in the saloon bar of the Blue Barsoomian, the Doctor was fêted by team-mates who no longer wore the air of a team which had already lost. Amy proposed a toast which was seconded by Flapper and Hari.

'To the Doctor. Saving the day!'

The Doctor had never felt at once so pleased and so burdened by responsibility. While the Gentlemen celebrated the winning of their first round, he was already wondering what strategy their captain, Bingo Lockesley, planned for the whackit matches. And so far, in spite of his promises to produce the missing Roogalator, Captain Abberley had not yet made his appearance.

Had he been lying about knowing where to find it? Did Quelch have it? Quelch always liked to pretend he was a major player when in fact he rarely was.

Or had he, the Doctor wondered, been completely deceiving himself?

'So what do you think, Bingo? Will we get the Arrer if we win?' He spoke to the Earl of Lockesley, but he was looking hard at Mr Banning-Cannon. The Earthman seemed startled.

'We're bound to win,' said Bingo, 'so we're bound to get the Silver Arrow, Doctor.'

'I admire your confidence, sir.' Mr Banning-Cannon held up a guilty shant. He had misjudged these lads. Spending so much time in their company, he had developed something of a liking for the Terraphiles. He would be taking some great ideas home. Money in the bank, this trip. 'Can I get anyone anything?'

'The Arrow will be ours. It will,' Bingo said. 'I know it. We'll win it. Do you know why, chaps?'

'Why, Bingo?' asked Amy, smiling at him. She had to love his innocent confidence.

'Because it's so important to us,' he said. 'You need it, don't you, Doctor? To straighten the multiverse out. That's what you're doing for us.'

'I told you I admired your confidence,' broke in Mr B-C, who was enjoying himself increasingly. 'Humans are remarkable in that respect.'

Bingo was surprised. 'You speak as if you're not one of us. But you are, aren't you?'

'Almost.' Mr B-C gestured with his glass and laughed loudly. 'Half-human, anyway, according to my wife.' He offered the decanter.

'Better not,' said Bingo. 'You know. Important game

tomorrow and all that. You want us to do what's right, don't you? I can tell you're a decent chap at heart. One of us. You want to see Mrs B-C present it to the winning team, eh, and you want that team to be—'

Mrs Banning-Cannon's powerful voice rang out from the private bar. 'All I want to find out is who stole my hat. The authorities here are absolutely useless. I was in the magistrate's office half the day! And could they offer so much as a clue? They gave me nothing but lame excuses. They said it was stolen outside their jurisdiction. I told him that all the likely suspects were bound to be here. We left no one on the ship did we? Except bots? I have learned a great deal about the police forces of half the universes on this trip. Where's my daring Doctor? He'll know what to do.'

The Doctor was heading for the door. 'Early night,' he said. 'Big game tomorrow.'

'I think I'd better call it a day too,' said Amy and about half the others there in chorus.

Mrs Banning-Cannon was left wondering why the pub had suddenly emptied.

Chapter 23

The Rising Sun

FOR A TIME THE Tournament followed a leisurely predictable course. Everywhere you looked were people in the formal 'greens' which showed them to be professional Terraphile Re-Enactors: Lincoln Green Sherlock hats, Lincoln Green hooded capes, Lincoln Green doublets, hose and boots with long toes which suited some of the competitors but did not, for instance, do much for a Judoon.

The Doctor proved a good all-rounder, doing some sturdy work at the various games allowing players to qualify for the serious matches ahead. He was knocked off his centaur more times than he might have liked at quintain, but he conducted himself usefully in the jousting. Amy and Flapper were, they both agreed, lucky to qualify, but they made it. Nano-tech tabs had helped them enormously, but natural skill could not be taught. Flapper, in fact, discovered a genetic talent for Skipping the Landlord, and Amy was unpleasantly surprised by how well she did at Hanging the Serf (a straw one these days – real ones wriggled and cursed too much for a family sport).

The beautiful deep blue of the sun spread its gorgeous light across amber and rust-coloured hills. Apart from the colours, Flynn might have been Old Old Earth, dreaming in some perpetual summer.

The Doctor said nothing of his own discomforting thoughts, remembering Edwardian England confident in her power to spread peace and justice across the world at the very moment before the first Great War began. He did his best to smile and join in the fun. Everyone's attention was on the games. The spectators were having a good time. Only someone who took pleasure in spreading anxiety would possibly want to spoil this mood. After all, he thought, forcing a grin and accepting a pint in the Blue Barsoomian the day before the first whackit match, this might be the last time they ever actually enjoyed life again.

The choice of order of play went to the Tourists who chose as first opponents the Visitors, believing they could pretty easily defeat the Gentlemen if they first beat the other team. They would be fresh for the first game. This gave the Gentlemen little to do but practise and observe. Both their rivals had Second Fifteens they could draw upon, though the rules concerning this were a bit complicated, which gave them a further advantage, and both were pretty much on top form.

The players in their fresh 'greens', some dressed in green armour consisting of leg, arm and body covering, huge helmets with visors and shoulder pads, made their way from the pavilion to the pitch. They looked magnificent outlined against the pulsing disc of the sun.

The first day's play had a few surprises, however, when J'n, a saurian who was the Visitors' second-best archer and a useful whacker, was caught by an arrow shot by Je'I'me Polucks, the famous half-Spooni known as the Battling Bow-Wright because he had made his own equipment as a poor boy in the infamous Jelly Ghetto on Ethel. Polucks took four more targets that afternoon, establishing a sticky off hundred which could not be regained in a hurry, though Argentino, the Visitors' star, would do it if anyone could. In fact, Argentino had been watching from the pavilion, and Amy could almost hear him gearing himself up to get that supplemental and change it in for spins. But meanwhile the spectators were applauding on both sides.

After that things settled in to a good, calm thwick-slamp of arrows being shot and arrows being whacked, with the Visitors keeping their lead for the next day and into the following morning until the captain decided to bring in Argentino. No one could have guessed that Argentino's mother had been a lab rat. He was tall, fit, personable, with a shock of white-blond hair that would have let him model for some great V-roles a few hundred years earlier, before public taste changed. His diamond-sharp blue eyes and his wide, honest features made him the darling of the lady spectators. He was the player to watch.

Standing on the pavilion deck, Mickey Argentino casually strung his bow, slipped his quiver over his back, and strolled onto the pitch to wild applause. Sum'in, the Cairene Dodger, was caught for 20 and Jill Jay managed to get to 29 before the cunningly placed arrow was caught off-slate by Kali-Kali rising into the air as if on winged feet, gracefully shooting the arrow back and slipping it past the wotsit keeper into the heart of the wotsit itself. Amy was sorry to see Jill be taken off so quickly. They had become friendly, since Jill claimed Scottish ancestry and wanted to hear anything Amy could tell her about Mackintosh the Tea Maker and so on. Amy had done her best not to bring Jill down too heavily on certain facts, like haggis-warrens, which she couldn't fudge and remain honest.

By now the Visitors had no advantage, but the Tourists still needed a good hundred rounds to win. This was first-class playing and, for another two hours until teatime, Argentino kept up a steady and varied strategy, sinking one 380 after another. When they broke, even the surliest Judoon on the other team could not help but congratulate Mickey A.

After tea, Argentino strode in to shoot against Pilliom Rekya, who was the best whacker left and a bit of a dark horse. Pilliom whacked Argentino's first arrow to left far point where O'Gruff caught it in a beautiful spinning lift, returning it to Brown at the Visitors' end wotsit. Brown attempted to slip it into the target with a millisecond to spare before Argentino's startled gaze just as something flickered in the early evening sunlight. From horizon to horizon the sky glowed blood red, and they all felt the ground shift beneath their feet.

The Doctor spoke quietly from behind Amy. 'I don't think that was nature responding to a fine bit of playing. I'm afraid that's Miggea getting ready to shift.' He paused, frowning. 'Oh! Oh, bother! I've just realised I might have made one rather crucial miscalculation…'

As umpires conferred, Argentino came off the Tournament pitch, his expression one of quiet resolution, his already unstrung bow over his shoulder. He saw the Doctor and lifted his heavy eyebrows to show that he knew his luck had turned. He didn't blame the sun any more than he would blame the rain, which now began to pour from sudden black clouds with tropical force. Besides which, he had scored the equaliser and left his team considerably better off. With the rain thundering down and everyone hurrying for the pavilion's shelter, the teams would play again with more or less equal strength now that Argentino was out of the shooting at least. He would be whacking, given the chance, when fresh targets were set up in the morning.

Gathering under the deck's roof, the teams and spectators had temporarily forgotten the game as they watched the great, brilliant blue sun seem to rock across the bloody horizon, back and forth, forcing some of the watchers towards the bathroom facilities, unable to hold the contents of their stomachs down.

Amy had been told by the Doctor about the first signs of the 'Ghost Worlds' beginning their orbit through the multiverse, but she had felt he was talking about a dream or a story. The reality was more spectacular and more terrifying than anything she had expected.

The rain stopped as suddenly as it had started and a delicious scent of wet grass and wild flowers filled the air. The black cloud passed and the remaining clouds were purple, breaking occasionally to let shafts of blue sunlight spear their way to the ground. Pitchmen hurried to put a force field over the whole grounds and turn up the heat within to begin drying the pitch. This had to be done gradually to ensure that there would be a proper spring to the turf when they played again.

Then everything within the pavilion started to shake. Amy wondered if this was an earthquake, and the Doctor laughed. He had that wild look he got in his eye when something big was about to happen. Something dangerous.

'This is it! This is it!' He was exultant. 'You'll probably never know anything like this ever again. Make the most of it, Amy Pond! Here we go!'

Through the windows she saw the purple clouds pass and the sun shiver and shake in the sky, beginning to spin like a monstrous Catherine wheel; the Doctor assured her it was only an illusion. Many of the watchers threw themselves to the floor, a few muttering prayers to whatever deity they had just rediscovered. Lightning began to run across the ground outside, crackling and shouting. Off in the distance they saw the village dairy explode and go up in smoke as if under attack. Then the lightning ran back exactly the way it had come and poured up a massive tree on the far side of the pitch, not harming it but causing its branches to glow and flicker as it formed a beautiful golden halo and slowly faded.

'I doubt there was anyone in the dairy at this time of the evening.' The Doctor's tone was intended to be reassuring. Amy was not altogether reassured.

'Is there any chance of getting off and back to the ship?' she asked.

'None at all,' he told her. 'The Ghost Worlds are moving. *Sideways* through time and space. Enjoy it, Amy. The shift won't be this spectacular every time, not once the orbit is established.'

'You told me people were lost in these orbital changes. Did you mean killed?' Her voice rose and fell with the wind. She watched as the trees began to dance, their branches bending down to the ground and then sweeping gracefully up, coming together before they spread out again, as if synchronised. A huge oak suddenly split and cracked all the way down the middle, falling apart in two perfect pieces. 'I think that *is* what you meant,' said Amy quietly.

There being no difference in their luck whether they stayed in the pavilion or went to the pub, a group of them agreed to make a dash for it. As soon as the rain stopped they set off along a relatively level road into the village.

The landlord of the Blue Barsoomian was pleased to see them. 'It's going to get chilly if what I've heard is true,' he said. 'I came here as a settler twenty-five years ago. Bloody agent told me Miggea was "shifted out" – whatever *that* meant!' He winced as the ground trembled again.

Rubbing his hands together, for all the world like a TV game-show host, the Doctor looked around. 'OK,' he said, 'what does everyone say to a good old-fashioned singsong?'

Bingo came to stand beside Amy and put a comforting arm around her shoulders. 'I know the words to "My World

Fell Apart When I Fell In Love With You",' he offered. He thought for a moment, then cleared his throat. 'Perhaps not,' he said.

In the end Amy remembered a song Mr Thompson in the village had sung. When he'd heard her accent, he'd even bought her a CD of Harry Lauder and a bunch of other early twentieth-century music hall performers singing their best-known numbers:

> *'I belong tae Glasgae, good auld Glasgae toon,*
> *Oh, there's somethin' the matter wi' Glasgae,*
> *She keeps goin' roond an' roond!*
> *Ah'm only a common old workin' man*
> *As anyone here can see,*
> *But when ah git lit oop on a Saturday –*
> *Glasgae belangs tae me!'*

The Doctor took down the big menu board on the bar and turned it round, using a bit of chalk to write the words out in Universal, which most of them knew. Of course hardly anyone had the faintest idea what the song was about, but they were glad to learn it, since that was better than trying to puzzle out the Ghost Worlds, where they were going, and what would happen.

Eventually the sun set –

And set again –

And again –

And again –

'I'm getting fed up with this,' said Amy sternly and stepped towards the nearest window as if she intended to admonish Miggea for its erratic behaviour. 'Oh, gosh!' she exclaimed. 'Oh, everybody! Come and look at the stars!'

In the soft darkness of the skies over Miggea the now-familiar constellations had never been more beautiful.

Everything was magnified and somehow sharper. The distant suns appeared to have been scattered like precious stones and metals over black velvet. Shimmering rubies, sapphires, emeralds; gold, silver, milk jade and onyx swirled in a magnificent pavane. You could hear the music swelling. No one attempted a rational explanation for this miracle; they simply stood in awe and watched. The constellations marched this way and that as if in celebration of Creation. They were closer, larger, brighter. The Doctor, who had seen so much of the multiverse, shook his head in amazement. 'I *think* we're still moving. The stars aren't. They only *seem* to be changing their positions. We're going from one level of the multiverse to another. That's what we're seeing. And we're keeping our atmosphere, our positions around Miggea. It's happening!'

Amy understood. 'So – do you mean we're moving through all the alternatives in the multiverse?'

'I don't think Miggea's orbit takes her through *every* alternative, only a relative few really – maybe thousands? A few million at most. Time determines the nature of space, you see.'

They heard more deep rumblings, saw deep green flashes.

'We're actually orbiting the black hole. We've no business existing, yet we *do* exist. I don't know how time relates to space here. Not really. Especially where gravity's an important part of the equation. But this isn't an aberration. I think all aspects of the multiverse have systems like this at their centre. It's part of that grand design, that logic we find so hard to grasp. Wheels within wheels. A quality of gravity that's barely begun to be examined. Gravity within gravity? Like electricity, we know it happens but we don't know how or why. We can learn how to use it because that's what we're good at. Yet – I'm not sure —' He shook his head.

'What, Doctor?' Urquart Banning-Cannon lifted his pewter shant to his lips. 'What aren't you sure about?'

'I think we're going to have to play these matches through, for a start. And then we might learn a bit more. I think we're heading for the centre – no, I don't mean *the* centre, do I? I mean *a* centre. There's more than one. I should have realised that. Yet each centre represents the other, just as each aspect of the multiverse represents the other. And each affects the other! It's beautiful! What a machine! I doubt if you could easily make a model of this. But maybe *you* could. Self-similarity. The part represents the whole. There's really no such thing as size, not in the way we've been taught to understand it.

'That's why these rituals are so important, see? Why we have to play the game or do the dance or say the prayers or whatever it is, yeah? I think we should try to keep things as ordinary as possible. So the clocks don't represent cosmic time. It doesn't matter. We stick to our rules. Our regulations. Our rituals. And that way we might just restore it all. Of course, there are the games to play. They're important. No, really, they are. Play the game. Win the prize. Do what we have to do. And the rest will follow logically. I don't mean by our logic but by the logic of the multiverse. What a privilege, eh? We can't let the multiverse down, can we?'

'It's the strain, poor beggar,' said the landlord of the Blue Barsoomian.

Outside, the stars continued their dance and the thunder boomed, the lightning flashed. The great ritual dance of the multiverse, driven by some unreasoning intelligence that was both Law and Chaos, Matter and Antimatter continued…

'I think we need to get to the Second Aether,' said the Doctor. 'Miggea will take us there. And then we'll know what to do.'

'But will you have the *means* of doing it, Doctor?' Mr

Banning-Cannon smiled as he raised his shant to his lips.

'I know. That's why I think we have to play on through. At least it'll help us pass the time.'

They had not predicted the rain which came as a result of their passage through the scales of the multiverse. Neither had they anticipated the pain or the sickness. More than once, as the colours of space melted and merged and the star that was Miggea blazed scarlet, they doubled up with appalling cramps, forced to abandon momentarily the game on which so much depended. 'Pain stopped play,' as the Doctor had it. Then there were the bloody blue screams which seared their way through their circulatory systems, as if they were attempting to warp them into entirely different creatures.

The blue screams affected the Judoon more than the humans, and they seemed ashamed when even the smallest moan escaped their brutal snouts. It was sound, it was colour and it was something else, maybe scent. Nobody could easily describe it, nor the bubbling mauve 'fizz' associated with phasing from one scale to another, which took over their muscles and made them good for something other than their original purpose, causing exhilaration.

When a good whack was scored, then came pleasure, glowing through them from feet to face, all gorgeous blues, the colours of the sun. They could not witness it for what it was, a rapid scale change in which everything on Flynn and everywhere else under the Shifter star's influence shifted upscale (or was it down?) from the star and planets to their ship, their bodies to their smallest possessions, the atoms of the air they breathed.

Those few like the Doctor who understood the mathematical theory knew why this happened to them but not how to describe it, nor how to stop it, only that resisting the process generally caused death. Once again the Doctor was forced to resort to his old admonition to 'go with the flow', even if that flow caused him to writhe and pulse with uncontrollable tremors. How they played so well when remembering and anticipating these horrible sensations they also could not begin to understand, but play they did, perhaps because their instincts told them that the ritual and replication involved in the game could bring resolution and an ending of the pain.

Once Amy saw a spoon and a cup on a table shake, crack and appear to *tear* as something in their constitution failed to match the scale which made them either too big or too small to be seen. The Doctor had told her that this could happen to anything or anyone failing to shift in concert with the indigo sun.

But then there were the pleasures the Shifter brought when enjoying food or a shower or some other pleasant physical sensation which became hugely intensified. Sometimes they could not exchange so much as a word without experiencing ecstasy; at other times the same sensations translated into agony.

Trailing the Visitors by 97 for 12, the Tourists did everything they could to save the game but they had very little left and, when the Cairene Dodger was taken 9 for 22, they were forced to acknowledge defeat. The Visitors would play the Gentlemen for the Silver Arrow of Artemis.

The final match of the tournament opened on a golden day when countless planets filled a sky with glorious reflected light and seemed to be jostling to get a view of the match between those old rivals.

Captain Bingo decided to put Hari Agincourt in to defend the wotsit while a Judoon fast archer went up against him. Both players were on top form, and Hari kept his ownership of the wotsit firmly against arrow upon arrow, hitting high sixes and tens, until he looked like a distraught hedgehog, with shafts sticking from every part of his well-padded armour. The Judoon did not break down his defence until just before teatime, when an arrow, whacked for six into the lower screens, was caught smoothly before Hari saw it out of the corner of his eye and rammed by the keeper deep into the 180 quarter causing a huge wave of applause from the Gentlemen's supporters. At teatime, Hari was congratulated by the Tourists for a fine score which they promised to even up.

After tea, they put Parker, the half-canine whacker, in as defender, indicating a more aggressive strategy against Je'I'me Polucks, which kept the game in their hands but failed to advance by the time change of wotsits was called. The rain came on again just before the planet began to grumble and struggle beneath their feet.

The Gentlemen had a good deal to celebrate, even though their ears felt as if they were swelling from the inside, and a rapid thump-thump-thump reminded Amy of a pneumatic drill going off right next to your head. Fortunately all this subsided and the sun returned to its usual colour just in time to offer them an astonishingly beautiful dusk.

That evening, looking around the crowd in the Blue Barsoomian, the Doctor opined that everyone was beginning to look the worse for wear, though he was proud of them all for their resilience and determination. 'I sometimes forget that it's not just humans who have kept going through all the various disasters the universe has sent. I'm honestly amazed at how well all these species perform under duress. Victory tends to be bad for the character if it's too easily won. Know what I mean?' He stuck his tongue out suddenly, his face contorted in disgust. 'This tea is rubbish, isn't it?'

'Made by a Ringai,' Amy said with a nod towards Mrs Aramone in her pretty false head and retaining glasses. 'And if there's one thing a Ringai can't do, it's make a decent pot of Darjeeling. Even when you give them second flush to make it with.'

The Doctor was laughing. 'Is this the wisdom you intend to take back to Earth with you some day?'

She shared his amusement. Bingo strolled over, attracted by the ordinary domesticity he'd spotted. 'Dashed good bit of playing on Hari's part, eh? You two seem to be enjoying yourselves.'

'We were talking about the tea,' Amy told him.

'Ranjun, isn't it? Not a patch on Darjeeling. I say, I wish the weather was a spot more predictable, don't you? Almost impossible to know who to put in from hour to hour. I was thinking of a Judoon before lunch tomorrow and then see how we go. What do you think, Doctor?'

For a while they discussed the merits of the various players until it became obvious to the Doctor that Bingo really wanted to talk to Amy alone, so he rose and made his excuses. He strolled over to the bar and was caught just as he reached it by Mrs Banning-Cannon who let him know she was pleased to hear he was well.

Amy, to tell the truth, found Bingo's attentions relaxing. She told herself off for leading him on, but then told herself again that he would have remained there talking to her no matter what she said, unless it was a straight bit of rudeness from her.

'Looking forward to the bleachers tomorrow, old thing?' he asked, when he came back to their seats with her half-shant and his full one. 'I thought I'd put you out there, given your spiffin' performance today.'

'Oh, come on, Bingo, there was nothing for me to do,' she said, grinning. 'I caught and returned four shafts which my dog Spot could have retrieved if they were Frisbees.'

'Oh, no,' he said seriously. 'You're a natural. I'm not the

only one who thinks it.'

She was glad when Flapper turned up with Hari Agincourt in tow. Hari had been hard to pull away from his admirers. He sat down with a weary thump and sipped his shant. 'Phew! That's better.'

They waited patiently for the earth-tremor to come and go as it usually did at about this time by the pub clock. Outside the rain bucketed down. By now they knew it would last about half an hour. Most of the other players groaned, but Amy said she found it quite soothing. 'It always reminds me of home,' she said. 'When I was a little girl.'

'Have you popped the question formally, yet?' asked Bingo of Hari, not sure how the notion had come into his head at that point.

'Um,' said Hari. 'Well, no. I know you told me it was OK with old man Banning-Cannon, but every time I start to ask him, Mrs B-C turns up with her wonderful imitation of a basilisk and transforms me pretty much to stone. Flapper tells me I'm going to have to get used to handling her, if we're to spend the rest of our lives together and all that, and I know it's jolly yellow of me, but so far I've got no closer to the important action than quacking like a duck...'

'A pretty feeble duck at that,' declared the Last of the Banning-Cannons, not without an edge of rancour to her dulcet tone as she gave Hari's arm something of a confusing squeeze. Mrs B-C had her back to them, still deep in conversation with the Doctor. 'But I suppose you're correct about after the game being the right moment. Assuming we win, of course.'

'As we must,' said Bingo.

'Quite,' said Flapper and examined a naked left finger rather pointedly.

Amy wasn't sure she liked the direction of the conversation but that wasn't what was making her uncomfortable. Looking up, she noticed someone at the bar. Captain Abberley was staring at her through the glass bottom of his shant. When he saw her looking back he gave a slight bow. There were sides, she decided, to the big, bluff Chaos Engineer.

What on earth did he really want from them? she wondered. The Doctor had agreed with her that he had a clear but so far unstated reason for being here. Perhaps he had not wished to risk his own ship by bringing it in so close to the galactic Hub? Perhaps he was moving through the Shifter orbit in the hope of reaching a particular scale where he expected to find something? Was he, too, looking for the Silver Arrow of Artemis? Did he mean to steal it if it ever turned up? She still had half an idea that it was already gone from Mrs Banning-Cannon's portable vault and that the theft of the hat had been nothing more than a cover-up.

As the pub shook and jingled, the customers were interrupted in their sing-song – 'He was a patient she kept in a can and she was a healer with feet out of line' – so full of triple and quadruple entendres that Amy was completely lost before the first verse was over.

She was relieved when the singers were drowned out by a bestial roar from the sky outside, tempting her to jump up and go to the window. Overhead was ragged with racing blackness recalling the dark tides Amy had seen during the storms. Tides now rimmed with deep, glowing blue, the exact colour of the old medicine bottles she had collected for a while as a teenager. Then it felt as if the sides of the pub were repeatedly kicked by a gigantic boot, except nothing was damaged. The strange lack of accompanying sensation made her, if anything, more frightened than earlier. She was glad when the shift ended even if the sun did suddenly rise again, in all its original glory, making the rain on the windows sparkle like glass beads.

She looked back towards the bar, directly into the eyes of

Captain Abberley. He smiled, not unpleasantly, and gestured to her to join him.

'I'll be back in a minute,' she told her friends.

Next morning by the clock, for there was no other way at the moment of measuring time on Flynn, the game continued. While the sky swept from dark grey to scarlet and the ground shook and squirmed, the Gentlemen again took their turn at the wotsit, and those old rivals continued to play what was in so many ways the game of their lives. The Gentlemen stayed ahead for most of the day but at teatime their luck changed drastically and they lost four whackers to Grimtok, the Visitors' number five archer. He was an elegant centaur, rather finely built, with large blue eyes and a palomino coat, another favourite with the ladies. Somehow the day, with its brilliant, unfamiliar colours, had invigorated him and he was at the top of his game.

Bingo Lockesley, as captain, was kicking himself. He knew he had made a bad judgement. Once he had seen the first two whackers go down so speedily he should have put a better whacker in to play against Grimtok. As it was, there would now be some important strategy required of him. By lunchtime, he had come to a decision and, as soon as tea was over, he put in W.G. Grace, who had been itching to play. With her huge, glistening beard she made a picturesque, as well as a confident, antagonist. Her confidence was not unfounded. Within twenty minutes of taking up her whacking bat she had sailed a beautiful arrow to Amy who sent it back to Flapper in wotsit who tucked it neatly into the Visitors' target as Grimtok galloped triumphantly around the 'stand', coming to a sudden stop as, open-mouthed, he heard the unexpected 'Howzat'...

And then the sun went out.

*

The pavilion's floodlights came on automatically as Grimtok cantered slowly back, while Amy and Flapper did their best to maintain their gravitas when what they really wanted to do was hug each other and jump up and down in celebration of their own unexpected success. With the centaur's run of luck over, the Gentlemen and the Visitors found themselves more or less level pegging.

The sun eventually appeared in the sky, but now there was no point in continuing until the next day. Back in the pavilion, and later the pub, Amy and Flapper were fêted by their fellow team-members. Though they protested that Grimtok had been unlucky, and everyone privately knew that it was more to do with the fact that the centaur had been playing on better form than he had ever demonstrated before, there was still good reason for congratulations given that until a short while earlier both women had been amateurs. The Doctor was the most enthusiastic of all, not counting Bingo, of course, who was ecstatic both as team captain and as suitor.

Amy felt more than a little overwhelmed by the attention she was receiving, so when Mrs Banning-Cannon burst into the pub wearing not only a triumphant smile but also a large, somewhat battered hat, she was relieved.

'Where did you get that hat?' she asked.

'Where did you get that tile?' asked the Doctor.

'Isn't it a lovely one?' Grimtok said, squinting through the mist which was now curling through the air of the pub like smoke.

'It's no longer in style,' said Mrs Banning-Cannon firmly. 'That's not the reason, of course, that I'm wearing it.'

'No!' The Doctor slipped from his barstool. 'You found it!'

'Actually, Doctor, I found the thief.' Mrs Banning-Cannon removed the huge, if dishevelled, piece of creative millinery work and floated it carelessly to the bar. 'With the hat.'

She whirled dramatically, her finger pointed at the young man who had followed her through the door.

'There he is! Our snake in the grass. The viper we have been holding to our bosom. The tie in the ointment.'

'I swear, Mrs Banning-Cannon, that the only reason I was there was because – because I-I-I…' Hari Agincourt was giving an impression of a dog whose paw-prints had been discovered on the best bedspread.

'Don't stand there addressing me like some stammering sailor, sir,' hissed the furious matron. 'I caught you red-handed!' She took a step towards him.

Hari flinched. 'Honestly, the only reason I was outside your door was because I couldn't find you. I was about to knock when—'

'Liar! You were leaving our apartments where you had left the hat in the hope that you would not be discovered with it.'

'Hang on.' The Doctor shook his head, puzzled. 'You have your hat back, Mrs Banning-Cannon?'

'Not that the hat is any longer of the slightest importance. Catching the thief, however, still remains an issue. Or did before I caught him.'

'That wasn't why I was there!' Hari declared desperately.

'What other reason would you have for being there?'

'I had come, you bullying old bat, to ask for your daughter Jane's hand in marriage!' Hari stopped himself, frowning. He wondered if he had phrased his reply quite as diplomatically as he might have done. 'I mean…'

But Flapper had thrown herself into his arms. Although she did not say the words 'My hero!' it was pretty clear that's what she was thinking.

And for once in her long life in the metaphorical driving seat, the heir to the Tarbutton zillions was at a loss for speech.

At this happy point, Mr Banning-Cannon entered the pub, his hand firmly holding the tailored collar of a lady's smart royal blue two-piece containing a struggling woman with tightly permed and blonded hair whom the Doctor immediately recognised.

'Why, Lady Peggy,' he said, 'I'd been wondering if you'd turn up in plain view, as it were, with the light altering so rapidly and unexpectedly all the time. This, ladies, gentlemen and others, is my old antagonist Lady Peggy Steele, the Invisible Thief. Logic's been pointing her unwavering finger at you for quite some while, Lady Peg. I'm so glad you decided to do the right thing and return Mrs Banning-Cannon's hat. Mm. Nice perfume.'

Enola Banning-Cannon, however, was gaping at Hari Agincourt and her daughter. 'Did you say "marriage"?' she asked.

'I did,' said Hari.

'I forbid it absolutely,' pronounced the second-to-last of the Banning-Cannons, and, with the proud air of a freshly launched battleship eager for business, she swept from the saloon bar.

'Actually,' murmured the Doctor from his corner of the bar. 'Amy put the hat there at my request. I finally caught up with Lady Peggy after searching for her for years. I guessed she had to be here somewhere. But I'm afraid she only stole the hat for the *second* time.'

'Then who took it the first time?' Flapper wanted to know.

'I've no idea, I'm afraid. Well, I have a suspicion...'

'And *why* did she pinch it?' asked Mr Banning-Cannon, who was rather beginning to warm towards Lady Peggy. Apologetically he released her collar. Lady Peggy shrugged her jacket back into shape, tugged at its bottom, and at once recovered her dignity. She took her handbag off her arm, opened it, removed a pink compact and added some powder to her nose and cheeks.

'Because I was convinced that damned arrow was hidden in it,' she announced. 'It smelled of the thing. Appears I made a mistake. Threw me off, I can tell you. I'm hardly ever wrong.'

'How much was Frank/Freddie Force going to give you for it?' the Doctor asked, staring at a poster of a picnic on Flynn.

'We hadn't agreed an exact price,' she replied glaring at Mr Banning-Cannon.

'So where is it now?' the Doctor asked.

'Wherever you hid it, Doctor.' Peggy patted the back of her hairdo reassuringly.

'I didn't exactly hide it,' he said. 'But we should find that out in good time, I'm sure.'

Chapter 24

The Filling Skies

POM'IK'IK WAS PROVING A pretty steady player and hard to budge. Even Hari's expert shooting couldn't faze him, and it was a bit of a disaster to see Hari go down for 8 thanks to Kali-Kali's beautiful catch at right quarter. Sum'in, the Cairene Dodger, took the whacker by eleven o'clock with W.G. Grace being put in just after lunch. They were 42 to the Visitors' 87 and it looked all up for the Gents until Grace brought out her treasured bow which looked like a Sumatan 50x to Bingo, though it was almost certainly modified. The Doctor also admired the antique bow. He could see why she had been so fussy about protecting it on the journey here. Placing one end against her foot, she showed her great strength as she bent it forward to string it, then walked with steady confidence onto the pitch, her hand raised to acknowledge her many fans cheering from the bleachers.

Just as W.G. reached the wotsit, the glowing sun went down with a faint sighing sound, a hard rain fell for a few moments and then stopped. Trees swayed along the horizon like a funeral procession in the deep purple haze. Rays of white-yellow light, like pillars they seemed so solid, spread from behind the trees and telescoped down to make way for

Miggea again, pushing the black and silver globe high into the air and causing a horrible round of sickness in everyone but the Judoon, who had anticipated the phenomenon and taken pills for it.

Ignoring all this, Grace put arrow after arrow into whackers, wotsits and wotsit keepers, slowly bringing the score up to something the Gentlemen could live with. By the end of play, Grace was not out and the score was 89 to the Visitors' 90: they had been awarded extra points after the umpires' decisions on a split arrow and an offside catch.

It was clear to all that the next day's match would be the crucial one, assuming there was anything resembling a next day as the Shifter moved through the multiverse bringing incredibly good displays of lights, moving trees and 'jupiter bushes' of primal energy which everyone did their best to avoid.

Then came a massive throbbing from what seemed the core of the planet's being. The sun began to sing a wild song that sent out ripples of music, visible in the air they breathed. The mere act of breathing caused them to absorb some of the notes until at last virtually every living creature on the planet was adding its song to the complex harmonies and the sky was full of planets – planet after planet stretching into infinity, sun into sun folding one into another, larger and larger and at the same time smaller and smaller. They watched a vast stretch of green-white curd curl around a corner and disappear. The Doctor began cheering, his arms around Amy. He came close to kissing the Team Captain because he recognised the tentacle for what it was.

'We've made it,' he said. 'We're in the Second Aether. That's Squid Mammy's Spill and – look!' He danced along the pavilion's deck, pointing. From out of the green-white tentacle emerged a tidy little steamboat, her paddles churning against the splashing colour, her captain in his wheelhouse booming out a song:

> *We're Rolling, Rolling, to the Roogalator Rhumba,*
> *We're dancing to the doom of the dumble drum Samba!*
> *How's the music doing down there, Mr Cappybera.*
> *Fill up the converters and let's boogy with the thunder.*

But it wasn't Captain Abberley. Instead a long, insectoid face with v-shaped mouth parts, a set of sunglasses with eight lenses and a scarlet Mohawk put its head out of the wheelhouse and waved at the Doctor. 'Good to see you, Doctor. Too-woo-da-whooo. How's life treating you?'

'Good enough, thanks, More-than-It. All well, I hope?'

'Never better, Doctor. I heard you were looking to score the arrer today and do a bit of jiggery-pokery for us.'

'Hoping. Young It, we've the rest of our game to play.'

'You're safe enough at the centre for the time being, if you don't mind over-vivid colours. They make my eyes ache, you know.'

'Do your best, pardner. And spread the word, if you don't mind. I was hoping Captain A and the Bubbly Boys would have something for me.'

'Aha,' sang More-than-It. 'That might explain the battle. Good luck, Doctor!'

The paddle-wheeler steamed off through the sky.

'Let's keep this game going!' Sum'in, the Cairene Dodger, was impatient. 'It's too tight to tell and it's getting on my nerves.'

The two captains conferred and agreed to play on. Their shadows were long against the backdrop of constantly shimmering stars and planets clustered around them. The dome of the great sky was like a richly decorated brocade, impossibly thick with multicoloured stars. Although encircled by such a variety of spheres in all directions, a sense of calm pervaded both the pitch and the village. They were playing for the existence of Creation, playing out a ritual which, by its very formality, might restore the worlds and the galaxies they knew.

As the minutes passed, the space immediately around them cleared and the Second Aether manifested itself again, an intense wash of thick yellow that was Mustard Beach. And hanging in this background were all manner of vessels from galleons to old-fashioned rocket ships, from coracles to torpedo boats, yachts, submarines, a Lancaster bomber, which indicated that Wing Commander Heidegger and his friends had come to check out what was going on.

'Have they come to watch the game?' Amy asked the Doctor.

'Oh yes,' he said. 'They love a good whackit match. Huge sums change hands when they bet on them.'

She marvelled at the jewelled skies.

'Pretty, isn't it?' said the Doctor. 'The weird thing about the Second Aether is the atmosphere. Because so much is reversed here, any planet you find in the Second Aether will not naturally have any atmosphere at all. The air we breathe is in the space between the worlds. Miggea's a bit of an exception because of the terraforming which went on before they realised what the star and its planets really were. But you can still travel about in the Second Aether as if it were water and breathe it as if it were air while if you landed on an untreated planet you'd need a spacesuit or you'd burst and die.'

'How did all these people get here in the first place?'

'They were born here, I suppose you'd say. Pretty much every species in the multiverse lives here. From preference, obviously.'

'And Lady Peggy, the Invisible Thief? Is she from round here?'

'I'm not sure. She's here most of the time, but she isn't much liked because of her thieving. She can't help herself. Anything she spots that can turn a penny she'll have it.'

'But how did she get to Peers™ and pinch the hat the first time?'

'She didn't. Someone else nicked it first. We got that one back on Peers™. We keep experiencing these nasty little time shifts. When Lady Peggy pinched it the *second* time she'd come aboard with Frank/Freddie Force and his Antimatter Men. Invisible, of course. He left her behind with us when he returned to their ship. She stole the hat but was forced to keep on wearing the hideous thing so it would stay invisible, too. Couldn't have done much for her morale. I think this had to be the rendezvous where she was supposed to hand over the hat to Frank/Freddie. But Mr Banning-Cannon caught her first. I was hoping Captain Abberley and the Bubbly Boys would have arrived by now.'

He looked up at all the different and strange varieties of ships hanging in the Second Aether. He was reminded of cars at a drive-in cinema getting ready for the Big Show. 'Frank/Freddie is playing a dangerous game. Even in the Second Aether he is still unsafe, not impervious. He could implode at any minute, and here he wouldn't even have the satisfaction of taking others with him. He wants the Roogalator, and somehow connects it with the hat. But the hat also contained something else and the person who took it had entirely different ambitions.'

'Who's that?'

'Well, remember the smell left behind in Lockesley Hall that first night?'

'Yes! Burnt seawater—perfume...'

'That's right. Well, one's the smell of...'

'HOWZAT!!!'

A fine bit of fielding from a Judoon and a centaur in wotsit, and another Visitor dragged herself off the field looking miserable.

'The Bubbly Boys were crucial to the search for the hat because for some reason, probably to do with their being born in the Second Aether, they can see the invisible when others can't.'

Amy looked a bit smug. 'I worked that out.'

'And very clever you were, too. Oh! Well played that Judoon!'

And so the game continued. 210 for 8 on the Visitors' board at lunchtime and 198 for 6 on the Gentlemen's. It could go either way.

Chapter 25

Doctor Whack

THE DOCTOR FOUND HIMSELF with his bow strung and his first twelve arrows in the quiver ready to go in to shoot with a Judoon at the other end. Amy was in field again and Jane was in wotsit. Although the Doctor conducted himself well, with arrow after arrow sent down to the Visitors' whackers with never-ending skill, he could not score more than the odd wotsit. But by the time the Doctor was caught ABW, in the fourth innings, he felt he had done his best, even though his best hadn't been quite good enough. Amy was looking pretty exhausted and Flapper was a little grim around the gills. Happily, lunch was called and the players stumbled in to the pavilion.

'I'm sorry, Bingo,' the Doctor said as he climbed wearily up the steps.

'Not a bit, old man, what? You've broken their run. All we have to do now is take up on the advantages you've left us!'

After lunch, Bingo put himself in bow and Grace at wotsit, a pretty good bit of strategy with only a few hours to go. They turned out to be a decidedly dynamic duo. It was Bingo's finest moment. And when he wasn't demonstrating some superb bowmanship, W.G. Grace took over. The Visitors never had a chance. They were stunned by Grace's amazing skill. Arrow after arrow slammed into the wotsits, leaving them as little more than heaps of hay wrapped in a bit of tattered material. The Visitors' captain put his best people in, but it was hopeless. Grace's scores advanced relentlessly. That ebony and ivory composite thrummed in victorious voice.

Rather than stay to watch the inevitable, the Doctor took Amy behind the pavilion where Captain Brian Abberley met them sans the Bubbly Boys and his ship *Now the Clouds Have Meaning*. 'What ho, Doctor! And good day to thee, lass. Nicest bit of whackawotsit I've seen in many a year. We'll all be there to see the finale. Was a time I wasn't so bad at the Good Old Whack mesel'. Any road, tha'll have tha' cargo by close of play, Doctor. Tha' knows t'trust us, 'appen.'

'I'll wait for you, captain. There's a lot depending on you and the Boys.'

As they strolled back beneath that quaking, shimmering, jewelled sky, the Doctor said to Amy: 'So was it you and Captain Abberley who set up that trap for old Lady Peg?'

Amy looked smug. 'Mr Banning-Cannon caught her hat-handed just after the Boys pinched her invisibility tiara.'

The Doctor began to laugh. 'She must have taken that hat with her wherever she went. She was so sure the Roogalator was in the hat and had promised it to Freddie/Frank for a price. She was determined to get it. They met on Venice shortly before the *Paine* arrived to take tribute. They'd found out where the star map they were looking for was: in the hands of an antiquarian who was able to carry it to the *Paine* before they caught him. They needed to get to Ironface's ship and persuade him to join forces with them to find the Roogalator, once Frank/Freddie and Co were sure it wasn't in the hat or on Venice. Lady Peggy still thought the hat contained something of worth, but she wasn't sure what. When Frank/Freddie went aboard the *Paine*, Lady Peggy slipped in with them. When they left, they left her behind, which is how she was able to get aboard the *Gargantua* with Captain Cornelius. She came down to Flynn with us, too. The last clue was when the bots counted an extra passenger on the tender. She could be sensed but not seen. She hadn't allowed for me working out who she was and how she'd been the second person to pinch the hat. The Roogalator wasn't in the hat, but something else was, giving it that basic spider shape which originally scared Mr Banning-Cannon. That, of course, was the—'

They turned the corner of the pavilion. Amy groaned loudly when she saw the scoreboard. W.G. was out, admittedly for a century and a half, but they had no other players of her class left to put in. W.G. tramped desolately back to the pavilion. Moodily, she handed her bow to Bingo as they passed on the pavilion steps. 'Here, see if she brings you more luck than she brought me.'

The Visitors were drawing ahead with a combination of luck and good playing. Bingo looked harried as he graciously accepted W.G.'s loan of her beautiful antique bow. He paused as Amy and the Doctor came up. 'We're in a bit of a spot, chums. I'm last archer in and we need to make a clear 75 to have any chance of beating 'em. Wish me luck.'

Bingo began with a tremendous shot. It put Pom'ik'ik the Aldebaran out for 27. Jill Jay went down next for 18, then Pilliom Rekya was out for a turkey. The Doctor and Amy left briefly to get a quick drink and some conversation in the pavilion.

They came back to the game in time to see Bingo loose a splendid shot straight into the Visitors' wotsit. Another score from Flapper in wotsit took a tremendous automatic 10.

Even Mrs Banning-Cannon had emerged to show a far keener interest in the game and was cheering heartily for the Gentlemen. 'When it comes time to award the Arrow of Law,

I shall of course do my duty,' she declared, 'but I shall not be amused if the Gentlemen lose.'

Bingo, aware how much depended on him, was shooting like a demon. Wotsit after wotsit fell to his relentless arrows. The bow loaned him by W.G. was in fact helping him to perform a wizardry far above his usual fine archery. Twang, thump. Twang, thump. Only occasionally now was Tarkus, a four-armed tireless Thark whackiteer, able to deliver a hefty thwack and keep the moment of defeat at bay.

Slowly the Gentlemen's score mounted, aided by some fine catches and returns once Bingo had put in Amy and the other best fielders.

But Bingo was tiring. The day was a warm one and the heat was getting to the Earl of Sherwood. One arrow after another found its target and then –

Lockesley to Tarkus. Tarkus whacked an easy 7. Pond, in the far coaxings, leapt up and sideways to catch the deflected arrow. Her hand closed around the shaft. She fitted it to her bow, took steady aim and –

'Howzat!' She screamed her triumph as her arrow took the wotsit at maximum score.

The umpire delivered the verdict:

'Three hundred and *eighteeeee*!'

And it was all over for the Visitors.

Between them, Bingo and Amy had saved the day.

The Visitors were the first to run up to their opponents and congratulate them on one of the finest games ever to be played anywhere.

From every side of the pitch, from spectators as well as players, came wild cheering. The exultant cheering did not stop. The bowmanship had been stunning; the wotsit defence and fielding would not be bettered for many a year.

The Doctor had his hands deep in his pockets and was lolloping about in that idiosyncratic way of his, whistling and humming to himself, singing under his breath. *'We won the cup / We won the sword / We won the staff / We won the word...'*

He looked expectantly up at the sky. The great star Miggea was casting long shadows across the afternoon field and glowing a deep, warm indigo.

Bots were setting up and decorating the banquet table, while Mrs Banning-Cannon had disappeared into the pavilion to emerge soon afterwards wearing a relatively small and simple creation from Mr Toni Woni. She was so pleased with their success she even allowed Flapper to run up to her and kiss her. Hari Agincourt shook her hand vigorously. 'Well done,' she said amiably and did not wince even a little as Hari stepped back, his arm now defiantly around Flapper's slender waist.

The underdogs had confounded the bookies.

'Just the sort of game we all love,' said the Doctor. 'I think we'd better go and pick up the traditional prize, yes?' He drew a deep breath of pleasure and advanced towards the table whistling the same silly little repetitive tune.

He seemed as surprised as anyone when the sky behind Mrs Banning-Cannon suddenly turned a lustrous pulsing blue, so intense that she almost ducked away from it.

The Doctor stopped whistling. 'This is all right, isn't it, Amy?' He winked at her. Then he began to whistle a more complicated tune. 'Know it? Duke Ellington. I saw him live at the Apollo in – um...'

'So what's going on?' she demanded firmly.

'What would you call that colour?' He indicated the sky.

She suddenly understood. 'Oh!' she said. 'Indigo!'

'Bingo!' he said triumphantly. And laughed.

The baffled team captain turned to see who was calling him. His head whirled round again as everyone else gasped. He followed the Doctor's gaze.

Mrs Banning-Cannon grasped her husband's arm. 'Oh,

look, Urquart! He was right! The Doctor was right! Here's my vault!'

A vision had appeared just above Mrs Banning-Cannon's head. About the size of a football, a round bright glittering bucky ball buzzed and fluttered overhead. Everyone watched in something approaching awe as slowly the ball moved through the air and began to descend from above Mr and Mrs B-C before coming to rest on the table.

'Is that all it is?' One of the Judoon sounded disappointed. 'What is it, ma'am? I thought we were playing for the Arrow of Artemis, not the Ball of Bacchus.'

'So we are!' said the Doctor, stepping up to stand beside Mrs Banning-Cannon. 'Very decent of you to agree to present the prize, Mrs B-C, but first I think we can safely take this out now.' He reached into the sparkling ball up to his elbow and brought up what looked like a toy of some kind. 'Indigo!'

And on his palm, for all to see, stood a tiny TARDIS about fifteen centimetres high, its little roof light flashing an intense blue. The crowd watched intently as the Doctor bent and placed it on the ground. 'There she is! Good hiding place, don't you think?'

Amy could not remember a time when she'd been so pleased to see it. 'But it's so tiny, Doctor! How?'

'Scale is determined by all sorts of factors in the multiverse, remember?' He frowned. 'As long as you can get everything to match up on the different planes, of course. But for now here's the most important thing.' Picking it up, he reached into the tiny TARDIS, this time feeling around inside, and brought out an arrow measuring about two and a half metres long. 'Look at that! Made of solid newtonium by the look of it, the rarest metal in the multiverse, precisely because it combines *all* metals in Creation, just as these jewels which seem to be built into it combine all the other jewels in Creation.' It shimmered and appeared to shake in the Doctor's hand. Its cold white light reminiscent of silver or platinum glittered with sapphires, rubies, diamonds and emeralds – every precious stone that existed. The gold fletchings shook and rustled in the breeze. The slender point was very stylised, certainly not made to kill, and the long shaft bore lettering in an unfamiliar runic alphabet.

The Arrow of Artemis. The Roogalator. The beam intended to rest on the fulcrum of the Cosmic Balance.

Chapter 26

The Arrow of Law

THE DOCTOR HANDED THE arrow to Mrs Banning-Cannon, who took it in both hands with sudden respect. Someone came forward with a plush cushion, and she placed the arrow on it. She turned toward the winning side, who stood grouped and waiting, and spoke in her poshest voice: 'Robin, Earl of Lockesley, who brought his team, the Gentlemen, to success against all odds, it is my great pleasure to present you with the winning Silver Arrow of Artemis! Jolly well played everyone.'

As Bingo, on behalf of the team, stepped forward to receive the arrow, it seemed to Amy that the entire multiverse glowed and pulsed in the sky in celebration.

Huge applause rang out from all supporters and team members. Everyone, including the Visitors and the Tourists, thought the Gents thoroughly deserved their victory. In the surrounding skies of Mustard Mull, the Chaos Engineers hung over the rails of their steam tugs and yachts and red-sailed Loondoon barges, intent on the ceremony, and roared and cheered with the best of them. Amy spotted the Bubbly Boys and recognised Captain Quelch's yacht.

The Doctor and Amy looked at the Arrow as it was passed

from hand to hand. 'So here's the Roogalator which is going to save all Creation!' Amy said, a little disbelievingly. 'I'll never understand.'

'It's a trick I used to pull a lot. Hide one thing in another thing you want to hide. I put the arrow inside the TARDIS, and the TARDIS inside the bucky ball before we left Peers™. It was much smaller then. That way, both things were safely hidden, yes? Now let's hope we can find a way to get the Roogalator back into place. We've only got one crack at it, you know. Whatever we do next, if we're successful, will be reproduced across the multiverse, as our story will be retold in some form for ever. But, if we fail, of course, that's the end of us all. And all our stories…'

A little impatiently Amy said, 'Are you going to make it any bigger. Or shrink us, or what?'

He became embarrassed. 'That's a snag I hadn't anticipated,' he said. 'It should have come back to its regular size when I took it out of the bucky ball.'

'You mean we're stuck here!'

'Only until we get back to the universe we left. I have to admit I thought that Miggea might keep all her characteristics and allow me to bring the TARDIS back to normal size. I think I might have been wrong…'

'Stuck here until Miggea returns to our own space-time? How long is that?'

'Local time or our time?' He scratched his head.

'Oh, god!' She looked around at the cheering people. 'So we're stuck here. Maybe for the rest of our lives.'

'Maybe.' He was beginning to look a bit shifty. 'But we can't leave here now anyway. We have things to do…'

'So what do we have to tackle next?' Her look of disgust would have sent a Barsoomian banth whimpering back to its cave.

'We're waiting for Captain Abberley and the Bubbly Boys.

They've set off to capture Quelch. See, they—'

Bingo came racing up, arrow in hand, flushed with pleasure and radiating confidence. 'I say, Amy! That was great playing today! Can I have a quick word?'

'Well, we're a bit busy, Bingo.'

'Come over here, where it's quieter.' He took her arm and pulled her towards the shade of the pavilion. 'Look. I wasn't going to say anything until a bit later, but I'm walking on air at the moment and my bally stupid nerve isn't likely to hold, so I'm doing it while the bowstring's sizzling, as it were. I'm only a backwoods countryman with an interest in whackin' and shootin', what?'

She had been dreading this moment, hoping to avoid it. 'Bingo. You're so sweet and brave and you're really, really kind...'

'Then there's some hope – I mean – will you – would you?'

She grinned, still hoping to deflect what was coming. 'Won't you join the dance?' she added, quoting Carroll. 'Sorry, you don't know Alice, do you? It's a lovely bit of nonsense.'

'Amy. This isn't nonsense.' Bingo gurgled. He fingered his bow. He seemed to be offering her the Silver Arrow. He kicked fiercely at the ground. 'I'm wondering if you'd like to be the next Lady Lockesley. Run the show with me, what?' He glared at the sod of turf he had kicked up. 'There it is. I've said it.' He stood panting like a retriever who has fetched at least three ducks in one go.

Amy could dodge and weave no longer. 'Bingo,' she began. 'You're a super bloke. A catch for any smart woman. But – oh, dear, Bingo, I'm afraid I *can't* accept. You see—'

'Oh, gosh. I've really made an ass of myself, haven't I?' Bingo was once again giving his celebrated impression of a stop light. 'You've already got someone at home or – oh, lor' – not the Doctor? I thought he was just your boss or something…'

'It's very complicated actually and it would be hard to give a complete explanation, but I'm not free to…'

'Dash it. I've turned up too late as usual.' Bingo kicked another large lump out of the turf. 'Missed the jolly old boat, what?'

'Oh, Bingo! You're a smashing bloke. A girl couldn't want anything more than what you offer. You're sweet, generous, funny, good-looking – most women would snap you up.'

'But not this particular woman,' he said. He looked rather like a punctured airship. The picture of deflation.

She kissed his cheek and squeezed his arm. 'Not this particular one,' she said. 'Sorry.' She felt so wretched as she watched him slump away.

Then, to her astonishment, she saw the Doctor come racing up, spot Bingo, grab the arrow out of his hand and carry on running. 'Come on, Amy! What on earth's happened to him? He promised…'

There was the faint lowing of a steam-whistle.

'Sounds like him now.' The Doctor perked up. 'Can you see him, Amy?'

'Hey!' cried Bingo behind them.

A familiar ship suddenly poked its prow out of the surrounding yellow matter of Mustard Mull. Amy recognised the *Now the Clouds Have Meaning* as the boat swung round and lay bobbing at anchor. With his bow in one hand, the Silver Arrow in the other, the Doctor waved.

Brian Abberley saluted him back. 'How do, Doctor? I see you've brought t'Roogalator. Shall we get on with it?'

Bingo followed them up the ladder. 'I say, Doctor. That arrow…'

Captain Abberley gave the arrow an approving onceover. 'That's t'beggar all right. Our sweet old Roogalator! Nice going, chaps!' He looked from the Doctor to Bingo to Amy. 'But is that *all* you have? It's no good…'

'What do you mean?' the Doctor looked totally bewildered. 'I've brought the ancient Arrow of Law and it's imbedded with the equally timeless Jewels of Chaos. It's the blooming Roogalator, boys. It's what makes the worlds go round, keeps the clocks ticking. We've been defending it against all comers. We played the game of our lives to win it. Just in time. Another few moments and we'll all be dissipating dust. At best. We've brought it as close to the centre of the multiverse as anyone's ever dared, and you're telling us it's *useless*!'

'I didn't say it was useless, Doctor. T'rod's t'beam. T'star's t'fulcrum and t'bloomin' planets are t'pans. Everything matches, see. But just having t'Arrer is like having an H-bomb. It's no good without a delivery system. That's what tha's missin', old chum. T' *delivery system*.'

Chapter 27

Running for the Centre

'DELIVERY SYSTEM?' NOW THE Doctor looked as deflated as Bingo. Amy was baffled, too.

'Of course! That's why they were after the hat!' The Doctor laughed aloud. 'That's what Frank/Freddie knew they needed. And why we've been confused about this all along. It was hidden in the hat. Diana of Loondoon's own. She disguised it. What was in it?'

Amy remained baffled. 'I don't know. Lace? Feathers? Rings and things? Buttons? And – oh, wow!'

'Exactly! I was using it. I had it in my hands. And *she had it all along! Under our noses!*' The Doctor vaulted over the side of the little steamboat. Followed by Amy and Bingo, he ran back towards the pavilion where triumphant players were still gathered discussing the win.

In the middle of these, strutting her stuff a little, as she had every right to do, stood the great W.G. Grace, leaning on her antique bow and shaking hands with her team and its opponents. 'Very kind,' she said. 'I didn't think I could do it at first. The bow's not really my strong point.'

'You were never sure, were you, W.G.?' The Doctor leaned forward and snatched the bow from her unsuspecting hands.

'But now you *are* sure, you won't want that! I need it rather more than you do. In fact everyone needs it more than you!'

'Eh? Have you gone barmy, Doctor?' Hari Agincourt stepped forward.

But the Bearded Lady was no longer triumphant. Indeed, she looked a little downcast. 'So you worked it out, eh, Doctor?' She moved to the railing of the pavilion and leaned against it. From somewhere nearby a steam-whistle sounded. Its note was urgent. 'Yes, it was me. I recognised the bow as the famous Bow of Diana which, according to legend, was lost with the Elgin Marbles and the British Museum centuries ago. I was disgusted, I have to say. I was going to liberate the bow from that dreadful hat shop when we stopped over in Loondoon. It was obscene what they were doing. I planned to buy it. But Mrs B-C got to it first. She had no intention, she said, of ever selling it. So I pinched the hat from her when we were all at Lockesley Hall. I used an anti-grav handler to float it out of the window and into the shrubbery. I was standing under the bedroom window pretending to have a smoke round the corner. Nobody saw me. A bit later, when all the fuss had died down, I retrieved the hat from the shrubbery and messed it up a bit, tugging the bow, which was used as support for a mere decoration, out of the hat. I'd seen a picture of the thing years ago so I knew what it was: a genuine religious relic! She used it in that ridiculous hat, which was nothing less than blasphemy. How she came by it, I'll never know. My plan was to donate it to the Archery Museum on Twang in Calypso, but I thought I'd use it first, to see if it improved my shooting. Which it did...'

'I remember now. You and the First Fifteen were going round the shops at the same time I was.' Mrs Banning-Cannon glared. 'You only had to ask...'

'I think that's what Diana found on Venice and took back to Old Old Earth with her,' said the Doctor. 'I wish I'd realised...

Still, it might never have come here if you hadn't wanted to improve your bowing, W.G. I suppose we have you to thank. But I think Diana knew what the bow was and how to get it here. Where's Diana now, Mrs Banning-Cannon? Captain Cornelius might want to know when – well, *if* – we get back to the *Gargantua*.'

'She's still in Loondoon, as far as I know,' murmured Mrs Banning-Cannon dreamily, suddenly aware of the astonishing Romance she was involved in. Her holiday experience had mellowed her considerably.

Amy had been listening. 'And that's who Captain Cornelius's lost love must be. Diana knew where we were going, knew old Ironface would probably recognise it and trace it back to her. Where can she be? Here, maybe? Or still in Loondoon – waiting...'

The steam-whistle sounded again.

The pair started running for it, with Bingo not far behind. 'Hang on! I'm coming with you.'

'Well, technically, I paid for it,' began the matriarch. But she understood, somewhere in her bones, that this wasn't really the most appropriate response. She watched as the Doctor, Bingo and Amy clambered aboard the little steamboat, while the others stood open-mouthed, still not altogether sure what was going on.

'I'm really sorry!' cried W.G. Tears were coursing down her cheeks, filling her beard and making it glint like diamonds. 'I'm such an idiot. I had no idea how important that bow was. I should have guessed that was why they thought we still had the hat. They'd sniffed the bow when I had it in my case.'

Then Captain Brian Abberley gave one last farewell blast on the steam-whistle and the little boat was paddling back up the sky which turned from yellow to dark mauve.

'Purple Pastures,' said the Doctor. 'It's been so long since

I was here!'

Through Purple Pastures with a dozen vessels chugging, whining and moaning behind them. Into Bluebell Bay and still going.

'So old W.G. was the culprit all along!' Bingo shook his head. He realised that Mr Banning-Cannon would now know the truth. In his mind's eye his deed to Peers™ was disappearing with all his other dreams. And poor Hari's and Flapper's dreams, too, for that matter.

'That's why she hung on to it through thick and thin,' said the Doctor. 'That's why she wouldn't let anyone else handle her bow case. She certainly confused any pursuit – and confused us into the bargain. Isn't it lovely? Ebony and ivory! The art of fusing the two into a bow has been lost but you see them sometimes represented on old Greek vases and friezes. The bow of Diana, the huntress. And the woman Captain Cornelius has sought for countless years.' The Doctor ran his hand along the stave's length.

'What?' exclaimed Amy. 'A goddess. A real goddess?'

'Real enough for Cornelius,' he said.

Now their surroundings shifted to a brilliant green.

'Emerald City, next stop,' said the Doctor.

'*What???*' exclaimed Amy again. She almost hit him when she realised he was laughing.

'Green Glades, I think,' Abberley told her.

Bingo was standing disconsolately at the rail looking over the side as the little boat steamed its way through the *colour-zones* of the Second Aether. Amy suppressed an urge to go over to him and comfort him. Then she gasped in wonder.

They had broken out of Green Glades into a place that smelled and looked like the roots of the universe, a great tangle of tubers, of purple and yellow, of gold, black, maroon and orange. And laid on that a matrix of dark green, brown, jade green, crimson, silver, amber and cerise. Gigantic roses, pink, white, yellow and scarlet, intertwined to form a canopy of coruscating colour which opened out into another view of the multiverse and another and another, with glimpses of crowded planets blazing like orbs, coronets and sceptres: the Crown Jewels of Olympus. And through all this the little steamboat chugged doggedly along until suddenly the engines stopped.

And there was silence.

Below them they saw blackness; a blackness so intense nothing could escape it. Spiralling into it and out of it came threads of vivid orange, pale greens, spatterings and swirls of light blue beaches, yellow jungles, orange, pink and ochre seas, burnt amber rivers, fields of gold and glowing maple, spouts of liquid rubies, flowing sapphire and fusions of black-green, foam-white, startling combinations of a thousand shades of green and the flickering powders of silver, dust grey, pewter and bronze, all creating a funnel through which they peered down into a soul-sucking blackness.

'What is it, Doctor?' Bingo asked, his heartbreak momentarily forgotten.

'We're looking through the Sagittarian Schwarzschild Radius from the perspective of the Second Aether,' explained the Doctor. 'I doubt if it would be possible for people like us to do this under any other circumstances. The heart of it down there is the black hole which represents the centre of our multiverse and all black holes and universes everywhere to quasi-infinity, although there is, paradoxically, no centre to the multiverse and yet countless centres. But that's what began to go wrong millennia ago...'

'When t'Roogalator were pinched,' muttered Captain Abberley. 'Some damned fool got in there – don't ask how – and stole that beam from the fulcrum which regulates the Great Balance. I'll thank thee not to ask me, because I can't explain it. But that's t'form it takes for us.'

'Because this isn't just physics we're talking about.'
The Doctor's eyes gleamed with fascinated curiosity. 'It's
metaphysics. It's the only way we can understand reality.
And both are represented by mythology, by legends, by
the shamanistic power of humanity to tell a story that is
an absolute lie beneath which hides an absolute truth. Life
and Death, Law and Chaos, Matter and Antimatter. What
a species! A poem creates a formula. A formula becomes
material. And so it goes on. And now one of us must do his
duty.'

'And shoot that arrow into the very heart of the black
hole,' said Captain Abberley. 'Probably up to me, eh?'

'I don't think so, captain,' said the Doctor. 'I'm the one
who got us into this. I'm the one who has to shoot it.'

'Correct me if I'm wrong,' said Captain Abberley. 'I've seen
what happens to anyone who goes into the Schwarzschild
Radius. Wouldn't it be instant death, lad, to shoot that arrow
down there?'

'Not necessarily,' said the Doctor. He bent to pick up a
long coil of rope which Captain Abberley had brought on
deck. He tied one end of the rope to a capstan. 'See, if we can
shoot the arrow accurately enough and ensure a minimum
reaction, we just might be able to haul me back up.'

'Doctor! You can't!' Amy was genuinely scared. 'I don't
care what happens. You just can't risk it! I'm a pretty good
shot. Why don't I —'

'No,' Bingo shook his head. 'You couldn't do it, if you'll
forgive me saying so, Amy. And you're just not that good an
archer, Doctor. I've watched you. Admittedly you're a very
solid shot, but not a great one. And you won't know your
bearings once you're over the side. I'm sorry.'

'I've got a handy recognition chart in my wheelhouse.'
Captain Abberley frowned. 'But given as—'

'Well, it's my idea and I'm going to be the one who does

it.' The Doctor took off his coat. He was shaking a little. He handed the bow and the arrow to Captain Abberley. 'Hang on to these for a minute. I'll need to check that chart just to be certain. Did you say I'd find them in the wheelhouse?' At the captain's nod he ran up the short companionway.

A sudden menacing rumbling erupted from the region of the black hole. The swirling stars shivered briefly. Thin black threads were tightening around the multiverse.

The Doctor seemed very tired as he disappeared up the steps.

'*Bingo!*' Amy's voice was a scream of anguish.

The Doctor came barrelling out of the wheelhouse. He saw exactly what had happened. His voice joined hers. '*No!*'

Bingo was climbing slowly and deliberately down the rope, the bow of Diana slung over one shoulder and the Arrow of Artemis clutched firmly between his teeth. He had a fixed, deliberate look in his eyes and only looked up once when Amy cried 'Bingo! No! Come back!'

He made a muffled response which might have been 'Sorry, old thing,' and then coiled the rope more firmly around his left leg. He continued to inch down, his image wavering and growing suddenly larger, then smaller, while Amy continued to call to him and the Doctor shouted at him not to be such an idiot.

Only he wasn't an idiot, as they all knew. They watched him as he seemed to lose his hold on the rope for a moment, the arrow dropping from his teeth only to be caught by an expert hand as Bingo used all the skills he had ever learned to keep moving bit by bit into position.

With Amy and the others still calling out to him, he seemed to fumble with the bow as he hung there in his impossible position, almost lose it, fumble with the arrow, trying to slot it to the bowstring, look up once more, his eyes saying so much more than he had ever been able to say in words.

Amy bent and grabbed hold of the rope, hauling on it. 'Bingo! Don't!' Captain Abberley stepped forward to help her.

Down below them, Bingo looked up again shaking his head. He was having trouble keeping the rope twisted around him as he struggled to fit the arrow to the strung bow.

The Doctor grabbed at the rope to help Amy and Captain Abberley, then shook his head, dropping his hands and leaning over the rail to watch Bingo who was now drawing the bowstring to his cheek, his eyes narrowed, fixed on the target, the very centre of the black hole.

Captain Abberley had given up. There seemed to be tears in the old space-dog's eyes. He turned his head away.

'No. You can't let him!' Amy still held the rope trying to pull Bingo back in, but the Doctor moved suddenly, grabbing it from her hands and then dropping it to the deck.

'Too dangerous now,' he said. 'We'd kill him and everyone else.' And he sat down suddenly with his head in his hands. 'What an *idiot*!' He was berating himself.

'Look! Look, Doctor!' Amy clutched the rail, her other hand pointing.

Wearily he hauled himself upright and joined Amy and Abberley at the side. By some trick of the dragging chasm, they could all see Bingo, his feet spread wide in the nothingness of all-space, the bowstring pulled back with the gleaming newtonium Arrow of Artemis long and silver and bright, ready to shoot, the ebony and ivory bow curving deeper as he took careful aim along the shaft.

Then, framed by a dark aura, Robin Lockesley, Earl of Sherwood, let fly.

The arrow left the bow. It flew straight for the middle of the black hole. As it flew it grew longer and longer still until it was no more than a slender rod of silvery light, growing thinner and longer until it touched, then pierced the exact centre of the black sphere.

Without thinking, Amy made a dash for the rail, grasped the rope again with every muscle straining. It slackened...

Weeping, she pulled at the rope, hauling it in, but all was gone, gone into what the Mercurian poet Stark called the lake-of-the-gone-forever. Arrow, bow and archer. Alive for eternity. Dead for eternity. Conscious for eternity. All gone.

The little steamboat bucked and swayed. The Doctor's attention shifted and he ran back to the wheelhouse, this time to help Captain Abberley keep the boat in order. The rope itself writhed and twisted like a dying snake until, running back down to shove Amy into the comparative safety of the wheelhouse, the Doctor pulled at its tightening knots. The rope now threatened to drag them into the chasm after Bingo and the Arrow of Law.

'That should have been my job.' The Doctor produced a knife and cut the last knot. Suddenly the ship righted herself, already chugging away from the mooring. The Doctor joined them in the wheelhouse.

'Probably *should* have been your job, Time Lord,' said Captain Abberley. 'But yon youngster were right. He was the only really decent shot amongst tha. Besides, there's tons of Bingos in the multiverse. And only one Doctor.'

Chapter 28

The Multiverse Restored

TRAILING CLOUDS OF BRILLIANTLY coloured steam, her engines coughing and screeching, the paddle-wheeler thundered out of the pastures and horizons of the Second Aether into the glaring crimson peace of Ketchup Cove. Captain Abberley gave a decent impression of Humphrey Bogart in *The African Queen*, with his grubby white cap on the back of his head, an oily rag in his hand and a huge grin on his lips.

Amy's eyes told Flapper what had happened to Bingo. 'I'm so sorry,' said Amy. 'Bingo was going to make Hari a lord or something, and you were going to have some land and be rich...' But, before Flapper could tell her that their fortunes were nothing to the loss of old Bingo, Amy felt her eyes welling with tears. Then Flapper cried with her.

In fact, there were many emotions expressed that night when the Doctor came back into the pavilion to attend a wake for Bingo. The Doctor proudly told them that dear old Robin 'Bingo' Lockesley had saved Creation, good and bad, sweet and sour, ugly and beautiful, the whole of it from the centre to the Rim, top to bottom, side to side. In short, the quasi-infinite was no longer under threat of an early death and/or transfiguration.

'Well, good for Bingo,' said many of his friends, sipping thoughtful shants. As well as feeling sorry for their departed captain, they were now worrying how they were going to get off the Ghost Worlds and back to their various homes. They had all assumed that the *Gargantua*'s tenders would simply return them to the mother ship, if necessary with the Doctor's help. It wasn't a particularly cheerful prospect, dying of old age on a primitive planet with only the most basic health and entertainment programmes.

Amy had guessed it first. They were now stranded in Miggea, experiencing the system's constant shifting through hundreds and thousands, possibly millions, of alien universes until such time as the orbit returned them to their starting point, which could well be after many of them were dead, there being no sophisticated cryogenics here. The locals, accustomed to isolation, were prepared for the experience and, apart from the nausea accompanying a shift, had few changes to worry about. This added to the teams' overall gloom and rather spoiled the pleasure of a game well played and won, saving the multiverse from oblivion.

'I mean, it was no fun making that first transition.' Uff Nuf O'Kay sipped a moody pint. 'I have a weak stomach as it is. The thought of a thousand more is pretty unbearable.' He watched without regret as a feline of some sort appeared through one wall and sauntered past him into another. 'It's not every day I envy a cat's abilities.'

Amy was still mourning Bingo and wondering if she were not somehow to blame for his death, even though the Doctor continued to reassure her that Bingo's act of self-sacrifice had saved the multiverse. He had done the only sane thing, if multiverse-saving was worth it.

Flapper felt guilty worrying about Hari's status while still knowing a deep sadness at the loss of Bingo. Any agreement Mr Banning-Cannon had made with Bingo was now decidedly null and void. 'Although, of course, if it hadn't been for Bingo there actually wouldn't be a future to worry about.' But things still looked a bit on the bleak side. If they were doomed to permanent exile on this provincial planet, maybe all bets, so to speak, were off. They had better start again, tilling the virgin earth of Flynn together. It took a lot of energy, she reflected, to look on the bright side.

That night, the sky became layer upon layer of complementary realities, one fitting into the other, one shade colouring the next, one blazing aura into another and all giving off a faint, distant noise, for sound actually travelled through the space between the worlds of the Second Aether while Miggea's planets had been soundless before the terraforming.

Spiralling out in every possible direction and dimension, the tapestry of worlds could scarcely be absorbed by the human senses. Amy thought that the peace she discovered in the presence of so many worlds was the most profound she had ever experienced, precisely because those other worlds were packed with life and people pretty much the same as those she already knew. All life throughout the millions of universes supported people and places much the same as her own, given a minor difference or two. That knowledge brought with it a sense of continuity. It meant that somewhere out there, maybe, a good few versions of reality away, all the other Bingos who had not taken part in this singular adventure were enjoying a cup of tea after a long day's innings, swapping bits of news with some lady friend called 'old thing' and who called him 'dumb twerp' and with whom he had an understanding.

Here on Flynn, where the most important game in the history of existence had been played, both residents and newcomers planned to club up and build some sort of monument to Bingo. They would all remember when, looking up into the sky where a black sun burned, they saw a long slender silver lance slide into the place where the Balance swayed, between Law and Chaos, Love and Hate and all the other opposing forces that determined the existence of Creation.

And, back in place at last, that good old Roogalator, the regulator of the great engine of space and time and of all the various abstracts which, thanks to our love of myth, so quickly become actualities, resumed its steady movement. The black tides no longer raced through the universe. Shadowy harlequins and pierrots no longer danced upon the ruins of countless realities. The multiverse could return to its stately natural cycle.

That night, while the sky was filled with alien stars, the Bubbly Boys, those spoiled and oily boys, jolly jacks all three of them, bounced in to greet their old skipper Captain Brian Abberley with whistles and song to show off who they still had trapped in a fat pinky-grey bubble: none other than General Frank/ Freddie Force and his scowling Antimatter Men, who had turned against their leaders for mistakes of judgement and blamed this last ignominy on them as well. They raged and quarrelled within the bubble, like varicoloured hamsters. Time bends again, decided the Doctor. They shared invisible Peggy's disgust for his failures and were glad General Force had his reward, even if they had to suffer it with him. A sense of justice now infects the multiverse. The Force twins and their followers would soon begin the same arc across the Schwarzschild Radius which Robin of Sherwood had made when he restored the Roogalator, which could change its own shape to preserve its existence, which maintained the order of eternity, and which employed mortals in its and therefore their own salvation. Now Force and Co were doomed to live for ever in that moment between life and death.

The Doctor alone might have escaped Bingo's fate, but he knew in his bones that the single shot down into that constantly moving spiral would have been almost impossible for anyone but Bingo to make. He had grown rather philosophical over his half-shant of M&E Vortex Water and decided he had better retire to bed. All that excitement could put centuries on a fellow. He stood up and was about to say 'good night' when a fresh, piercing rumble filled the skies and he joined the others running from the pub to see what was happening.

A massive shadow blotted out the stars. A few spots of light gleamed in that huge shape. Framed against the deep blue disc of the setting sun it stood at anchor in the stratosphere, menacing the world, no longer moving. Waiting.

Nothing happened. Another flush of bronze and silver sparks erupted, faded, enough for them to think they might have recognised the shape.

'Could it be what I think?' The Doctor's voice was low, disbelieving.

Amy grasped his arm, as if afraid she would fall.

'It – it might be...' said Hari, equally unwilling to speak his thoughts.

A cosmic pause.

'We'll take a stroll to the landing field in the morning,' said the Doctor. 'Mm?'

'Good idea,' said Amy.

Sure enough, when they got to the landing field next morning, there she was, looking as if she had sailed down from heaven, a faint mist rising from her decks and masts, defying the gravities of a million worlds and riding the winds of the distant sky. How she had been able to sail here, how she resisted the pull of the black hole in order to perform this all-but impossible feat, nobody knew, but it spoke of superb spacemanship and an instinct for the multiverse only a few possessed.

They looked around them. Two black and brass boats had already landed on the space-field, joining the other beautiful, slender space tender steaming, bright brass and silver, in the cool, dawn air where high overhead, her sails reefed, lay the star clipper. Somehow, the *Paine*, of all ships, had risked the horrors of inter-multiversal space. She had managed to sail through the scales of the multiverse and find them, following the course of the Ghost System, a feat never performed until now. To find a needle in a needle stack. Here were her passenger tenders, waiting to take them off. And there before the trio of ships stood a tall figure in a navy blue and gold uniform whisking off his cap and bowing. Amy wondered what his expression might be behind that cold iron mask. She imagined he was smiling at their astonishment. Now, at least, she understood why he had demanded the necklace aboard the *Gargantua*.

Two hours later, they were preparing for take-off. By the time everyone was settled in their seats Captain Cornelius had enjoyed a small demi-shant and a good breakfast and, from his seat across from Amy, offered her the celestial necklace lying in the flat of his hand and no longer moving. She took it gingerly.

'The vitality will return, don't worry.' He had noticed her disappointment. 'That necklace has done a lot of good work. And believe me it was mine to give away. It was my map as well as my compass. That's how I could find Miggea. It took some tricky sailing and I'll admit to you that I was frightened we wouldn't make it, with only your celestial necklace to lead me to you. I'll explain the rest when we're aboard.' He seemed to relish her fresh awareness of what the celestial necklace actually was.

An hour later, in his spacious and comfortably austere

cabin aboard the *Paine*, Captain Cornelius explained how the necklace had been his. 'A gift from my Diana. She wanted to be sure I was here when you needed me. She left it with an antiquarian on Venice when she decided it was time to leave, presumably for Loondoon. Stolen by Frank/Freddie Force when they visited me. They knew what it was, of course. There's nothing stupid or uneducated about General Force. That's what makes them so dangerous.'

She had left Ironface the map not to lead him to her but to help him find Miggea. Somehow she knew he would play a part in the cosmic drama, knew he would either take them to Miggea or be there to save them from being marooned in Miggea once they had fulfilled their task and used the Bow of Diana to shoot the Arrow of Artemis into the heart of the multiverse.

'I have to say, you did a wonderful job, steering your way through all those different systems to reach us,' said the Doctor, 'even with that map and compass. It's so intricate. To calculate all those orbits within orbits demands mathematical skills beyond most of us. Wheels within wheels within wheels...' He raised his glass in salute. 'We'd have been marooned in Miggea for a lifetime if you hadn't worked it out. Thanks, captain.'

Captain Cornelius bowed in acknowledgement. 'Wheels within wheels, as you say, Doctor. Shadows of shadows. Self-similarity is the key to all as all our actions are reproduced throughout the multiverse. Resonances. Echoes...'

And, as Captain Cornelius observed when he made his plans to visit a certain milliner in Old Loondoon, travelling as usual under his alias, he would spare Lady Peggy the planned punishment. After all, she had actually helped him discover his lost Diana and, with W.G. Grace, who knew the most about hats and so forth, she would go with him to Loondoon to find Diana, or at least perhaps a warm trail.

'Won't you come with us, Doctor?' Cornelius tapped out his pipe in his cupped hand. 'We're natural friends. So much in common.'

'Except I try to hold things together. And you…'

'Oh, I don't blow stuff up any more. You must know that. I'm a reformed individual.'

They shook hands. And Amy decided to keep the already enlivened necklace.

As the *Paine* prepared to sail back to its own space-time where the *Gargantua* awaited them, Hari and Flapper became increasingly gloomy. Bingo's death, though the worst calamity they could imagine, had definitely destroyed their anticipated happiness. The *Paine* began her journey back through the multiverse, out of the Second Aether and into their home universe. Every few hours saw another sickening twist into single reality until, far too soon, they emerged at last beneath familiar stars laid against the darkness of normal space-time where the *Gargantua* hung to take them home. Now the time of parting drew closer. Flapper no longer hid her tears and Hari's back became stiffer and stiffer as he prepared for their final moments. There was nothing he could offer her. A man had no right to declare his love to a woman if he could not pay his own way at the very least. Flapper knew that she could not offer Hari any help, having no money of her own. Besides, his pride would not let him marry if he could not provide for her.

In the second-class lounge, the night after they were on their way, Hari and Flapper held hands over quarter-shants of VW and discussed how life might have been so much better but for a subtle twist of fate.

Entering from the first-class deck, Mr and Mrs Banning-Cannon nodded to the lovers who each defiantly retained a sturdy grip on the other's hand. But when Mr Banning-Cannon summoned Hari to his table and Mrs Banning-

Canning ordered her daughter to the bar, common politeness made the couple comply.

Hari immediately blurted his feelings to the Tiger of the Terraforming business.

'Look here, sir, I'm not going to lie to you, I love your daughter but if my hanging around spoils her chances of making a decent marriage—'

'Don't give me that!' declared the planet-master. 'I have something to say to you, young Agincourt and I won't be interrupted.'

Hari drew a deep breath and waited for the worst. 'Right, sir.'

'Good. Now you and Lord Robin were the best of friends, I take it.'

'Like brothers, sir. Since we were nippers.'

'Exactly. And he had no relatives, I'm told, except a distant uncle who is a magistrate in your neck of the woods.'

'That's right, sir. He isn't wealthy, unfortunately; rather depends on his stipend...'

'Yes, yes. Well, you'll be able to sort all that kind of thing out. I was going, as you might be aware, to give Lord Robin the deeds to the planet. Lock, stock and barrel.'

'He'd mentioned something of the sort, sir, yes,'

'Out of which, I understand, he was going to give you some local land and a title or some such, thus enabling you to make a bid – that is, ask me for the hand of my beloved daughter, Jane.'

'Uh umyum,' said Hari.

'Quite,' said Mr Banning-Cannon. 'Well, in the circumstances, and considering I have had a chance to see how you go about things and so on – well, sir, I'm going to give you what I was going to give young Bingo. But there's a condition. You have to take some sort of title – preferably the one Bingo can't take now. Say, Hari, Lord Sherwood.

Earl of Hood or however these things go. I have to admit,' said the tycoon dropping his voice, 'I have a motive here. If Flapper gets a title, I can't see Mrs Banning-Cannon having any further objection to the marriage.'

'Gosh, sir!' Hari was ecstatic. 'I say!'

Rather strenuously, he began pumping Mr Banning-Cannon's hand.

Meanwhile, by the bar, Mrs Banning-Cannon was confiding something to her daughter. 'In all my days, I have not had a young man – or indeed a man of any age – stand up to me the way Hari Agincourt stood up to me the other day, and I realised that I rather admired his quality of command. Therefore, Jane dear, I have thought things over and, if there's some sort of decent job your father can find for Mr Agincourt, who presumably, by some ancient tradition my husband explained but which I don't quite understand, ascends to the title, I am prepared to give you both my blessing. As for your dowry, well, I have something rather disgraceful to admit to you.' She coloured a little and sipped her drink. 'I fear I gave in to an old weakness before we went down to Flynn to watch the match. I had, I must state in my own defence, become horribly bored.'

'Gosh, ma, I'm not going to have to visit you in jug, am I?'

Mrs Banning-Cannon's normally grim features softened into a broad, rather charming smile. 'Good heavens, no! But I did break five years of abstinence. I'm afraid I put rather a lot down for the Gentleman to win the Tournament. As a result I returned to the *Gargantua* to discover that I had won a somewhat handsome sum of bluebacks – several million, in fact. And, because I should not profit from breaking my promise to Professor Disch, my psychiatrist, you know, I intend to bestow the whole amount on you and Hari, so that you can start life with a nice little nest egg!'

'Gosh! Oh, I say, ma, that's awfully good of you!' Flapper threw her arms about her mother and embraced her more enthusiastically than she had ever embraced her before. 'Oh, I *say*!'

She looked around her. The bar was filling up. Hari was nowhere to be seen. Maybe he'd stepped out for some clear oxygen, given his mood. She went to look for Amy.

Amy was in the reception area standing outside some kind of antique monument Flapper didn't remember seeing before. A big blue box with archaic writing on it. Amy was not in good spirits. Flapper thought perhaps Amy had had stronger feelings for Bingo than she realised. Also, of course, Amy had been with Bingo when he went over the side.

'I was wondering where you were,' Amy said. 'We'll be leaving soon.'

'Yes. Four or five days, eh? Of course.'

'We won't be going with you to the next port. We're leaving tonight.'

'Oh, that's a ship of some kind is it? Gosh. That's awful, Amy. You're off, then. In that little thing. I say!' A fresh tear blossomed in Flapper's left eye.

'I'm afraid this is the last night I'll be seeing you, Flapper. I hope you and Hari can get things sorted…'

'Oh, don't worry about that. I think we're going to be OK. But I'd rather hoped you'd be my maid-of-honour…'

'You're actually, really, really getting *married*?! That's absolutely marvellous, Flapper!' Amy did that hugging and jumping up and down thing girls do to show pleasure.

'You're the first to know!'

Hari came beaming out of the bar. 'I was looking for you, Flaps. Your pa's proven to be an absolute brick. Your ma, too, actually.' And he told her what had transpired.

When all the hugs and jumps were over, Hari said: 'I ought to thank the Doctor. Any idea where he is, Amy?'

'Well, he's—'

The door of the TARDIS swung open and the Doctor's face peered out at them. His eyes were positively sparkling. 'Everything ship-shape and Bristol fashion, Jim lad! Ready to come aboard?'

'Aye, aye, captain.' She gave him a mock salute.

A few minutes later, they stood together in the TARDIS while the Doctor fiddled with some old electrical equipment complete with big vacuum tubes, an antique microphone and a pair of 'head-cans'.

'Now I understand a bit better how you think,' she said. 'Who you are.'

'How's that, Amy Pond?'

'I think it's because of you being one of a kind,' she said.

'Yeah? Put your finger on that for a minute, could you?'

'Well, anyway. I hated Bingo going the way he did. But I was glad it was him and not the rest of us. Do you know what I mean?'

'Yup,' said the Doctor. 'Pass me that hammer, would you?'

'So in all these universes there might be more Amy Ponds, more – I don't know – Jonathan Rosses and Will Smiths and Gabe Byrnes?'

'Yep. More or less.'

'And more Doctors?'

'Ah, well…'

'You really are the only one?'

'Time Lord. The Time War got a bit desperate towards the end.'

'But you said our actions were echoed over and over again as if to infinity.'

'But by us. I'm not sure. There are people who take the same actions, fulfil, if you like, the same destinies.

Everywhere, throughout the multiverse there are people like us trying to put things right or sometimes just trying to stop things getting any worse – echoes of echoes, shadows of shadows. Call some archetypes. Jung did. But maybe we're all archetypes. Maybe there's no such thing as an original? Maybe the multiverse has no original. The World Snake eats its own tail. No beginning and no end.' He looked into her eyes. He grinned. 'We carry on for ever. Paradox upon paradox,'

'That's a thought,' she said. Then she clapped her hands together and looked business-like. 'So! Where *are* we going?' She again gave her attention to the controls.

'First off, I think we need to get back to your own time, don't you?' He smiled. 'Check a few things out. What's the scanner showing?'

Amy peered up at the screen. And there was the Milky Way in all her golden, scintillating glory.

'So what do you see?' He was busy with some retro switches.

'Well, it's our galaxy. What else should I be looking at?' And then she gasped as the truth dawned on her. 'Oh! They've gone! You did it, Doctor! The black tides have *gone*!' She sat down suddenly. 'Oh, wow!'

'Well, *we* did it,' he said. 'And Bingo was the true hero. Not at all bad, eh, for a gentleman amateur. That's his real monument… out there. We can celebrate later with the Bubbly Boys and I suspect we'll see more of Captain Cornelius, too.'

From somewhere they heard faint funky music. The toot of a distant foghorn.

The Doctor stopped. Rubbing his chin he looked out at the galaxy. 'Clean as a whistle, eh? Well, clean as she needs to be. We'd best be getting back to base. OK with you? I'm expecting an urgent message.' He turned a few knobs and flicked a few switches. 'Oh, sweet duroo, how I love you…'

'What are you doing?' she wanted to know.

'Something I shouldn't,' he told her. 'It's pretty much against all the rules. Physical or metaphysical. But the risks had to be – will have to be – taken.'

'What?' She sat down, more pleased than she could have guessed that they were heading for home. Home? She looked about her at the strange mixture: alien engineering, intelligent and wise. Arrogant and intuitive science, as much magic as machine by now. Humane and yet utterly inhuman...

There came the usual sound of rusty shopping carts being dragged over sheets of corrugated tin, and the TARDIS began to shudder. The Doctor leaned forward and started to tap out a message. 'I'll keep it on "send later". But since you never know how the time streams flow...'

'Who's it to?'

'Somebody has to do it,' he said, grinning like a wicked schoolboy. 'I've *always* wanted to. Totally against the Laws of Time, physical, metaphysical, natural or supernatural. There's a Gilbert and Sullivan song in there somewhere. Tum tumpety-too.' He bent towards the old microphone. 'Here goes – *Cling duroo. Cling duroo. Frank/Freddie Force, don't I know you? Tom Mix. Tom Mix, Oogalator, babies. No longer got the rabies. I love to mix, don't you? To them mean old Roogalator blues.. Ooo! Dark tides flowing up the wadi al gloo...*' Covering the mike with his hand he turned and winked at her. 'Time Lords used to have to go before the Grey Council if they started talking to themselves like this. But it worked, didn't it, Amy Pond? That's the power of positive Paradox. Without it we wouldn't *exist*. *Couldn't* exist.' He frowned suddenly and sighed. 'Neither, unfortunately, could that old dark tide.' He flipped a disconsolate switch.

She pointed at the screen. 'I told you, Doctor. Look for yourself. It's gone! Dark matter, yes, but no dark tide. It's *gone!*'

He grinned that grin of his.
'Give it time,' he said.
And pulled a lever.

Acknowledgements

To Justin Richards, who helped shape this story. (No living nuts were harmed during the writing of this book. Do not try any of these games anywhere, especially home.)

Also for the Roogalators, Martin Stone, the Hawkwinds, Janis Ian, Mac McLagan and other good musicians and friends who kept the work on this book rocking; to Billy and Betty and to Barry Pain, an inspiration to many; to the original Bubbly Boys, their mums, dads, aunts and uncles for whom Saturday fun always started with the Doctor and for whom it still starts, and of course for Linda.

Also available from BBC Books:

*Thrilling, all-new adventures featuring the Doctor, Amy and
Rory, as played by Matt Smith, Karen Gillan and Arthur Darvill
in the spectacular hit series from BBC Television*

Touched by an Angel
by Jonathan Morris
£6.99 ISBN 978 1 849 90234 2

Paradox Lost
by George Mann
£6.99 ISBN 978 1 849 90235 9

Borrowed Time
by Naomi A. Alderman
£6.99 ISBN 978 1 849 90233 5

DOCTOR WHO

The Dalek Handbook

by Steve Tribe and James Goss

£9.99 ISBN 978 1 849 90232 8

Exterminate!

The chilling battle cry of the Daleks has terrorised and terrified countless billions across thousands of worlds throughout time and space, from Skaro, Vulcan and Exxilon to the Medusa Cascade, Churchill's War Room and the opening of the Pandorica. This is the comprehensive history of the greatest enemies of the Doctor.

Learn about the Daleks' origins on the planet Skaro, how a Time Lord intervention altered the course of Dalek history, and how they emerged to wage war on Thals, Mechonoids, Movellans, Draconians and humans. With design artwork and photographs from five decades of *Doctor Who*, *The Dalek Handbook* also reveals the development of their iconic look and sound, and their enduring appeal in television, radio, books, comics and more.

Including the full story of the Daleks' centuries-long conflict with the one enemy they fear, the Doctor, *The Dalek Handbook* is the complete guide to the Daleks – in and out of their casings!